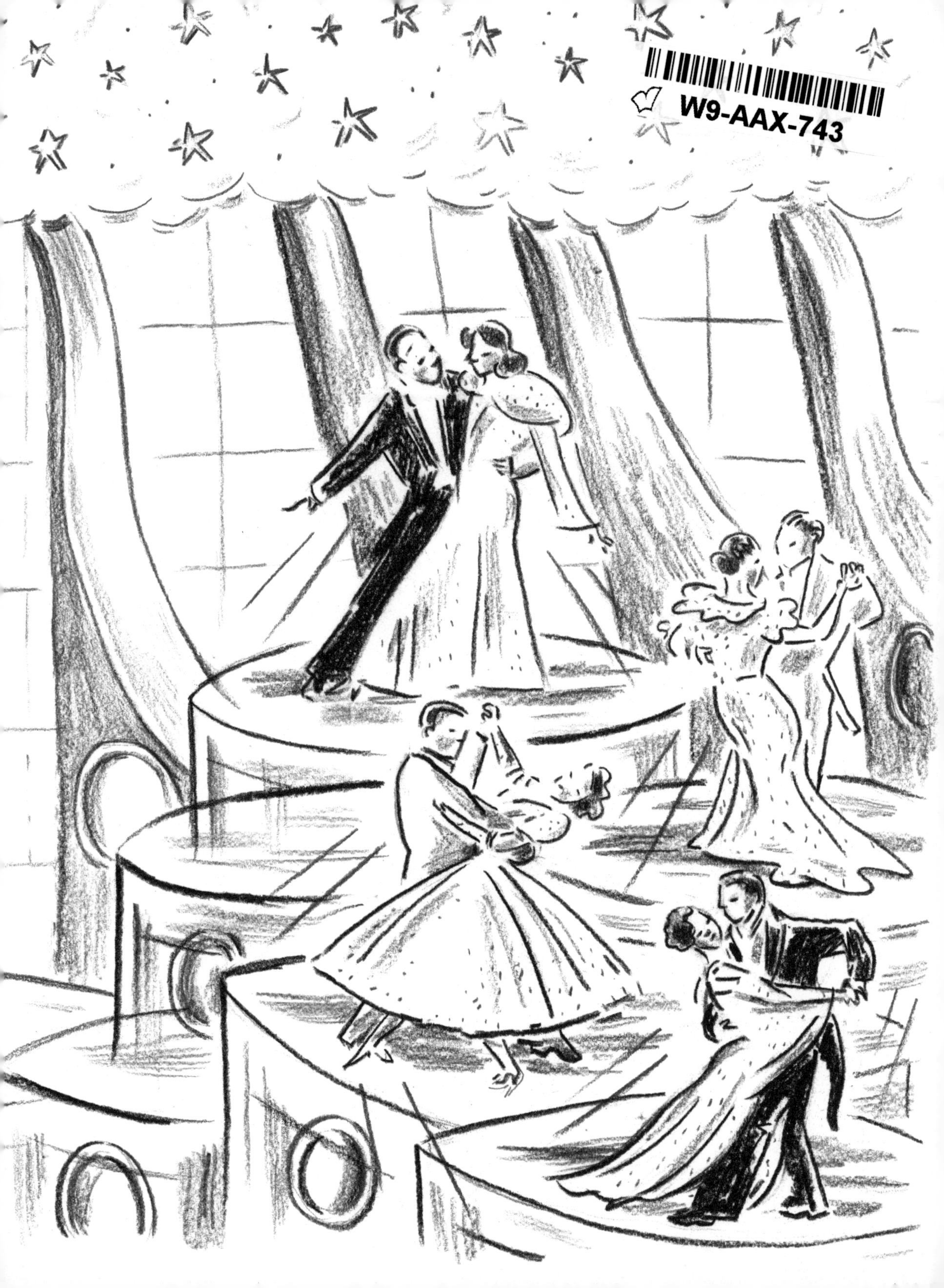

drawnandquarterly.com
rinaayuyang.com

ISBN 978-1-77046-318-9
First Edition: October 2018
Printed in China
10 9 8 7 6 5 4 3 2 1

Cataloguing data available from Library and Archives Canada

Published in the USA by Drawn & Quarterly, a client publisher of Farrar, Straus and Giroux. Orders: 888.330.8477

Published in Canada by Drawn & Quarterly, a client publisher of Raincoast Books. Orders: 800.663.5714

Published in the United Kingdom by Drawn & Quarterly, a client publisher of Publishers Group UK. Orders: info@pguk.co.uk

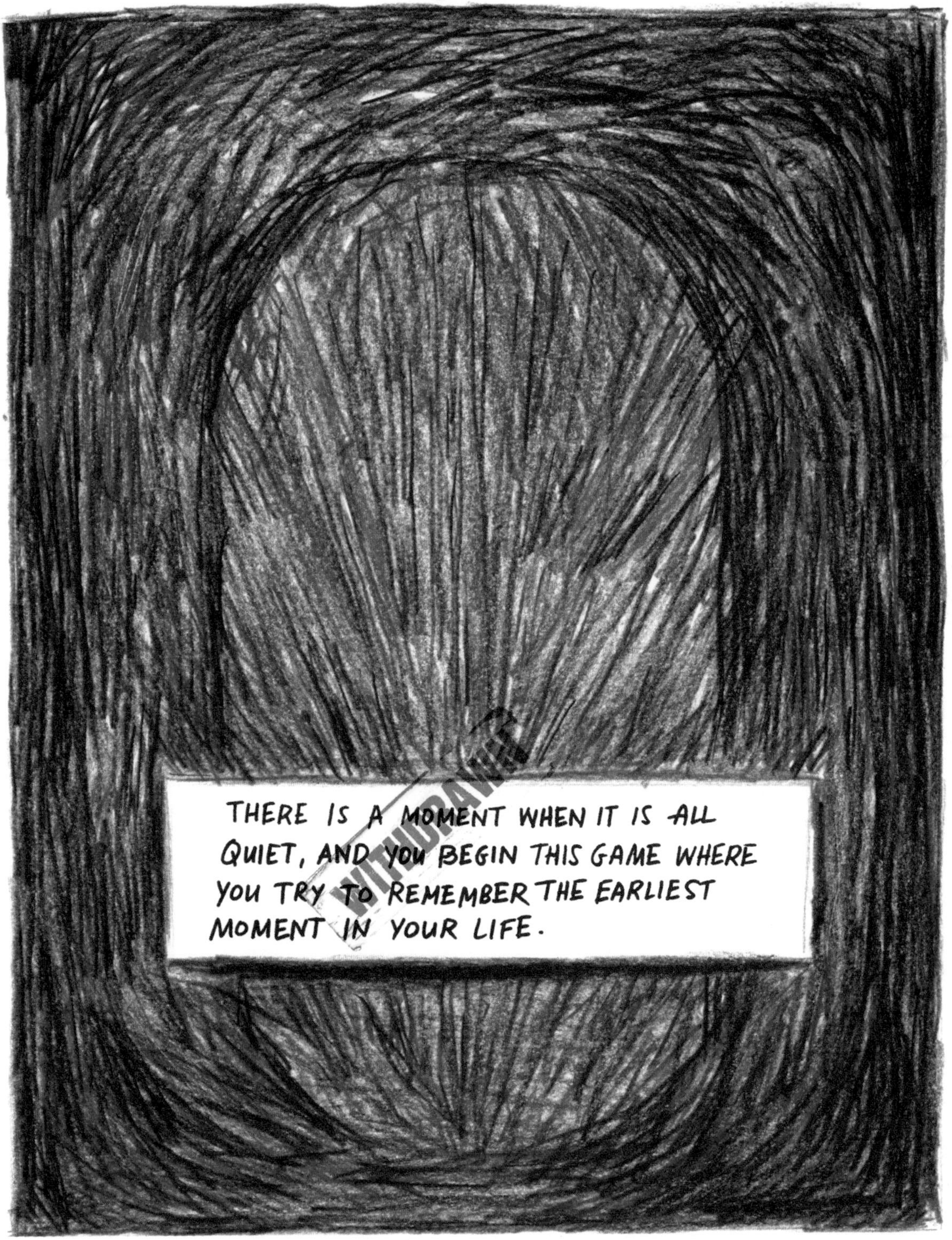
THERE IS A MOMENT WHEN IT IS ALL QUIET, AND YOU BEGIN THIS GAME WHERE YOU TRY TO REMEMBER THE EARLIEST MOMENT IN YOUR LIFE.

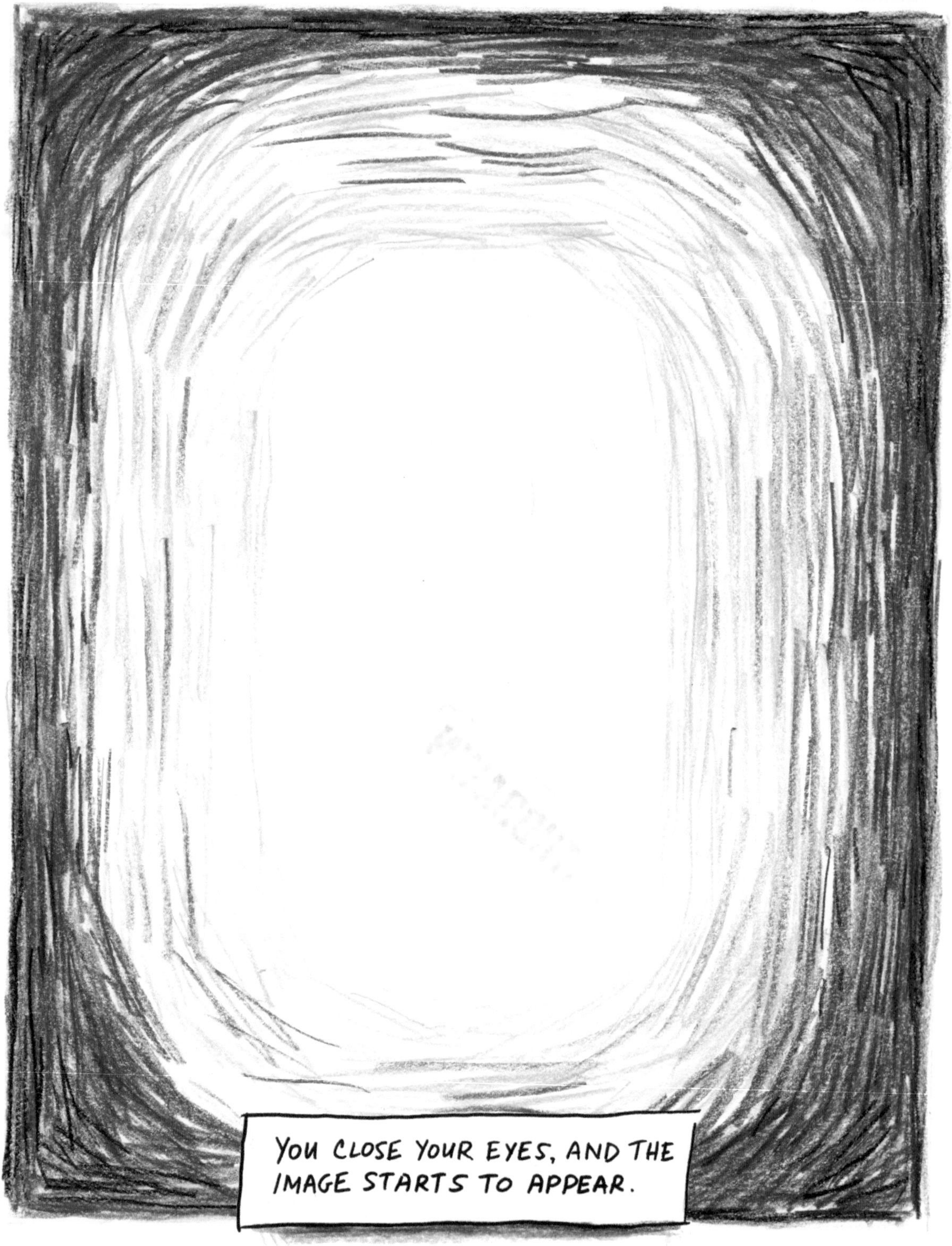
YOU CLOSE YOUR EYES, AND THE IMAGE STARTS TO APPEAR.

HERE IT IS.

SO EXCITING.

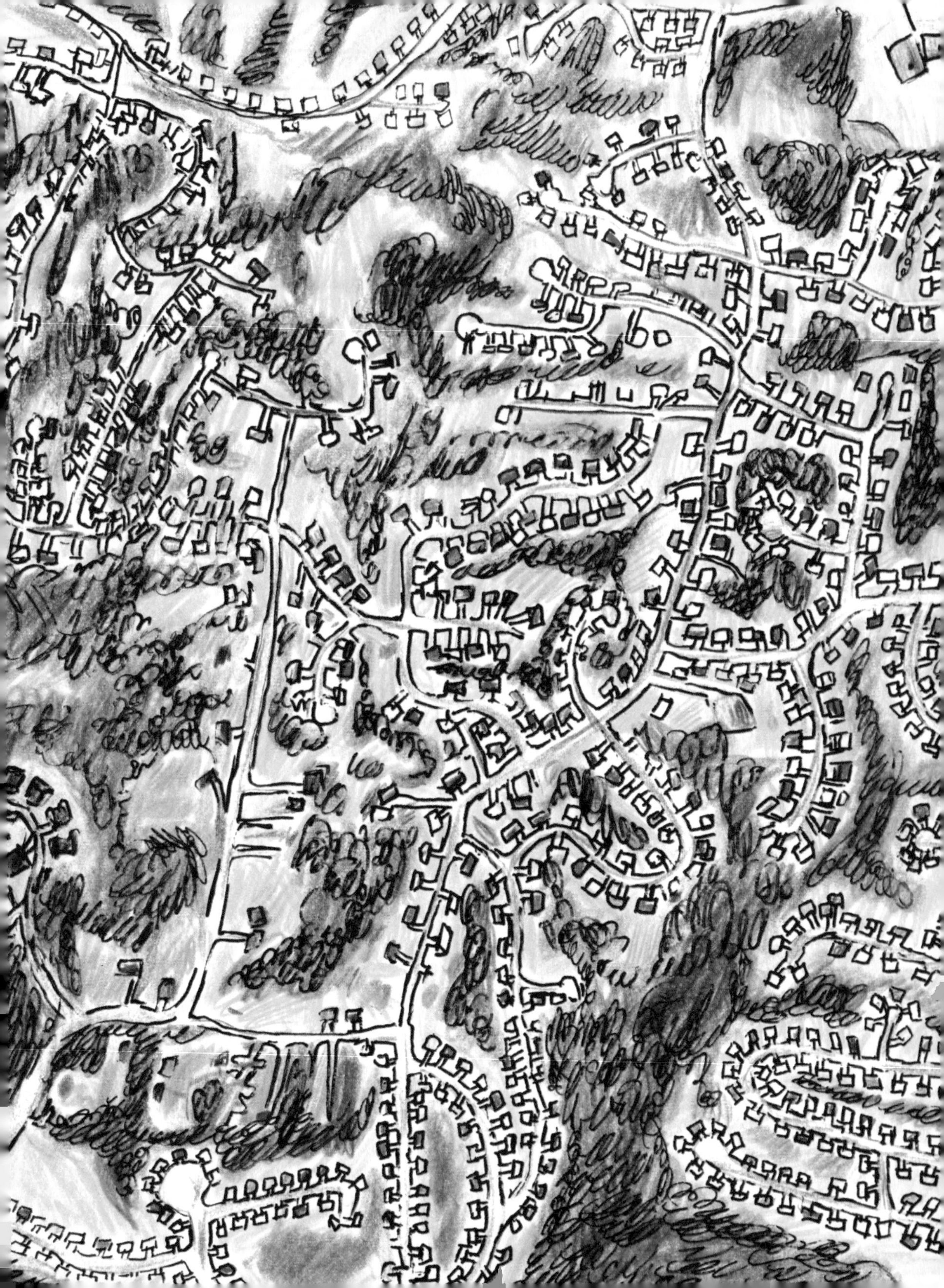

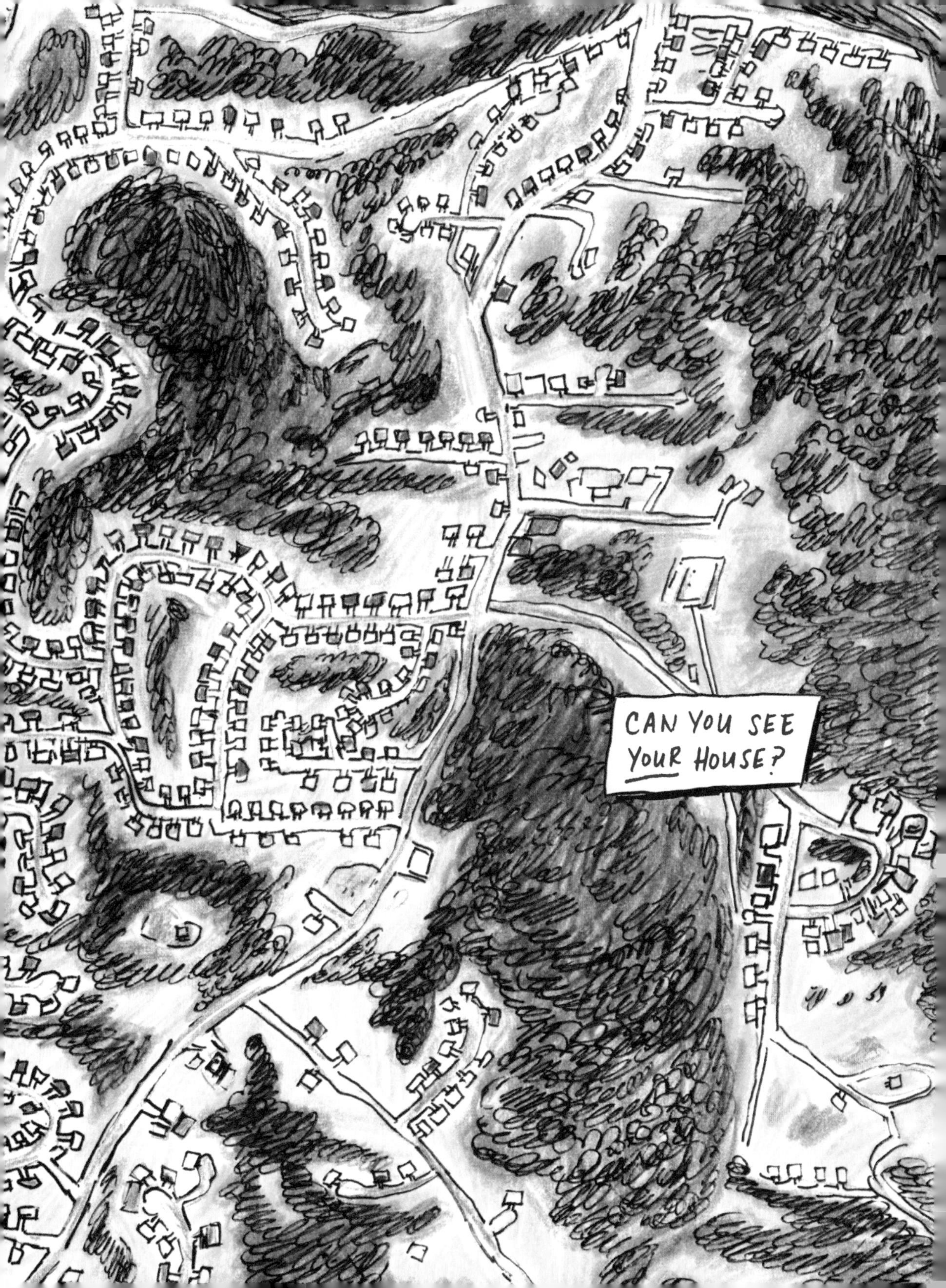
CAN YOU SEE
YOUR HOUSE?

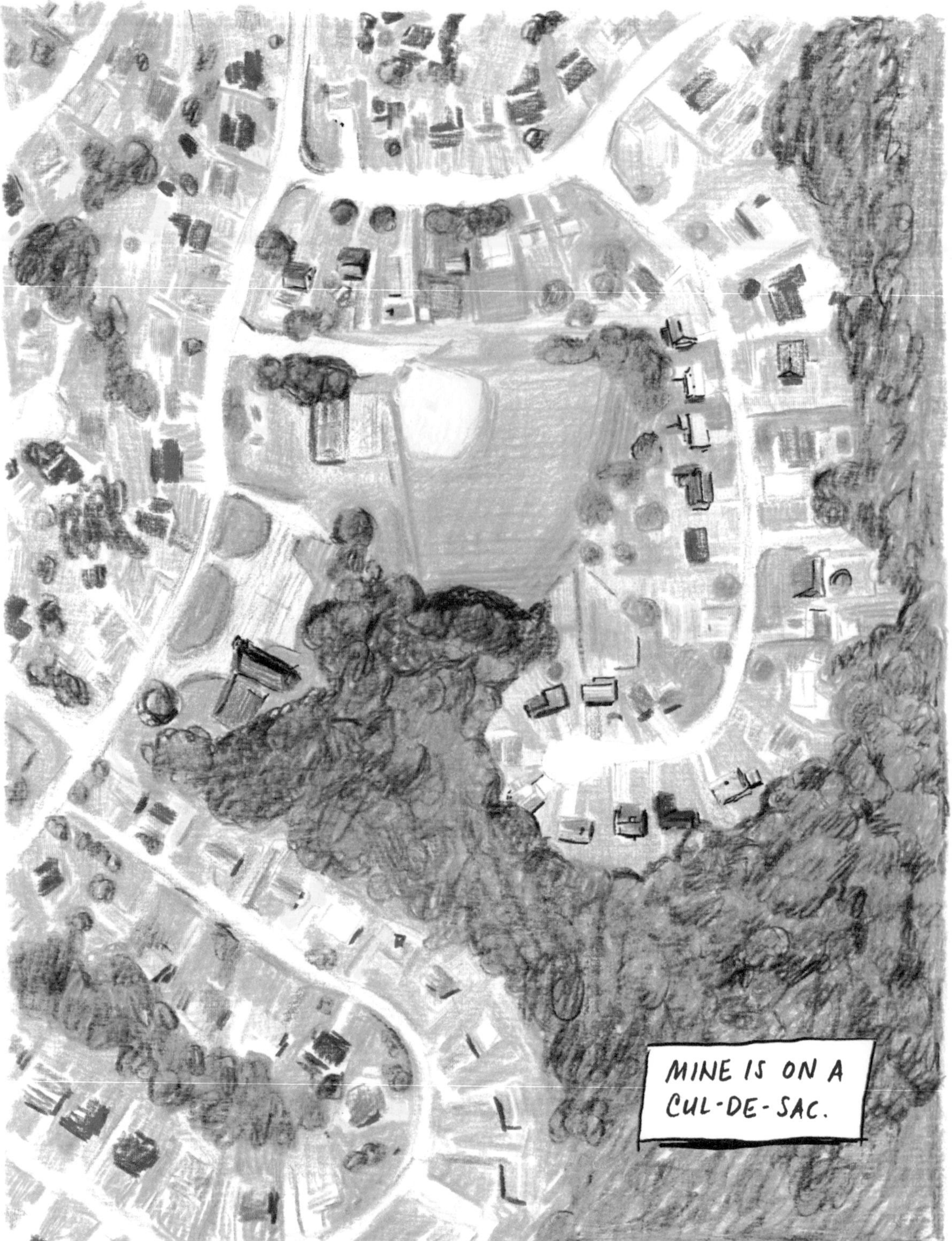
MINE IS ON A
CUL-DE-SAC.

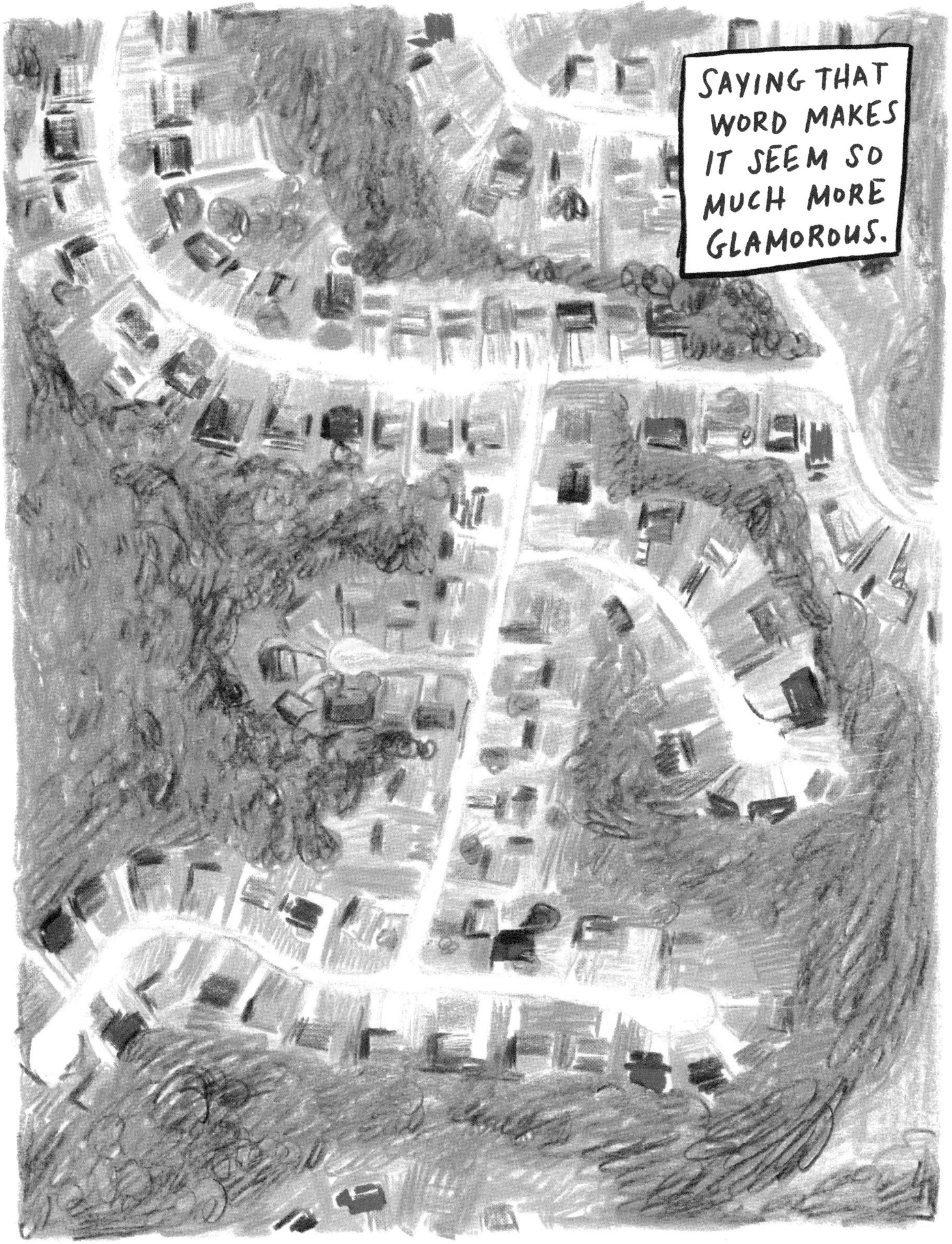
SAYING THAT WORD MAKES IT SEEM SO MUCH MORE GLAMOROUS.

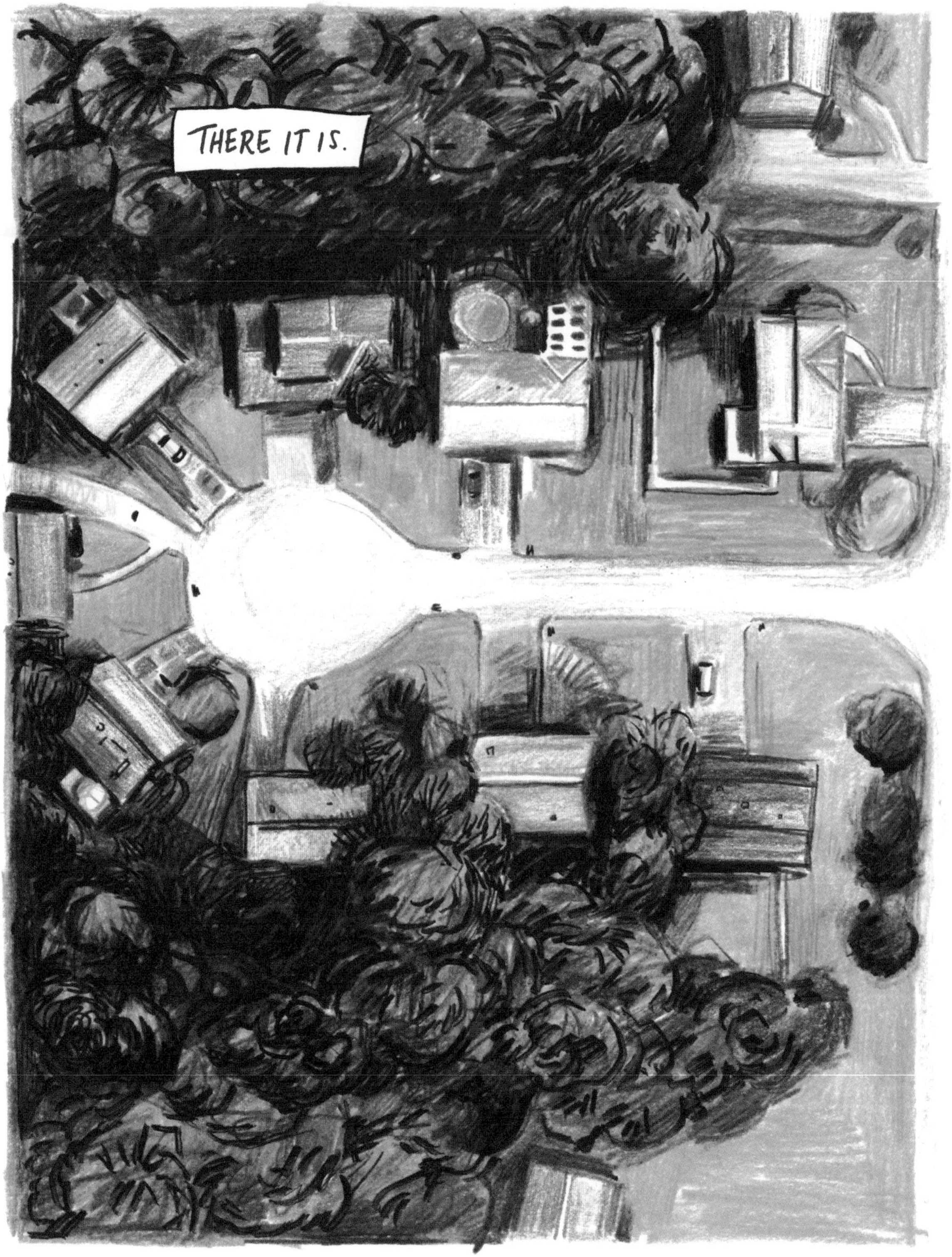
THERE IT IS.

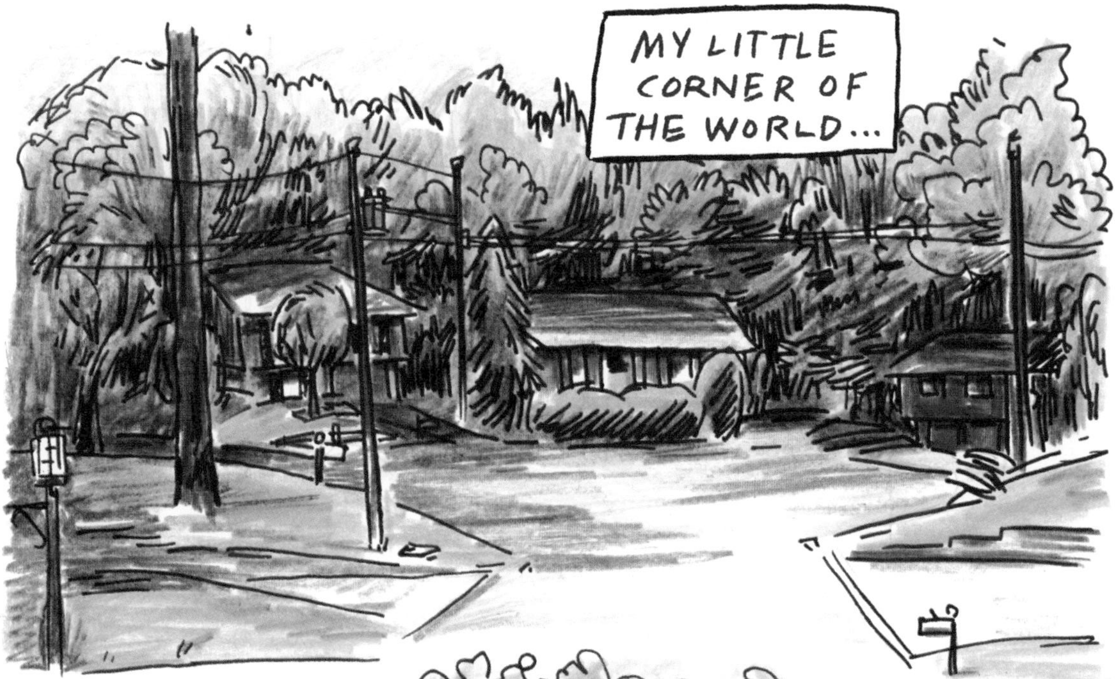
MY LITTLE CORNER OF THE WORLD...

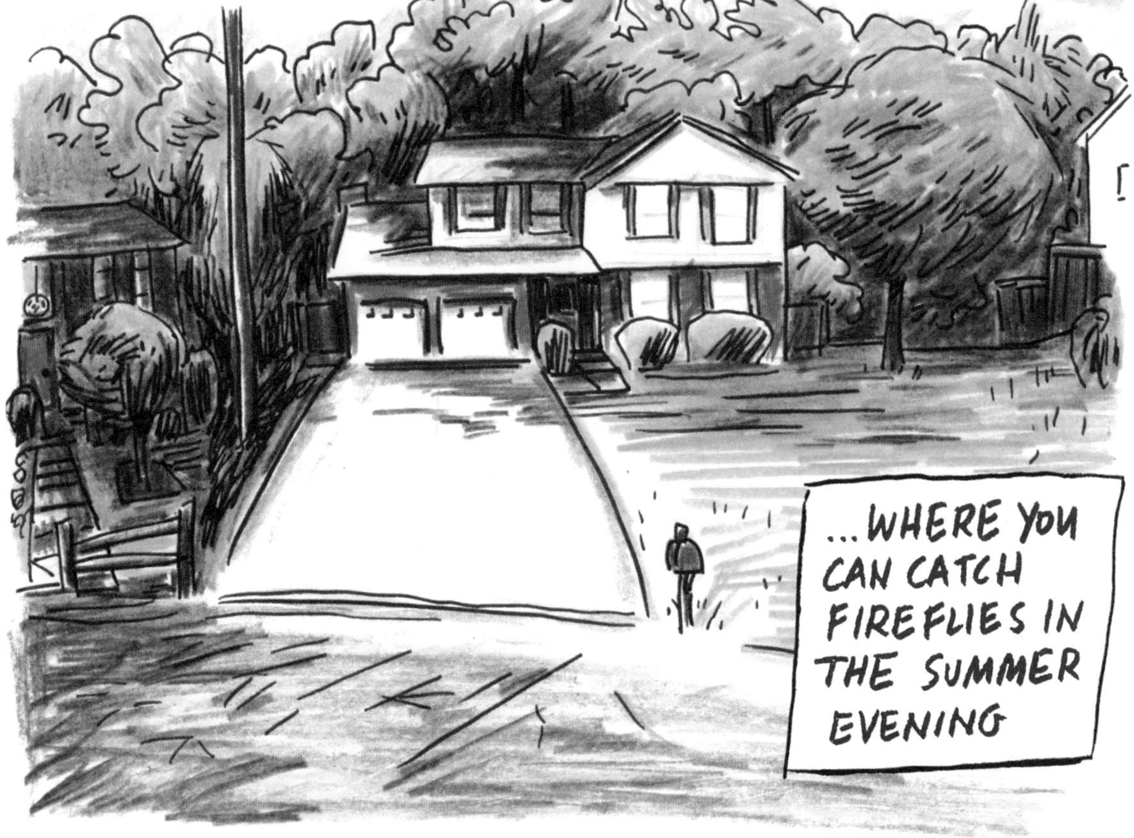
...WHERE YOU CAN CATCH FIREFLIES IN THE SUMMER EVENING

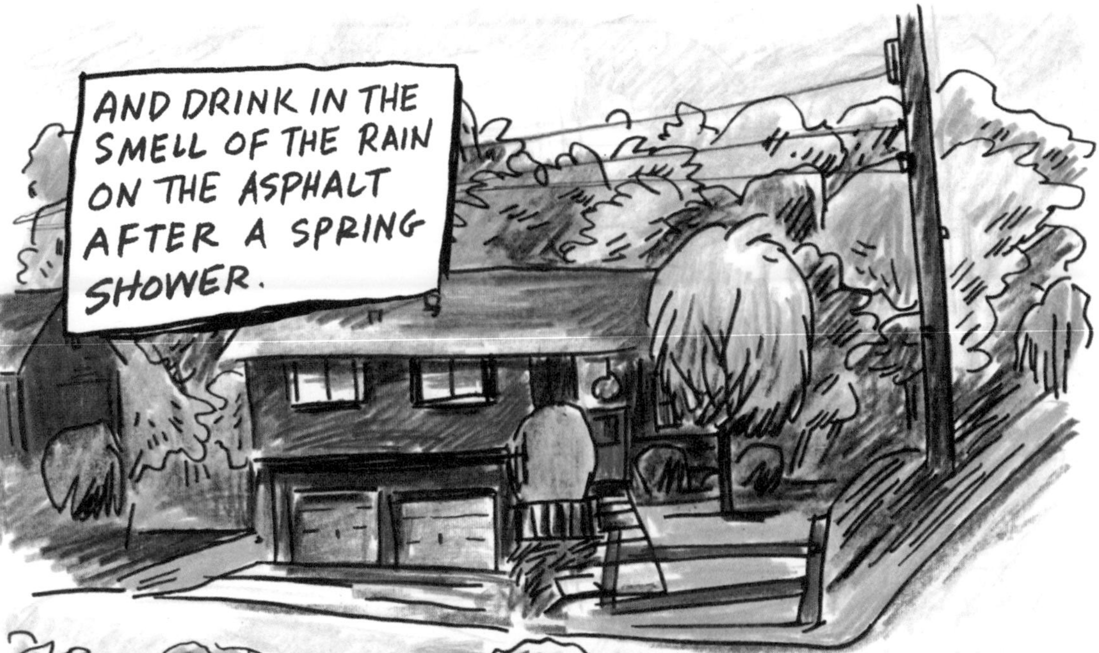
AND DRINK IN THE SMELL OF THE RAIN ON THE ASPHALT AFTER A SPRING SHOWER.

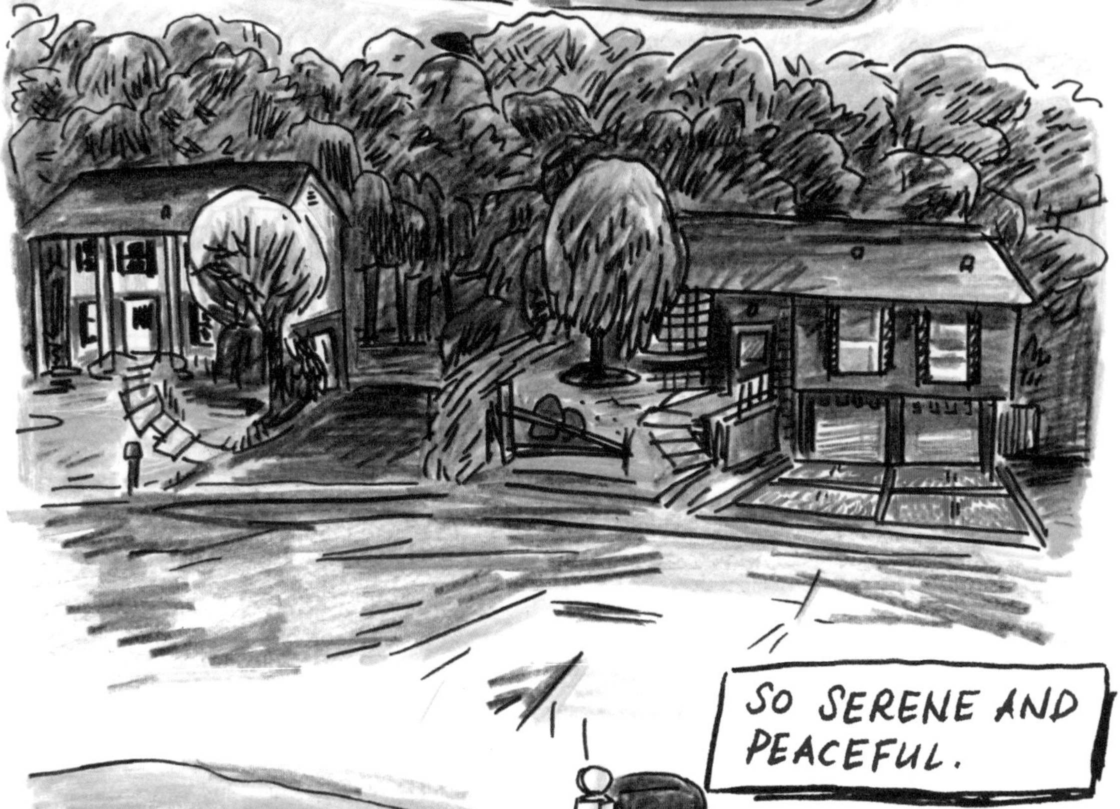
SO SERENE AND PEACEFUL.

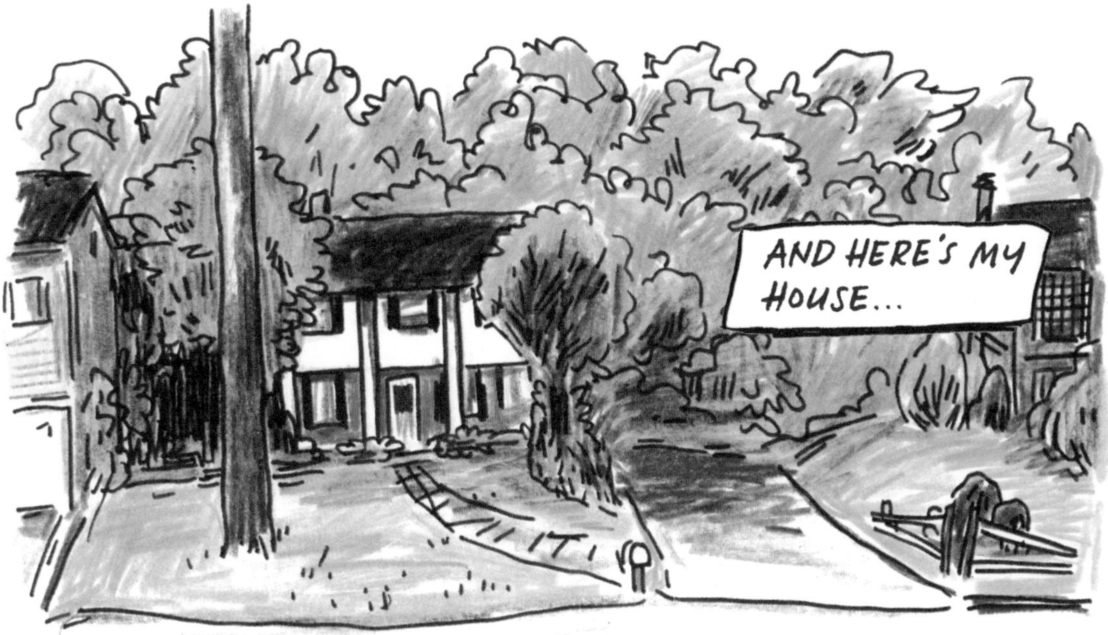
AND HERE'S MY HOUSE...

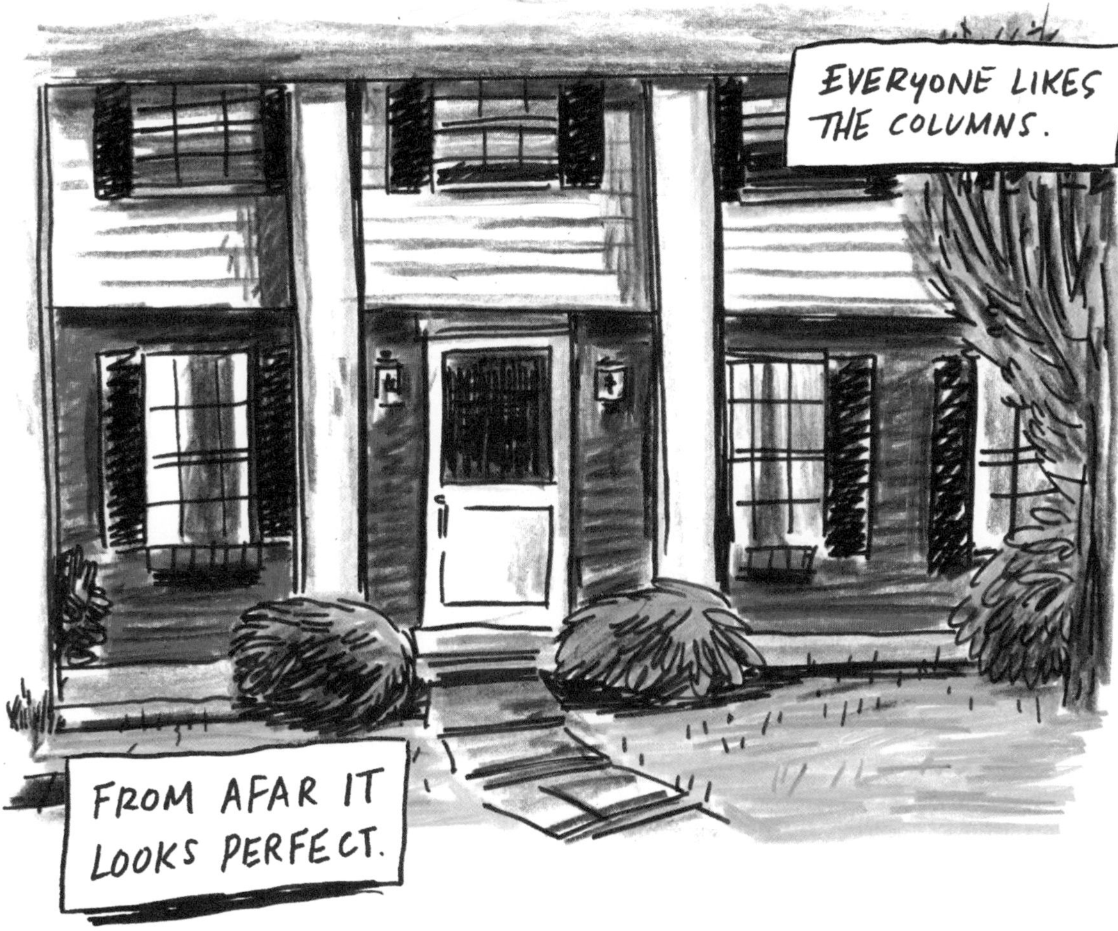
EVERYONE LIKES THE COLUMNS.
FROM AFAR IT LOOKS PERFECT.

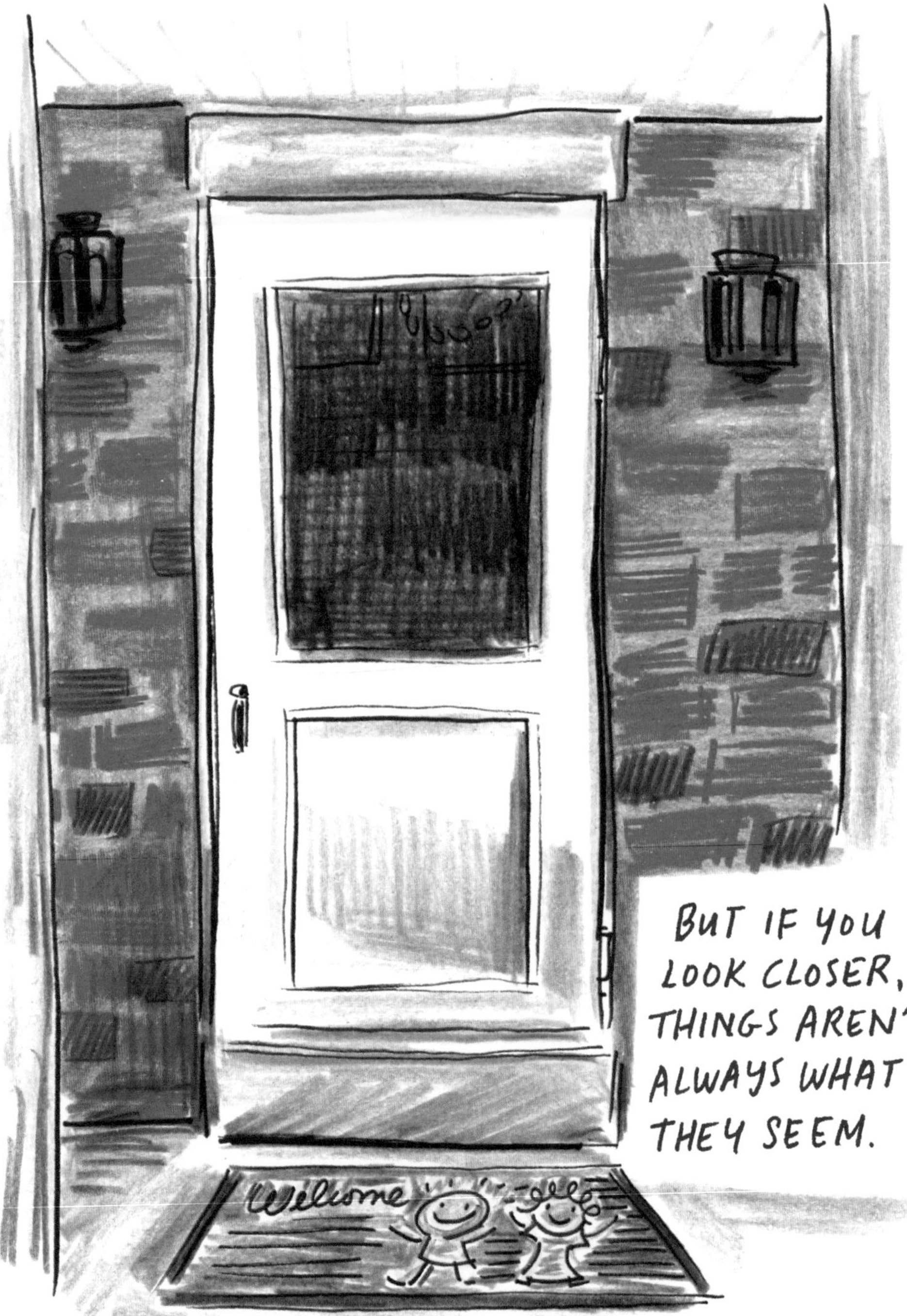
Welcome
BUT IF YOU LOOK CLOSER, THINGS AREN'T ALWAYS WHAT THEY SEEM.

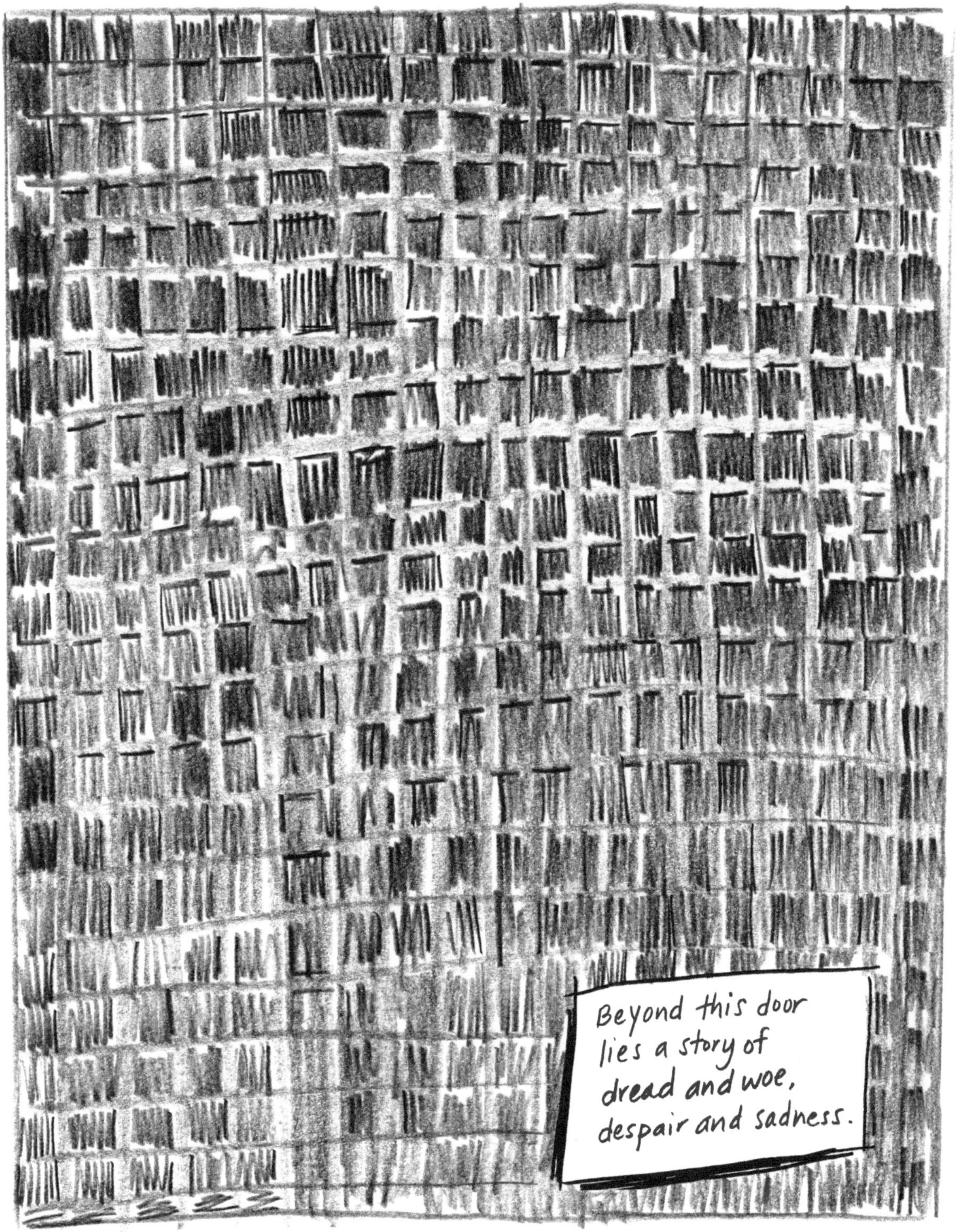
Beyond this door lies a story of dread and woe, despair and sadness.

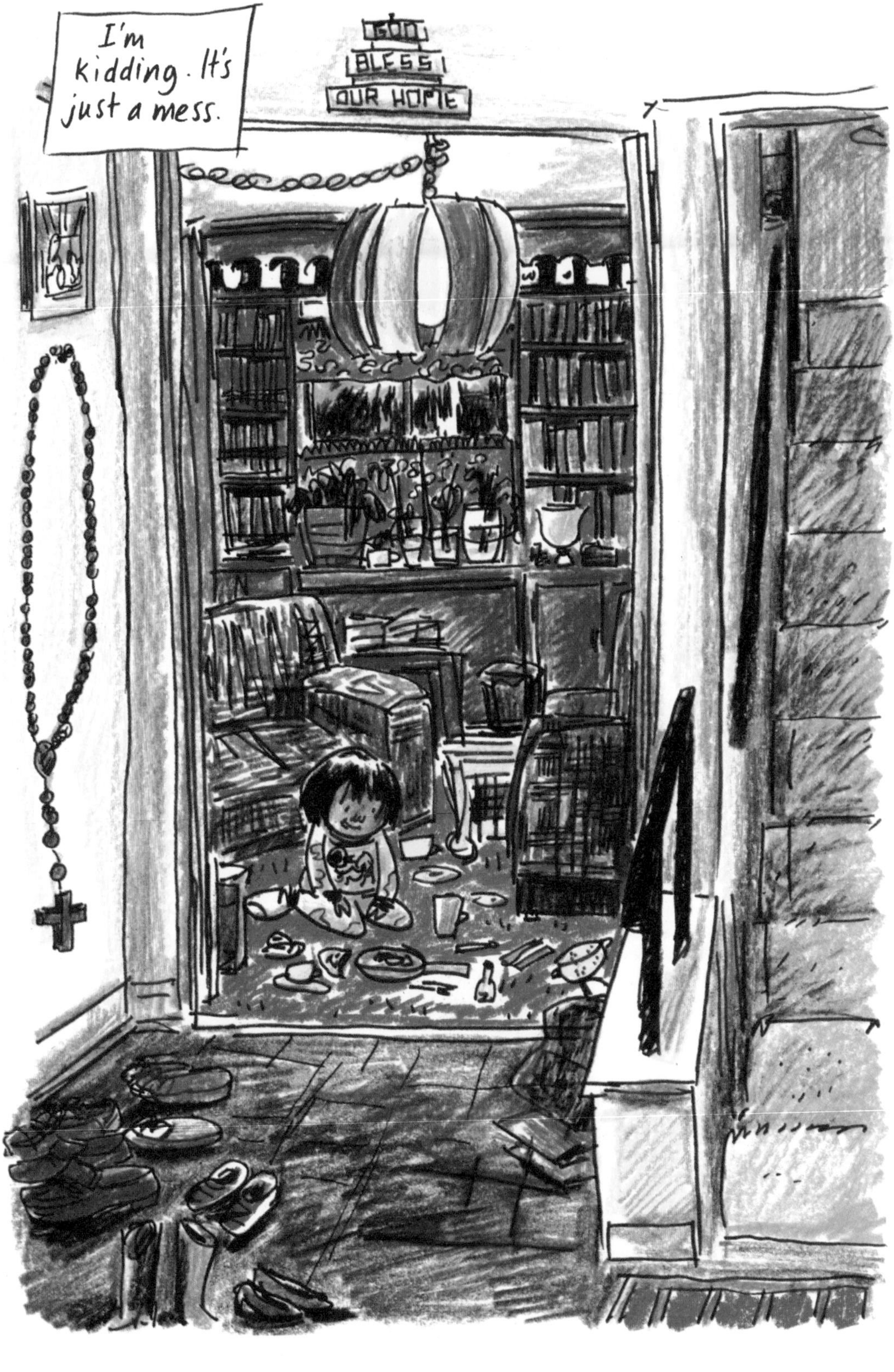
I'm kidding. It's just a mess.
GOD
BLESS
OUR HOME

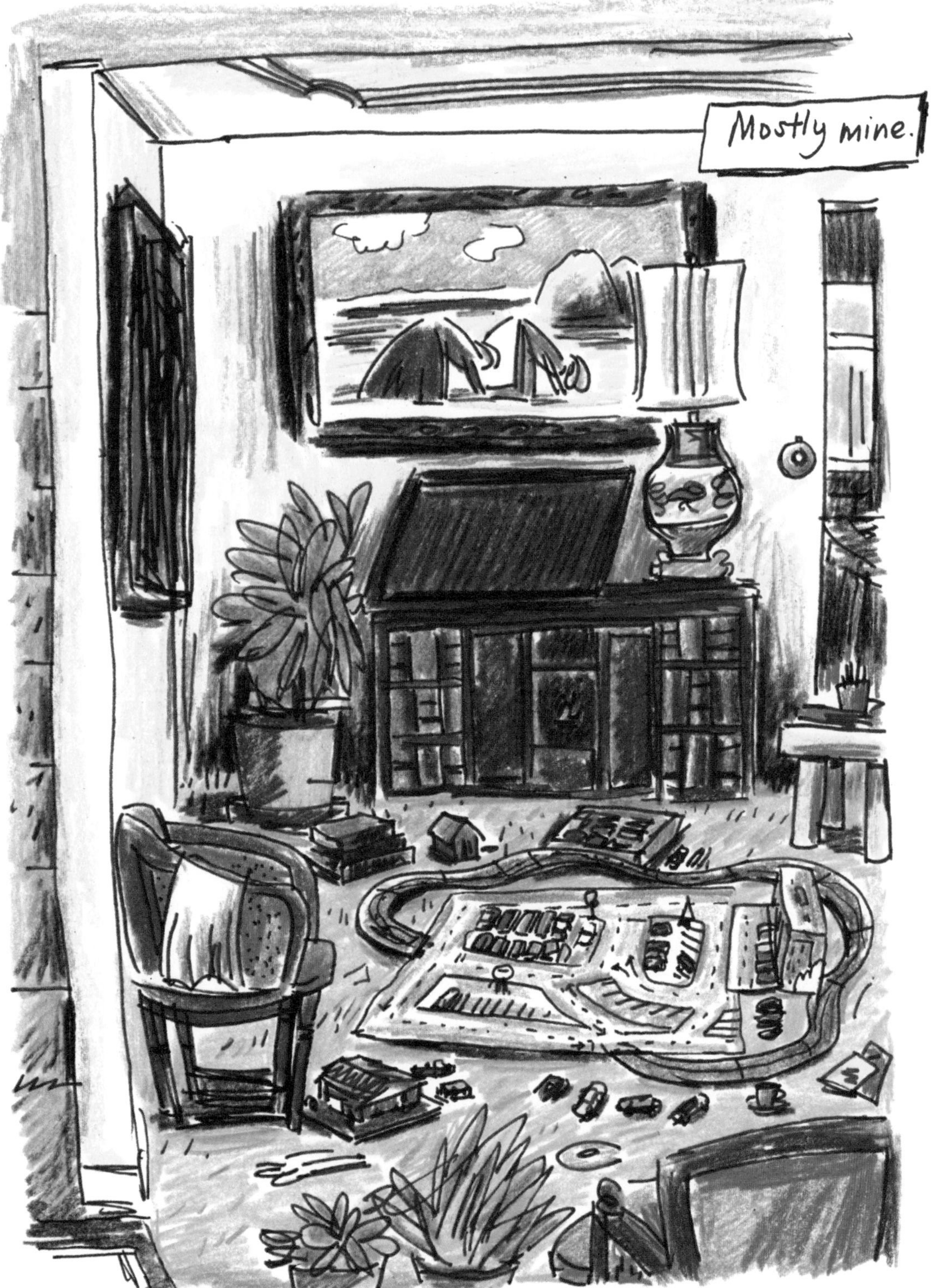
Mostly mine.

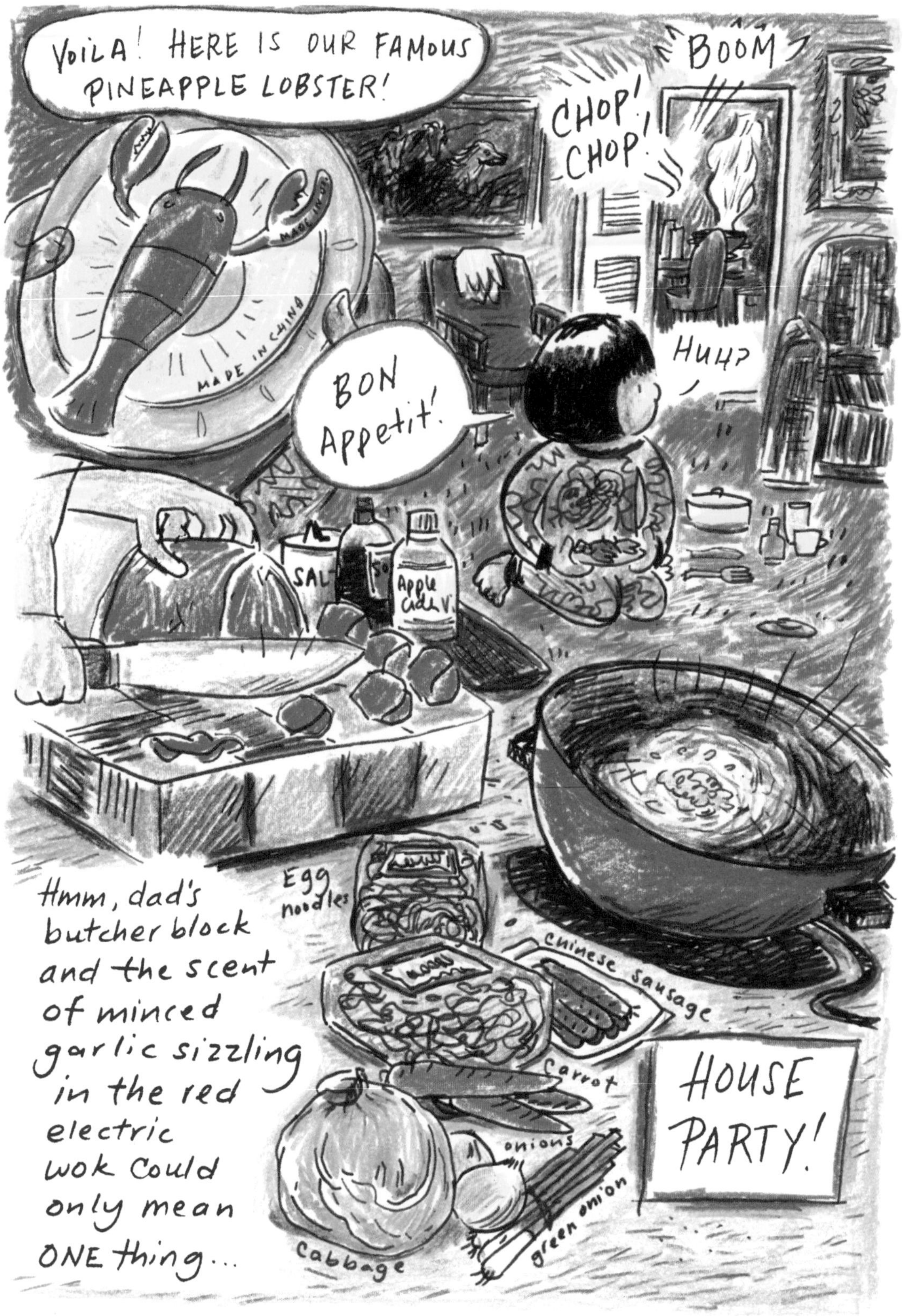
VoiLA! HERE IS OUR FAMOUS PINEAPPLE LOBSTER!
BOOM
CHOP! CHOP!
MADE IN CHINA
BON Appetit!
HUH?
SALT
Apple Cider Vi
Egg noodles
Chinese sausage
carrot
onions
green onion
Cabbage
HOUSE PARTY!
Hmm, dad's butcher block and the scent of minced garlic sizzling in the red electric wok could only mean ONE thing...

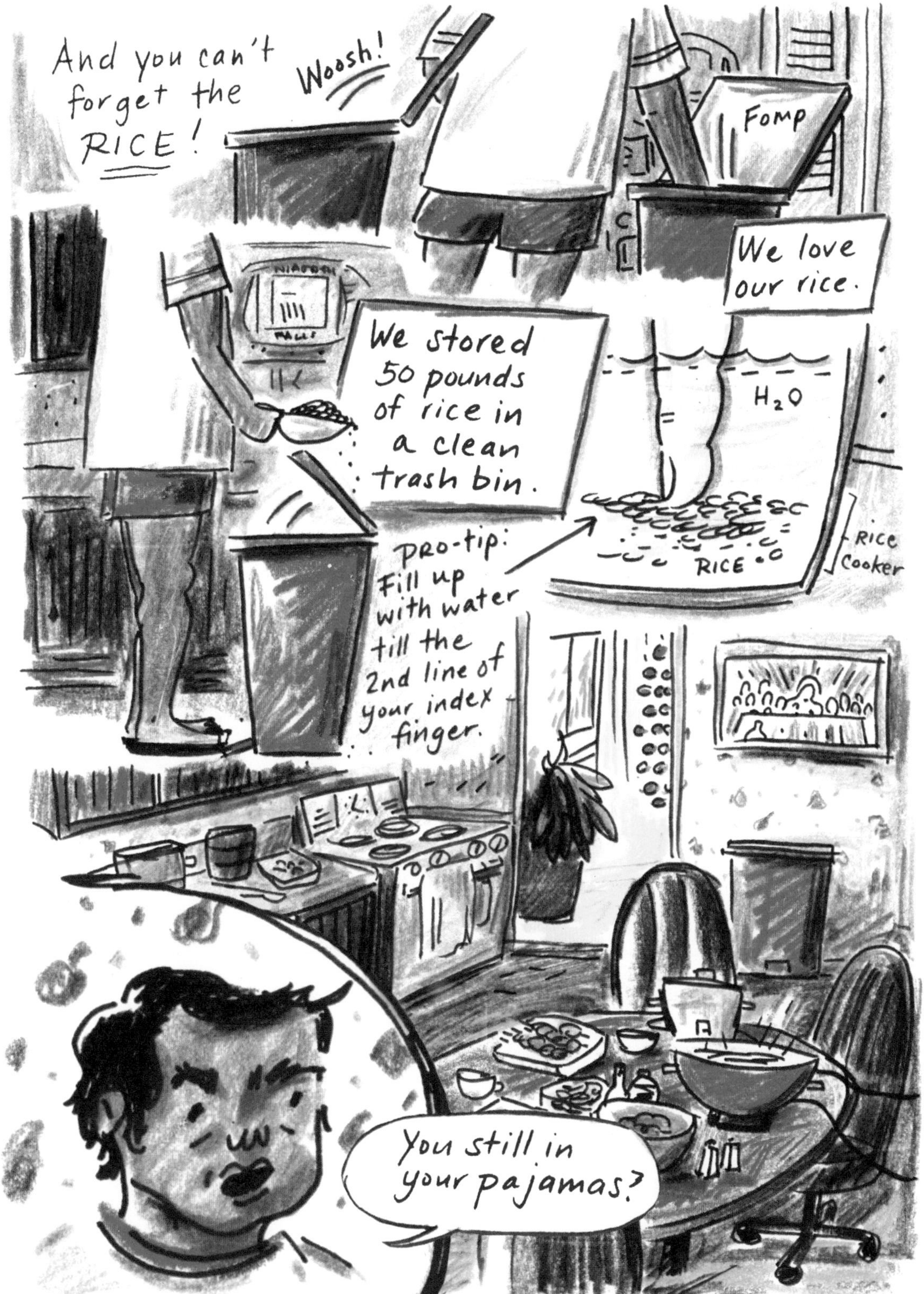
And you can't forget the RICE!
Woosh!
Fomp
We love our rice.
We stored 50 pounds of rice in a clean trash bin.
H2O
RICE
RICE Cooker
PRO-tip: Fill up with water till the 2nd line of your index finger.
You still in your pajamas?

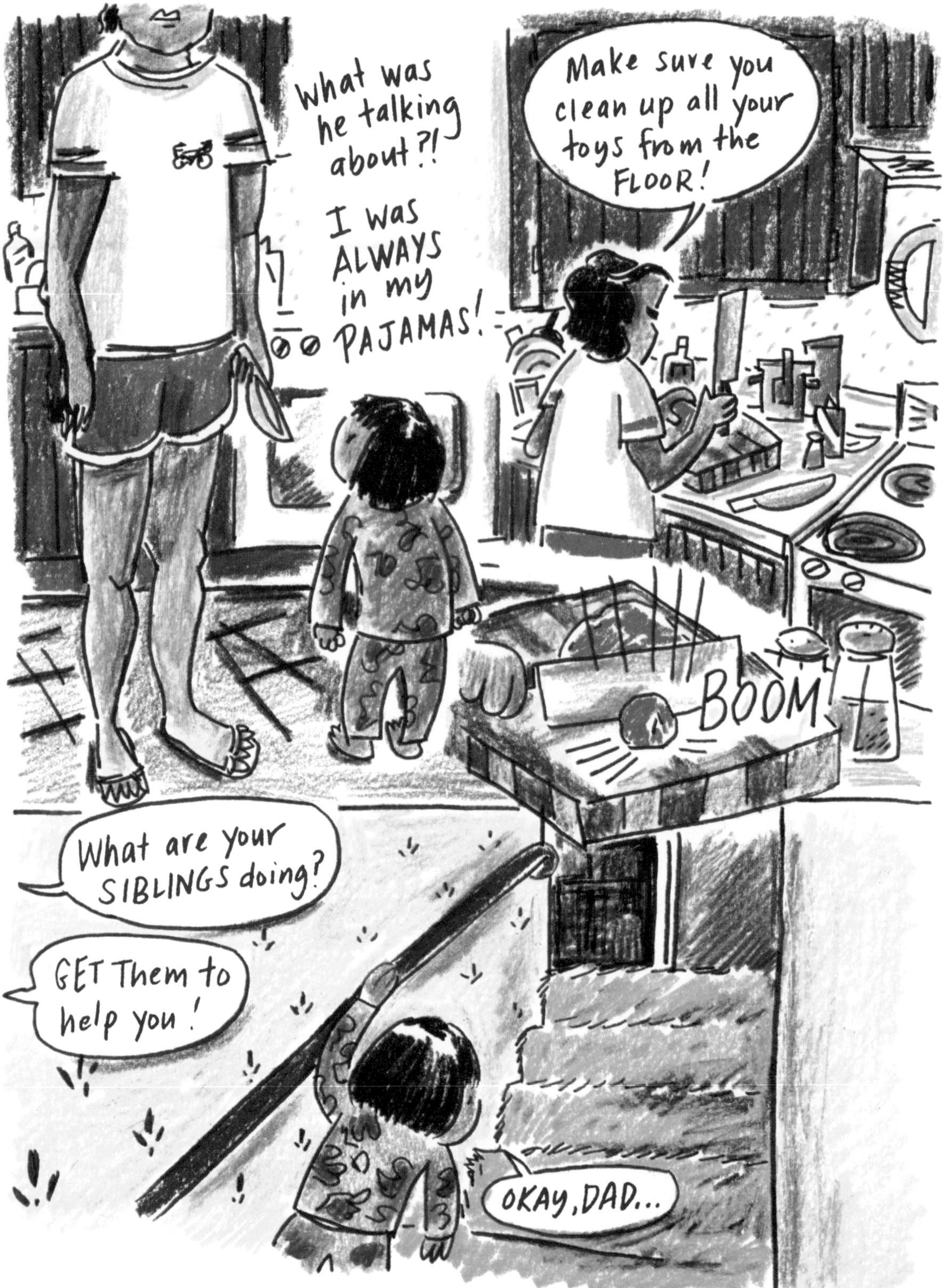
What was he talking about?!
I was ALWAYS in my PAJAMAS!
Make sure you clean up all your toys from the FLOOR!
BOOM!
What are your SIBLINGS doing?
GET Them to help you!
OKAY, DAD...

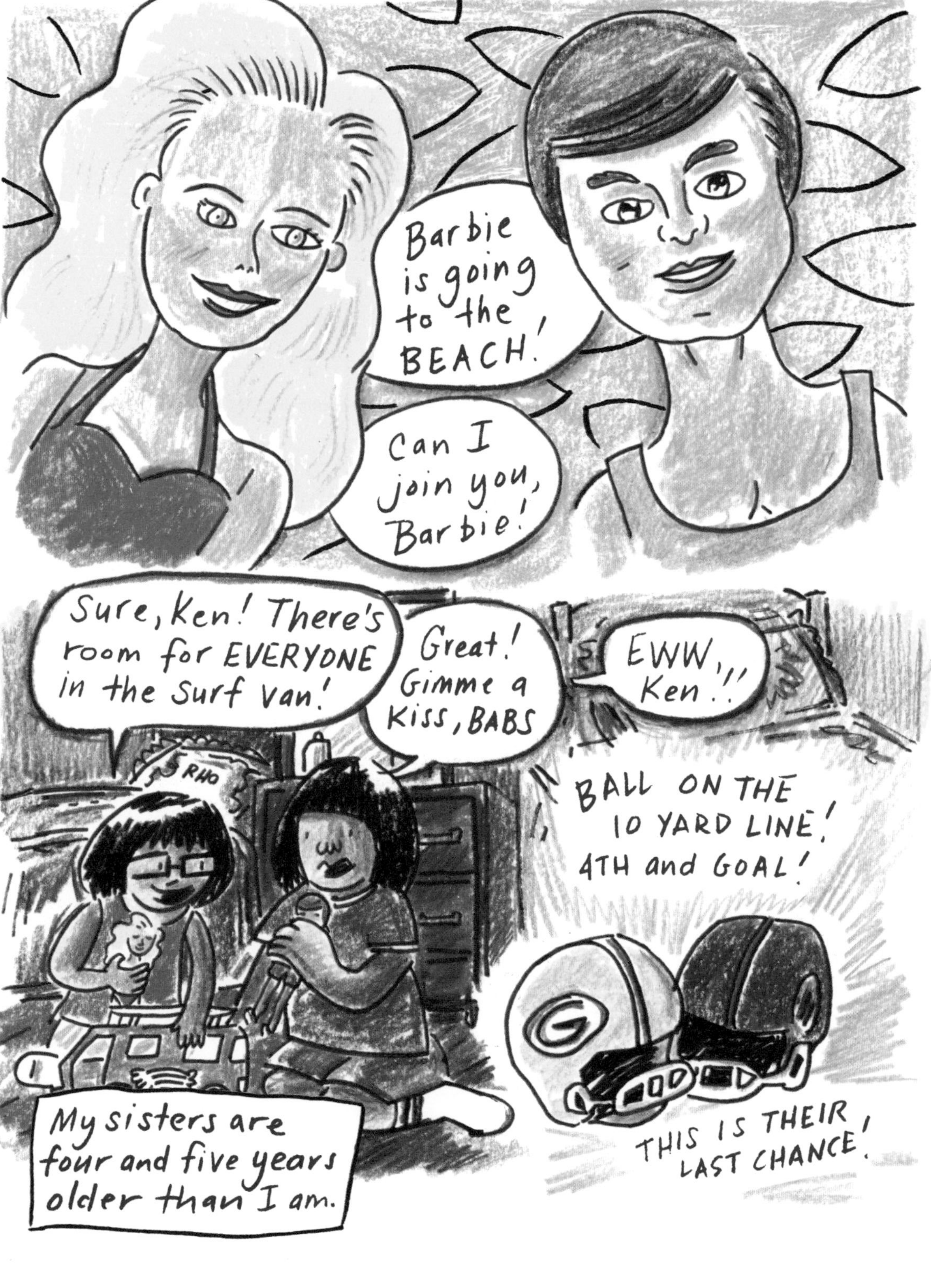
Barbie is going to the BEACH!
Can I join you, Barbie!
Sure, Ken! There's room for EVERYONE in the surf van!
Great! Gimme a kiss, BABS
EWW, Ken!!!
RHO
BALL ON THE 10 YARD LINE! 4TH and GOAL!
My sisters are four and five years older than I am.
THIS IS THEIR LAST CHANCE!

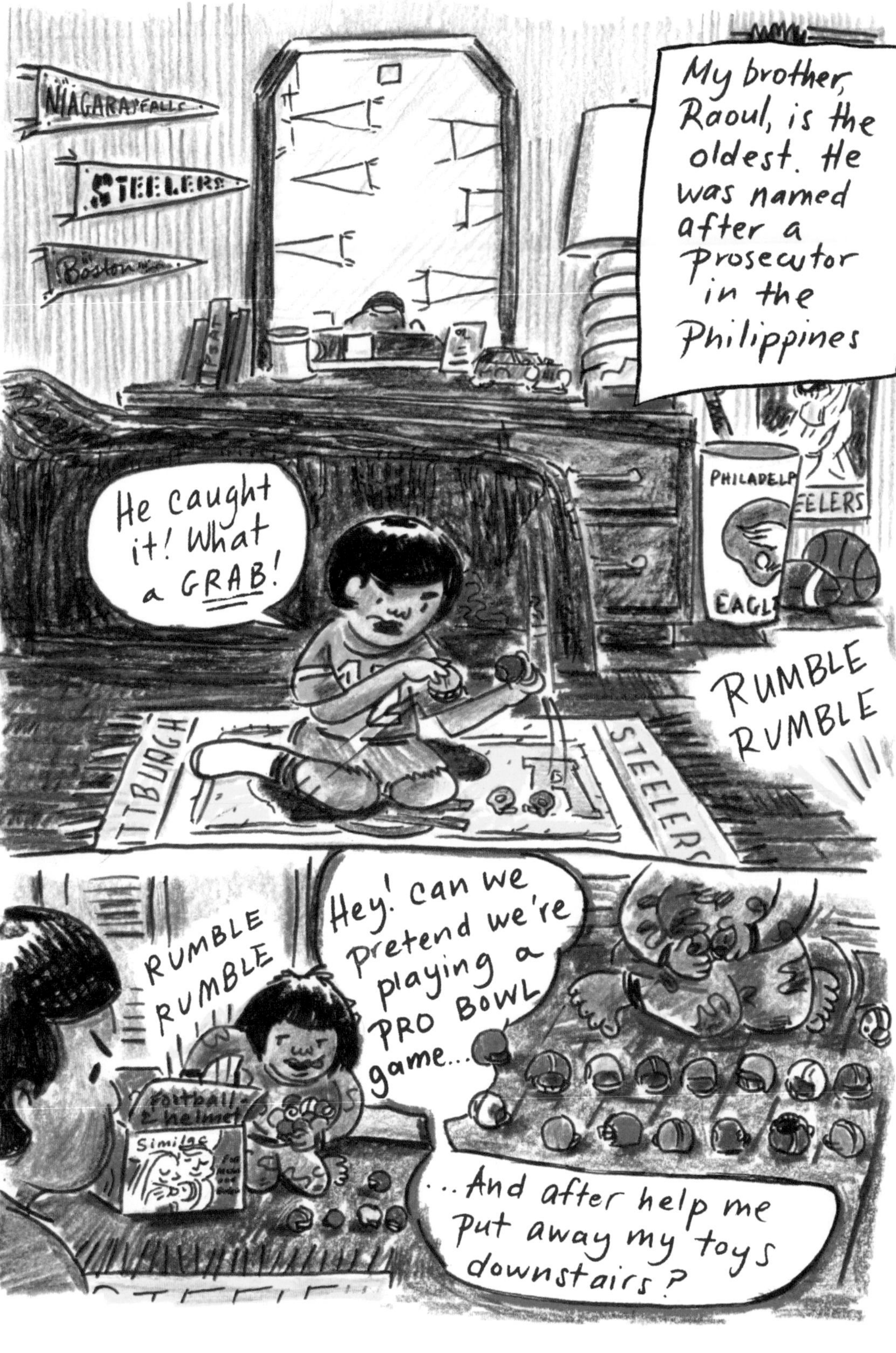
NIAGARA FALLS
STEELERS
Boston
My brother, Raoul, is the oldest. He was named after a prosecutor in the Philippines
PHILADELP
EAGL
EELERS
He caught it! What a GRAB!
RUMBLE RUMBLE
PITTSBURGH
STEELERS
RUMBLE RUMBLE
Hey! can we pretend we're playing a PRO BOWL game...
Football helmet
Similac
...And after help me put away my toys downstairs?

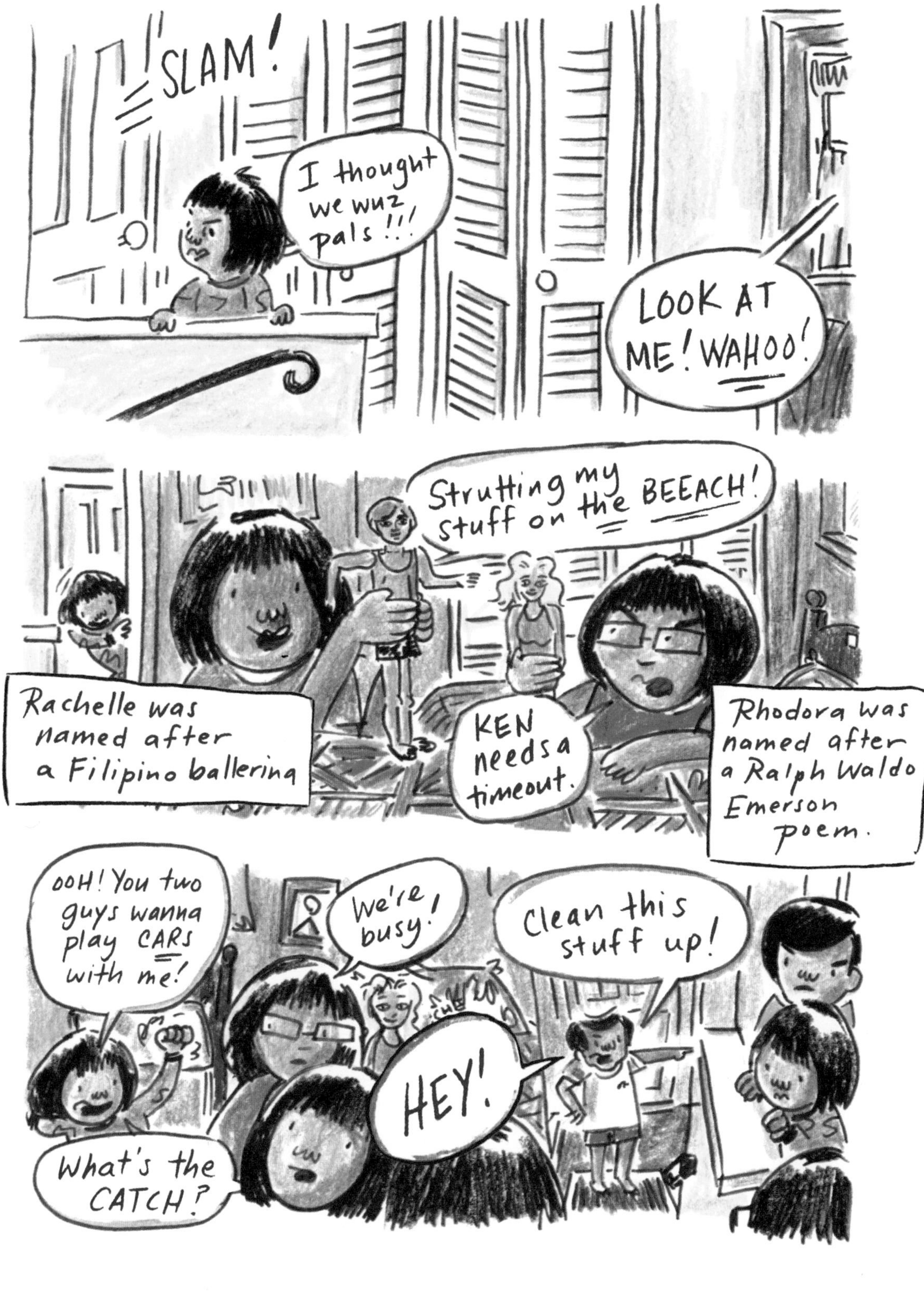
SLAM!
I thought we wuz pals!!!
LOOK AT ME! WAHOO!
Strutting my stuff on the BEEACH!
Rachelle was named after a Filipino ballerina
KEN needs a timeout.
Rhodora was named after a Ralph Waldo Emerson poem.
OOH! You two guys wanna play CARS with me!
We're busy!
Clean this stuff up!
HEY!
What's the CATCH?

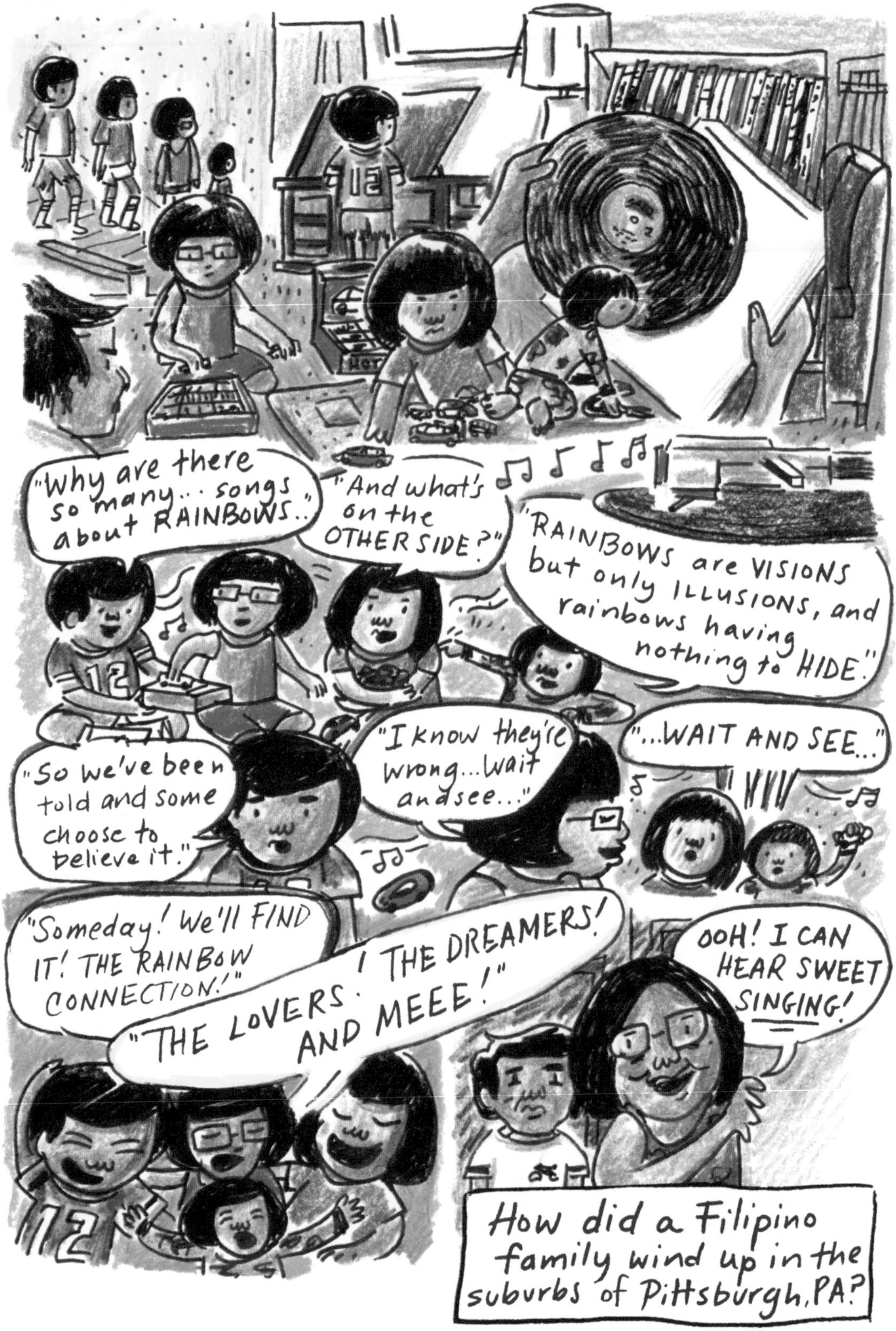
"Why are there so many... songs about RAINBOWS..."
"And what's on the OTHER SIDE?"
"RAINBOWS are VISIONS but only ILLUSIONS, and rainbows having nothing to HIDE."
"So we've been told and some choose to believe it."
"I know they're wrong... wait and see..."
"...WAIT AND SEE..."
"Someday! We'll FIND IT! THE RAINBOW CONNECTION!"
"THE LOVERS! THE DREAMERS! AND MEEE!"
OOH! I CAN HEAR SWEET SINGING!
How did a Filipino family wind up in the suburbs of Pittsburgh, PA?

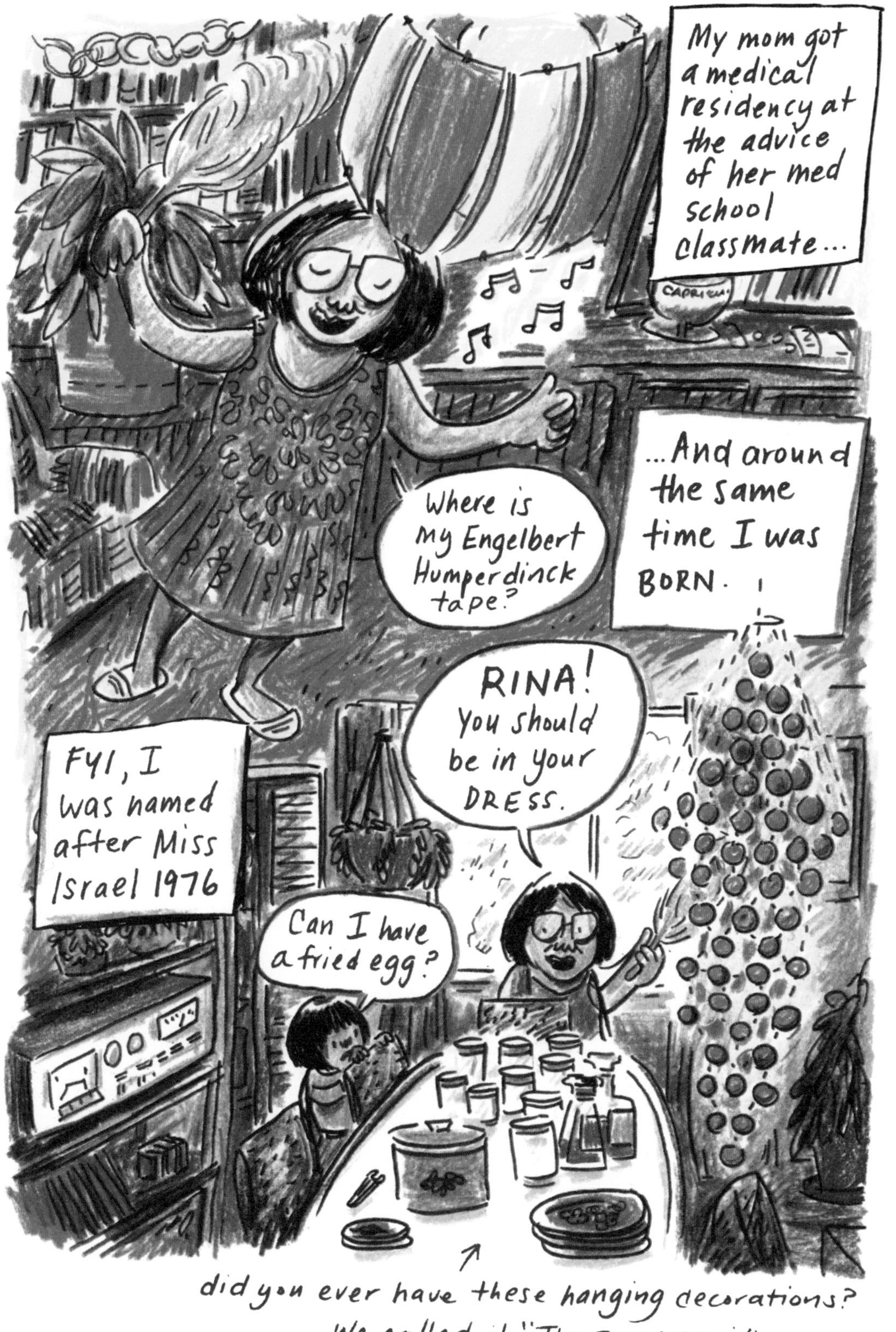
My mom got a medical residency at the advice of her med school classmate...
Where is my Engelbert Humperdinck tape?
...And around the same time I was BORN.
RINA! You should be in your DRESS.
FYI, I was named after Miss Israel 1976
Can I have a fried egg?
CAPRICE
did you ever have these hanging decorations? We called it "The pepperoni."

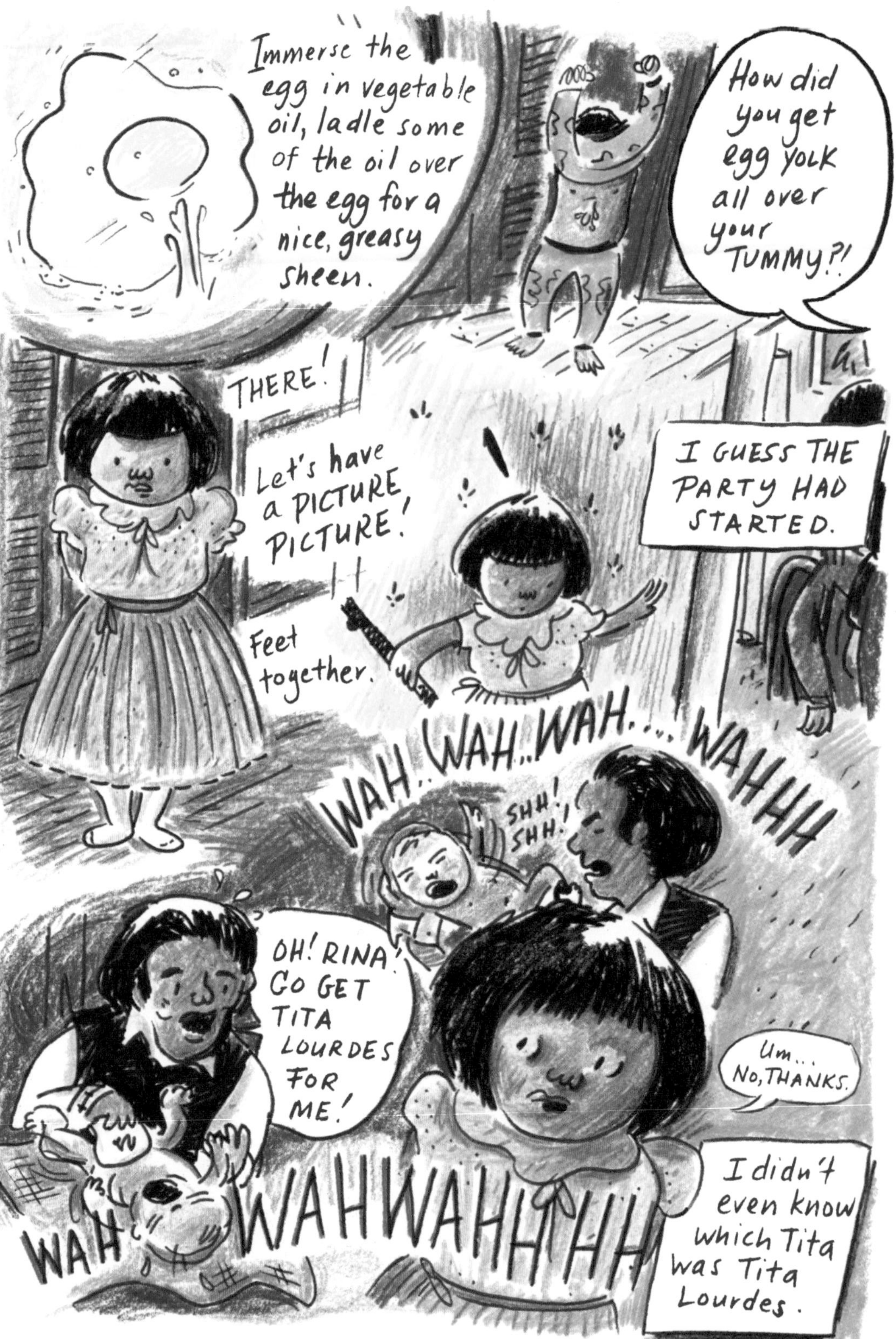
Immerse the egg in vegetable oil, ladle some of the oil over the egg for a nice, greasy sheen.
How did you get egg yolk all over your TUMMY?!
THERE!
Let's have a PICTURE, PICTURE!
Feet together.
I GUESS THE PARTY HAD STARTED.
WAH.. WAH.. WAH.... WAHHH
SHH! SHH!
OH! RINA! GO GET TITA LOURDES FOR ME!
Um... No, THANKS.
WAH WAHWAHHHH
I didn't even know which Tita was Tita Lourdes.

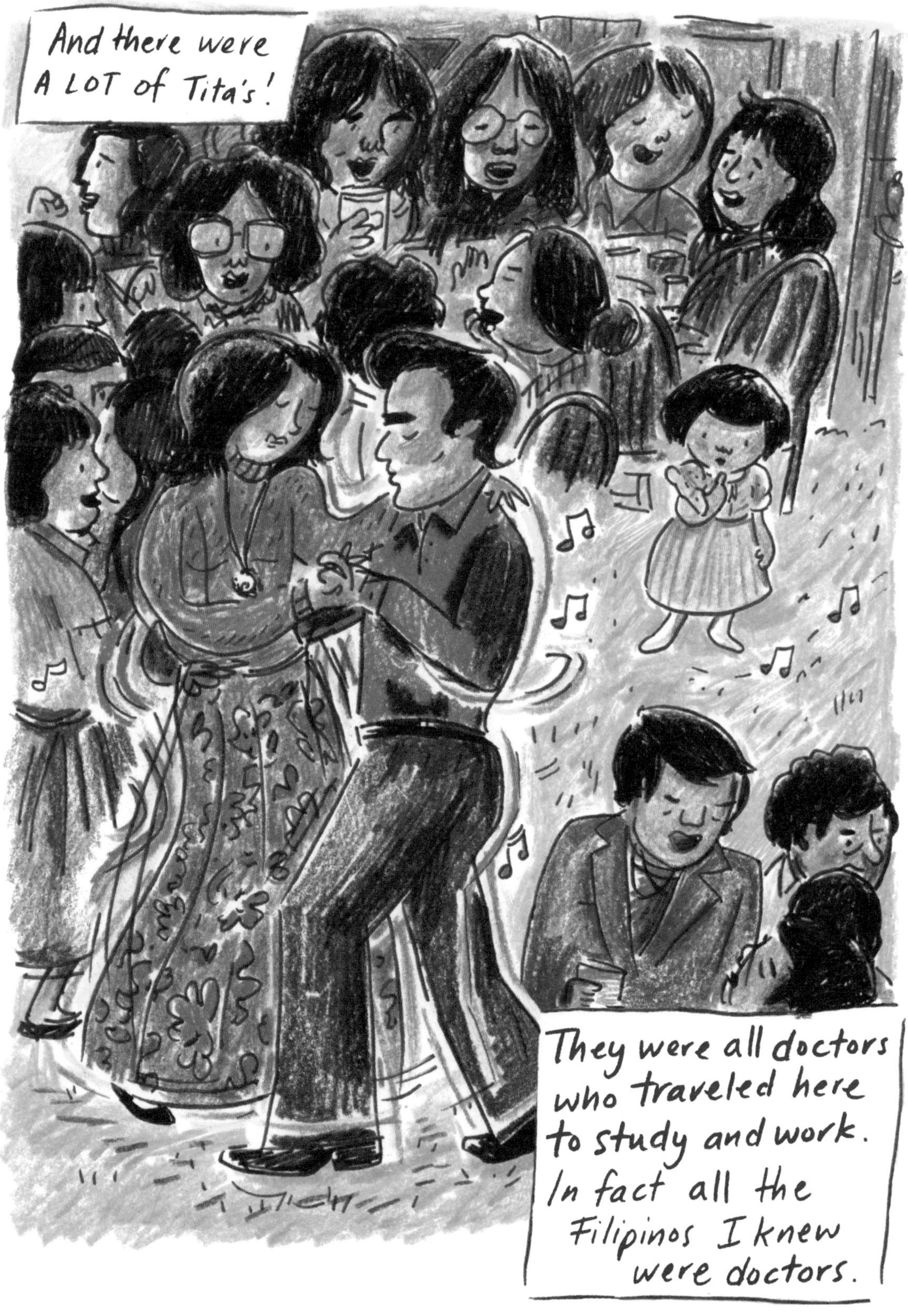
And there were A LOT of Tita's!
They were all doctors who traveled here to study and work. In fact all the Filipinos I knew were doctors.

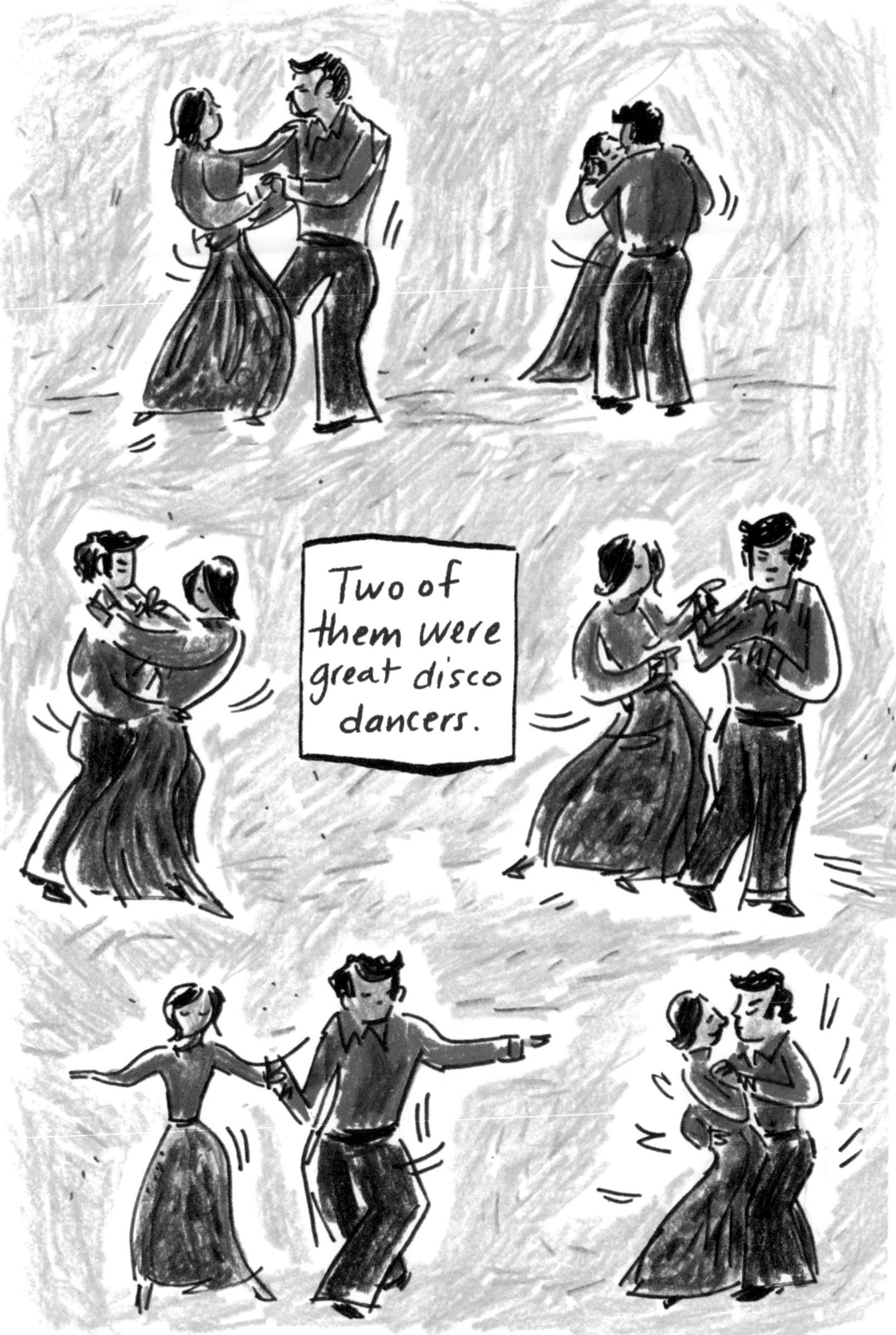
Two of them were great disco dancers.

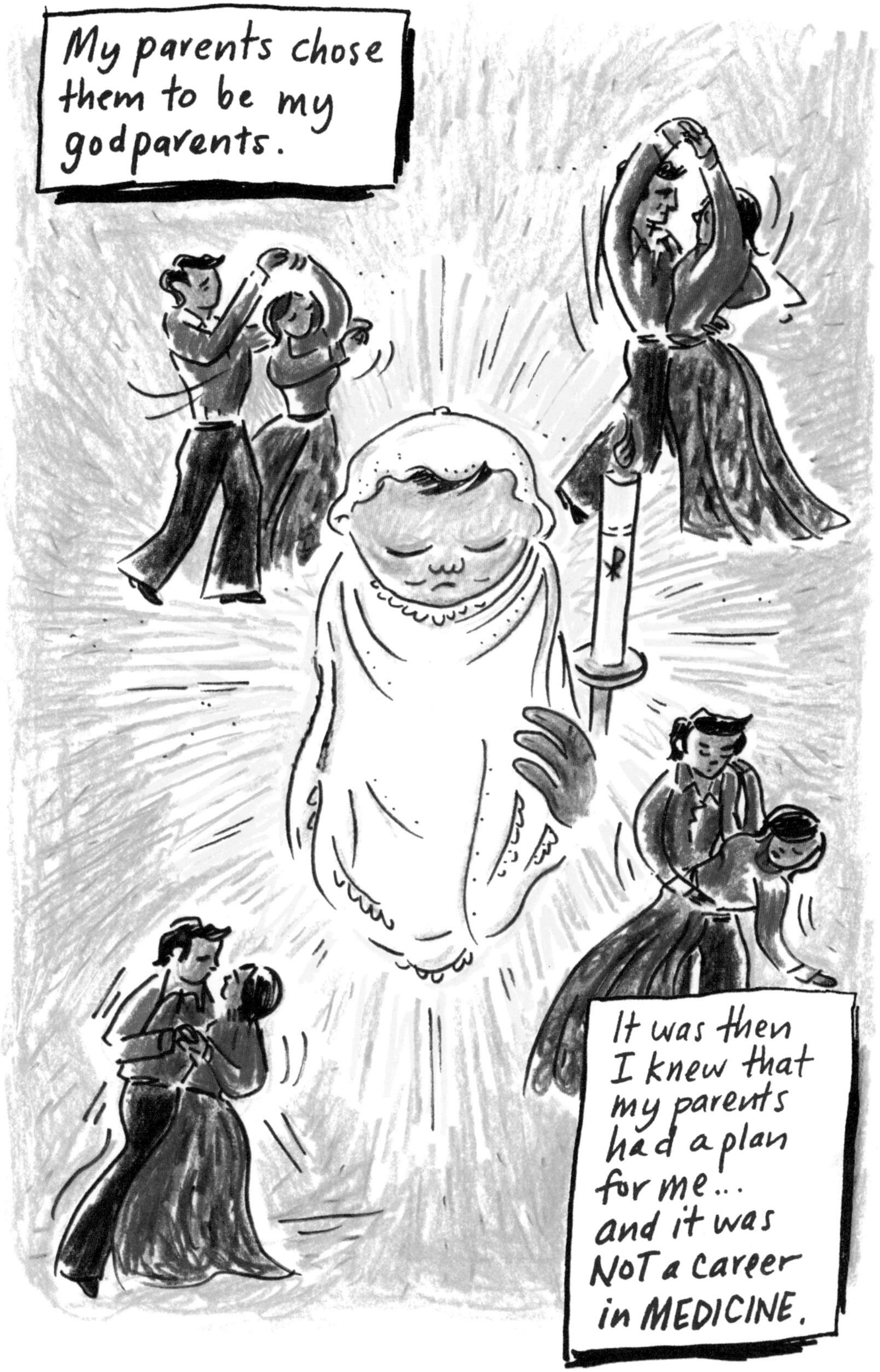
My parents chose them to be my godparents.
It was then I knew that my parents had a plan for me... and it was NOT a career in MEDICINE.

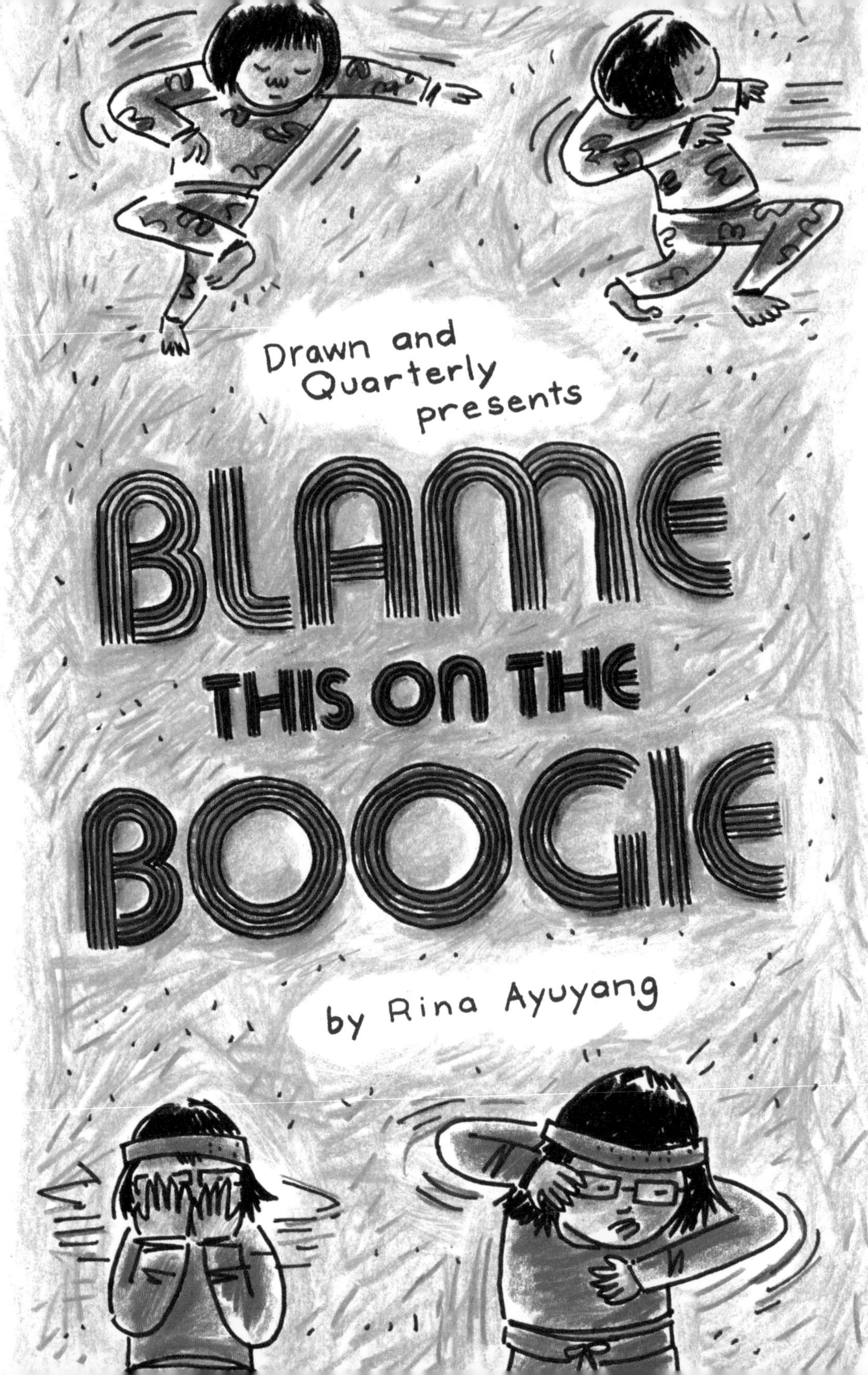
Drawn and Quarterly presents
BLAME THIS ON THE BOOGIE
by Rina Ayuyang

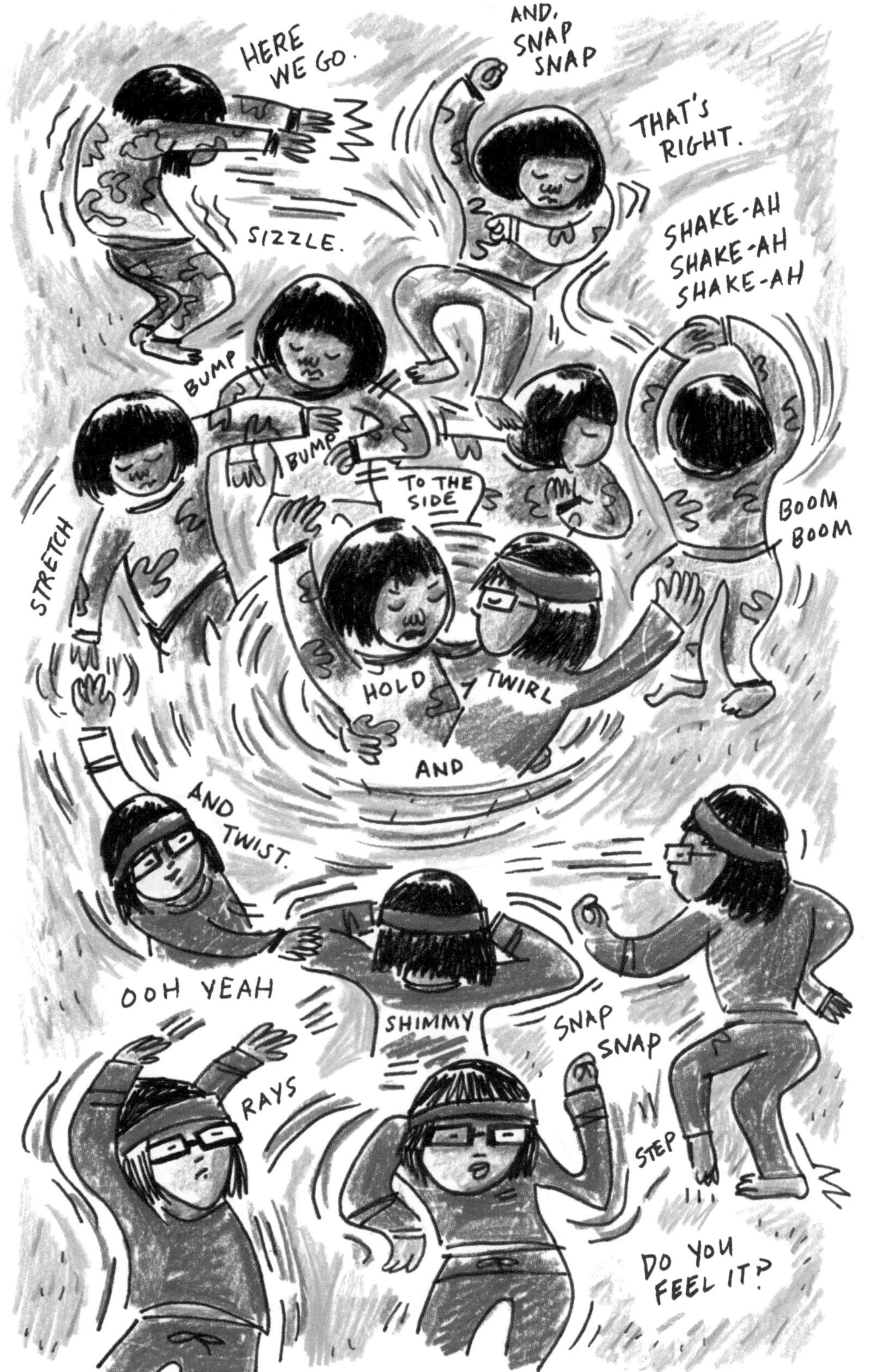
HERE WE GO.
AND, SNAP SNAP
THAT'S RIGHT.
SIZZLE.
SHAKE-AH SHAKE-AH SHAKE-AH
BUMP
BUMP
TO THE SIDE
STRETCH
BOOM BOOM
HOLD
TWIRL
AND
AND TWIST.
OOH YEAH
SHIMMY
SNAP SNAP
RAYS
STEP
DO YOU FEEL IT?

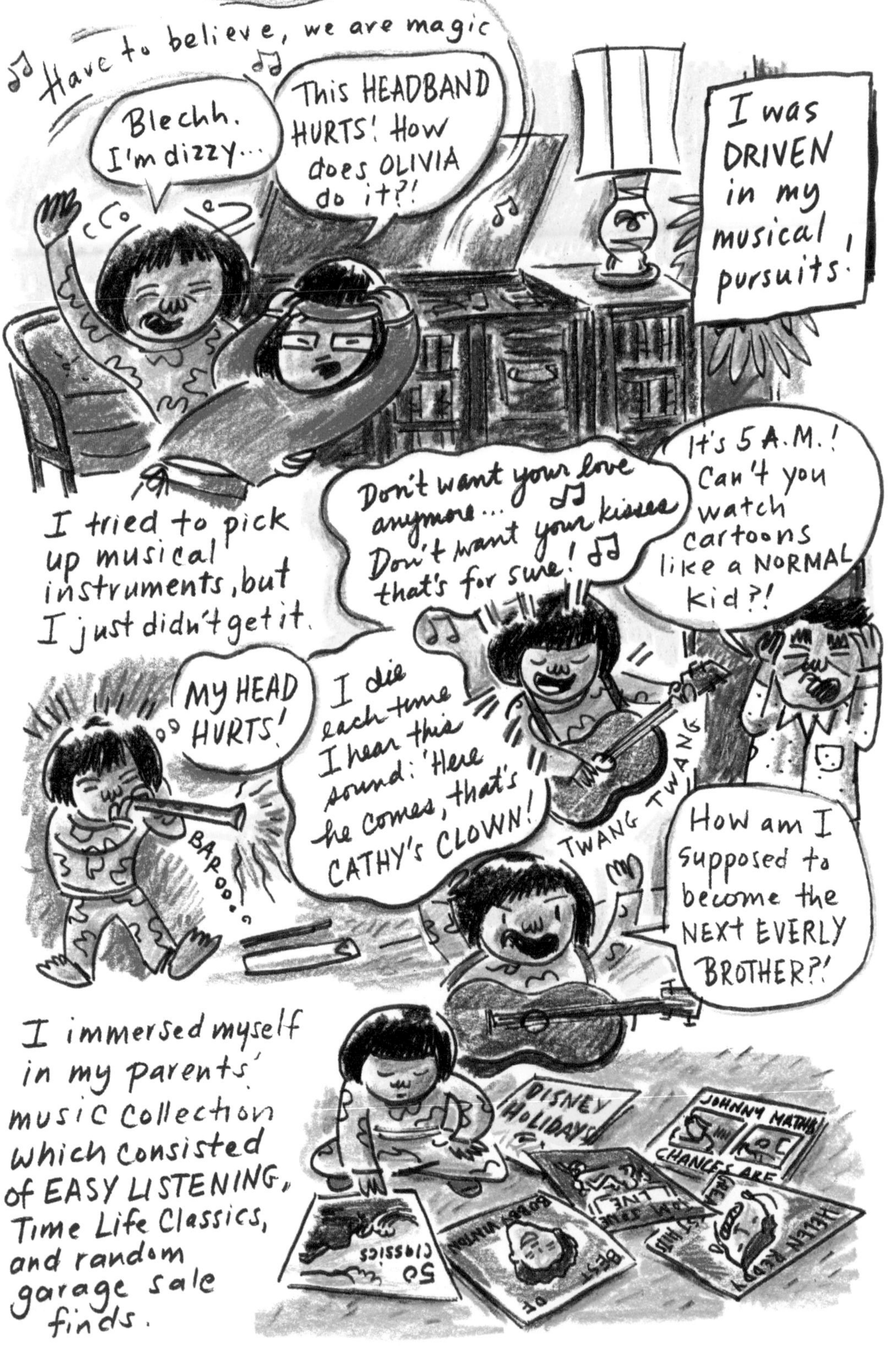
Have to believe, we are magic
Blechh. I'm dizzy...
This HEADBAND HURTS! How does OLIVIA do it?!
I was DRIVEN in my musical pursuits!
I tried to pick up musical instruments, but I just didn't get it.
Don't want your love anymore... Don't want your kisses that's for sure!
It's 5 A.M.! Can't you watch cartoons like a NORMAL kid?!
MY HEAD HURTS!
BAROOO!
I die each time I hear this sound: 'Here he comes, that's CATHY'S CLOWN!
TWANG TWANG
How am I supposed to become the NEXT EVERLY BROTHER?!
I immersed myself in my parents' music collection which consisted of EASY LISTENING, Time Life Classics, and random garage sale finds.
DISNEY HOLIDAY
JOHNNY MATHIS
CHANCES ARE
BOBBY VINTON
HELEN REDDY

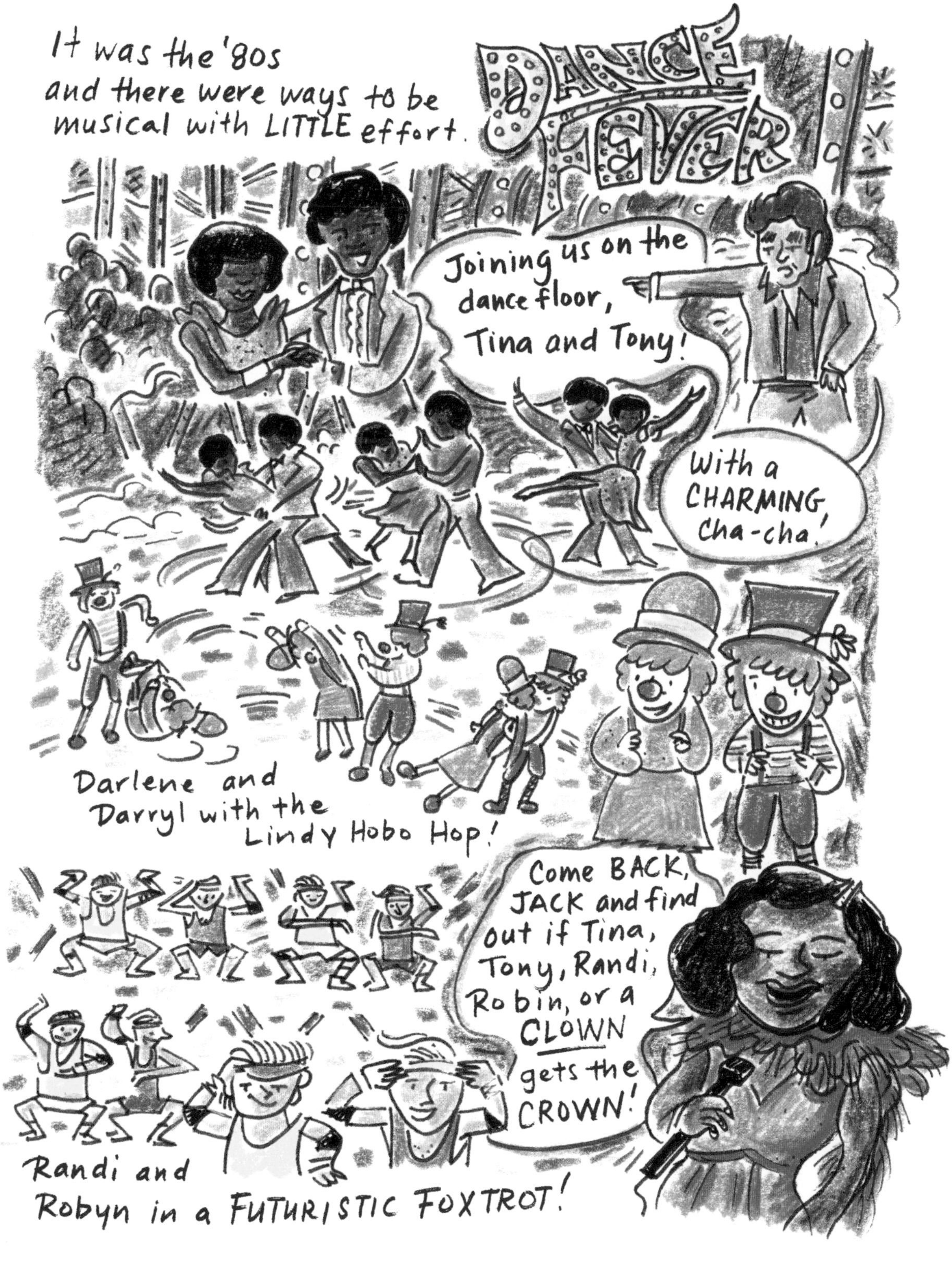
It was the '80s and there were ways to be musical with LITTLE effort.
DANCE FEVER
Joining us on the dance floor, Tina and Tony!
With a CHARMING Cha-cha!
Darlene and Darryl with the Lindy Hobo Hop!
Come BACK, JACK and find out if Tina, Tony, Randi, Robin, or a CLOWN gets the CROWN!
Randi and Robyn in a FUTURISTIC FOXTROT!

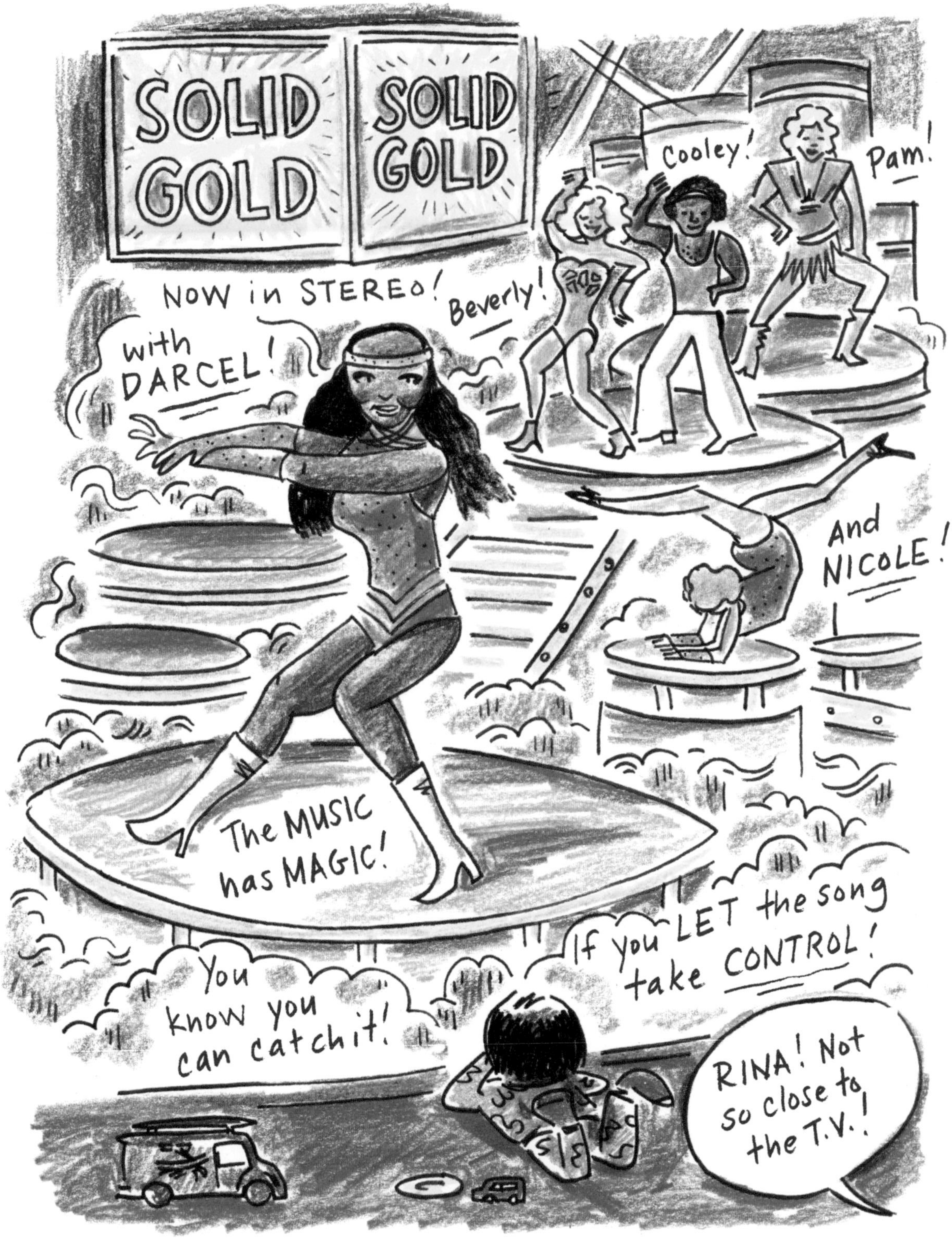
SOLID GOLD
SOLID GOLD
Cooley!
Pam!
NOW in STEREO!
Beverly!
with DARCEL!
And NICOLE!
The MUSIC has MAGIC!
You know you can catch it!
If you LET the song take CONTROL!
RINA! Not so close to the T.V.!

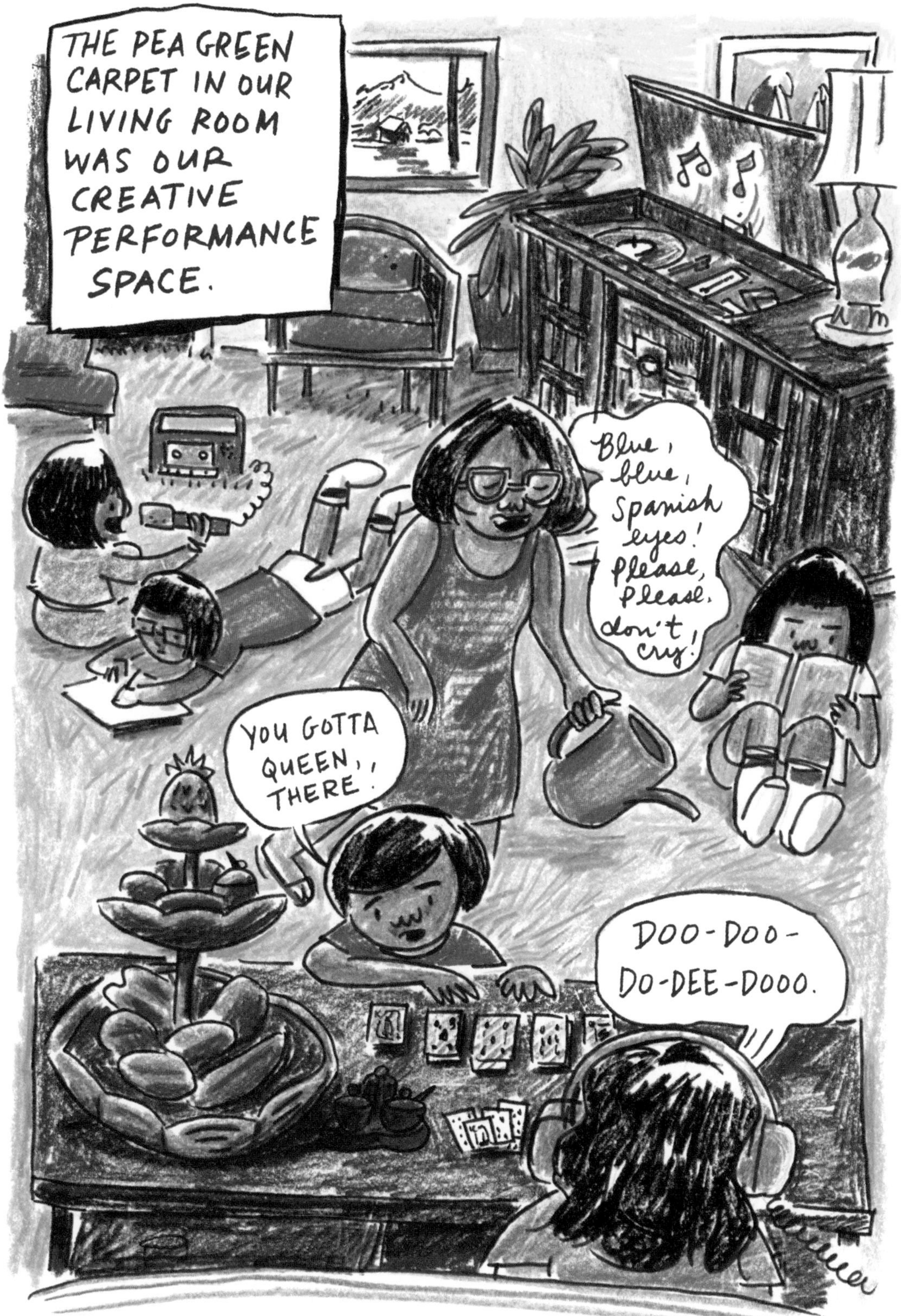
THE PEA GREEN CARPET IN OUR LIVING ROOM WAS OUR CREATIVE PERFORMANCE SPACE.
Blue, blue, Spanish eyes! Please, Please, don't cry!
YOU GOTTA QUEEN, THERE!
DOO-DOO-DO-DEE-DOOO.

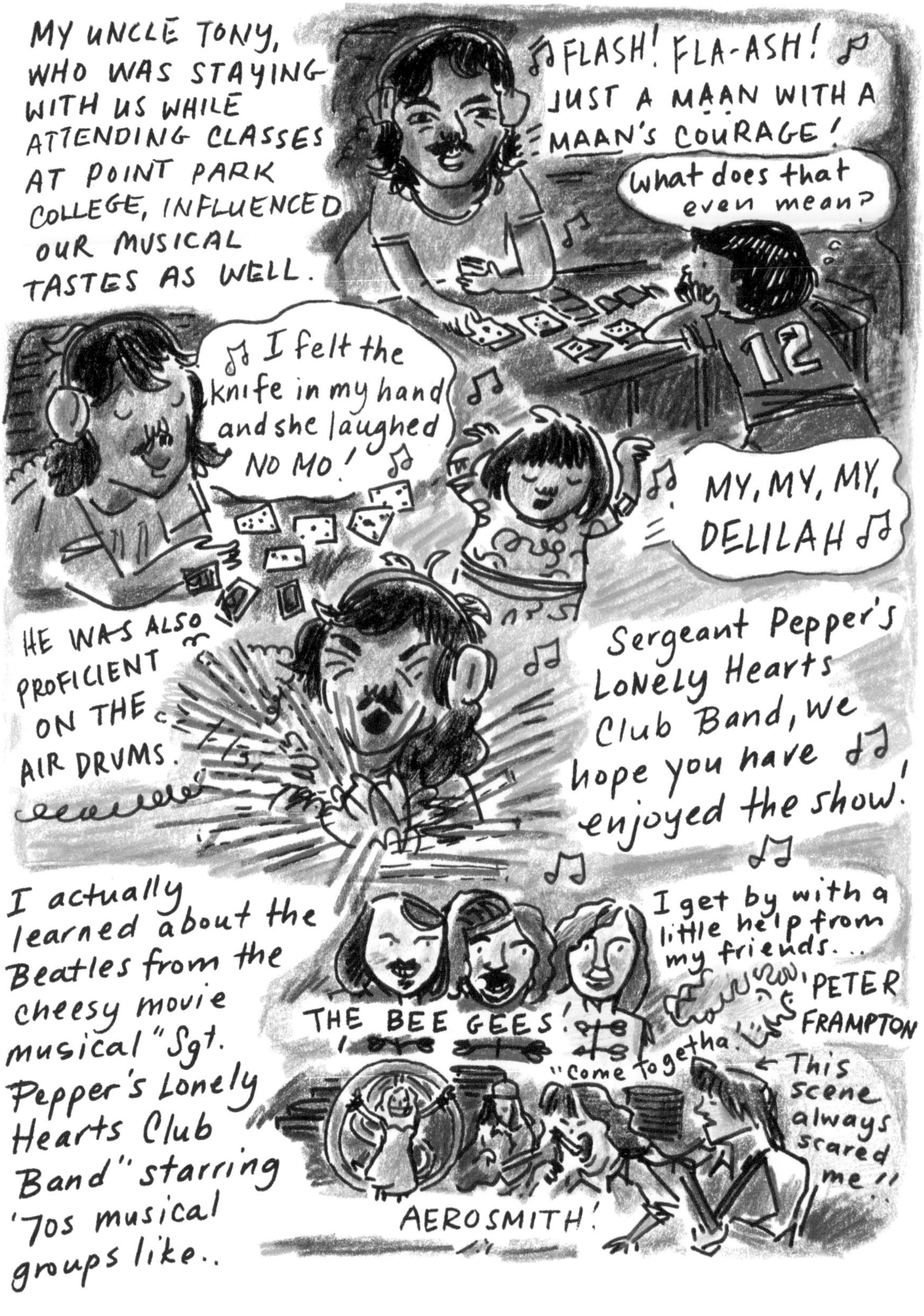
MY UNCLE TONY, WHO WAS STAYING WITH US WHILE ATTENDING CLASSES AT POINT PARK COLLEGE, INFLUENCED OUR MUSICAL TASTES AS WELL.
FLASH! FLA-ASH! JUST A MAAN WITH A MAAN'S COURAGE!
what does that even mean?
12
I felt the knife in my hand and she laughed NO MO!
MY, MY, MY, DELILAH
HE WAS ALSO PROFICIENT ON THE AIR DRUMS.
Sergeant Pepper's Lonely Hearts Club Band, we hope you have enjoyed the show!
I actually learned about the Beatles from the cheesy movie musical "Sgt. Pepper's Lonely Hearts Club Band" starring '70s musical groups like..
I get by with a little help from my friends...
THE BEE GEES!
PETER FRAMPTON
"come togetha!"
This scene always scared me!!
AEROSMITH!

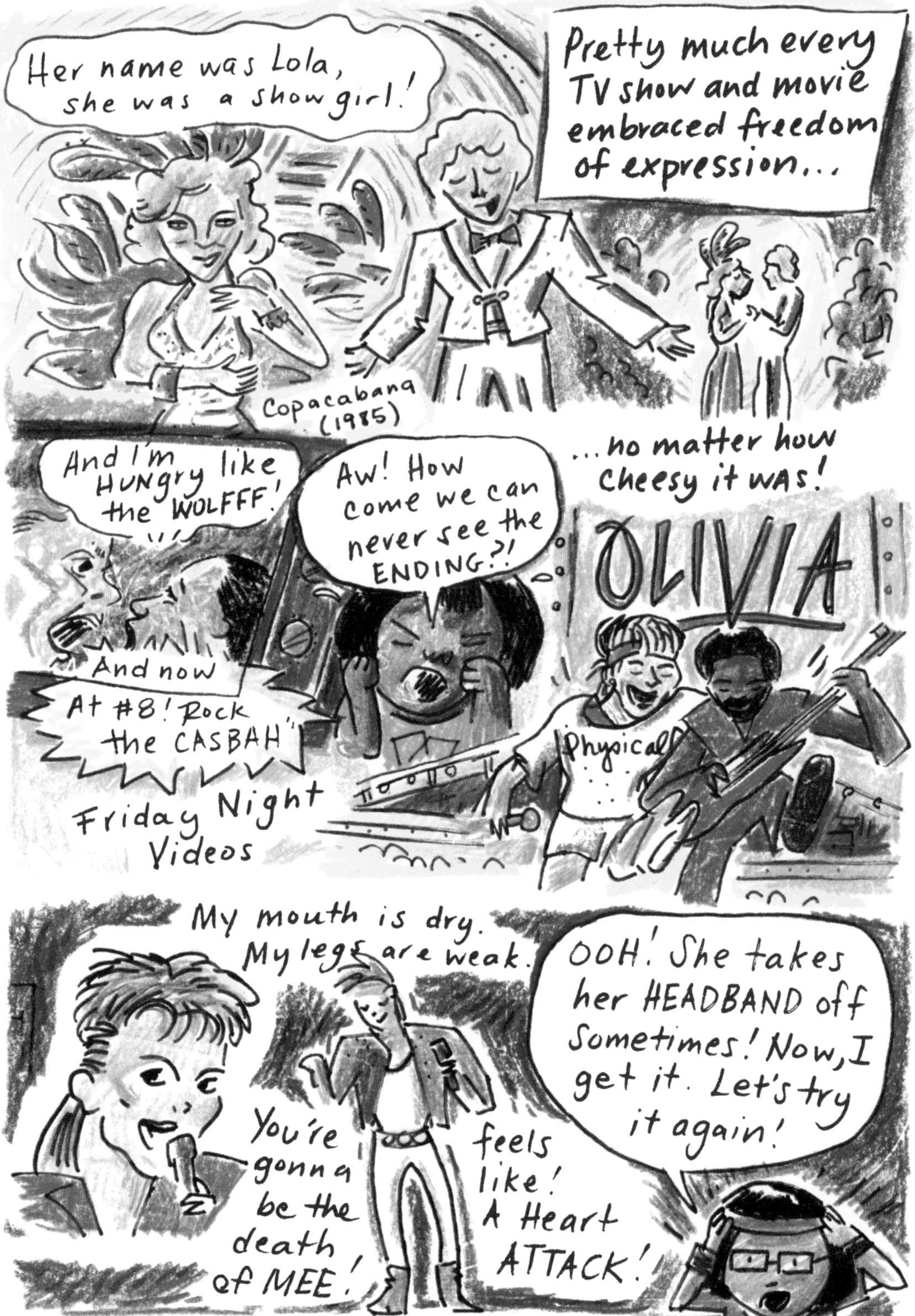

Her name was Lola, she was a show girl!
Pretty much every TV show and movie embraced freedom of expression...
Copacabana (1985)
And I'm HUNGRY like the WOLFFF!
Aw! How come we can never see the ENDING?!
...no matter how cheesy it was!
OLIVIA
And now
At #8! Rock the CASBAH
Physical
Friday Night Videos
My mouth is dry. My legs are weak.
OOH! She takes her HEADBAND off Sometimes! Now, I get it. Let's try it again!
You're gonna be the death of MEE!
feels like! A Heart ATTACK!

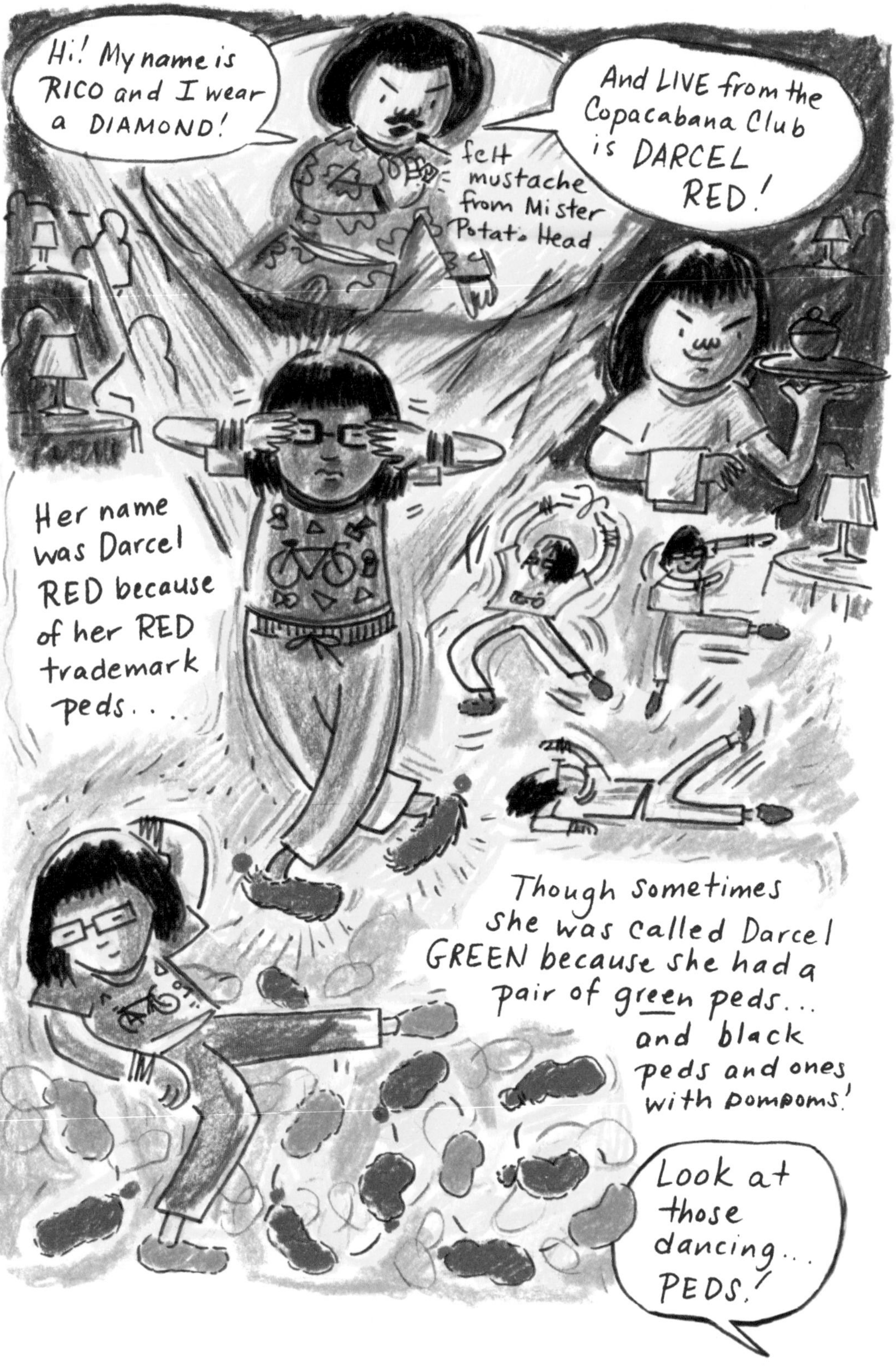
Hi! My name is RICO and I wear a DIAMOND!
And LIVE from the Copacabana Club is DARCEL RED!
felt mustache from Mister Potato Head.
Her name was Darcel RED because of her RED trademark peds...
Though sometimes she was called Darcel GREEN because she had a pair of green peds... and black peds and ones with pompoms!
Look at those dancing... PEDS!

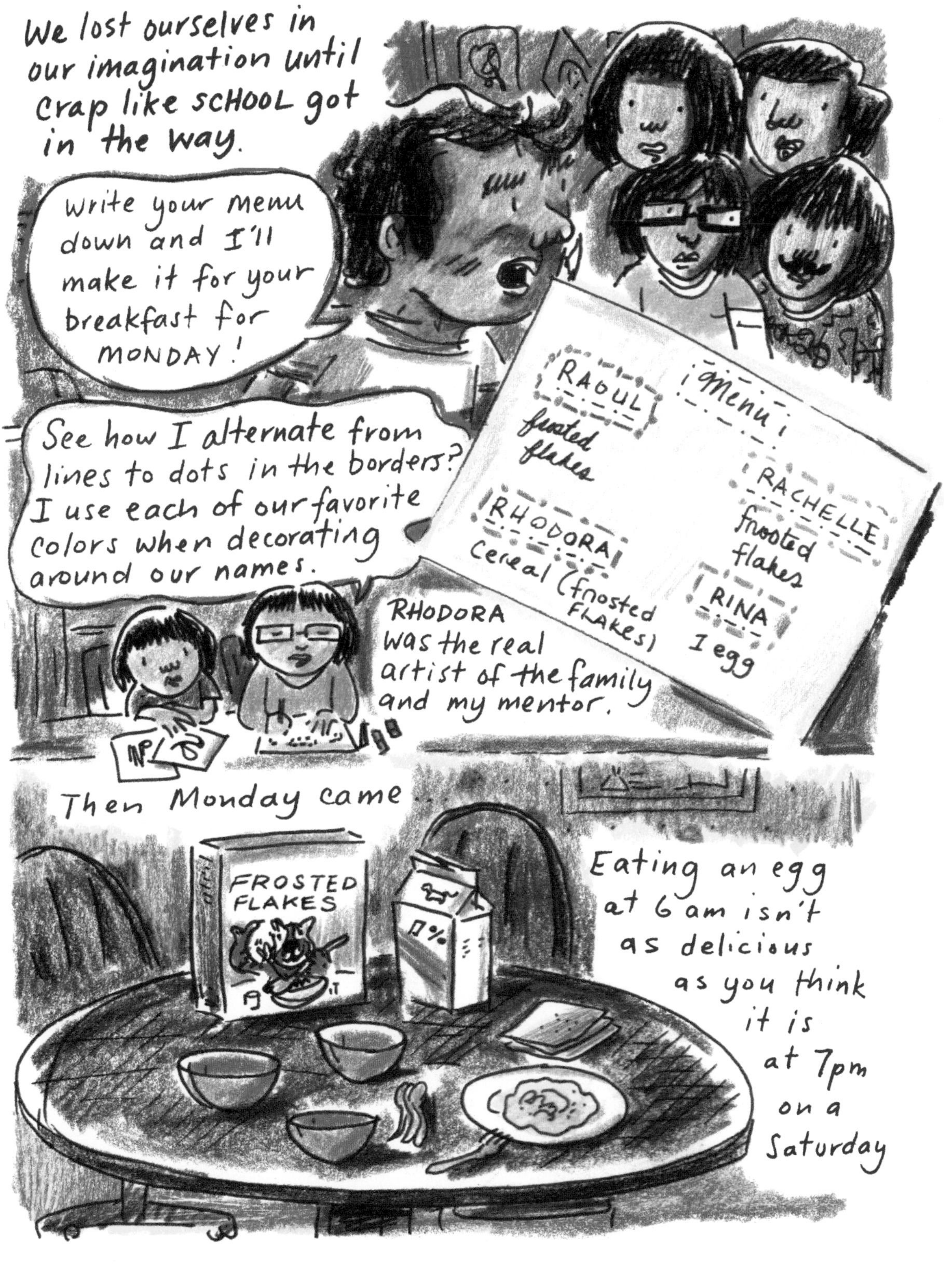

We lost ourselves in our imagination until crap like SCHOOL got in the way.
Write your menu down and I'll make it for your breakfast for MONDAY!
See how I alternate from lines to dots in the borders? I use each of our favorite colors when decorating around our names.
Menu
RAOUL
frosted flakes
RACHELLE
frosted flakes
RHODORA
Cereal (frosted FLAKES)
RINA
I egg
RHODORA was the real artist of the family and my mentor.
Then Monday came...
FROSTED FLAKES
Eating an egg at 6 am isn't as delicious as you think it is at 7pm on a Saturday

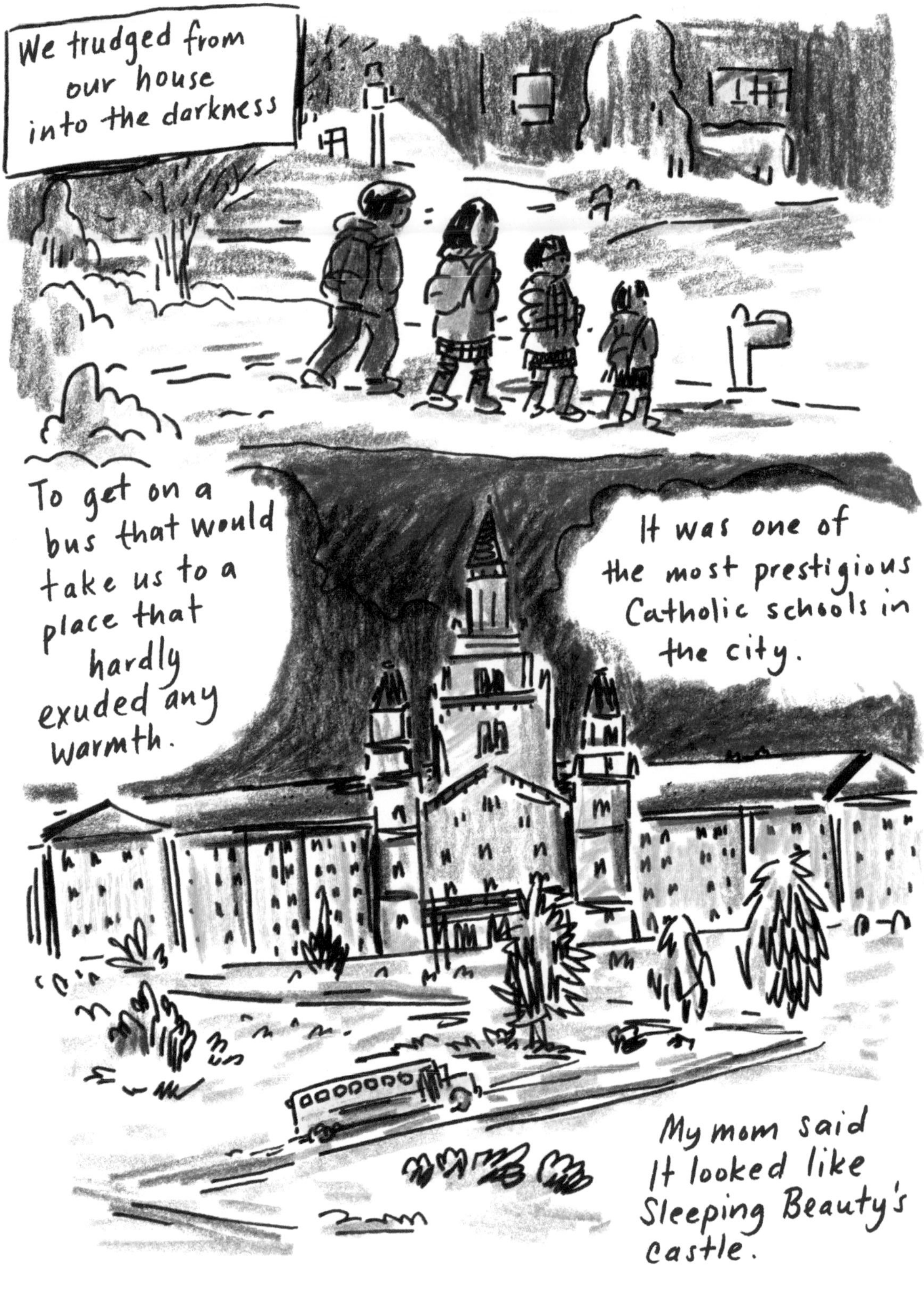
We trudged from our house into the darkness
To get on a bus that would take us to a place that hardly exuded any warmth.
It was one of the most prestigious Catholic schools in the city.
My mom said It looked like Sleeping Beauty's castle.

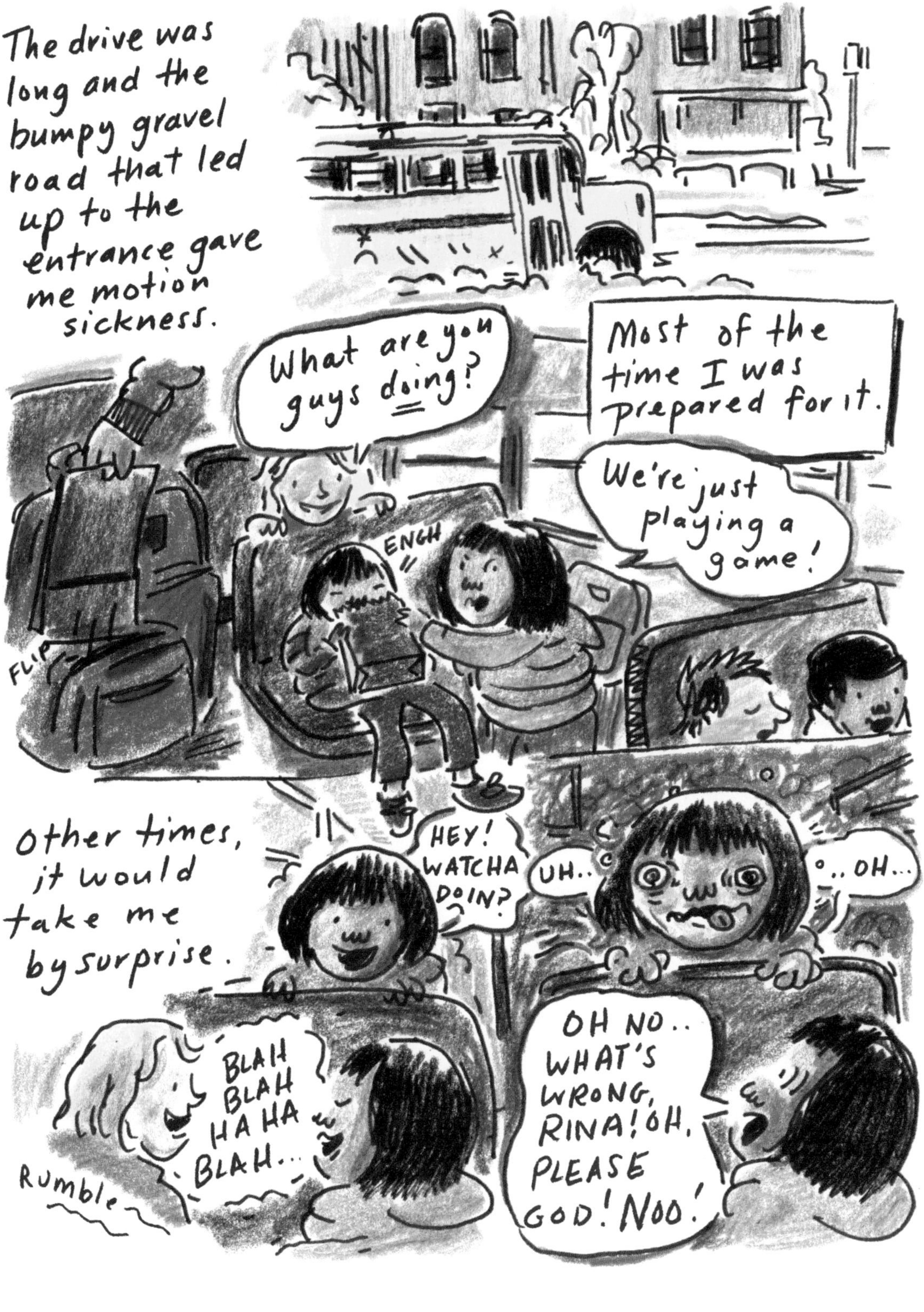
The drive was long and the bumpy gravel road that led up to the entrance gave me motion sickness.
What are you guys doing?
Most of the time I was prepared for it.
We're just playing a game!
ENGH
FLIP
Other times, it would take me by surprise.
HEY! WATCHA DOIN?
UH..
..OH...
BLAH BLAH HA HA BLAH...
RUMBLE
OH NO.. WHAT'S WRONG, RINA! OH, PLEASE GOD! NOO!

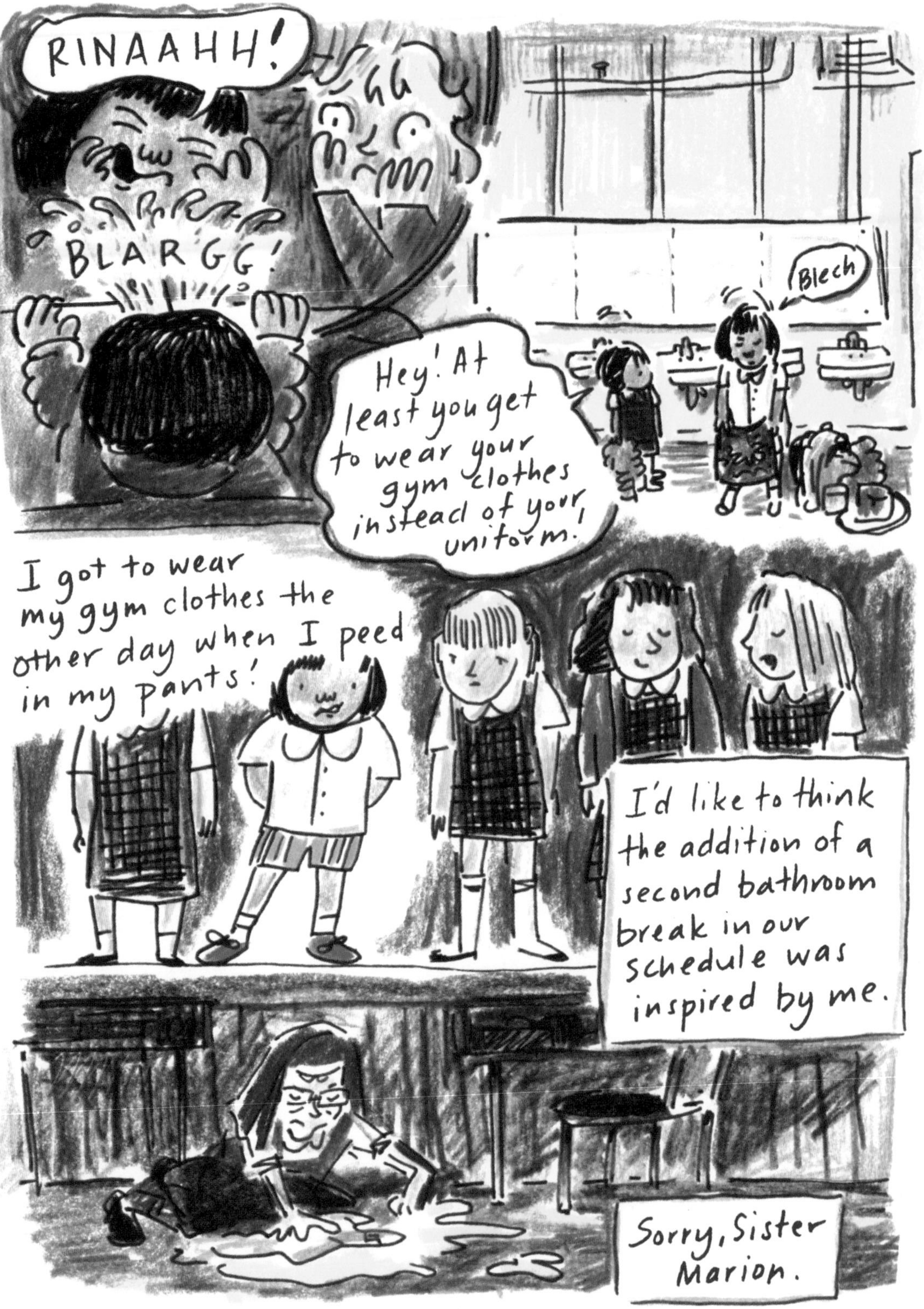
RINAAHH!
BLARGG!
Blech
Hey! At least you get to wear your gym clothes instead of your uniform!
I got to wear my gym clothes the other day when I peed in my pants!
I'd like to think the addition of a second bathroom break in our schedule was inspired by me.
Sorry, Sister Marion.

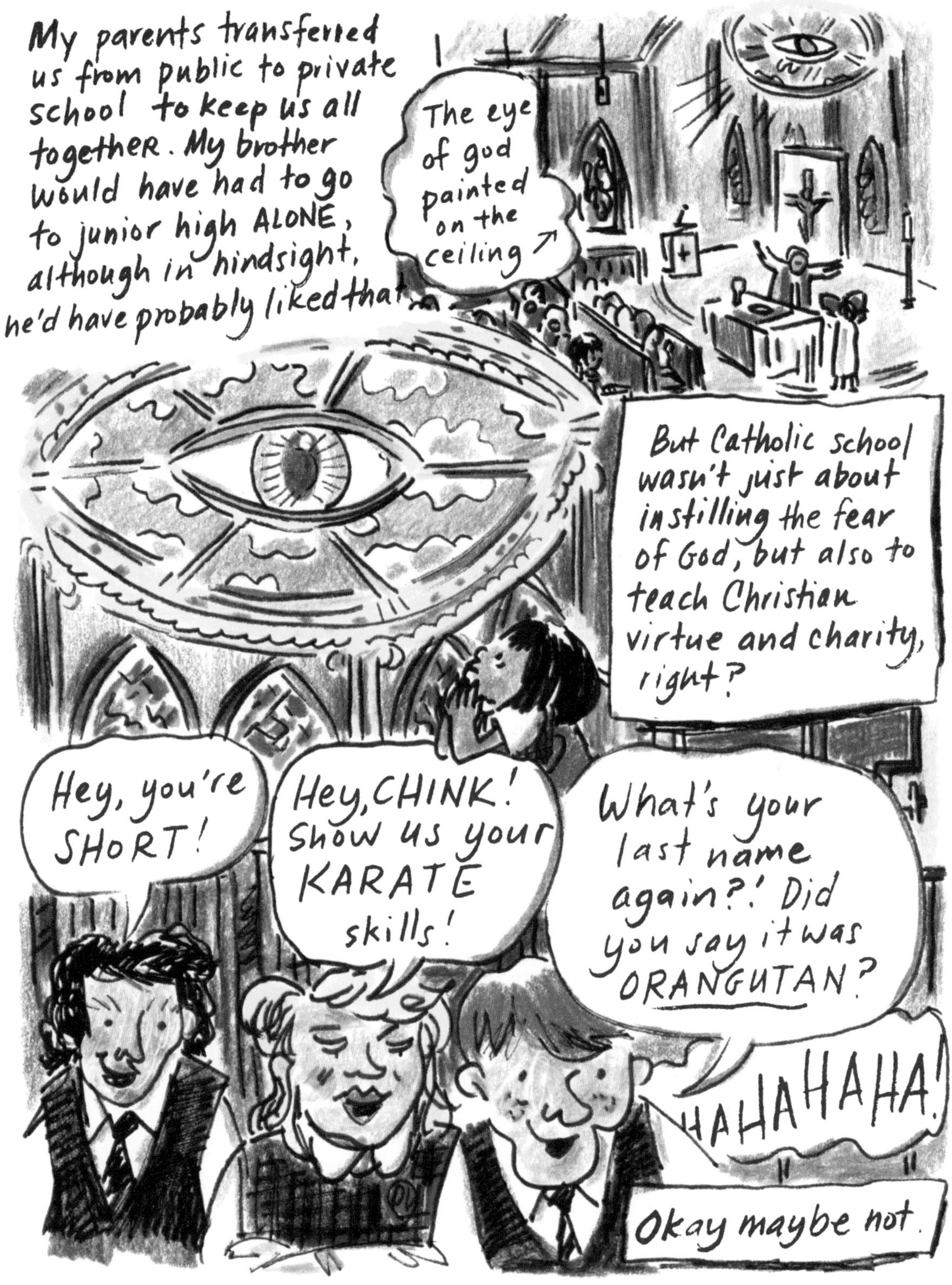
My parents transferred us from public to private school to keep us all together. My brother would have had to go to junior high ALONE, although in hindsight, he'd have probably liked that.
The eye of god painted on the ceiling
But Catholic school wasn't just about instilling the fear of God, but also to teach Christian virtue and charity, right?
Hey, you're SHORT!
Hey, CHINK! Show us your KARATE skills!
What's your last name again?! Did you say it was ORANGUTAN?
HAHAHAHAHA!
Okay maybe not.

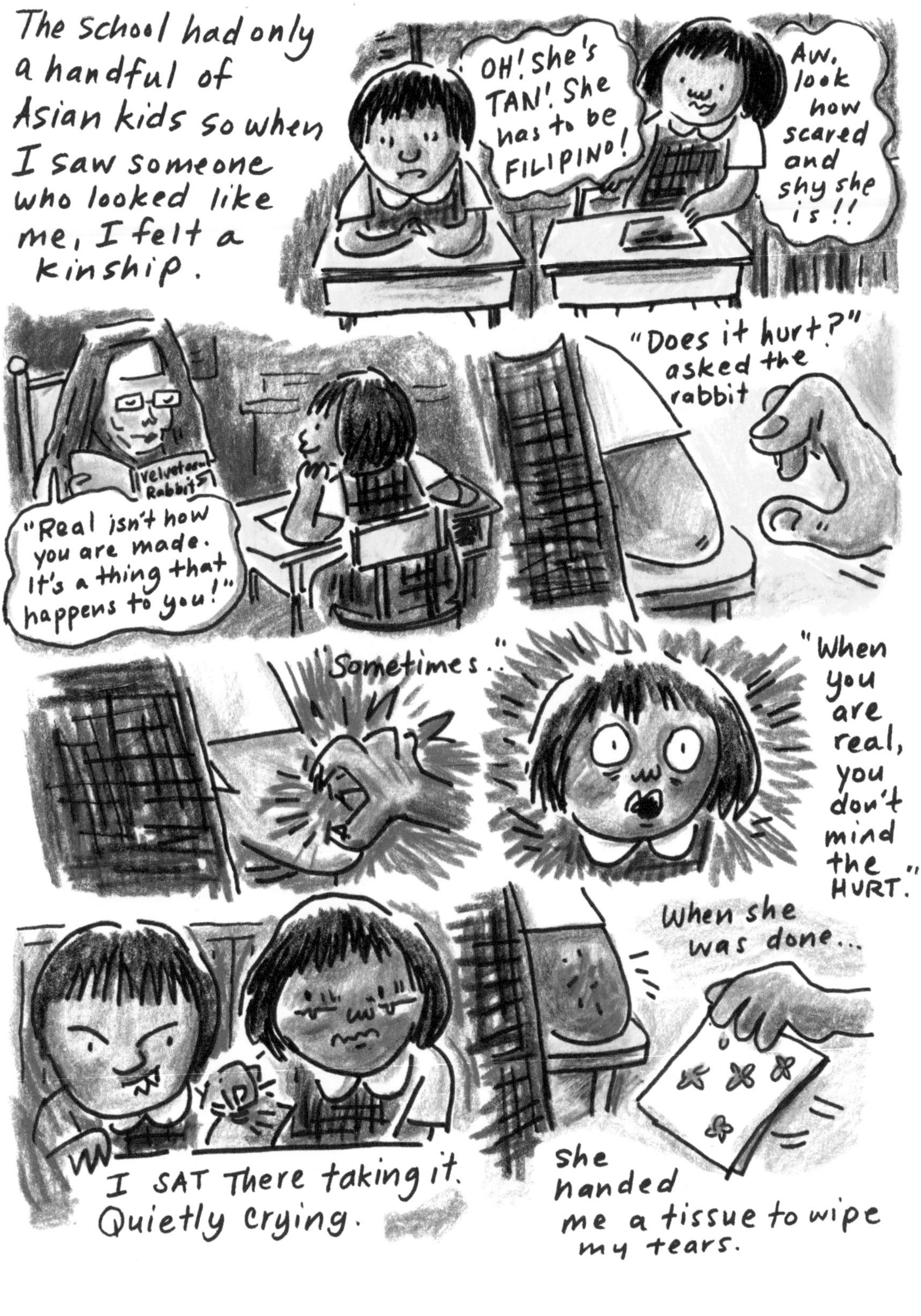
The School had only a handful of Asian kids so when I saw someone who looked like me, I felt a kinship.
OH! she's TAN! She has to be FILIPINO!
Aw, look how scared and shy she is!!
Velveteen Rabbit
"Real isn't how you are made. It's a thing that happens to you!"
"Does it hurt?" asked the rabbit
"Sometimes.."
"When you are real, you don't mind the HURT."
YIP
I SAT There taking it. Quietly crying.
When she was done...
She handed me a tissue to wipe my tears.

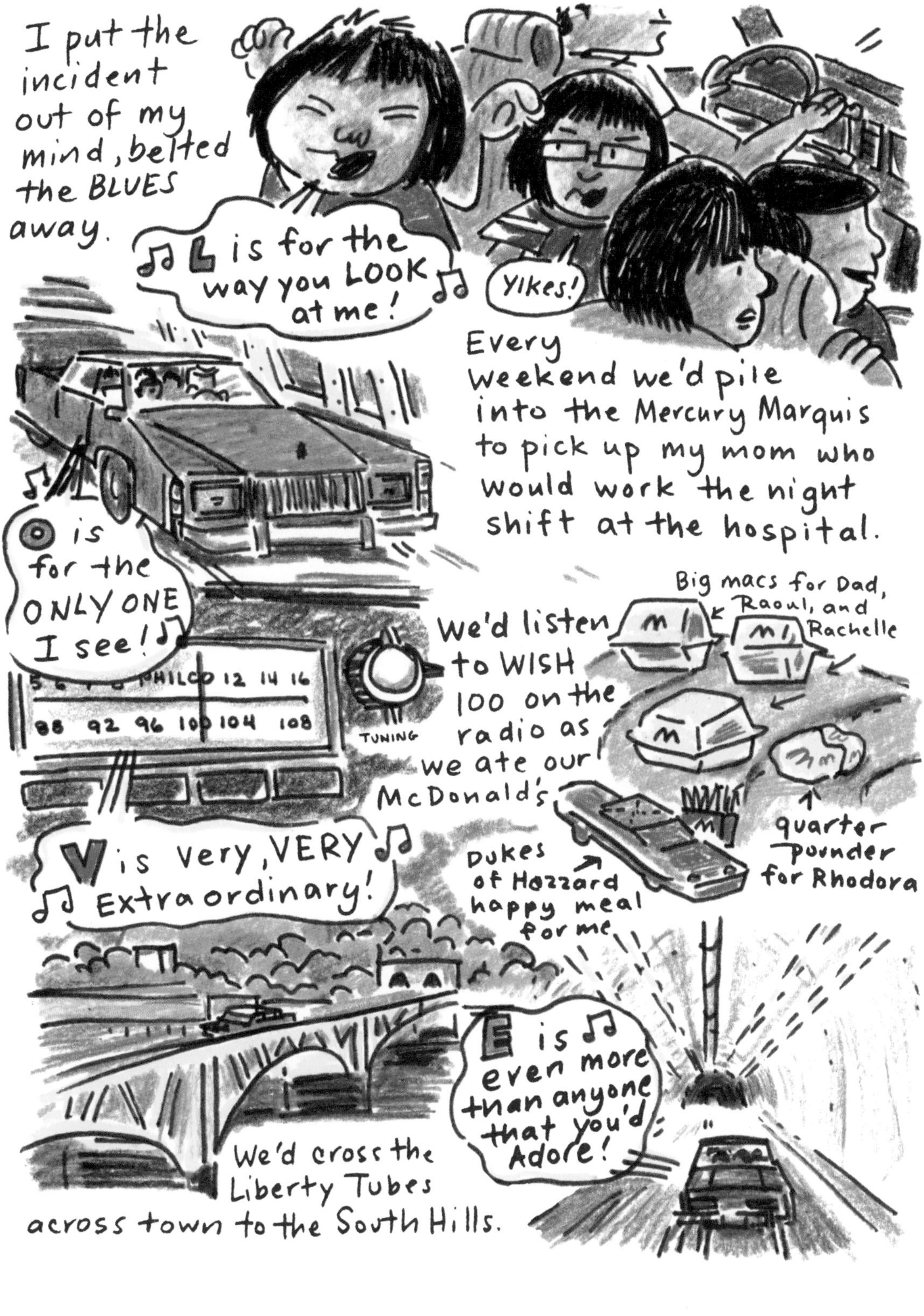
I put the incident out of my mind, belted the BLUES away.
L is for the way you LOOK at me!
Yikes!
Every weekend we'd pile into the Mercury Marquis to pick up my mom who would work the night shift at the hospital.
O is for the ONLY ONE I see!
Big macs for Dad, Raoul, and Rachelle
We'd listen to WISH 100 on the radio as we ate our McDonald's
PHILCO 12 14 16
88 92 96 100 104 108
TUNING
quarter pounder for Rhodora
Dukes of Hazzard happy meal for me
V is very, VERY Extraordinary!
E is even more than anyone that you'd Adore!
We'd cross the Liberty Tubes across town to the South Hills.

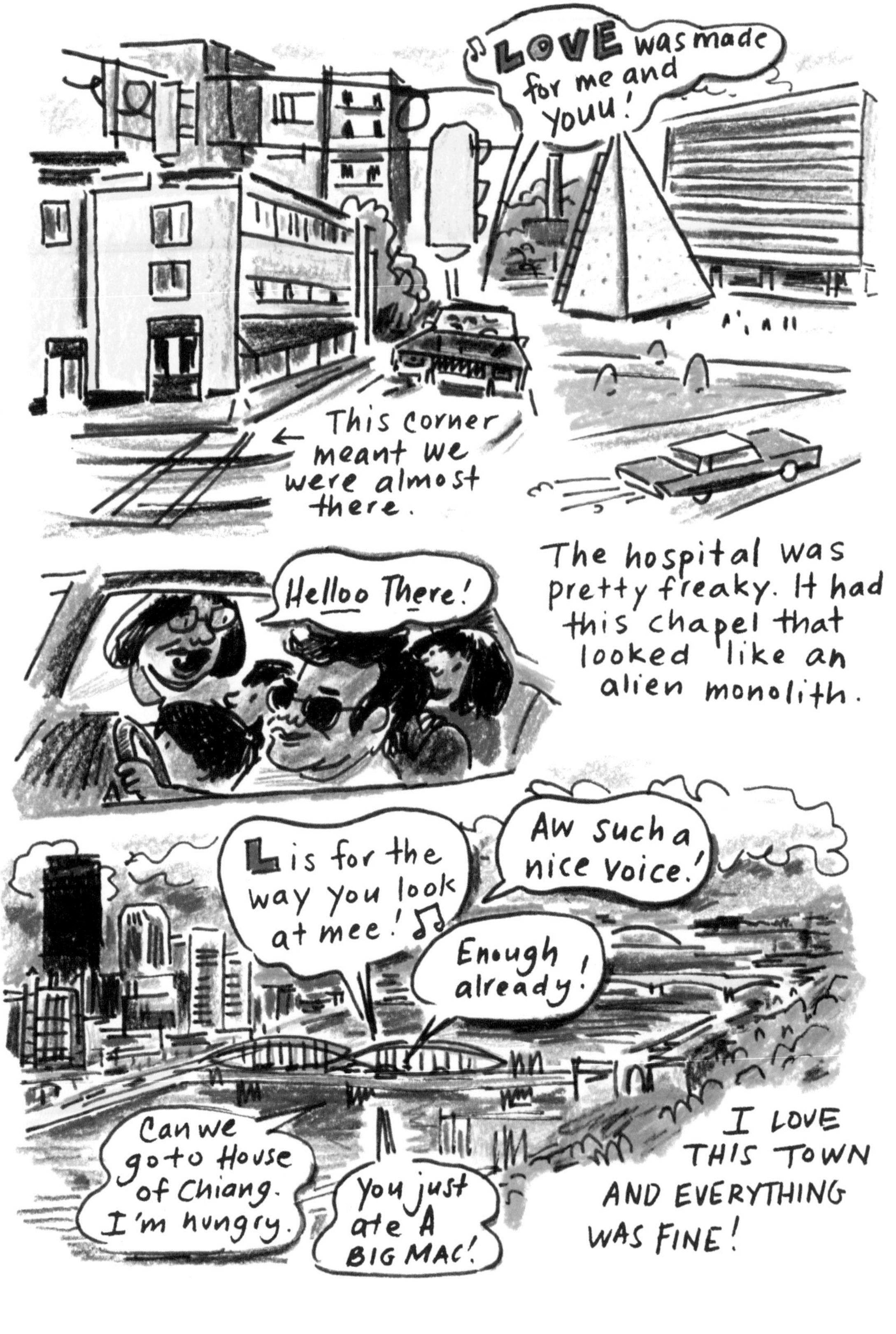
LOVE was made for me and youu!
This corner meant we were almost there.
Helloo There!
The hospital was pretty freaky. It had this chapel that looked like an alien monolith.
L is for the way you look at mee!
Aw such a nice voice!
Enough already!
Can we go to House of Chiang. I'm hungry.
You just ate A BIG MAC!
I LOVE THIS TOWN AND EVERYTHING WAS FINE!

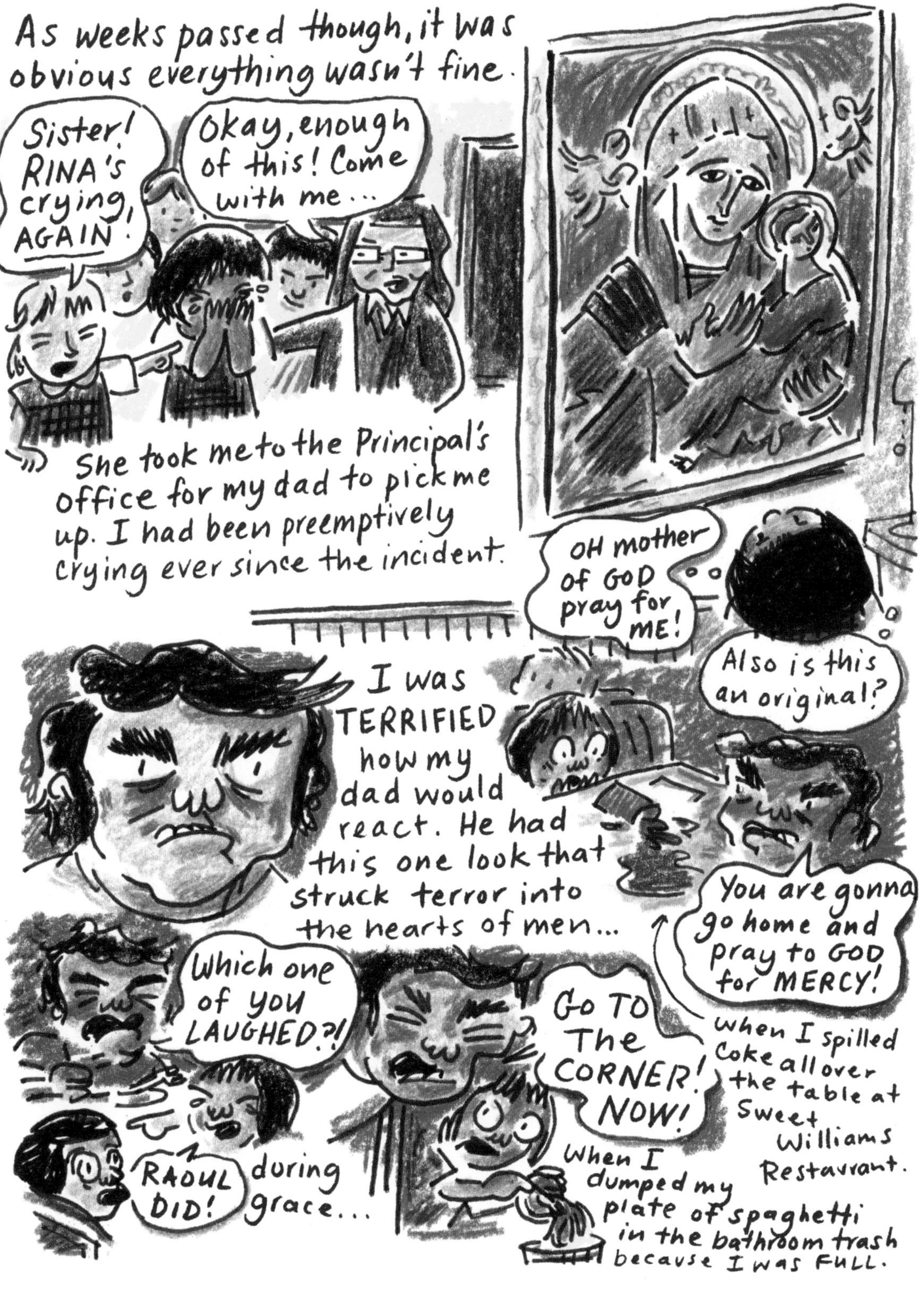
As weeks passed though, it was obvious everything wasn't fine.
Sister! RINA's crying, AGAIN!
Okay, enough of this! Come with me...
She took me to the Principal's office for my dad to pick me up. I had been preemptively crying ever since the incident.
OH mother of GOD pray for ME!
Also is this an original?
I was TERRIFIED how my dad would react. He had this one look that struck terror into the hearts of men...
You are gonna go home and pray to GOD for MERCY!
when I spilled Coke all over the table at Sweet Williams Restaurant.
Which one of you LAUGHED?!
RAOUL DID!
during grace...
GO TO The CORNER! NOW!
When I dumped my plate of spaghetti in the bathroom trash because I was FULL.

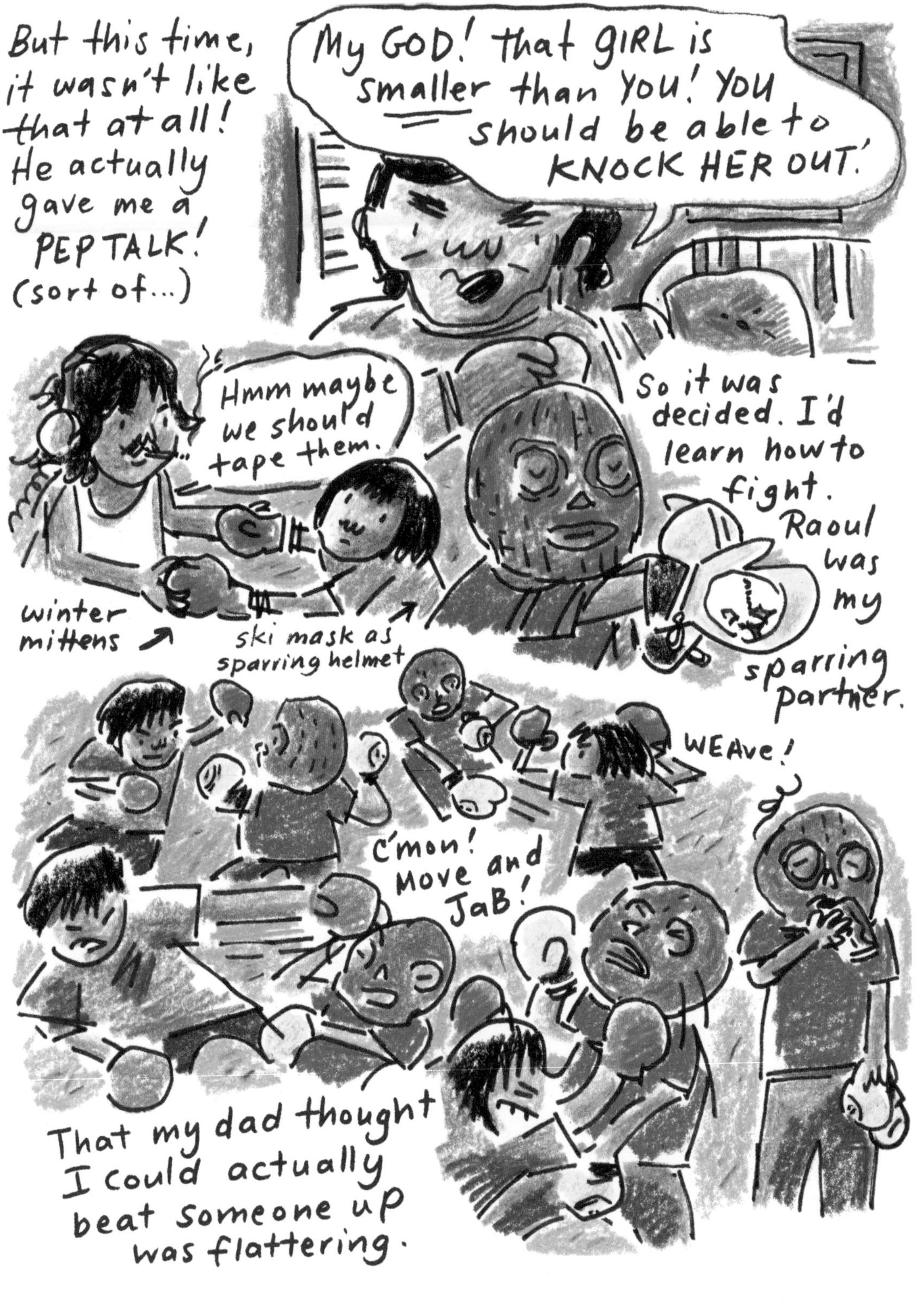

But this time, it wasn't like that at all! He actually gave me a PEP TALK! (sort of...)
My GOD! that GIRL is smaller than YOU! YOU should be able to KNOCK HER OUT!
Hmm maybe we should tape them.
So it was decided. I'd learn how to fight. Raoul was my sparring partner.
winter mittens
ski mask as sparring helmet
WEAve!
C'mon! Move and JaB!
That my dad thought I could actually beat someone up was flattering.

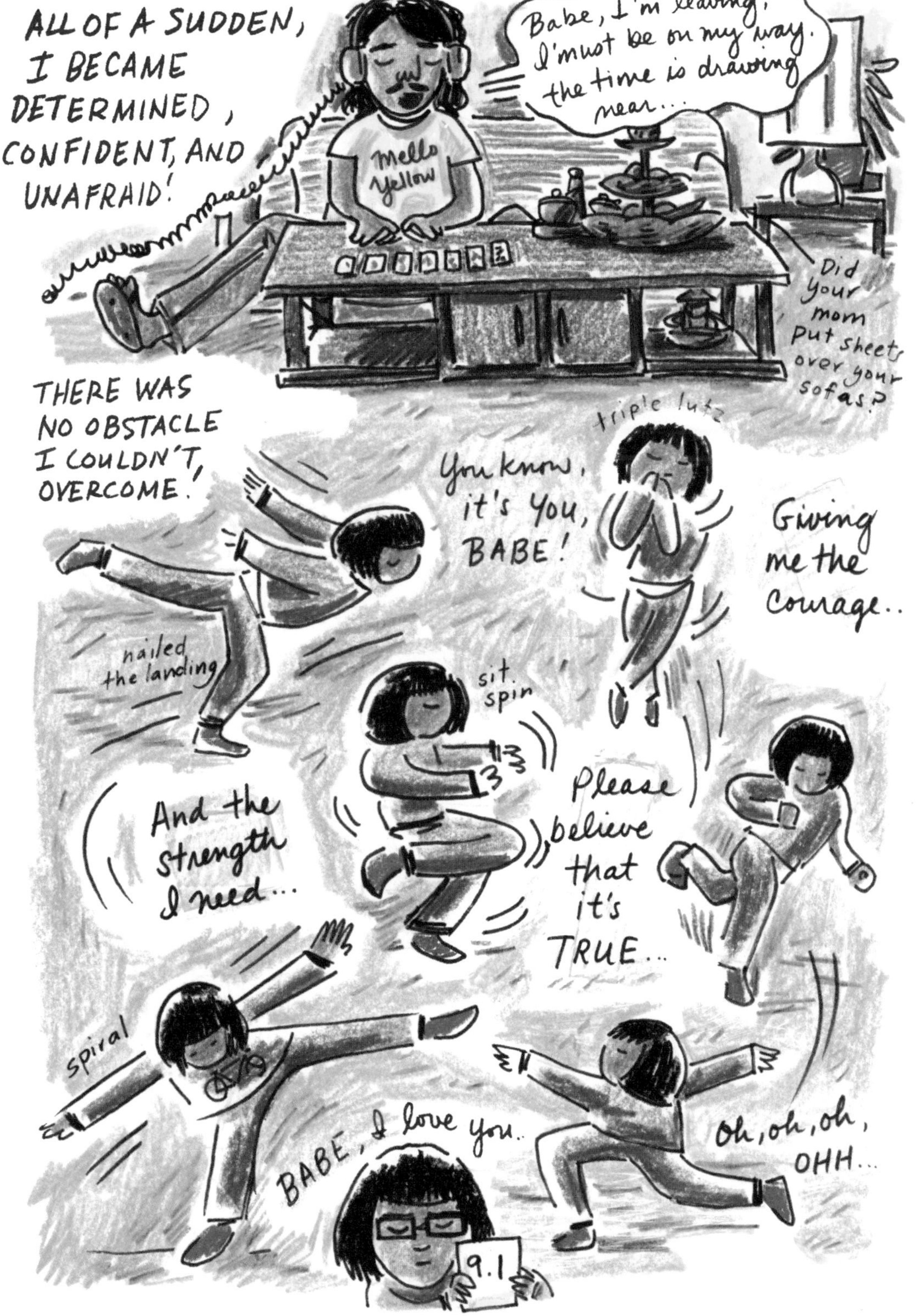

ALL OF A SUDDEN, I BECAME DETERMINED, CONFIDENT, AND UNAFRAID!
Babe, I'm leaving, I must be on my way. the time is drawing near...
Mello Yellow
Did your mom put sheets over your sofas?
THERE WAS NO OBSTACLE I COULDN'T OVERCOME!
triple lutz
You know, it's You, BABE!
Giving me the courage..
nailed the landing
sit spin
And the strength I need...
Please believe that it's TRUE...
spiral
BABE, I love you..
Oh, oh, oh, OHH...
9.1

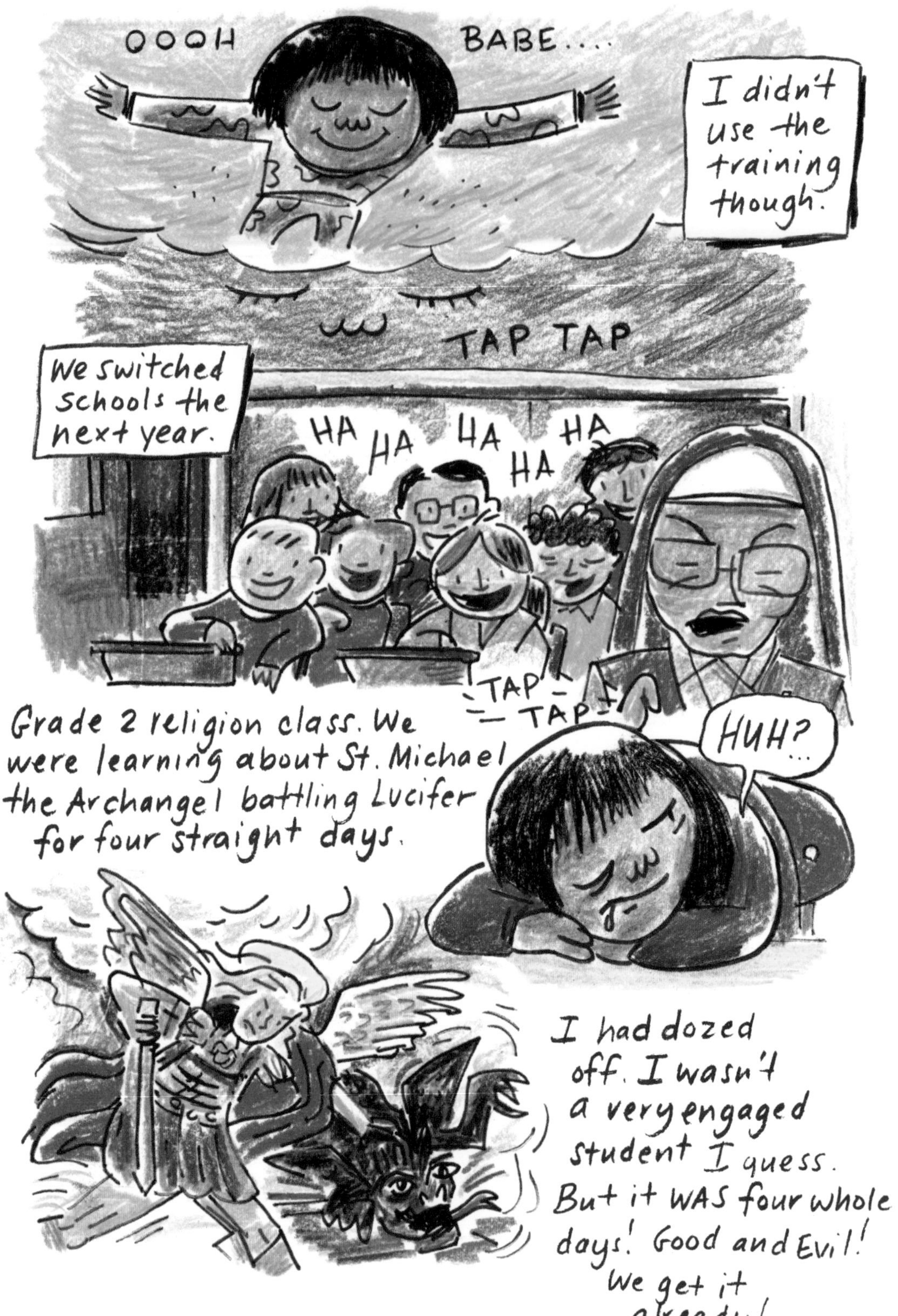
OOOH BABE....
I didn't use the training though.
TAP TAP
We switched schools the next year.
HA HA HA HA HA
TAP TAP
Grade 2 religion class. We were learning about St. Michael the Archangel battling Lucifer for four straight days.
HUH?...
I had dozed off. I wasn't a very engaged student I guess. But it WAS four whole days! Good and Evil! We get it already!

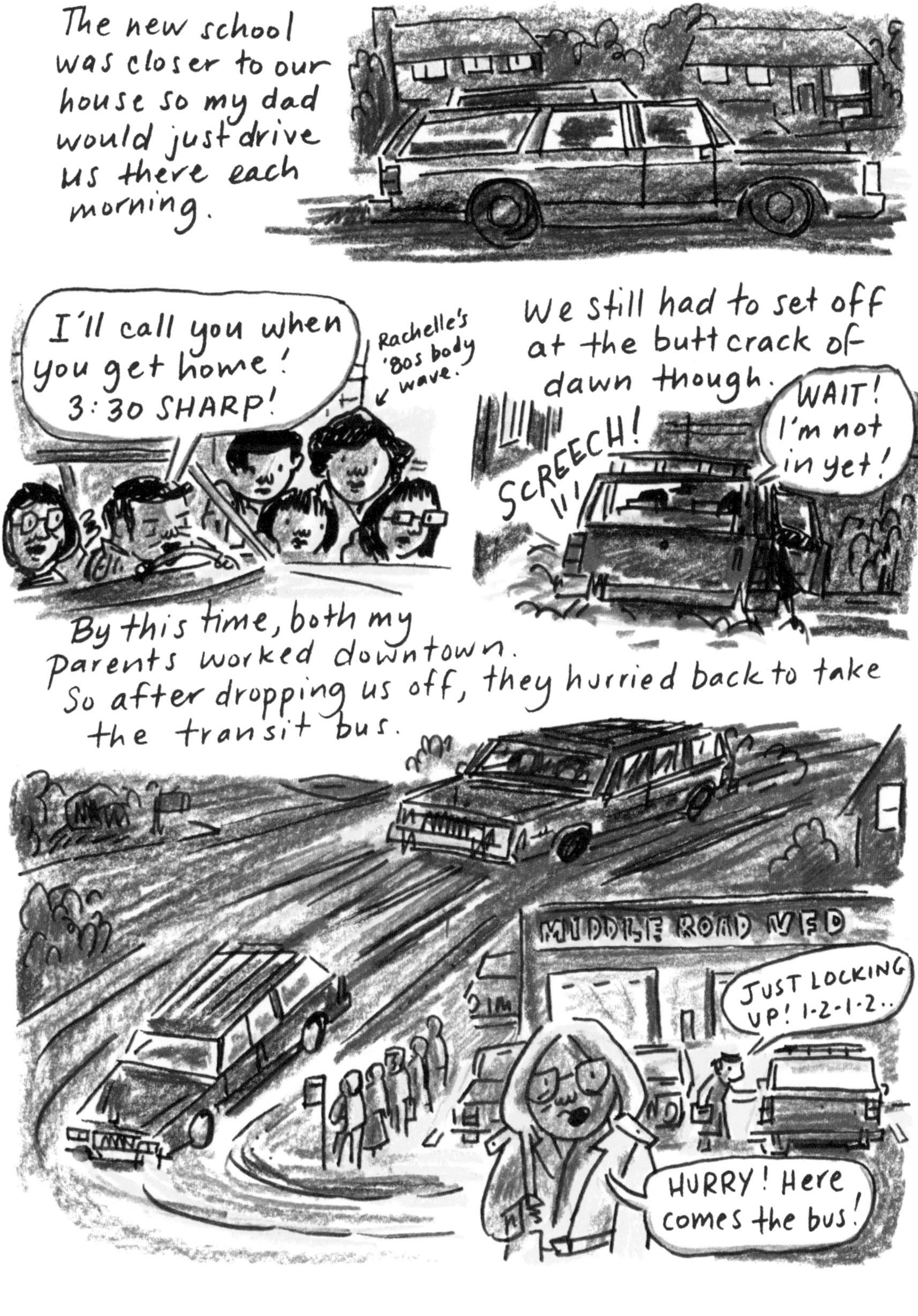
The new school was closer to our house so my dad would just drive us there each morning.
I'll call you when you get home! 3:30 SHARP!
Rachelle's '80s body wave.
We still had to set off at the butt crack of dawn though.
SCREECH!
WAIT! I'm not in yet!
By this time, both my parents worked downtown. So after dropping us off, they hurried back to take the transit bus.
MIDDLE ROAD VFD
JUST LOCKING UP! 1-2-1-2..
HURRY! Here comes the bus!

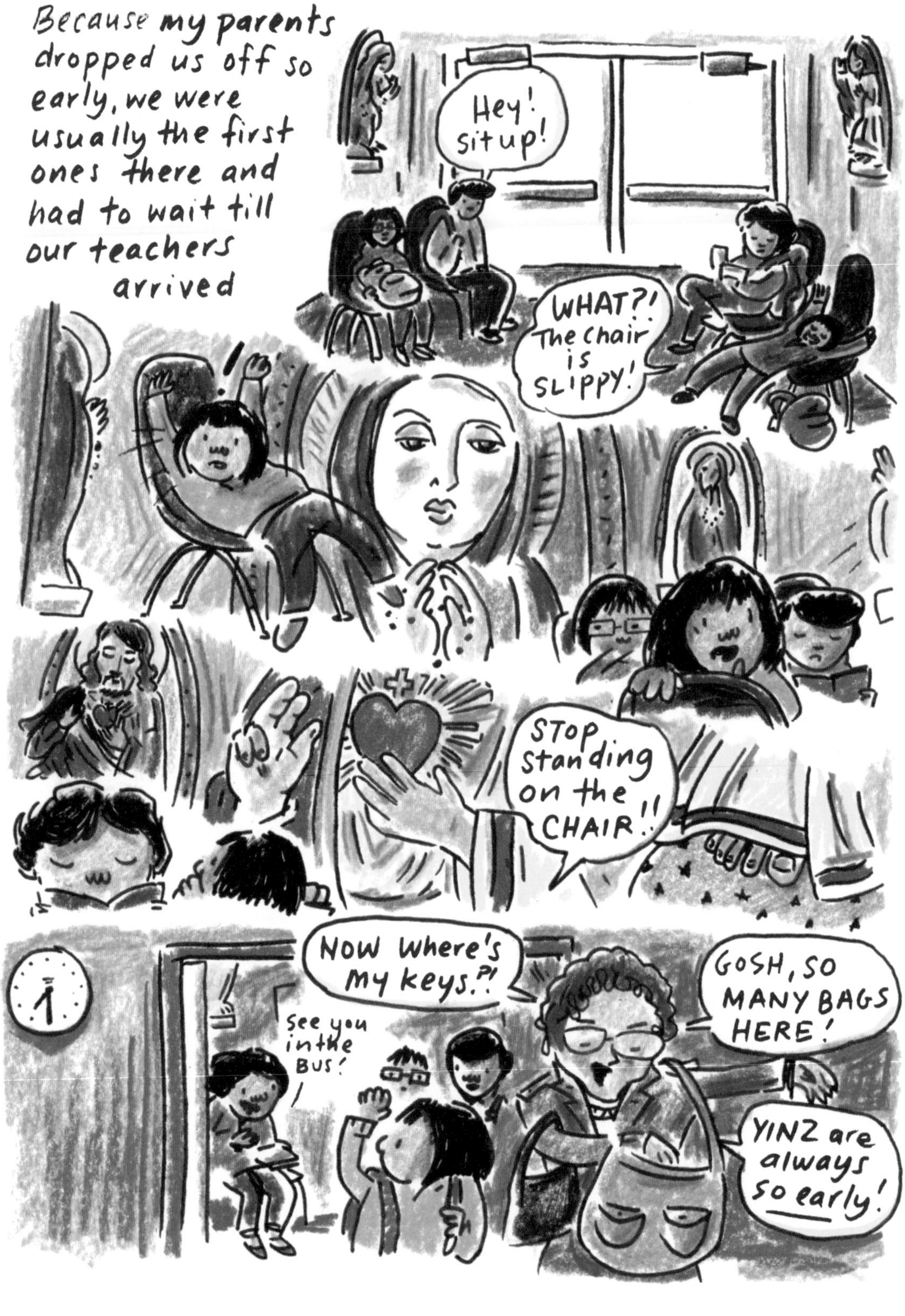
Because my parents dropped us off so early, we were usually the first ones there and had to wait till our teachers arrived
Hey! sit up!
WHAT?! The chair is SLIPPY!
STOP standing on the CHAIR!!
NOW where's my keys?!
see you in the BUS!
GOSH, SO MANY BAGS HERE!
YINZ are always so early!

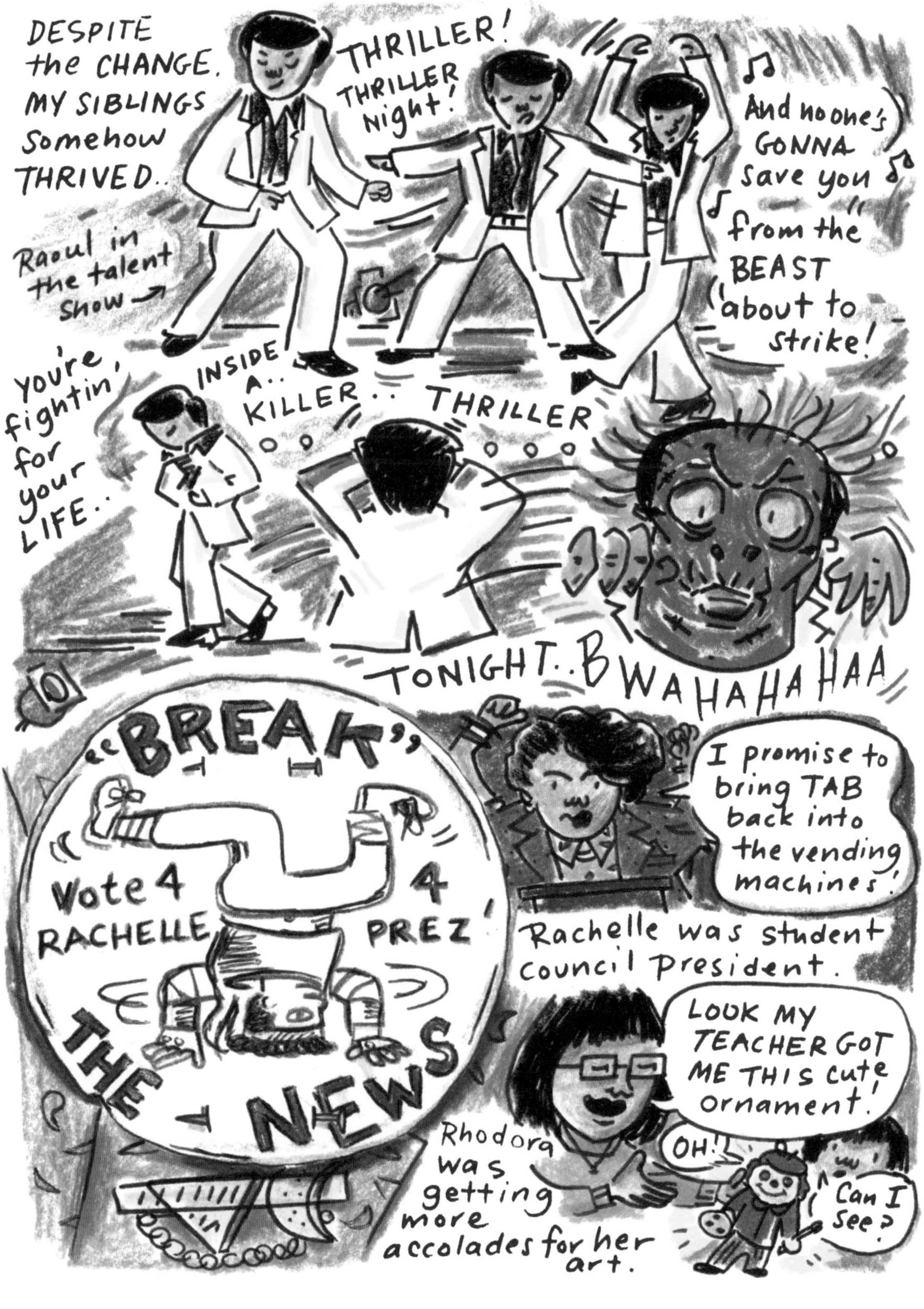
DESPITE the CHANGE, MY SIBLINGS Somehow THRIVED..
Raoul in the talent show →
THRILLER!
THRILLER Night!
And no one's GONNA save you from the BEAST about to strike!
You're fightin' for your LIFE..
INSIDE A.. KILLER.. THRILLER
TONIGHT..
BWAHAHAHAA
"BREAK" THE NEWS
Vote 4 RACHELLE 4 PREZ
I promise to bring TAB back into the vending machines!
Rachelle was student council president.
LOOK MY TEACHER GOT ME THIS cute ornament!
Rhodora was getting more accolades for her art.
OH!
Can I See?

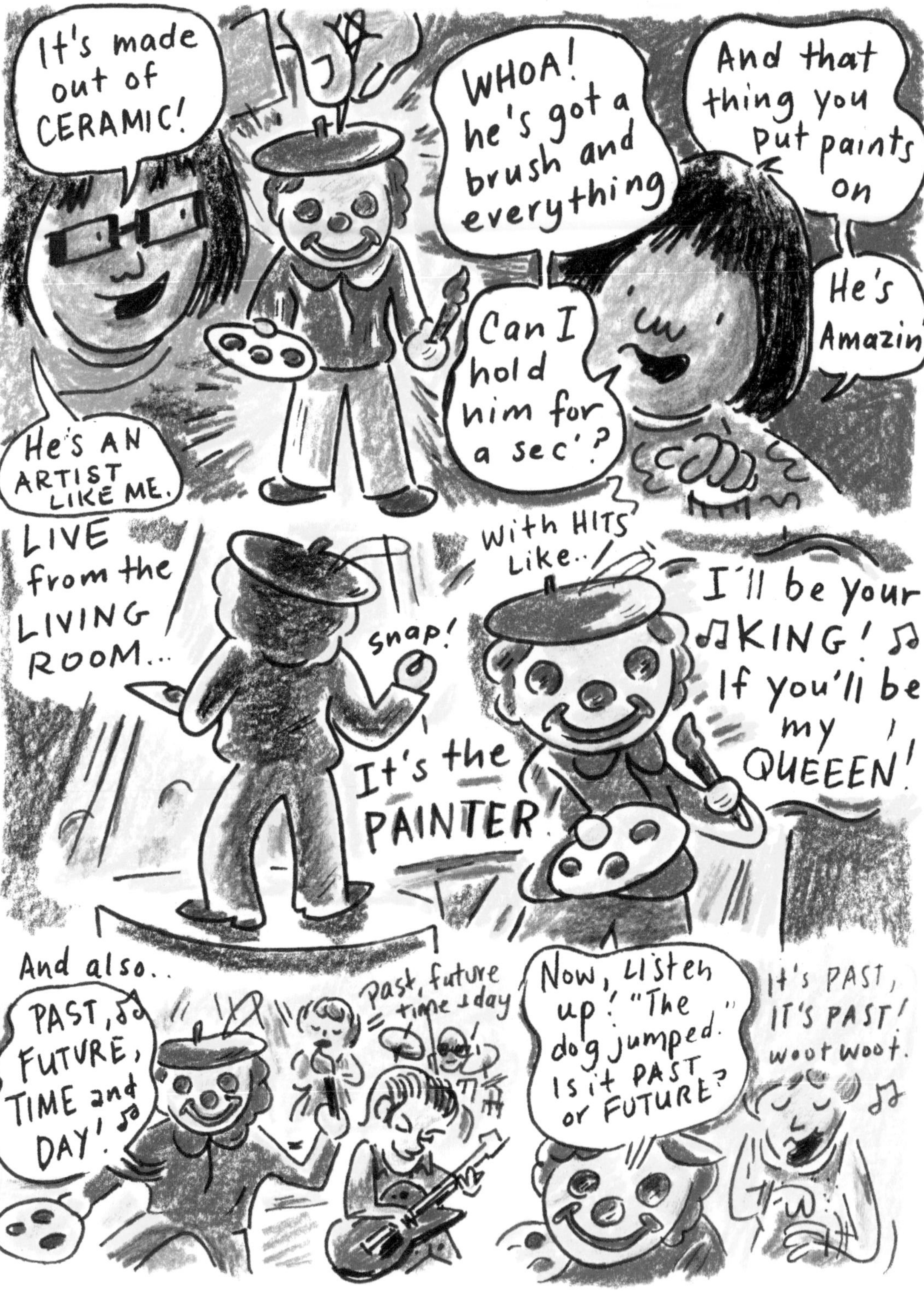
It's made out of CERAMIC!
He's AN ARTIST LIKE ME.
WHOA! he's got a brush and everything
Can I hold him for a sec'?
And that thing you put paints on
He's Amazin'
LIVE from the LIVING ROOM...
snap!
With HITS like..
It's the PAINTER
I'll be your ♫KING!♫ If you'll be my QUEEEN!
And also..
PAST,♫ FUTURE, TIME and DAY!♫
Past, future time & day
Now, listen up! "The" dog jumped. Is it PAST or FUTURE?
It's PAST, IT'S PAST! woot woot.

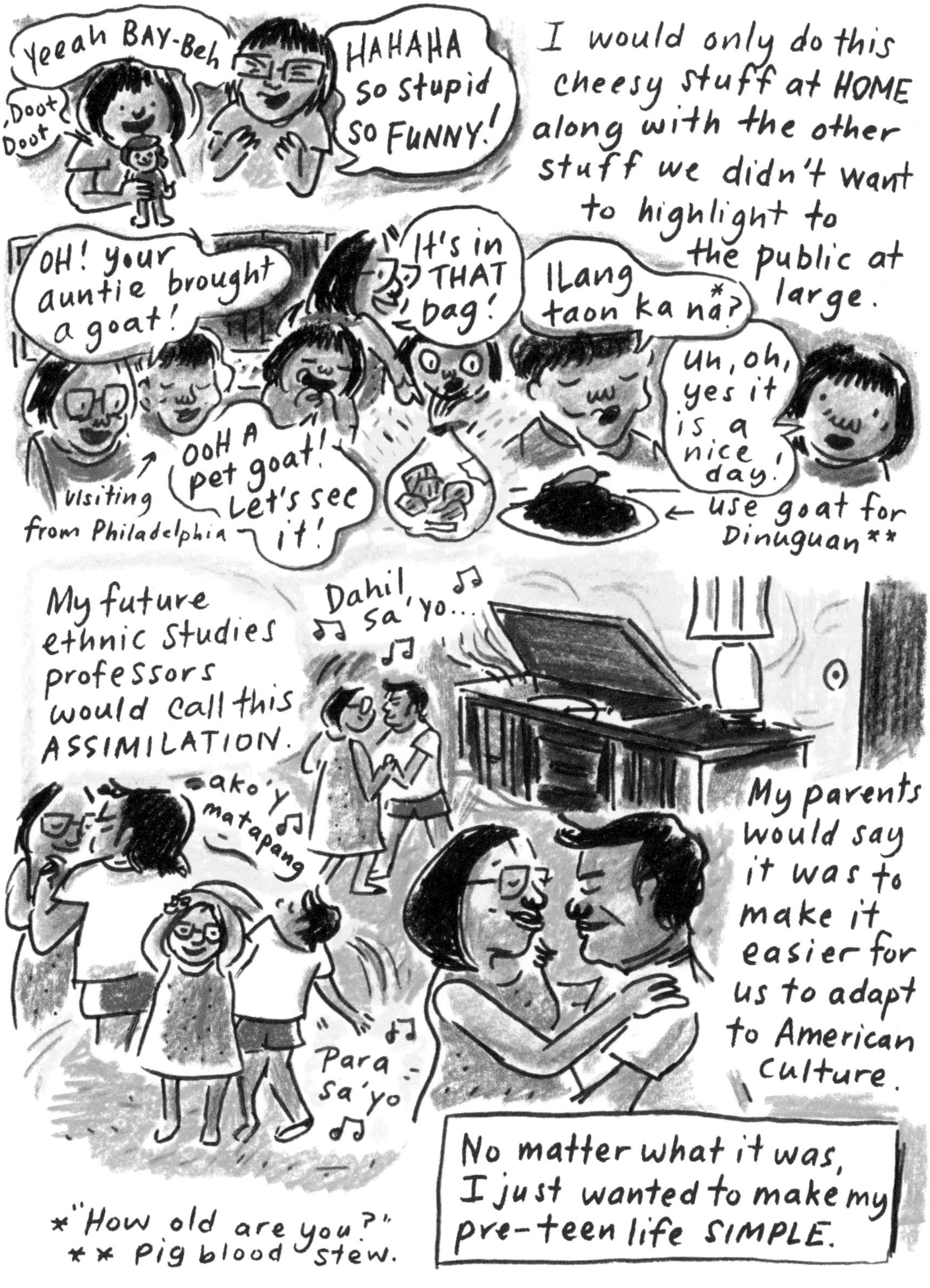
Yeeah BAY-Beh
Doot Doot
HAHAHA so stupid so FUNNY!
I would only do this cheesy stuff at HOME along with the other stuff we didn't want to highlight to the public at large.
OH! your auntie brought a goat!
It's in THAT bag!
ILang taon ka na?*
Uh, oh, yes it is a nice day!
visiting from Philadelphia
OOH A pet goat! Let's see it!
use goat for Dinuguan**
My future ethnic studies professors would call this ASSIMILATION.
Dahil sa'yo...
ako'y matapang
Para sa'yo
My parents would say it was to make it easier for us to adapt to American culture.
No matter what it was, I just wanted to make my pre-teen life SIMPLE.
*"How old are you?"
** Pig blood stew.

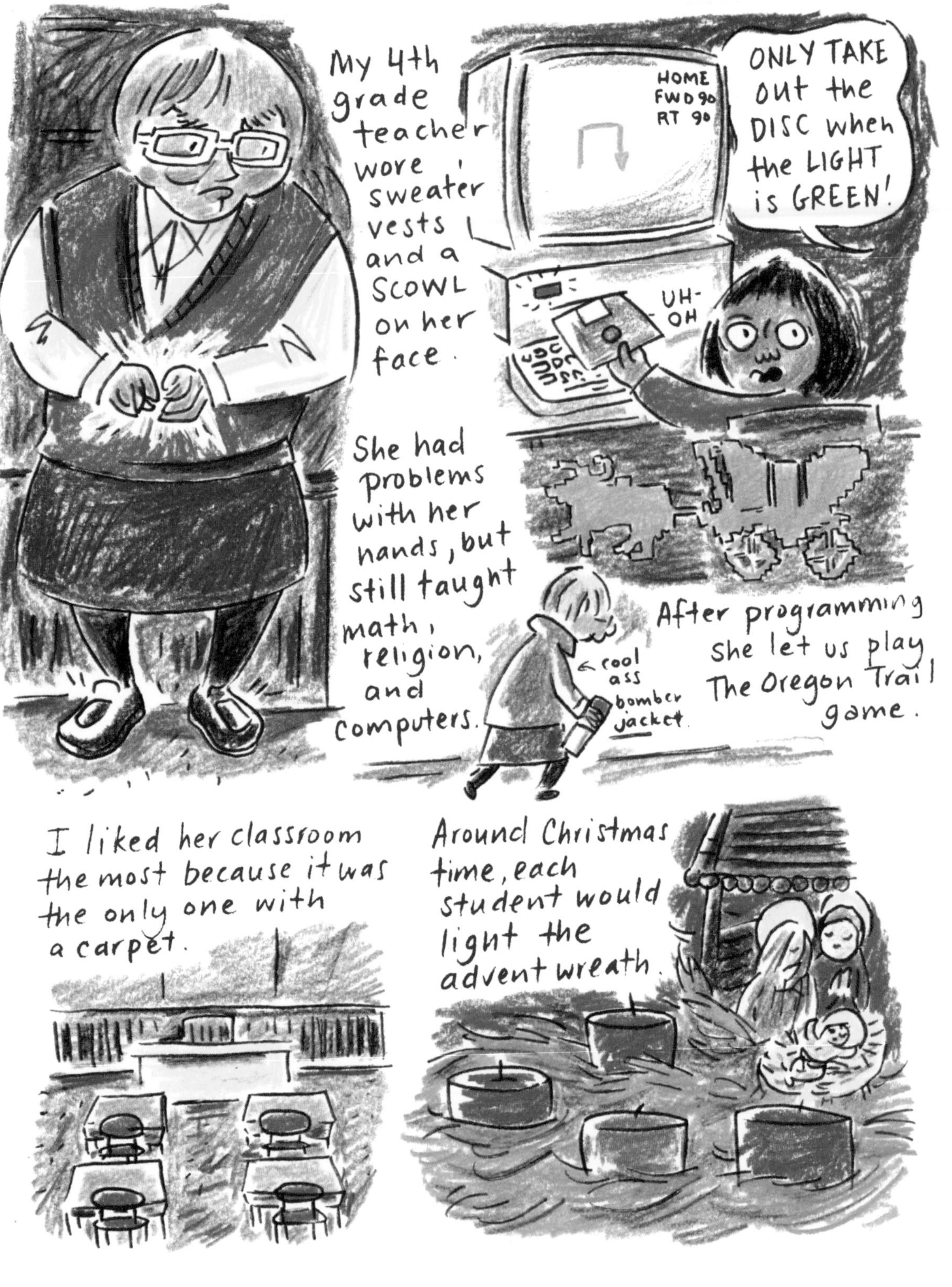
My 4th grade teacher wore sweater vests and a SCOWL on her face.
HOME
FWD 90
RT 90
ONLY TAKE out the DISC when the LIGHT is GREEN!
UH-OH
She had problems with her hands, but still taught math, religion, and computers.
cool ass bomber jacket
After programming she let us play The Oregon Trail game.
I liked her classroom the most because it was the only one with a carpet.
Around Christmas time, each student would light the advent wreath.

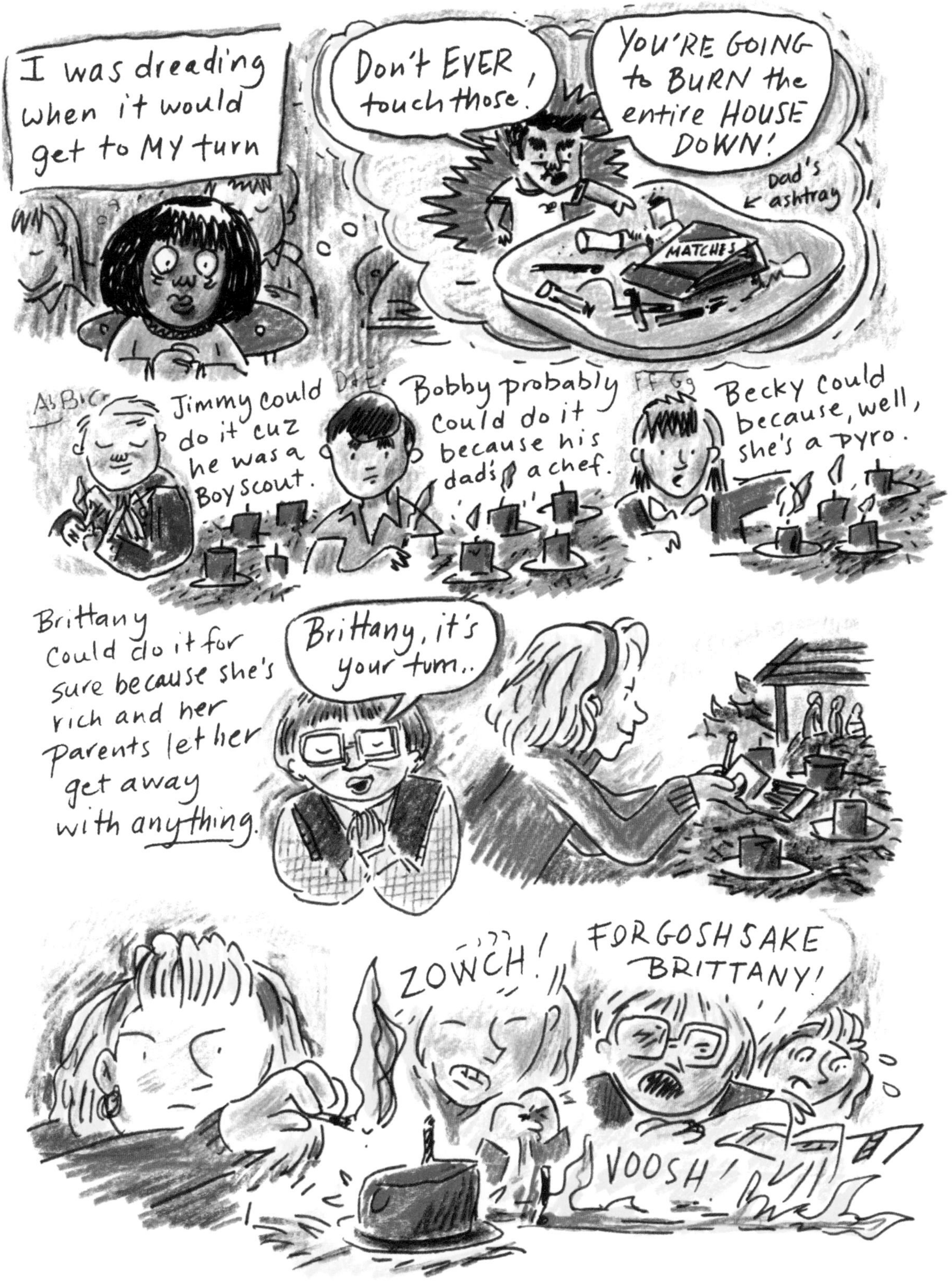
I was dreading when it would get to MY turn
Don't EVER touch those!
YOU'RE GOING to BURN the entire HOUSE DOWN!
Dad's ashtray
MATCHES
Jimmy could do it cuz he was a Boy Scout.
Bobby probably could do it because his dad's a chef.
Becky could because, well, she's a pyro.
Brittany could do it for sure because she's rich and her parents let her get away with anything.
Brittany, it's your turn..
ZOWCH!
FORGOSHSAKE BRITTANY!
VOOSH!

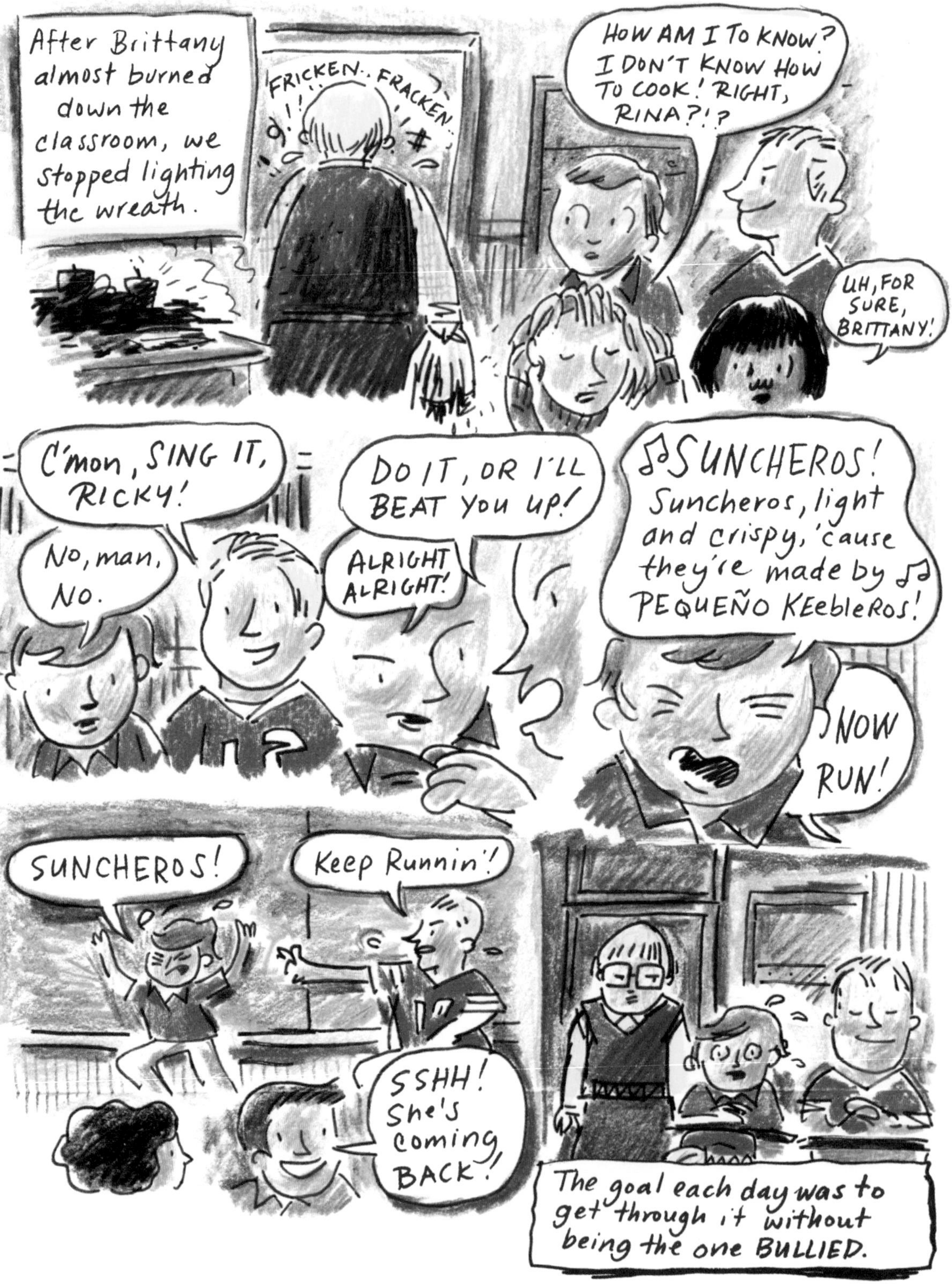
After Brittany almost burned down the classroom, we stopped lighting the wreath.
FRICKEN.. FRACKEN
HOW AM I TO KNOW? I DON'T KNOW HOW TO COOK! RIGHT, RINA?!?
UH, FOR SURE, BRITTANY!
C'mon, SING IT, RICKY!
No, man. No.
DO IT, OR I'LL BEAT YOU UP!
ALRIGHT ALRIGHT!
♫SUNCHEROS! Suncheros, light and crispy, 'cause they're made by ♫ PEQUEÑO KEEBLEROS!
NOW RUN!
SUNCHEROS!
Keep Runnin'!
SSHH! She's coming BACK!
The goal each day was to get through it without being the one BULLIED.

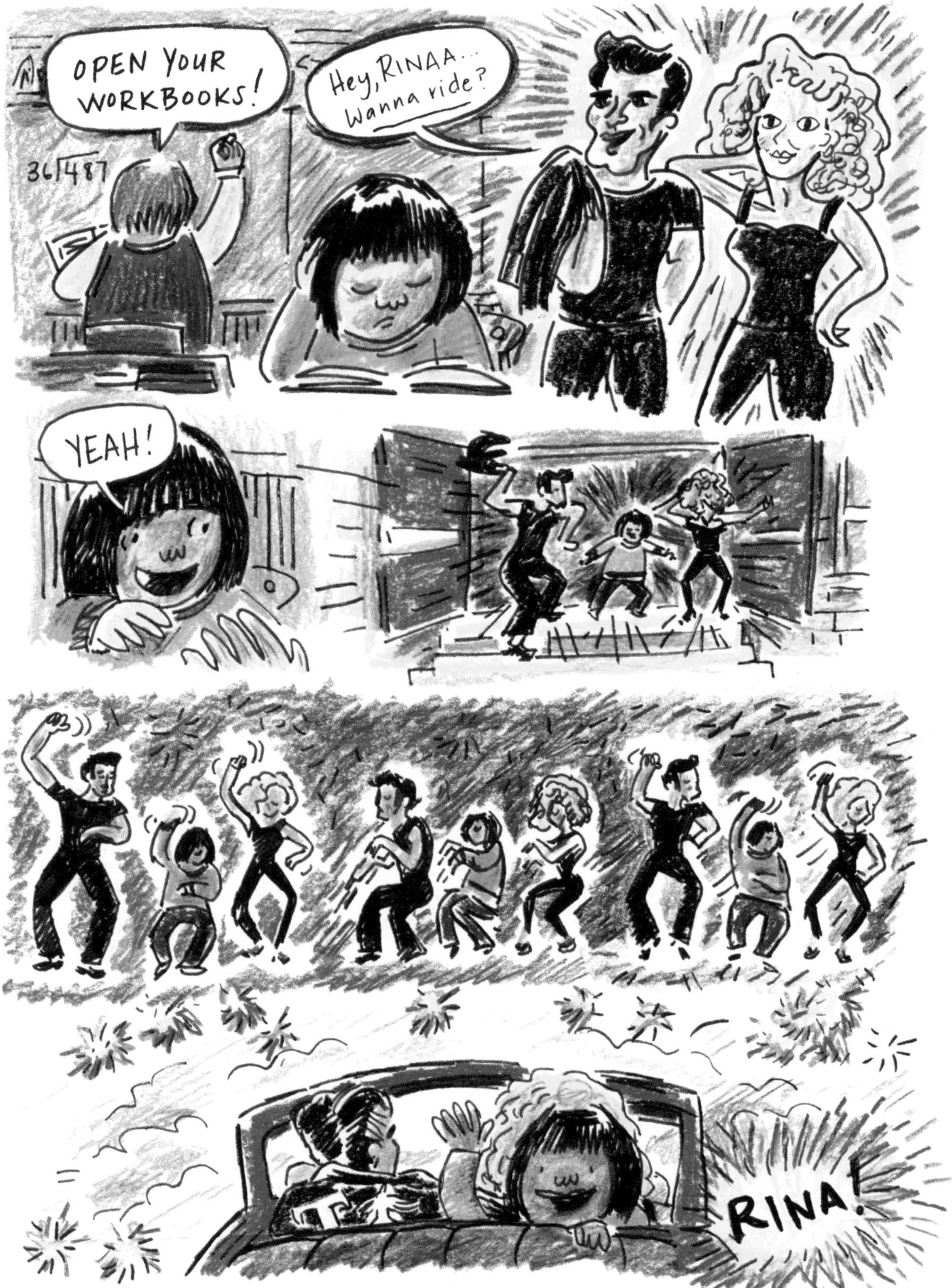
OPEN YOUR WORKBOOKS!
36⟌487
Hey, RINAA... wanna ride?
YEAH!
RINA!

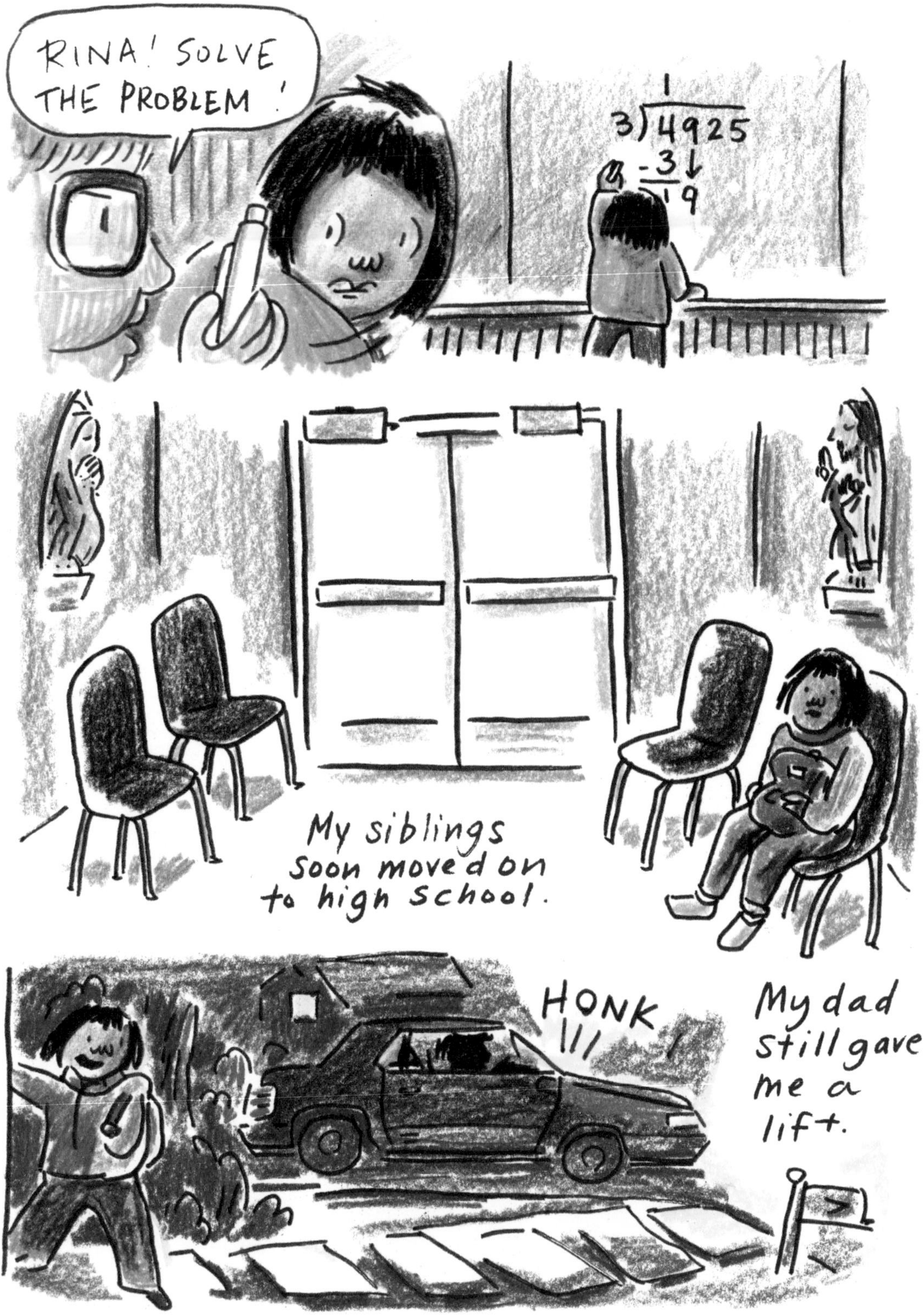

RINA! SOLVE THE PROBLEM!
3)4925
My siblings soon moved on to high school.
HONK
My dad still gave me a lift.

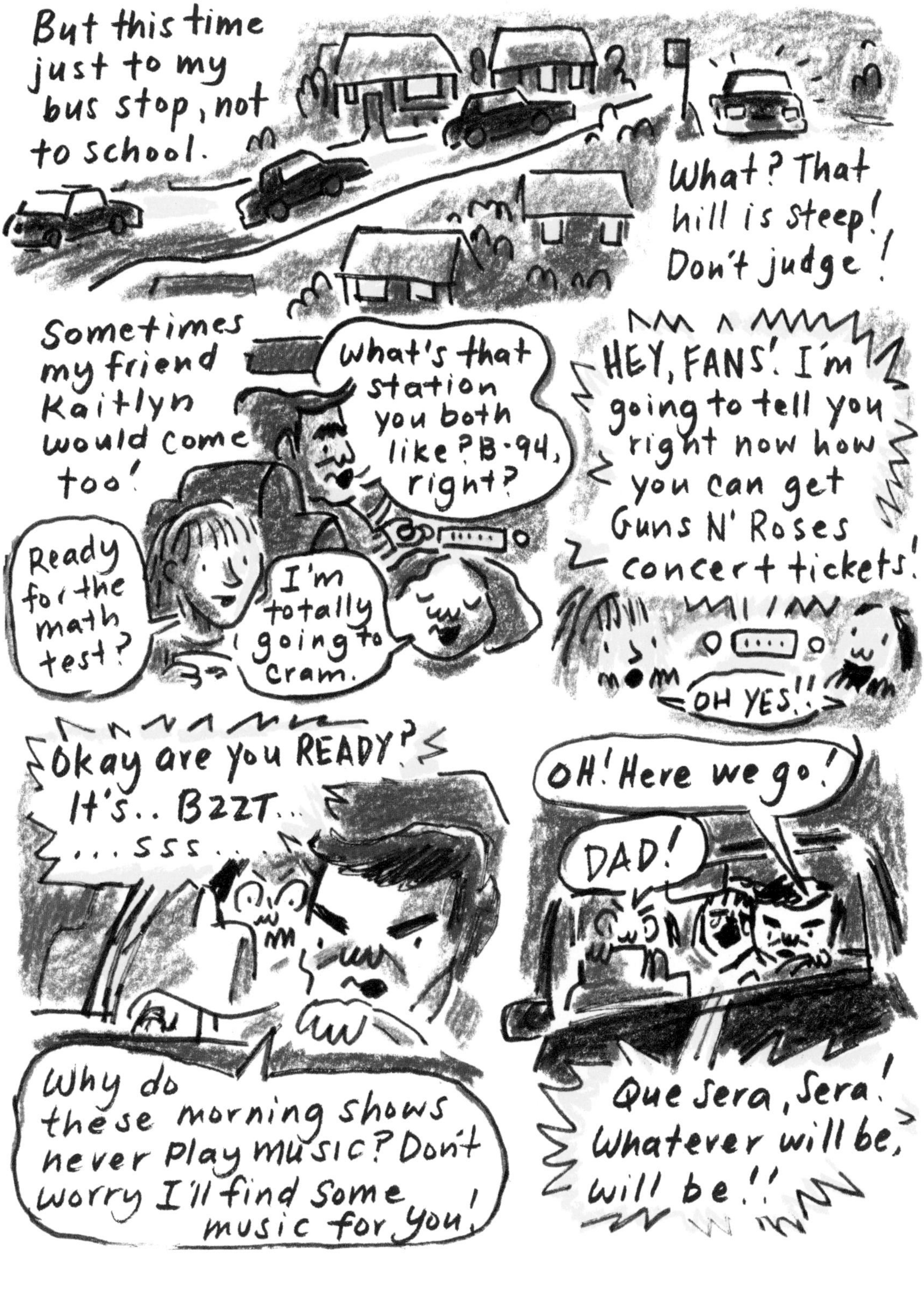
But this time just to my bus stop, not to school.
What? That hill is steep! Don't judge!
Sometimes my friend Kaitlyn would come too!
What's that station you both like? B-94, right?
Ready for the math test?
I'm totally going to cram.
HEY, FANS! I'm going to tell you right now how you can get Guns N' Roses concert tickets!
OH YES!!
Okay are you READY? It's.. BZZT... ...SSS...
Why do these morning shows never play music? Don't worry I'll find some music for you!
OH! Here we go!
DAD!
Que Sera, Sera! Whatever will be, will be!!

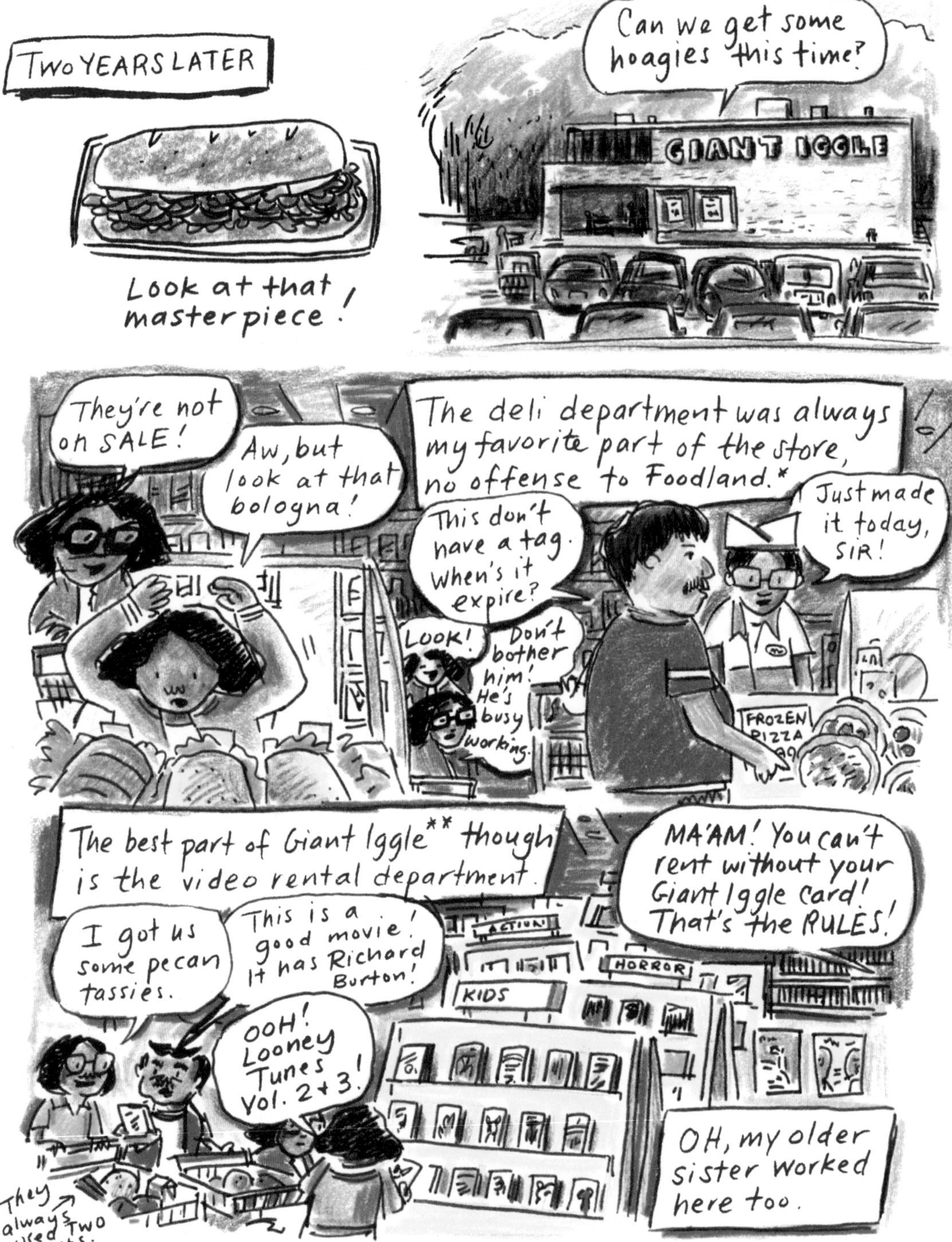
TWO YEARS LATER
Look at that masterpiece!
Can we get some hoagies this time?
GIANT IGGLE
They're not on SALE!
Aw, but look at that bologna!
The deli department was always my favorite part of the store, no offense to Foodland.*
This don't have a tag. When's it expire?
Just made it today, SIR!
LOOK!
Don't bother him! He's busy working.
FROZEN PIZZA
The best part of Giant Iggle** though is the video rental department.
MA'AM! You can't rent without your Giant Iggle card! That's the RULES!
I got us some pecan tassies.
This is a good movie! It has Richard Burton!
ACTION
HORROR
KIDS
OOH! Looney Tunes Vol. 2+3!
OH, my older sister worked here too.

They always used two carts.

Drives me CRAZY!

* Foodland didn't have a deli. I ♡ U Foodland.

**It's really Giant EAGLE, but this is how we Pittsburghers pronounce it.

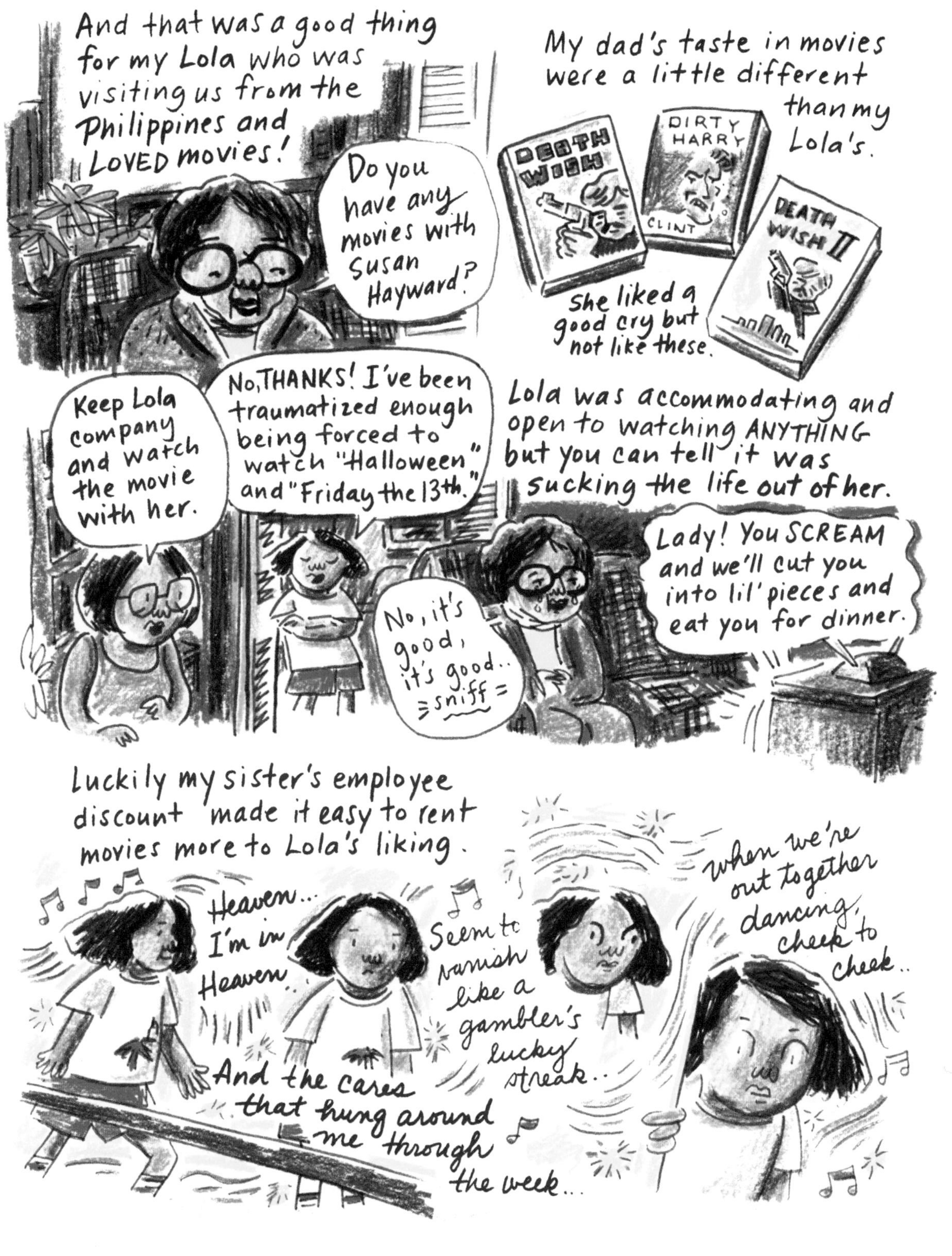
And that was a good thing for my Lola who was visiting us from the Philippines and LOVED movies!
Do you have any movies with Susan Hayward?
My dad's taste in movies were a little different than my Lola's.
DEATH WISH
DIRTY HARRY
CLINT
DEATH WISH II
She liked a good cry but not like these.
Keep Lola company and watch the movie with her.
No, THANKS! I've been traumatized enough being forced to watch "Halloween" and "Friday the 13th."
Lola was accommodating and open to watching ANYTHING but you can tell it was sucking the life out of her.
Lady! You SCREAM and we'll cut you into lil' pieces and eat you for dinner.
No, it's good, it's good.. =sniff=
Luckily my sister's employee discount made it easy to rent movies more to Lola's liking.
Heaven... I'm in Heaven...
And the cares that hung around me through the week...
Seem to vanish like a gambler's lucky streak...
when we're out together dancing, cheek to cheek...

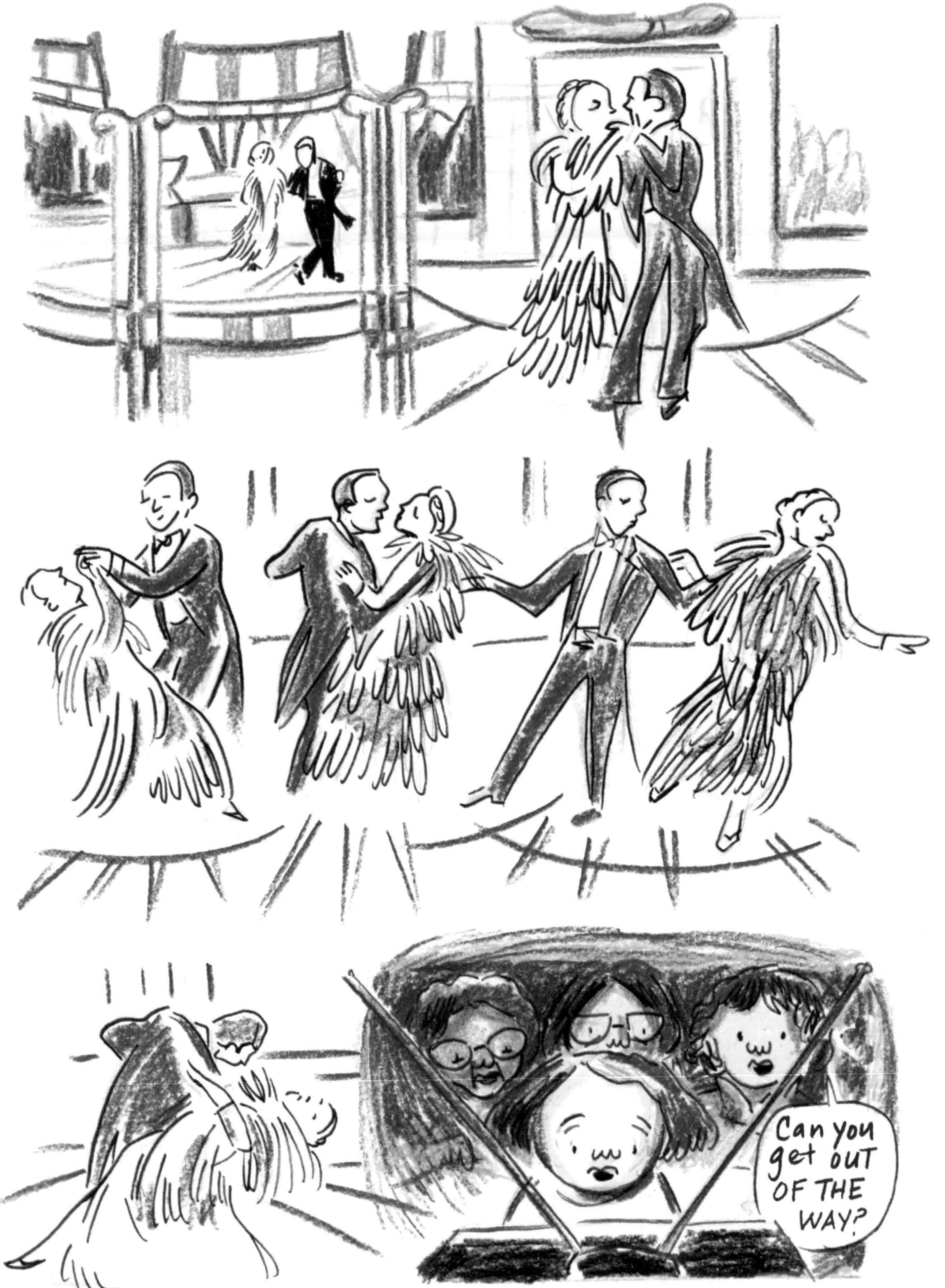
Can you get out OF THE WAY?

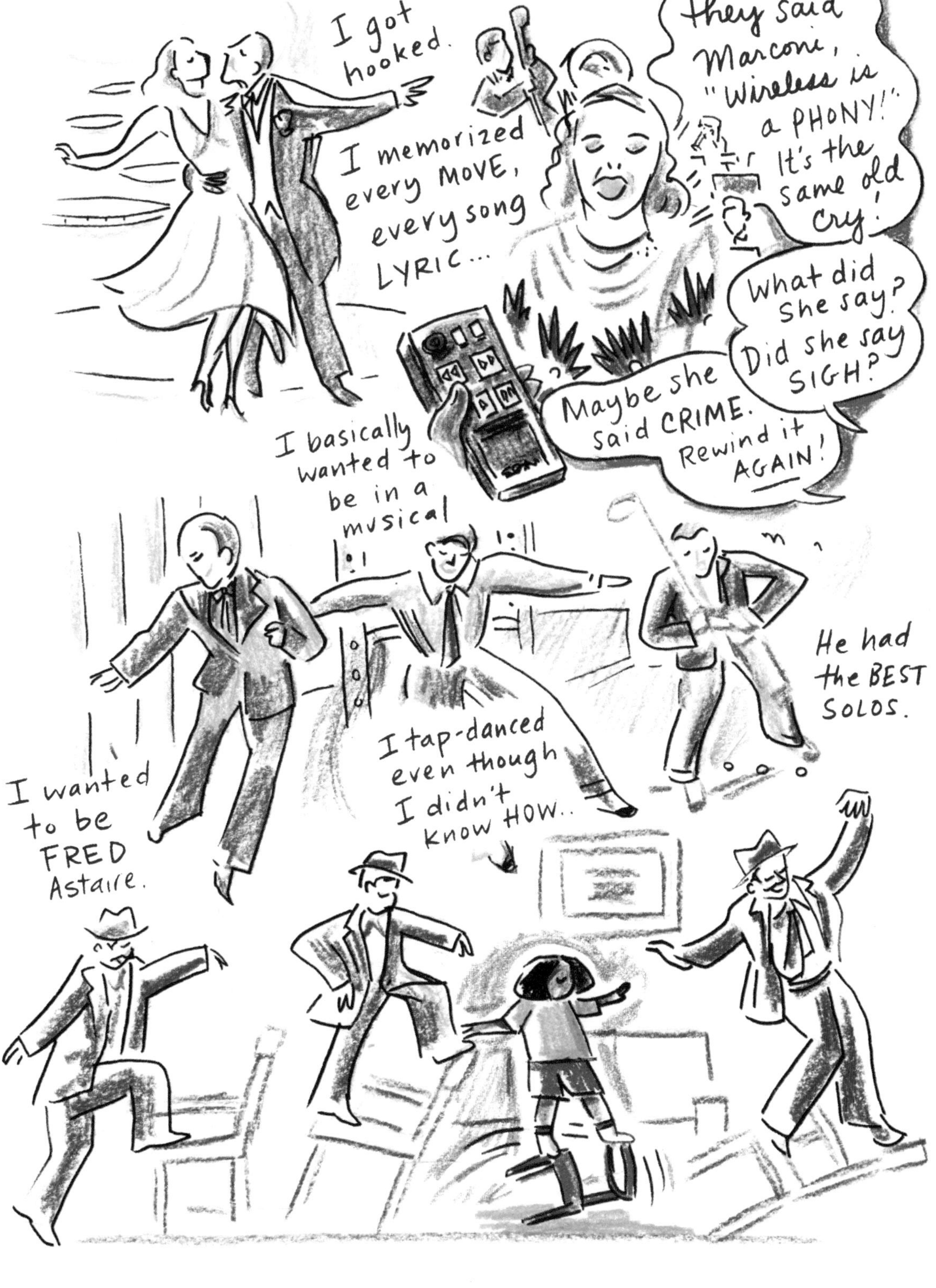

I got hooked.
I memorized every MOVE, every song LYRIC...
They said Marconi, "Wireless is a PHONY!" It's the same old cry!
What did she say? Did she say SIGH?
Maybe she said CRIME. Rewind it AGAIN!
I basically wanted to be in a musical
He had the BEST SOLOS.
I tap-danced even though I didn't know HOW..
I wanted to be FRED Astaire.

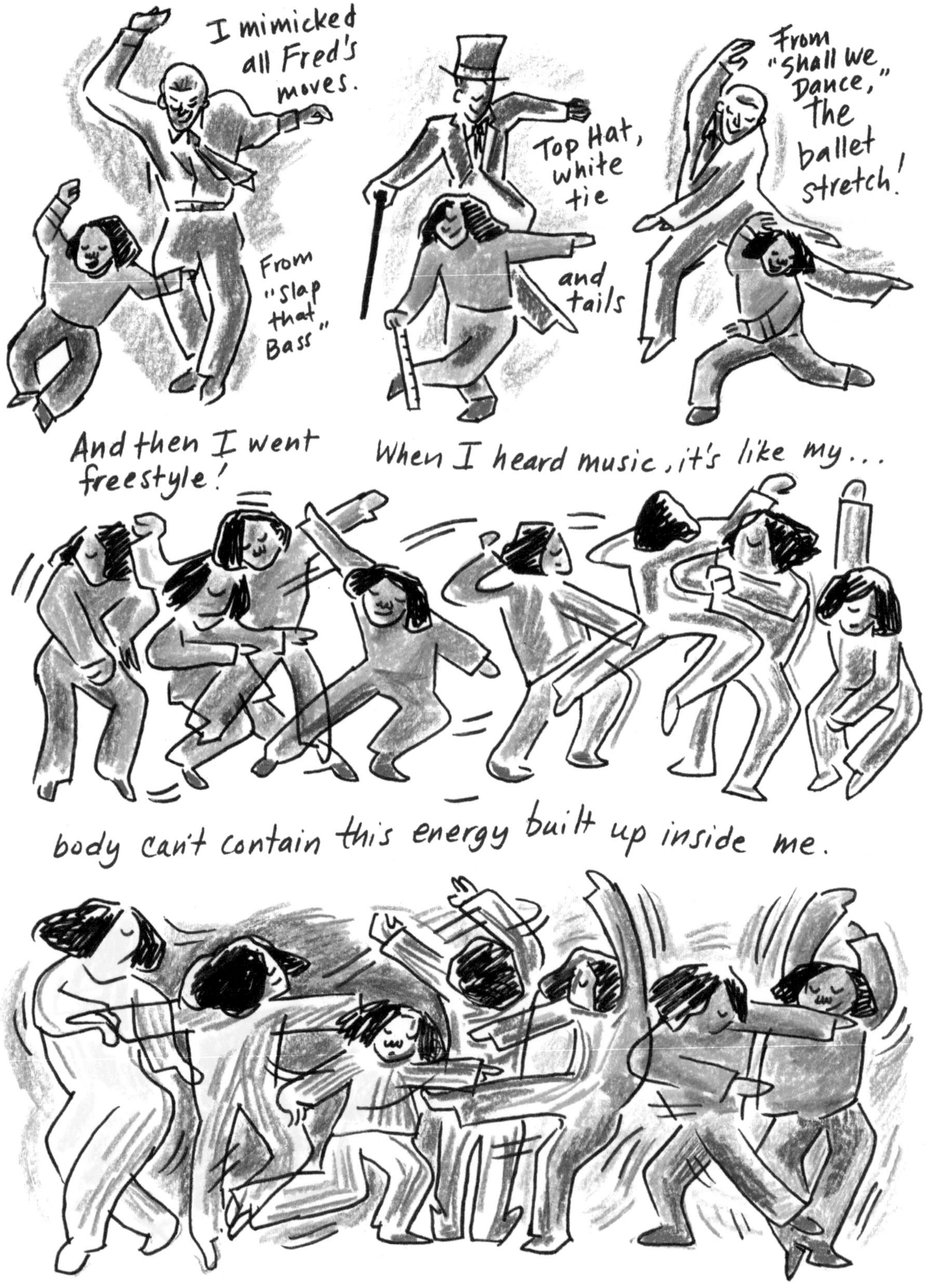
I mimicked all Fred's moves.
From "Slap that Bass"
Top Hat, white tie
and tails
From "Shall We Dance," the ballet stretch!
And then I went freestyle!
When I heard music, it's like my...
body can't contain this energy built up inside me.

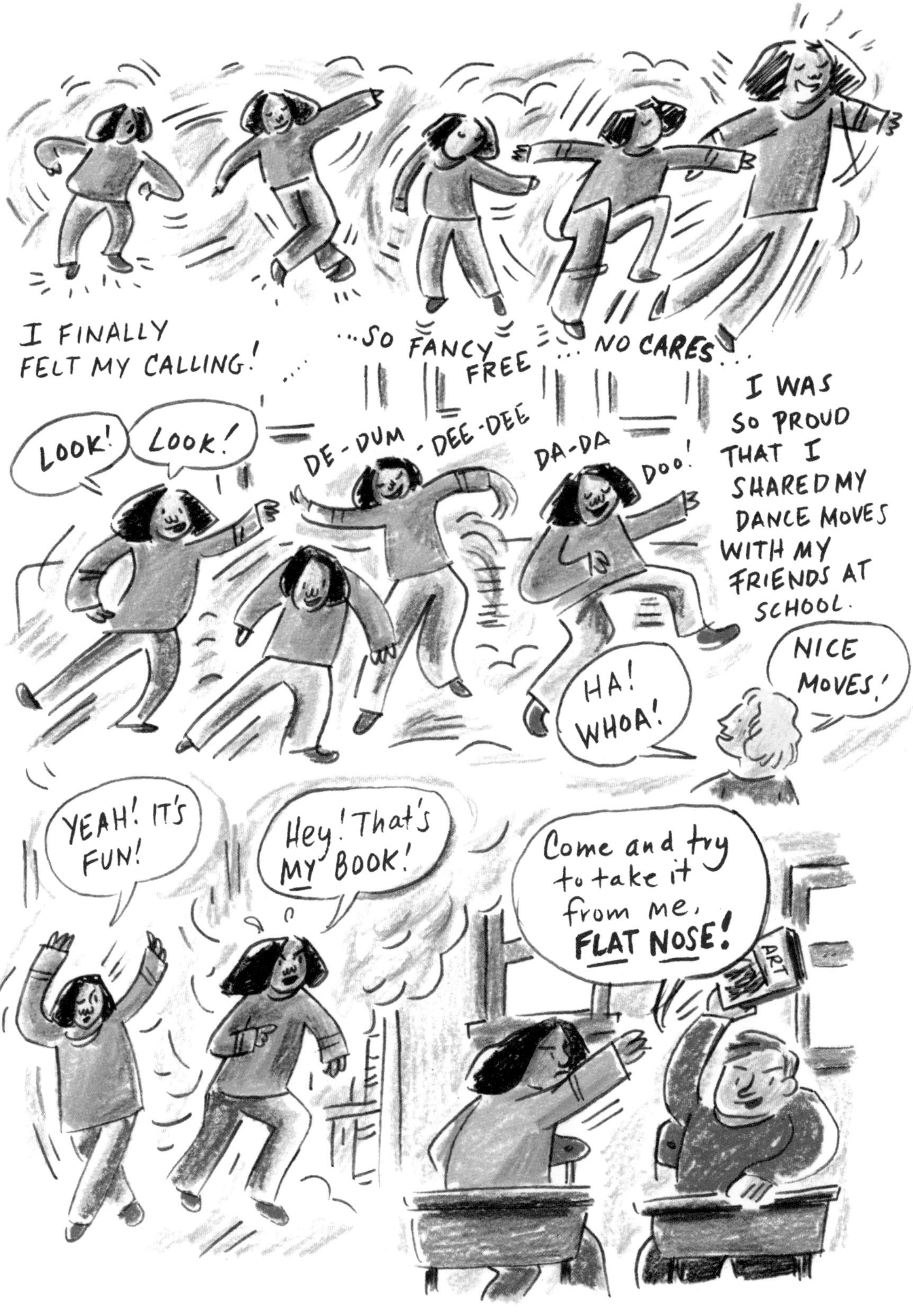

I FINALLY FELT MY CALLING!
...SO FANCY FREE ... NO CARES...
LOOK! LOOK!
DE-DUM - DEE-DEE
DA-DA DOO!
I WAS SO PROUD THAT I SHARED MY DANCE MOVES WITH MY FRIENDS AT SCHOOL.
HA! WHOA!
NICE MOVES!
YEAH! IT'S FUN!
Hey! That's MY BOOK!
Come and try to take it from me, FLAT NOSE!
ART

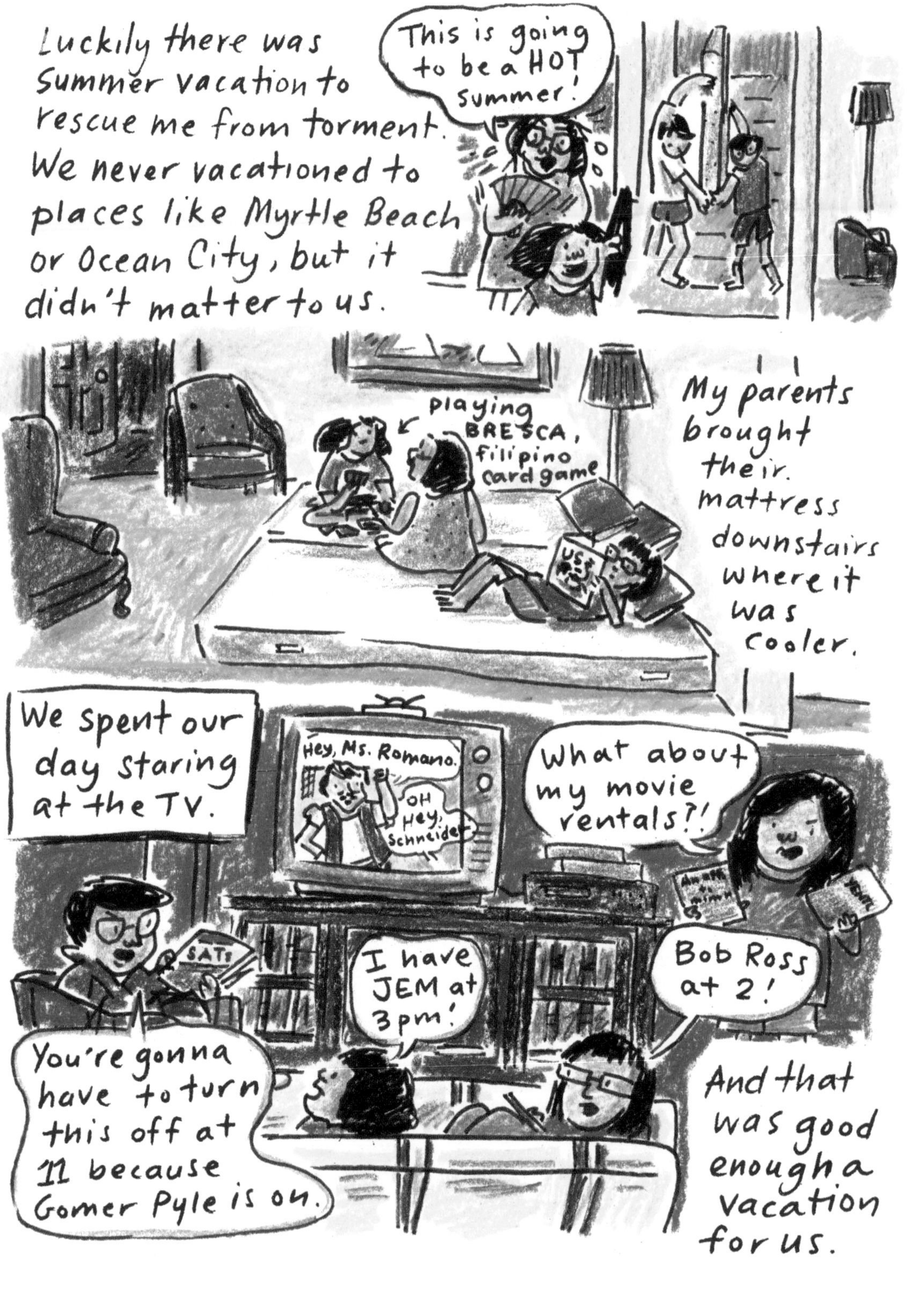
Luckily there was summer vacation to rescue me from torment. We never vacationed to places like Myrtle Beach or Ocean City, but it didn't matter to us.
This is going to be a HOT summer!
My parents brought their mattress downstairs where it was cooler.
playing BRESCA, filipino card game
We spent our day staring at the TV.
Hey, Ms. Romano.
OH Hey, Schneider
What about my movie rentals?!
SATs
I have JEM at 3pm!
Bob Ross at 2!
You're gonna have to turn this off at 11 because Gomer Pyle is on.
And that was good enough a vacation for us.

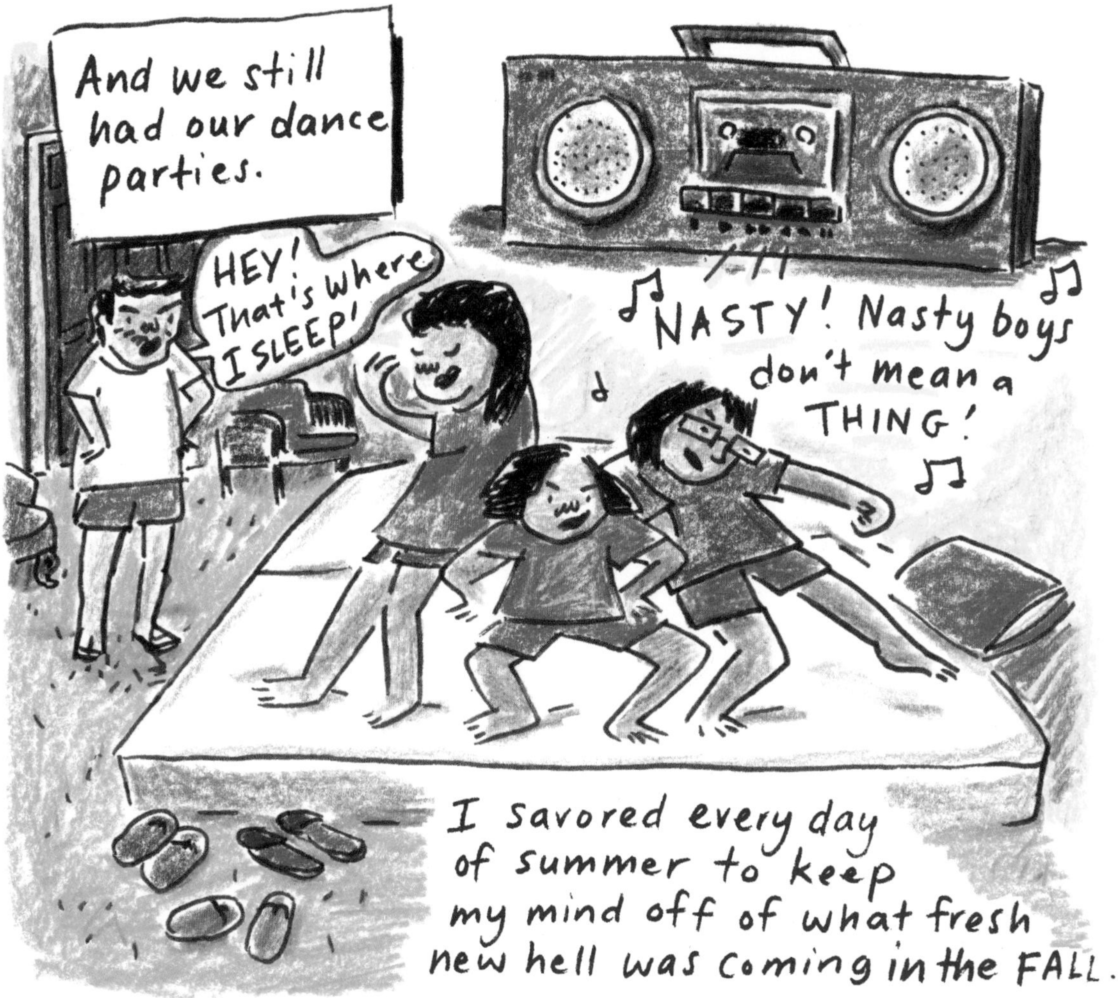
And we still had our dance parties.
HEY! That's where I SLEEP!
NASTY! Nasty boys don't mean a THING!
I savored every day of summer to keep my mind off of what fresh new hell was coming in the FALL.

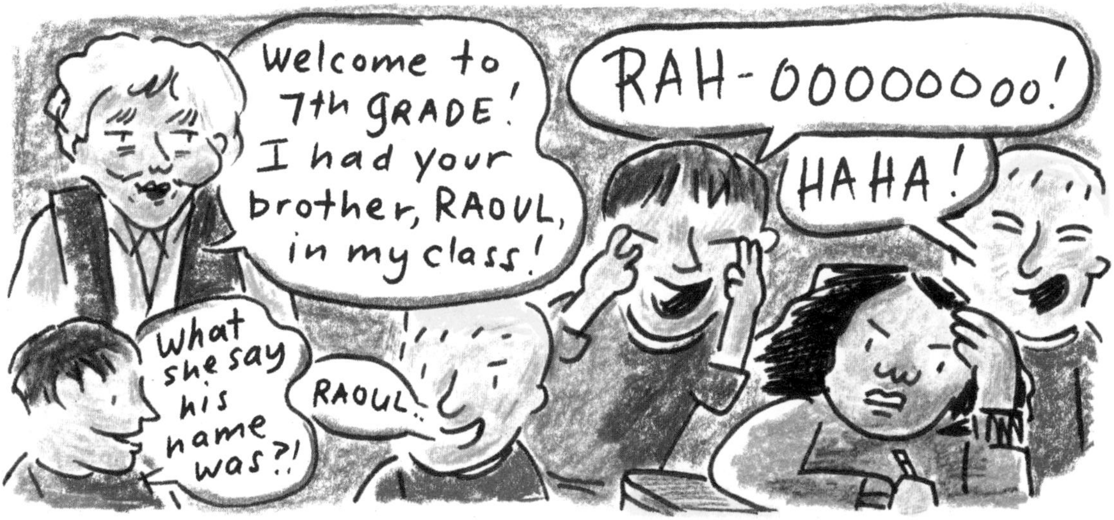
Welcome to 7th GRADE! I had your brother, RAOUL, in my class!
RAH-OOOOOOOO!
HAHA!
What she say his name was?!
RAOUL..

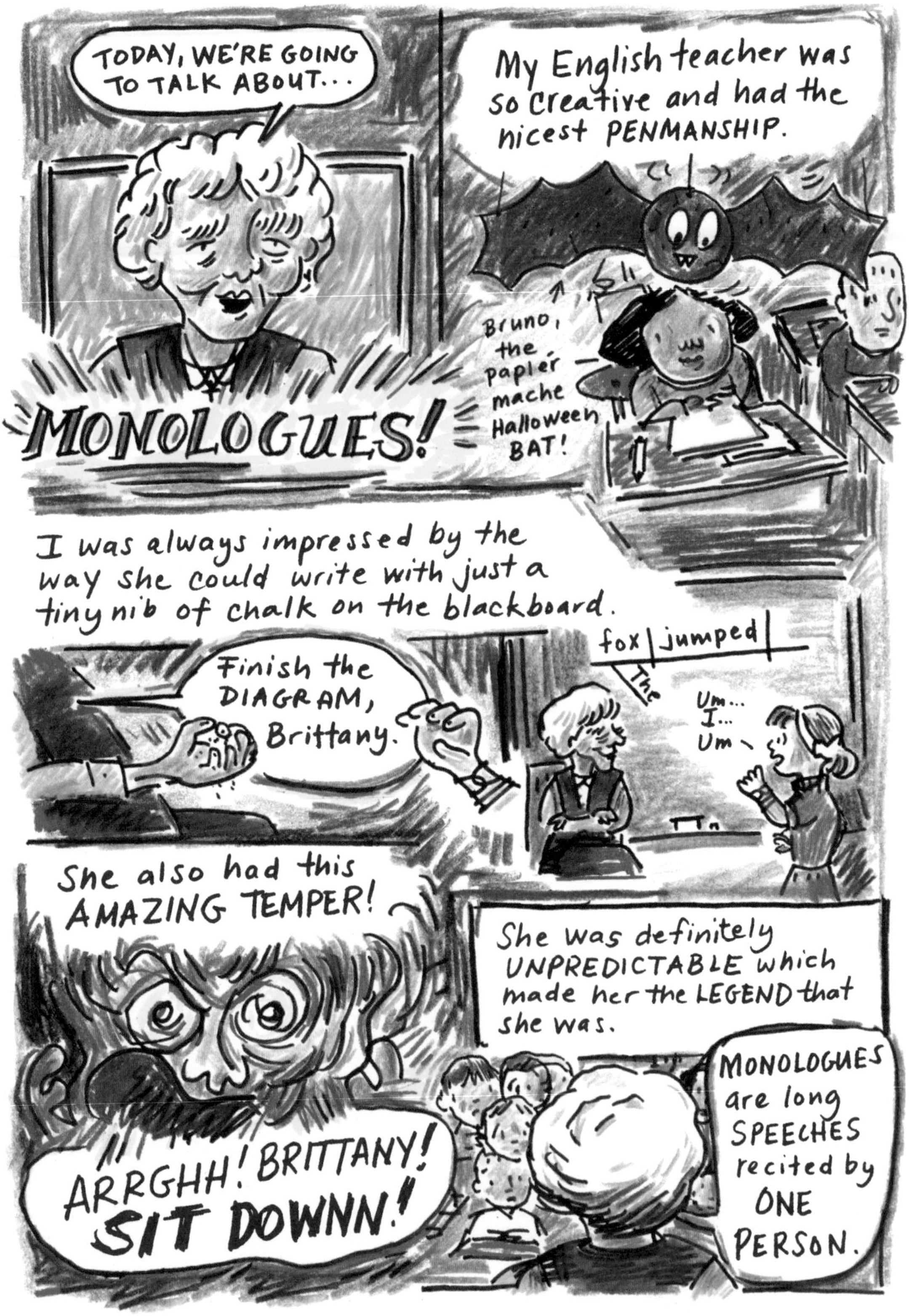
TODAY, WE'RE GOING TO TALK ABOUT...
MONOLOGUES!
My English teacher was so creative and had the nicest PENMANSHIP.
Bruno, the papier mache Halloween BAT!
I was always impressed by the way she could write with just a tiny nib of chalk on the blackboard.
Finish the DIAGRAM, Brittany.
fox
jumped
The
Um... I... Um
She also had this AMAZING TEMPER!
ARRGHH! BRITTANY! SIT DOWNN!
She was definitely UNPREDICTABLE which made her the LEGEND that she was.
MONOLOGUES are long SPEECHES recited by ONE PERSON.

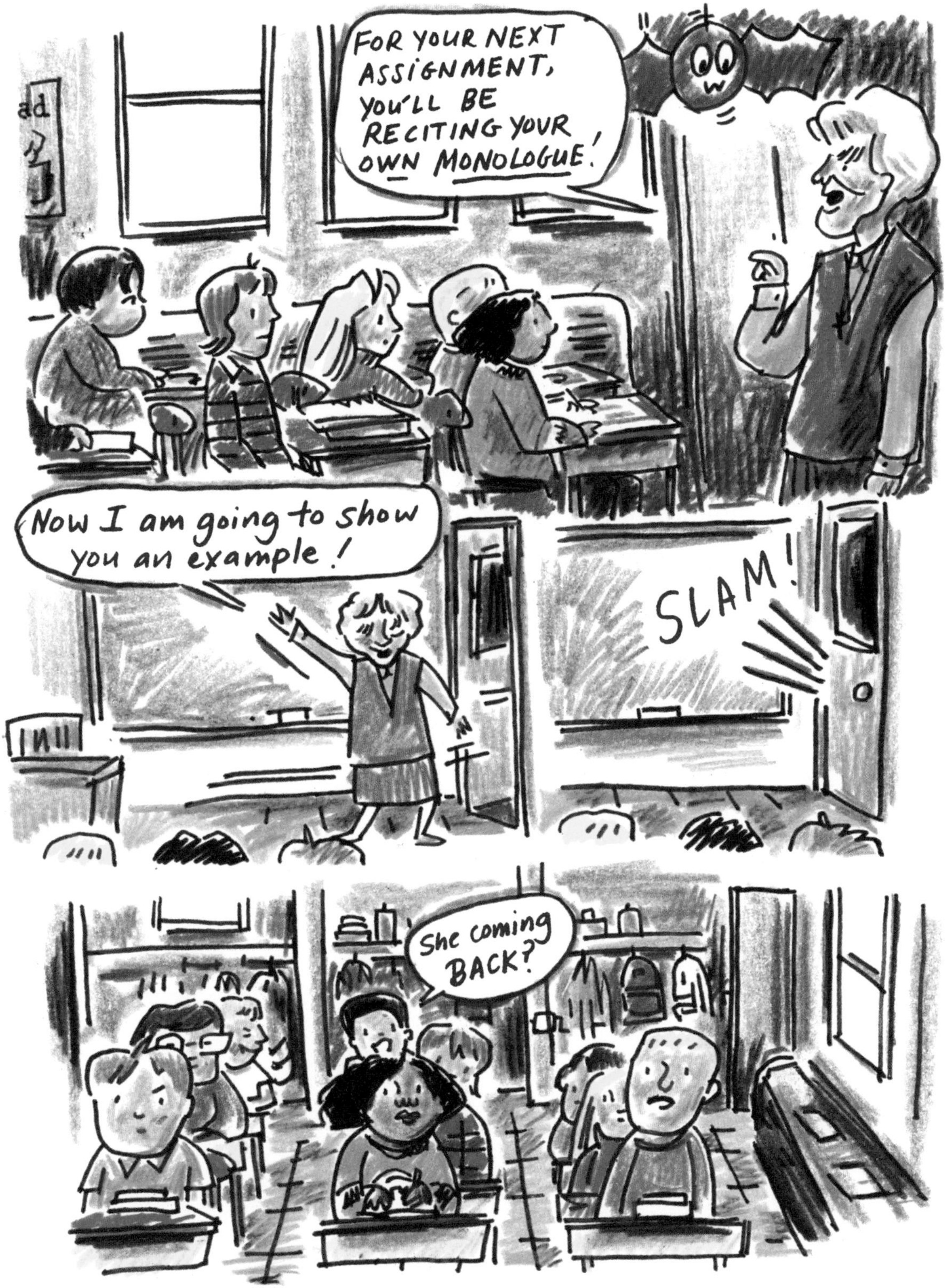
FOR YOUR NEXT ASSIGNMENT, YOU'LL BE RECITING YOUR OWN MONOLOGUE!
Now I am going to show you an example!
SLAM!
She coming BACK?

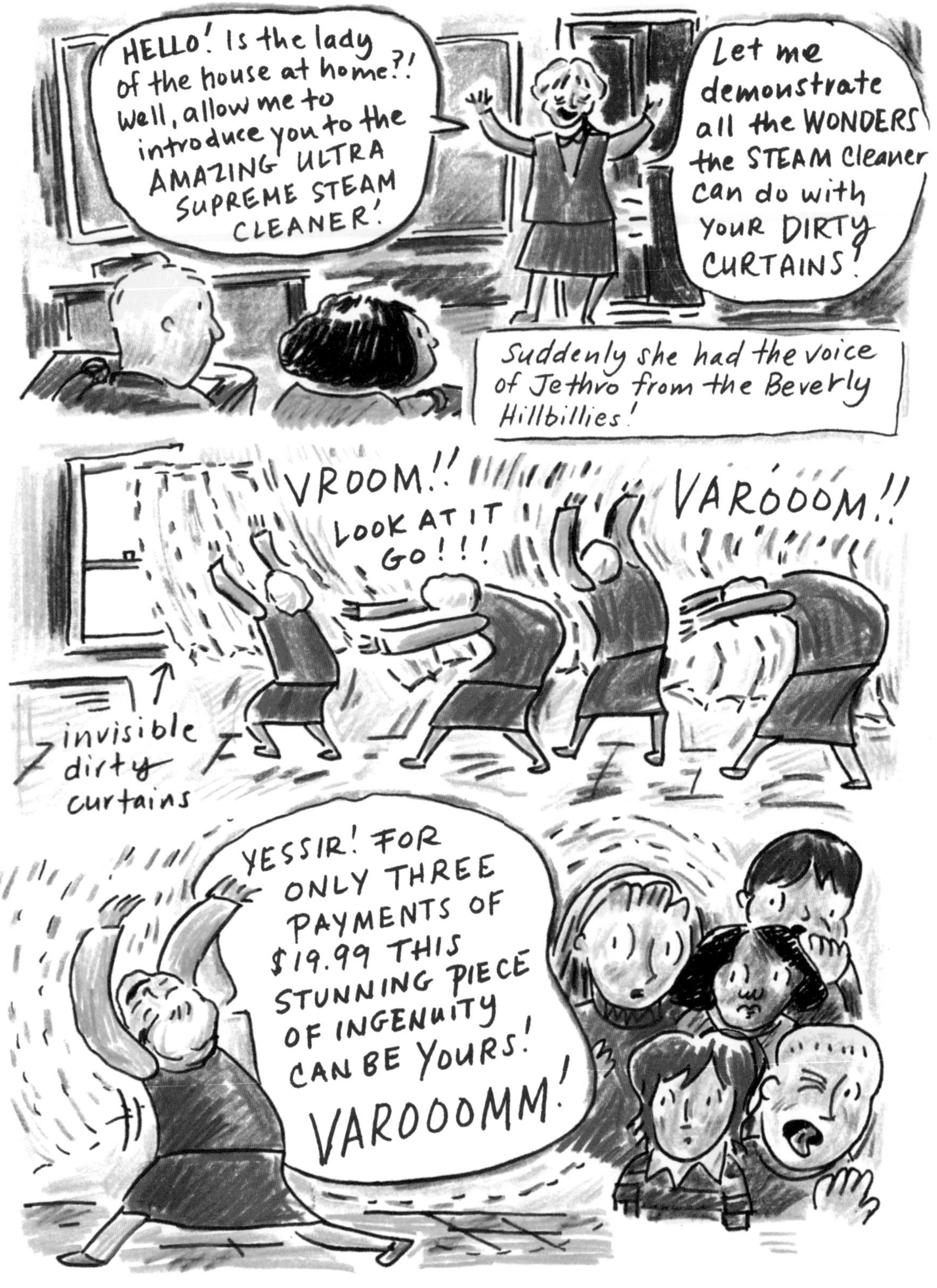
HELLO! Is the lady of the house at home?! Well, allow me to introduce you to the AMAZING ULTRA SUPREME STEAM CLEANER!
Let me demonstrate all the WONDERS the STEAM Cleaner can do with YOUR DIRTY CURTAINS!
Suddenly she had the voice of Jethro from the Beverly Hillbillies!
VROOM!!
LOOK AT IT GO!!!
VAROOOM!!
invisible dirty curtains
YESSIR! FOR ONLY THREE PAYMENTS OF $19.99 THIS STUNNING PIECE OF INGENUITY CAN BE YOURS!
VAROOOMM!

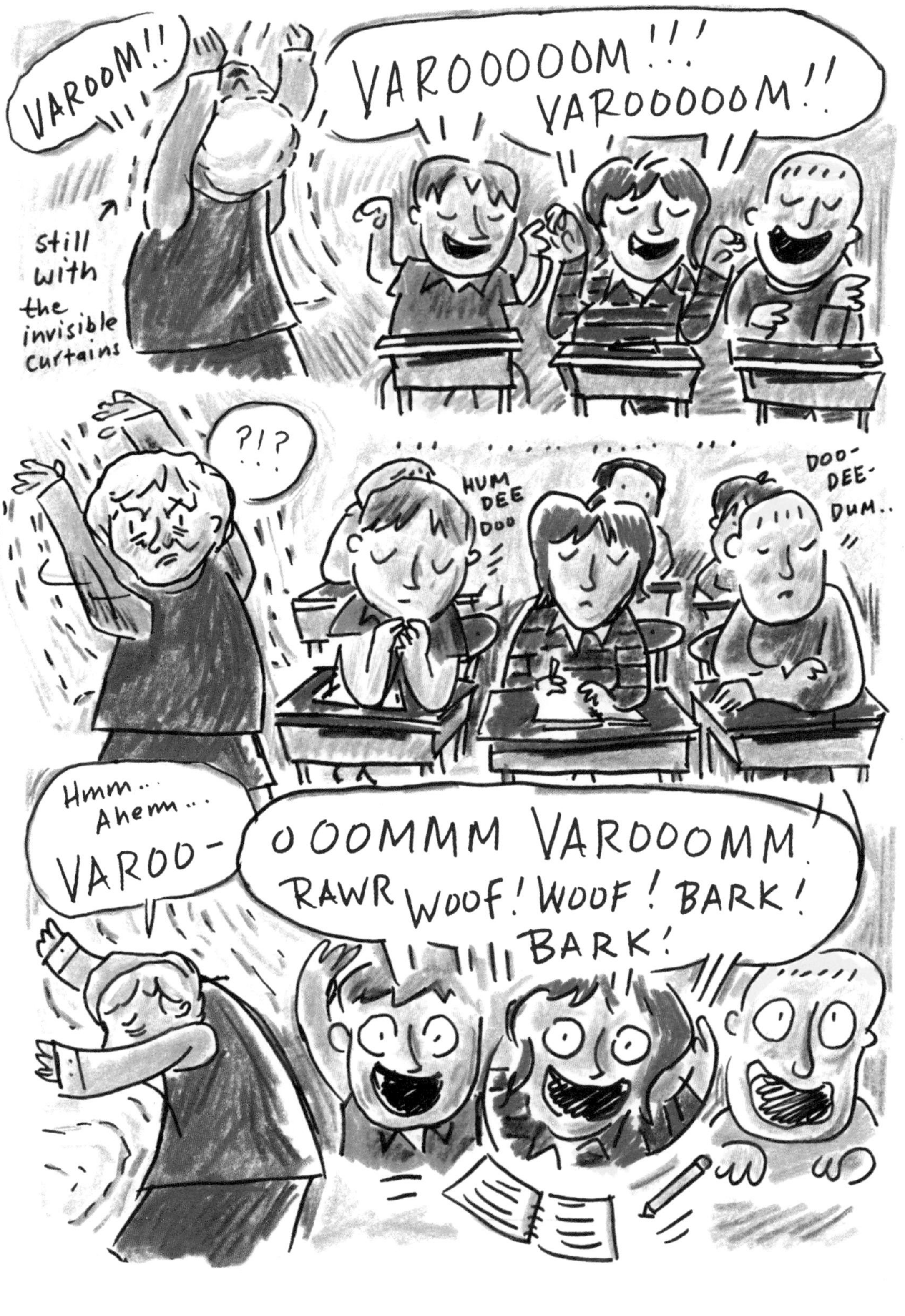
VAROOM!!
still with the invisible curtains
VAROOOOOM!!!
VAROOOOOOM!!
?!?
HUM DEE DOO
DOO-DEE-DUM...
Hmm... Ahem...
VAROO-
OOOMMM VAROOOMM!
RAWR WOOF! WOOF! BARK! BARK!

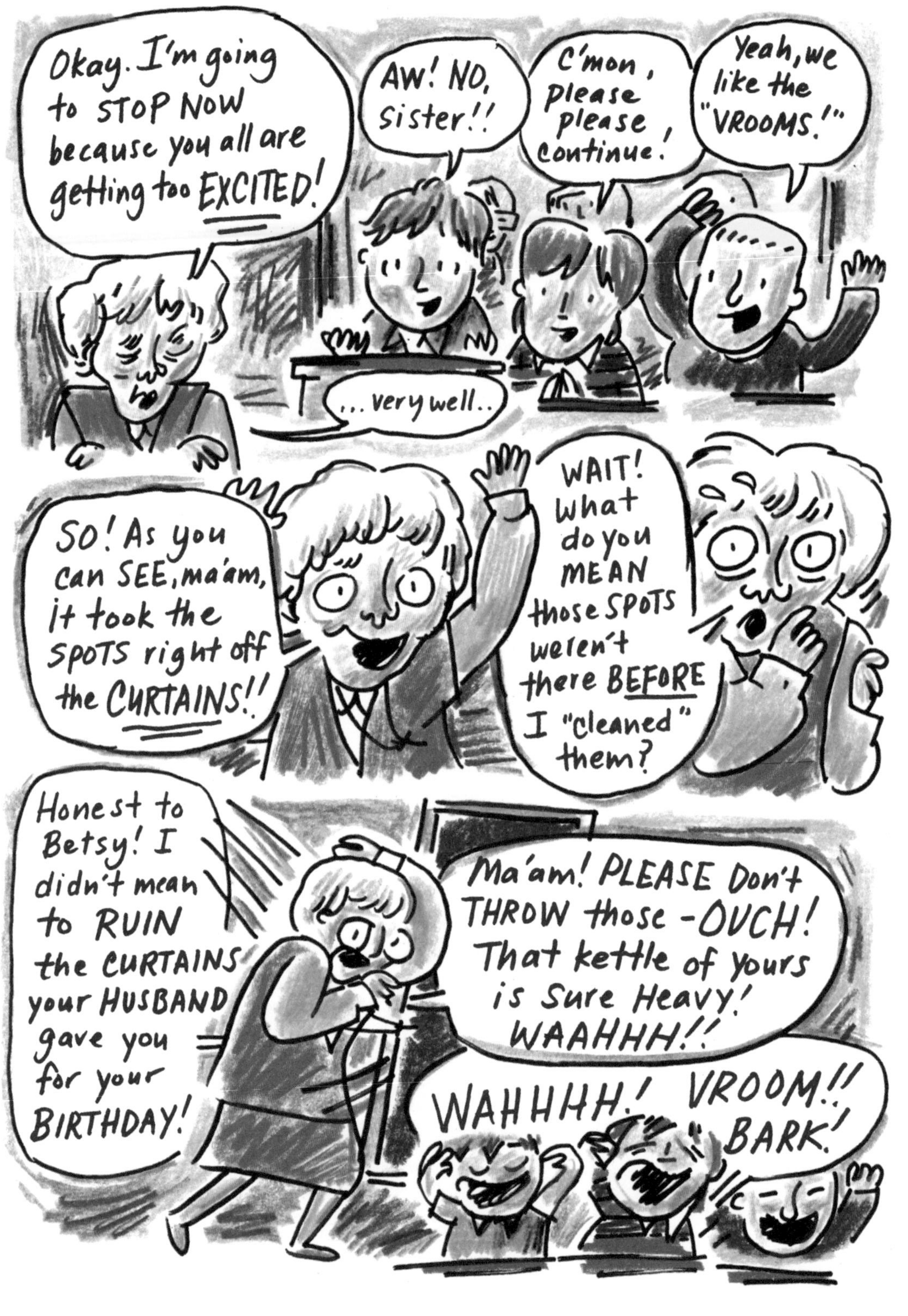
Okay. I'm going to STOP NOW because you all are getting too EXCITED!
AW! NO, Sister!!
C'mon, please please continue!
Yeah, we like the "VROOMS!"
...very well..
SO! As you can SEE, ma'am, it took the SPOTS right off the CURTAINS!!
WAIT! What do you MEAN those SPOTS weren't there BEFORE I "cleaned" them?
Honest to Betsy! I didn't mean to RUIN the CURTAINS your HUSBAND gave you for your BIRTHDAY!
Ma'am! PLEASE Don't THROW those -OUCH! That kettle of yours is Sure Heavy! WAAHHH!!
WAHHHH! VROOM!! BARK!

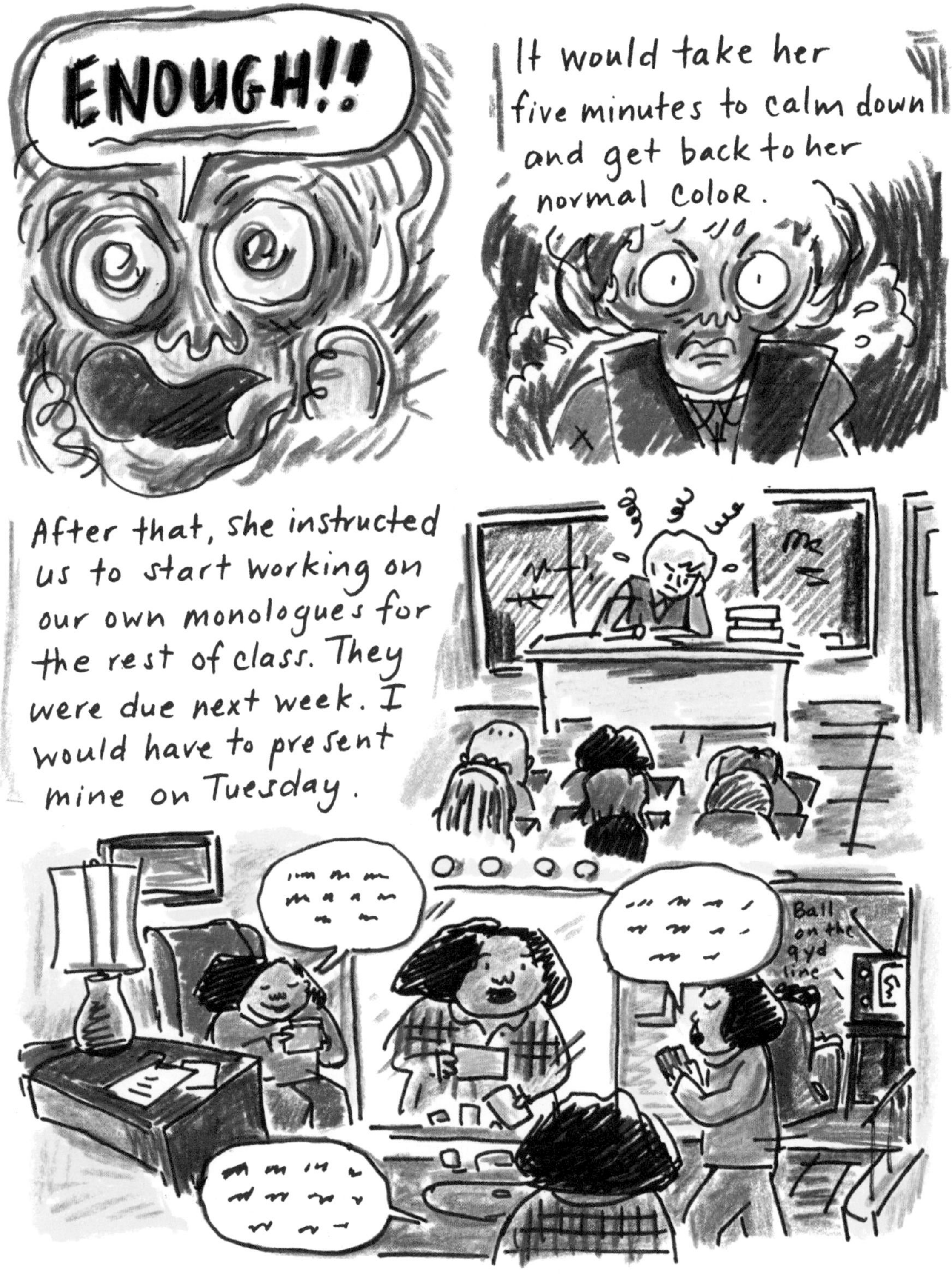
ENOUGH!!
It would take her five minutes to calm down and get back to her normal color.
After that, she instructed us to start working on our own monologues for the rest of class. They were due next week. I would have to present mine on Tuesday.
Ball on the 9yd line

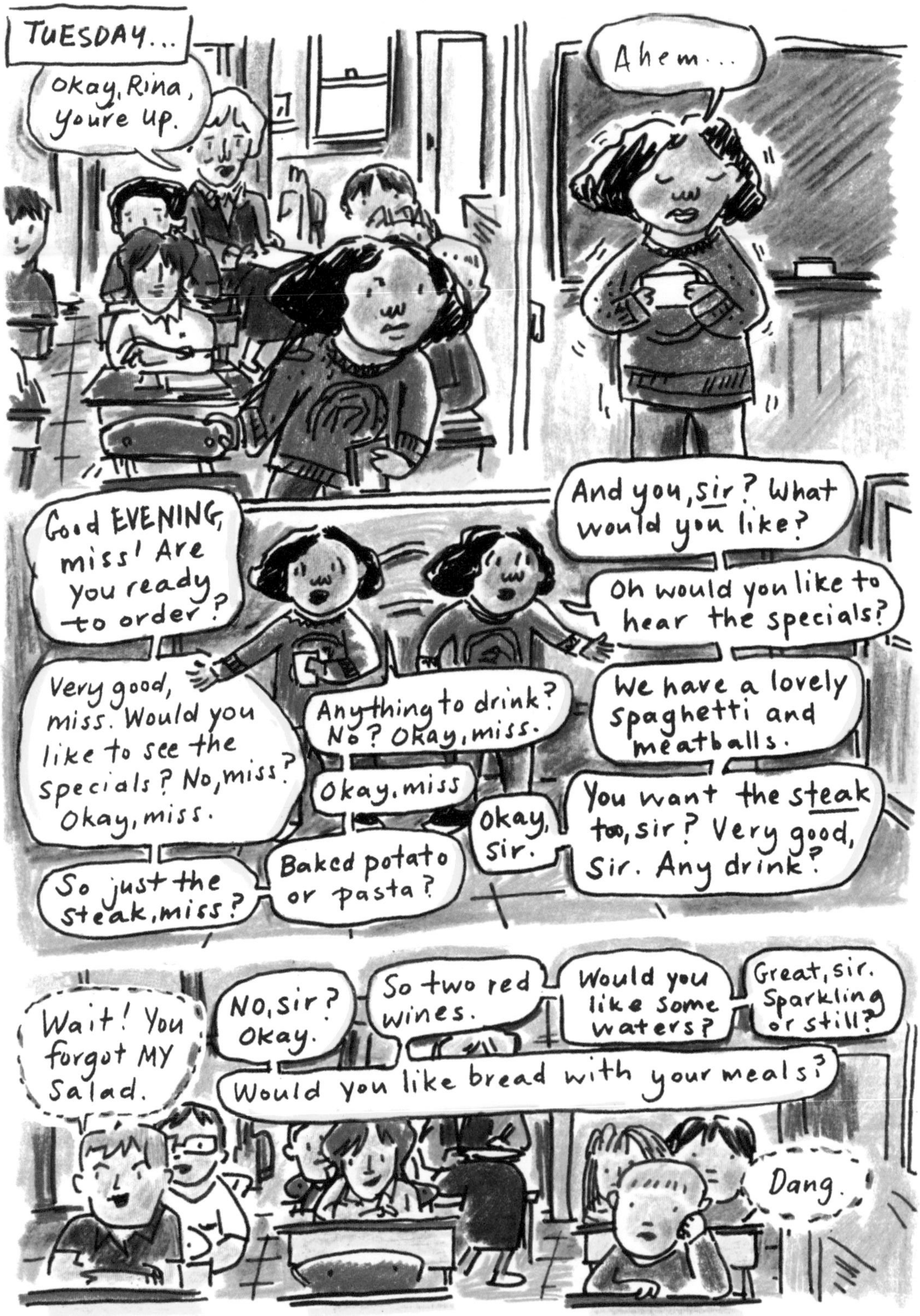
TUESDAY...
Okay, Rina, you're up.
Ahem...
Good EVENING, miss! Are you ready to order?
Very good, miss. Would you like to see the specials? No, miss? Okay, miss.
Anything to drink? No? Okay, miss.
Okay, miss
So just the steak, miss?
Baked potato or pasta?
And you, sir? What would you like?
Oh would you like to hear the specials?
We have a lovely spaghetti and meatballs.
You want the steak too, sir? Very good, sir. Any drink?
Okay, sir.
Wait! You forgot MY salad.
No, sir? Okay.
So two red wines.
Would you like some waters?
Great, sir. Sparkling or still?
Would you like bread with your meals?
Dang.

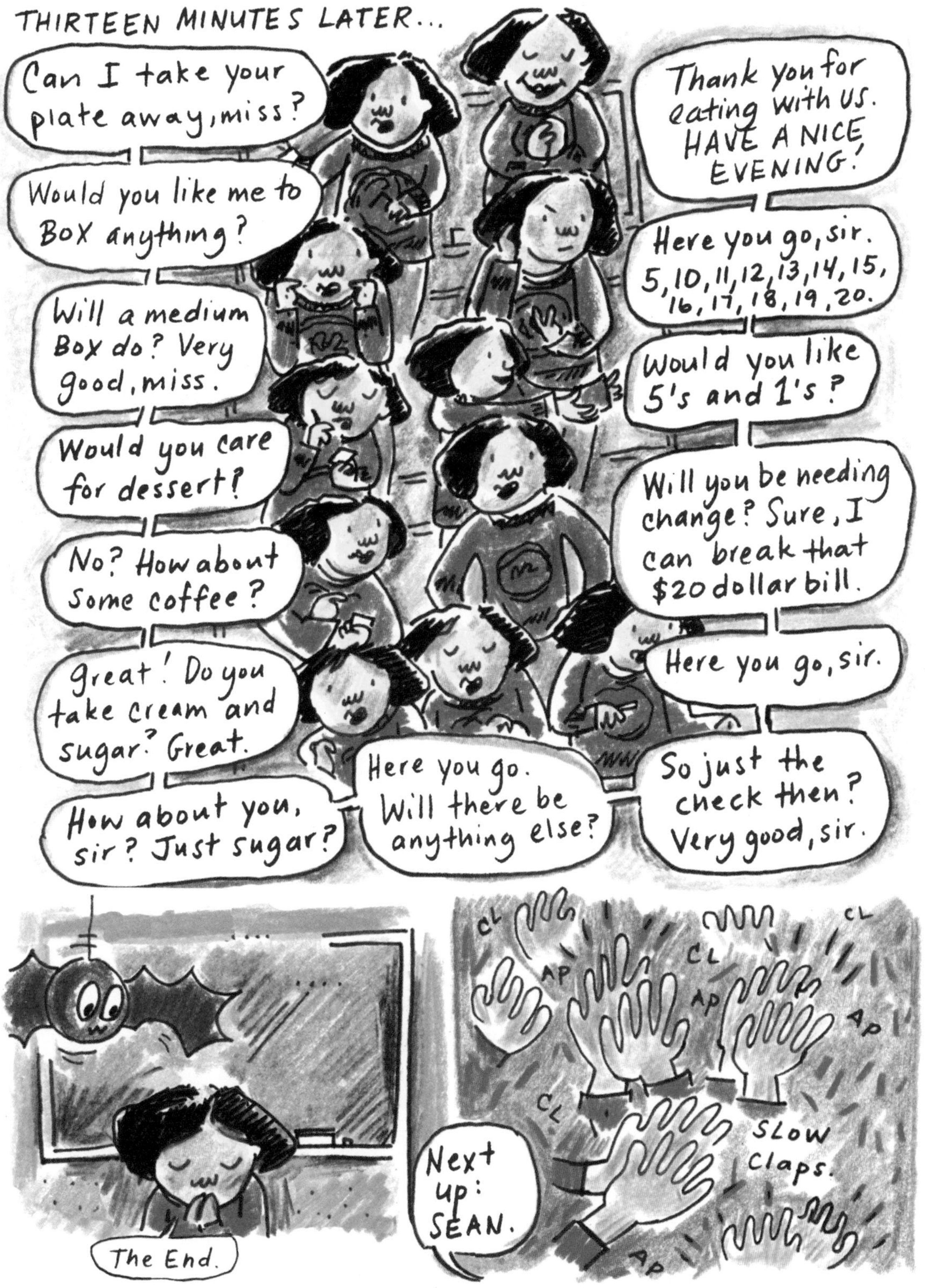
THIRTEEN MINUTES LATER...
Can I take your plate away, miss?
Would you like me to Box anything?
Will a medium Box do? Very good, miss.
Would you care for dessert?
No? How about some coffee?
Great! Do you take cream and sugar? Great.
How about you, sir? Just sugar?
Here you go. Will there be anything else?
So just the check then? Very good, sir.
Here you go, sir.
Will you be needing change? Sure, I can break that $20 dollar bill.
Would you like 5's and 1's?
Here you go, sir. 5, 10, 11, 12, 13, 14, 15, 16, 17, 18, 19, 20.
Thank you for eating with us. HAVE A NICE EVENING!
The End.
CL
AP
CL
AP
CL
AP
CL
AP
SLOW Claps.
Next up: SEAN.

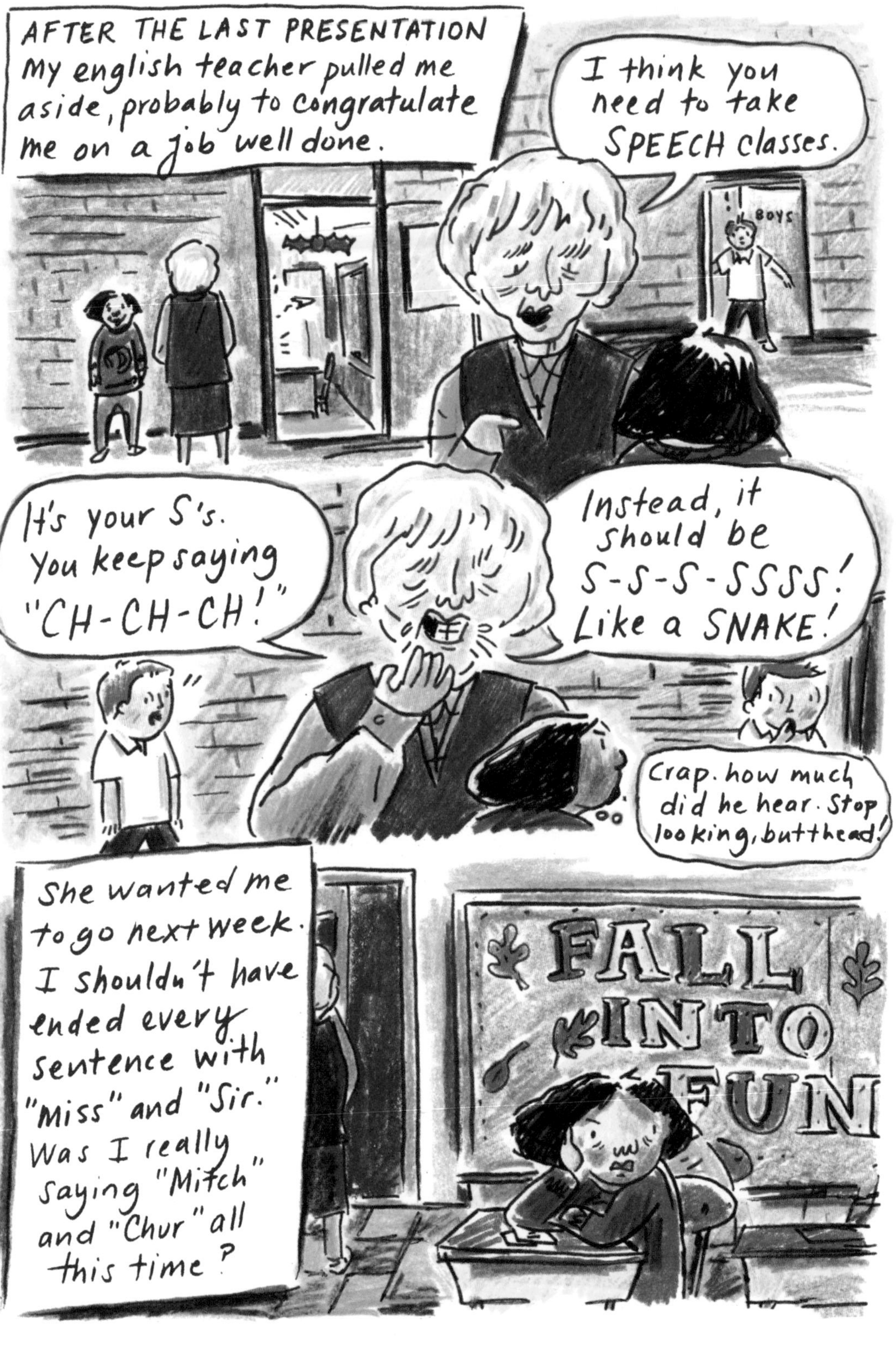
AFTER THE LAST PRESENTATION My english teacher pulled me aside, probably to congratulate me on a job well done.
I think you need to take SPEECH classes.
BOYS
It's your S's. You keep saying "CH-CH-CH!"
Instead, it should be S-S-S-SSSS! Like a SNAKE!
Crap. how much did he hear. Stop looking, butthead!
She wanted me to go next week. I shouldn't have ended every sentence with "Miss" and "Sir." Was I really saying "Mitch" and "Chur" all this time?
FALL INTO FUN

zzz

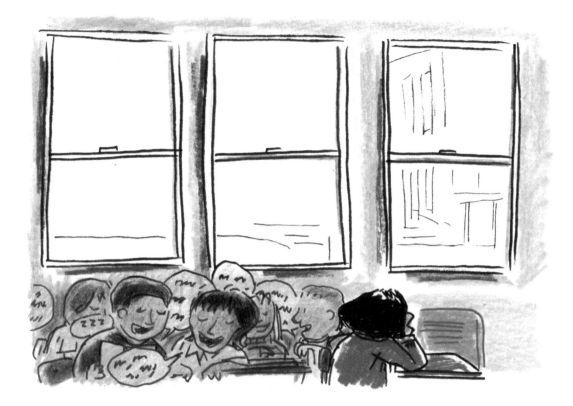

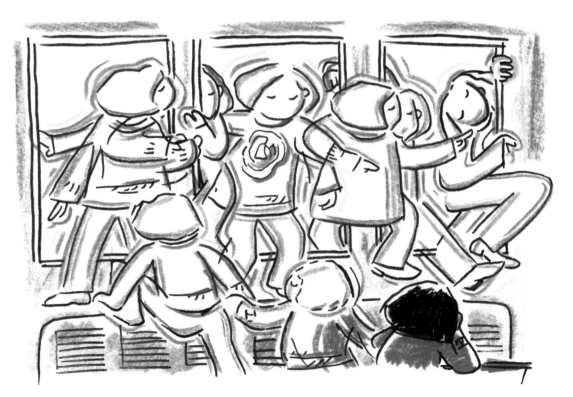

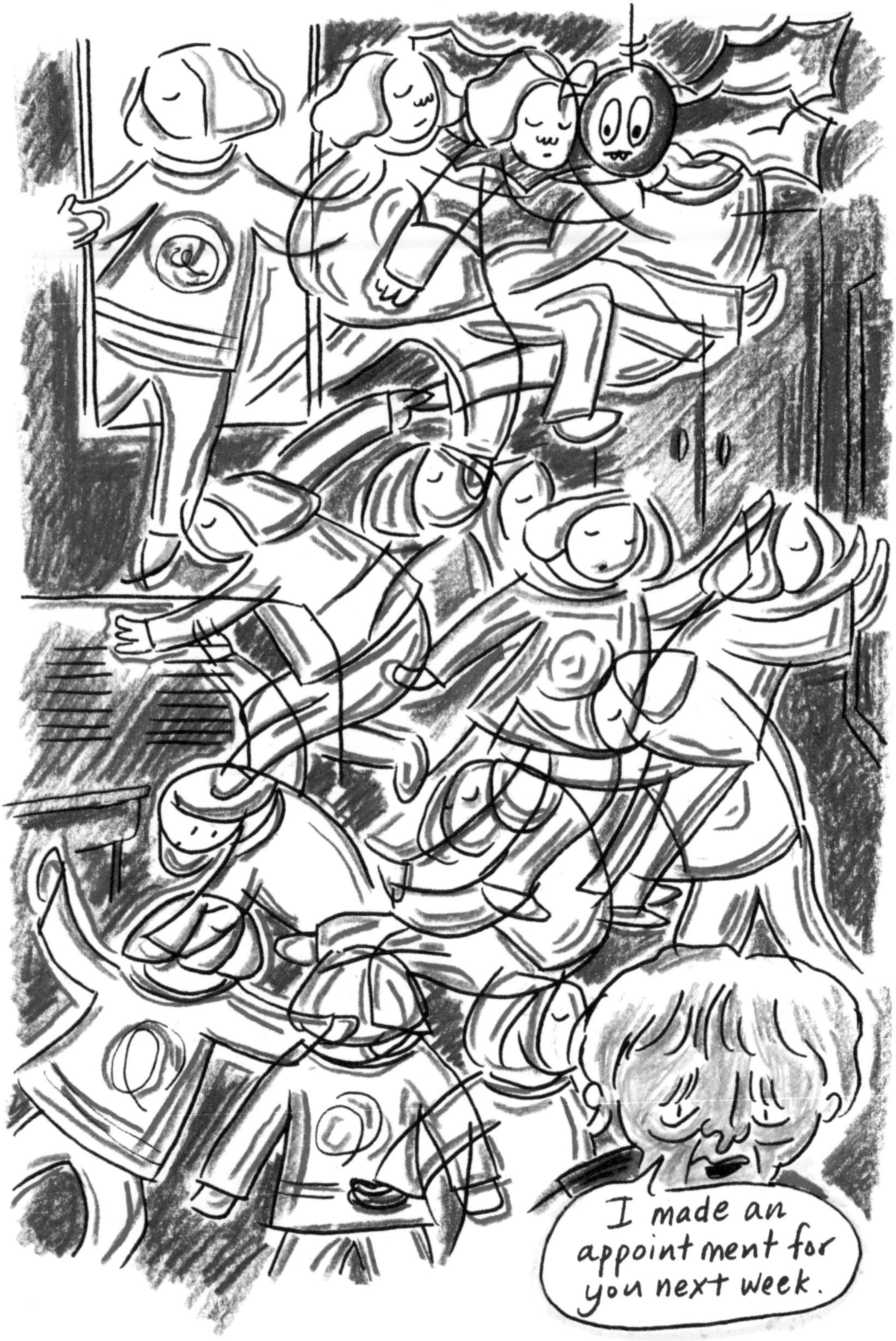
I made an appointment for you next week.

Five years earlier, I had to take speech classes in 2nd grade, for my "L's." Who goes to speech class for "Ls?!?" The classes were in a parked van next to the school. It always felt like a walk of SHAME.

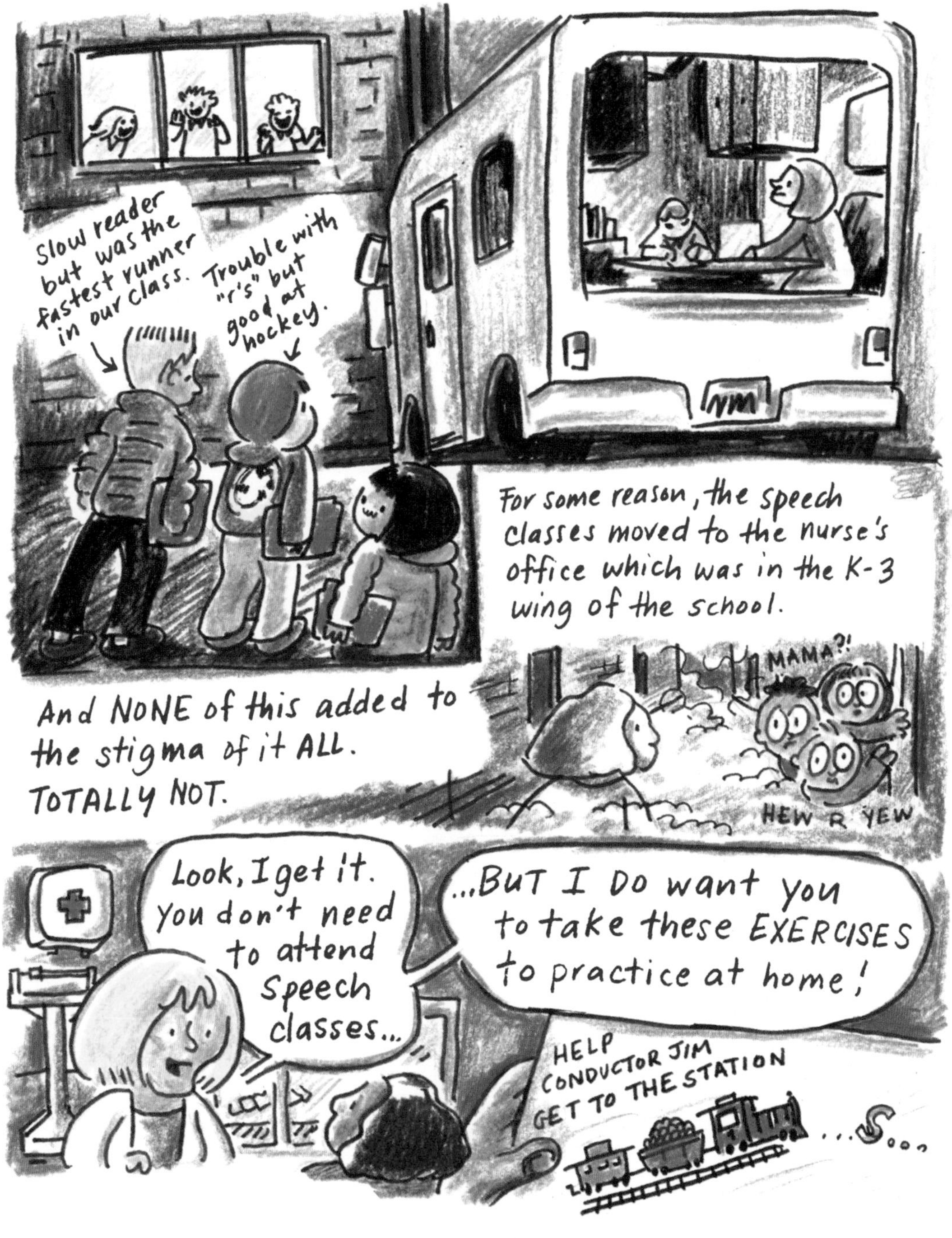
Slow reader but was the fastest runner in our class.
Trouble with "r's" but good at hockey.
For some reason, the speech classes moved to the nurse's office which was in the K-3 wing of the school.
MAMA?!
HEW R YEW
And NONE of this added to the stigma of it ALL. TOTALLY NOT.
Look, I get it. You don't need to attend speech classes...
...BUT I DO want you to take these EXERCISES to practice at home!
HELP CONDUCTOR JIM GET TO THE STATION
...S...

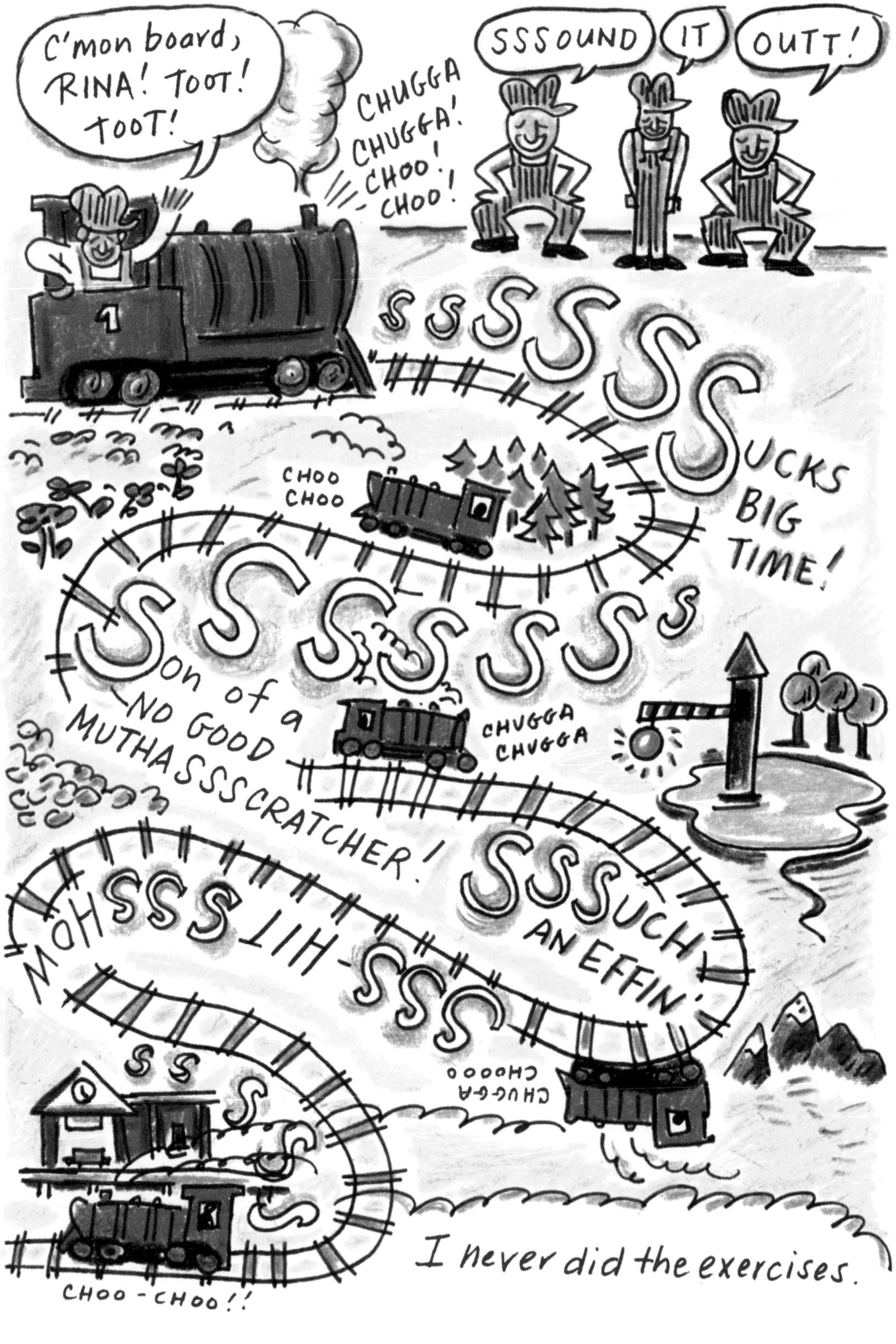

C'mon board, RINA! TOOT! TOOT!
CHUGGA CHUGGA! CHOO! CHOO!
SSSOUND
IT
OUTT!
SUCKS BIG TIME!
CHOO CHOO
Son of a NO GOOD MUTHASSSCRATCHER!
CHUGGA CHUGGA
SUCH AN EFFIN'
HIT
SSSHOW
CHUG-GA CHOOOO
CHOO-CHOO!!
I never did the exercises.

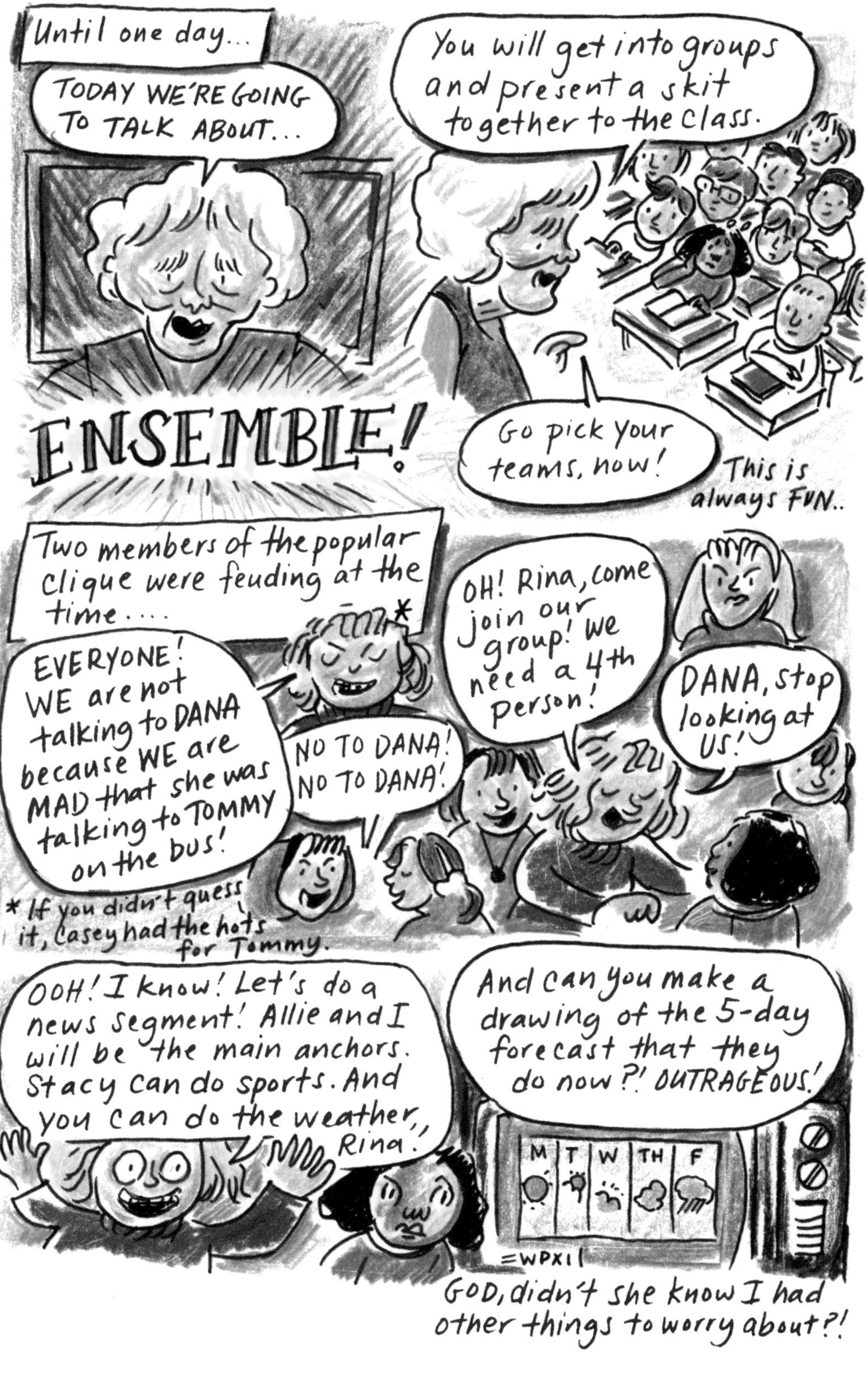

Until one day...
TODAY WE'RE GOING TO TALK ABOUT...
ENSEMBLE!
You will get into groups and present a skit together to the class.
Go pick your teams, now!
This is always FUN..
Two members of the popular clique were feuding at the time....
EVERYONE! WE are not talking to DANA because WE are MAD that she was talking to TOMMY on the bus!
NO TO DANA! NO TO DANA!
OH! Rina, come join our group! We need a 4th person!
DANA, stop looking at US!
* If you didn't guess it, Casey had the hots for Tommy.
OOH! I know! Let's do a news segment! Allie and I will be the main anchors. Stacy can do sports. And you can do the weather, Rina.
And can you make a drawing of the 5-day forecast that they do now?! OUTRAGEOUS!
M T W TH F
WPXI
GOD, didn't she know I had other things to worry about?!

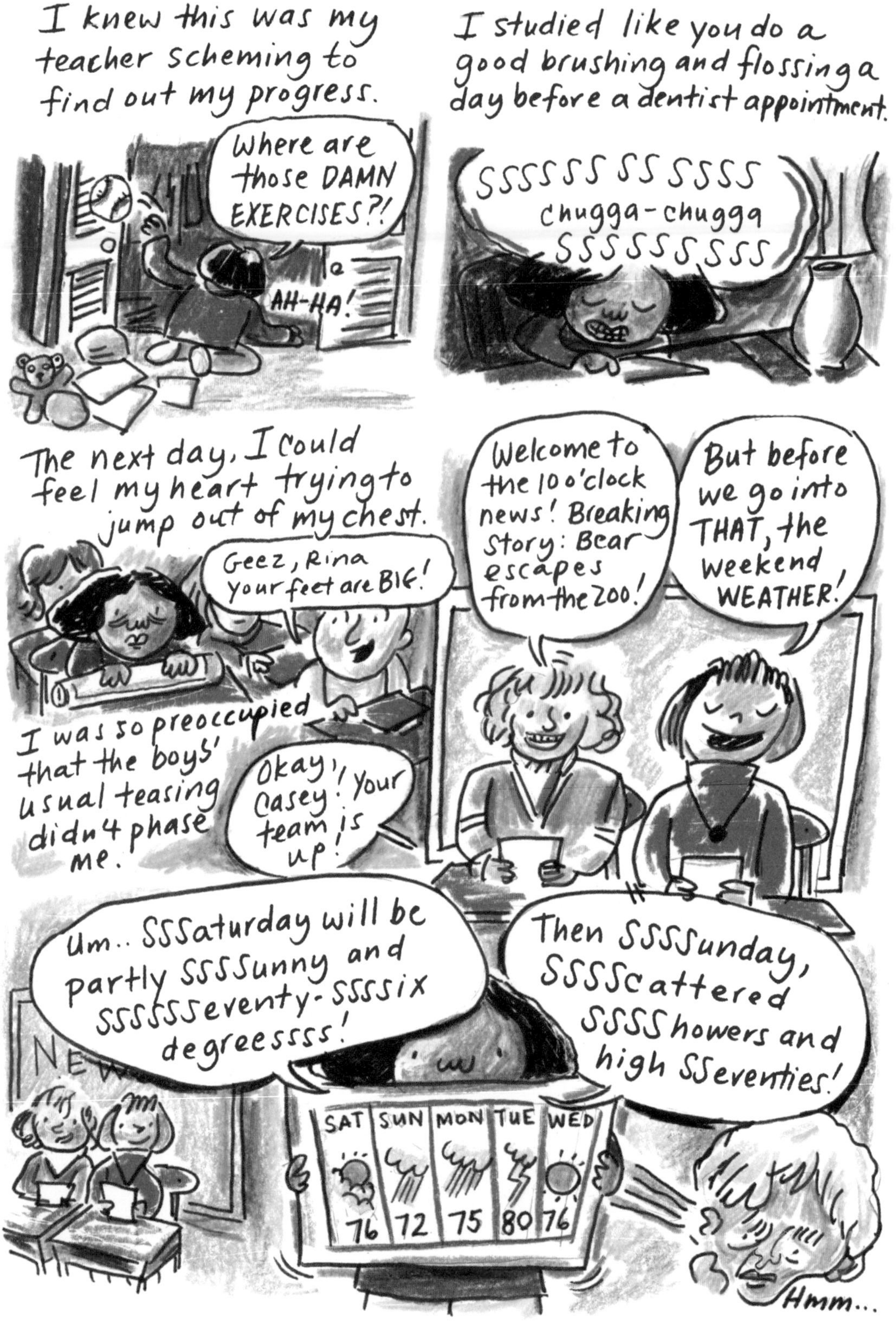
I knew this was my teacher scheming to find out my progress.
Where are those DAMN EXERCISES?!
AH-HA!
I studied like you do a good brushing and flossing a day before a dentist appointment.
SSSSSS SS SSSS chugga-chugga SSSSSSSSS
The next day, I could feel my heart trying to jump out of my chest.
Geez, Rina your feet are BIG!
I was so preoccupied that the boys' usual teasing didn't phase me.
Okay, Casey! Your team is up!
Welcome to the 10 o'clock news! Breaking Story: Bear escapes from the zoo!
But before we go into THAT, the weekend WEATHER!
Um.. SSSaturday will be partly SSSSunny and SSSSSSeventy-SSSSix degreessss!
Then SSSSunday, SSSScattered SSSShowers and high SSeventies!
SAT SUN MON TUE WED
76 72 75 80 76
NEWS
Hmm...

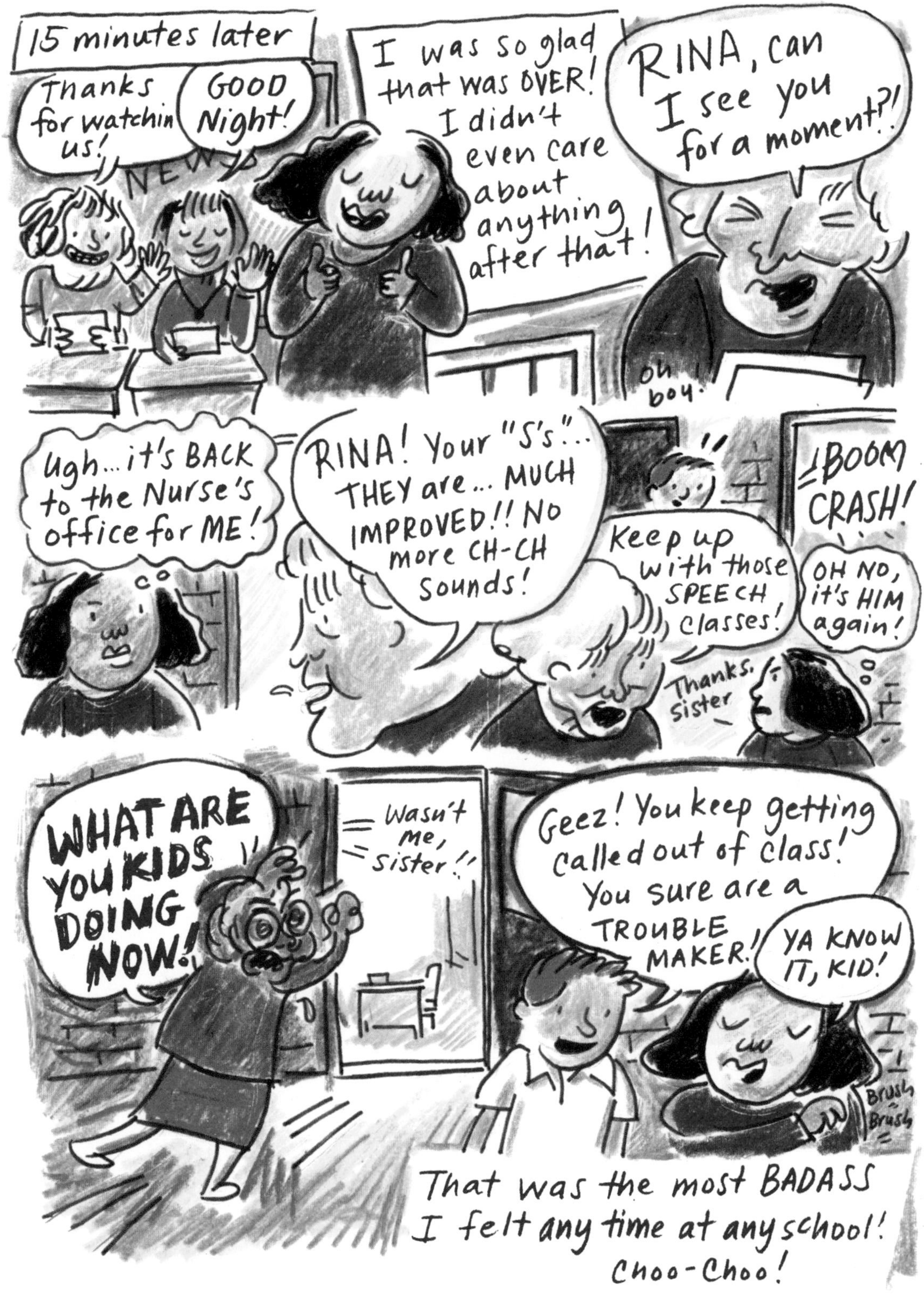
15 minutes later
Thanks for watchin us!
GOOD Night!
NEWS
I was so glad that was OVER! I didn't even care about anything after that!
RINA, can I see you for a moment?!
oh boy.
Ugh... it's BACK to the Nurse's office for ME!
RINA! Your "S's"... THEY are... MUCH IMPROVED!! No more CH-CH sounds!
Keep up with those SPEECH classes!
Thanks, sister
BOOM CRASH!
OH NO, it's HIM again!
WHAT ARE YOU KIDS DOING NOW!
Wasn't me, sister!!
Geez! You keep getting called out of class! You sure are a TROUBLE MAKER!
YA KNOW IT, KID!
Brush Brush
That was the most BADASS I felt any time at any school! Choo-Choo!

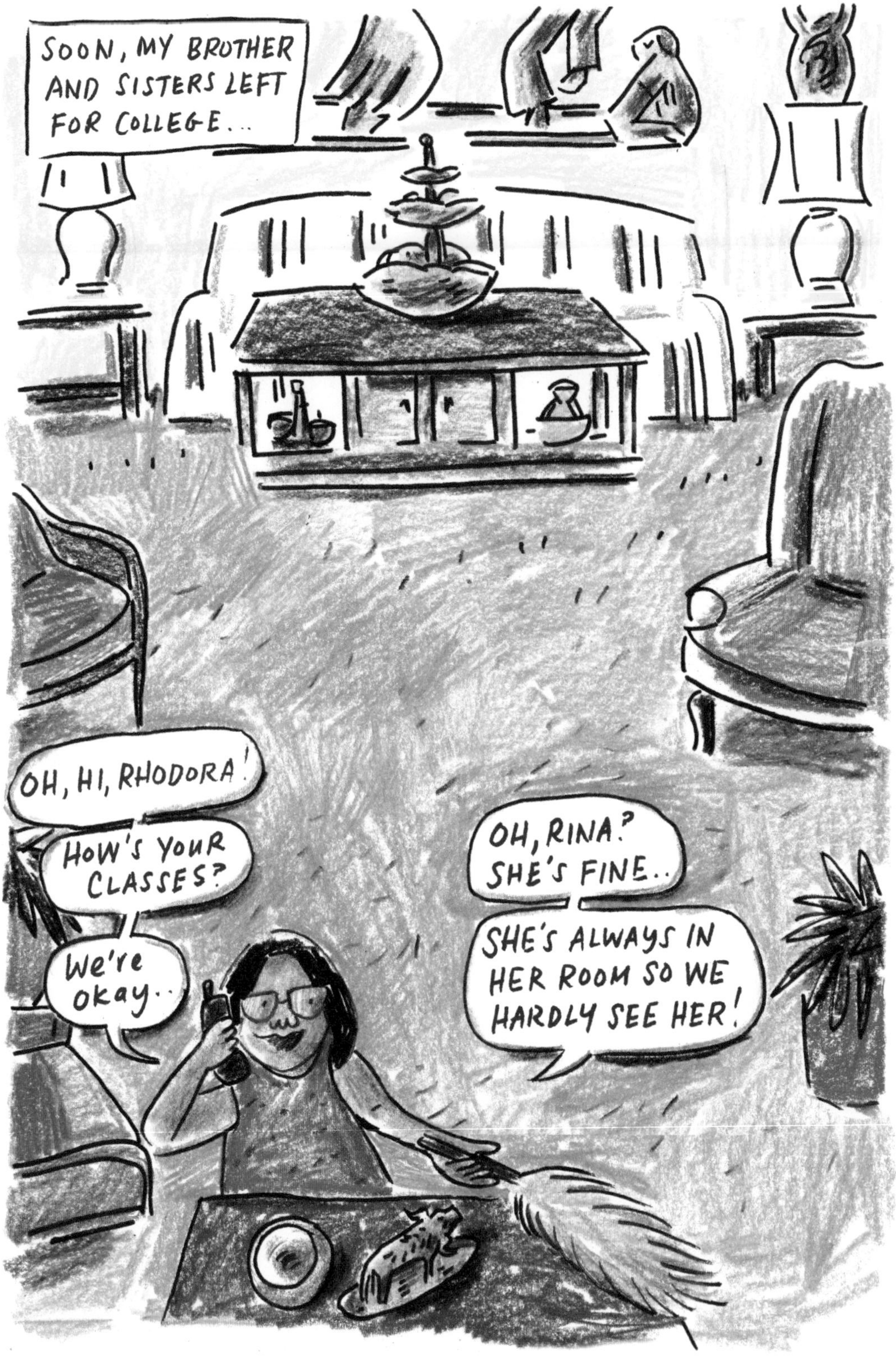
SOON, MY BROTHER AND SISTERS LEFT FOR COLLEGE...
OH, HI, RHODORA!
HOW'S YOUR CLASSES?
WE'RE OKAY..
OH, RINA? SHE'S FINE..
SHE'S ALWAYS IN HER ROOM SO WE HARDLY SEE HER!

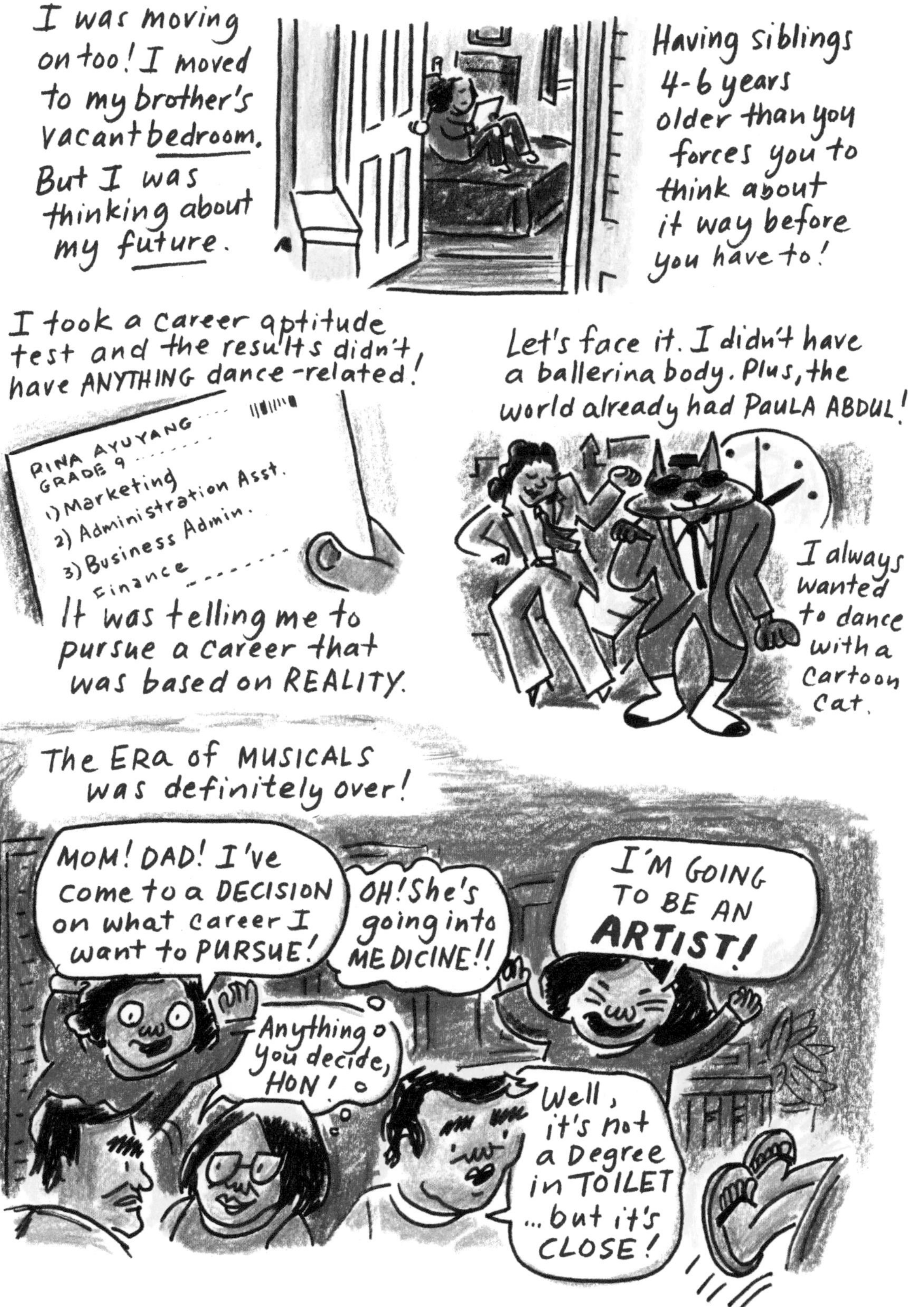
I was moving on too! I moved to my brother's vacant bedroom.
But I was thinking about my future.
Having siblings 4-6 years older than you forces you to think about it way before you have to!
I took a career aptitude test and the results didn't have ANYTHING dance-related!
RINA AYUYANG
GRADE 9
1) Marketing
2) Administration Asst.
3) Business Admin.
Finance
It was telling me to pursue a career that was based on REALITY.
Let's face it. I didn't have a ballerina body. Plus, the world already had PAULA ABDUL!
I always wanted to dance with a cartoon cat.
The ERA of MUSICALS was definitely over!
MOM! DAD! I've come to a DECISION on what career I want to PURSUE!
OH! She's going into MEDICINE!!
I'M GOING TO BE AN ARTIST!
Anything you decide, HON!
Well, it's not a Degree in TOILET ...but it's CLOSE!

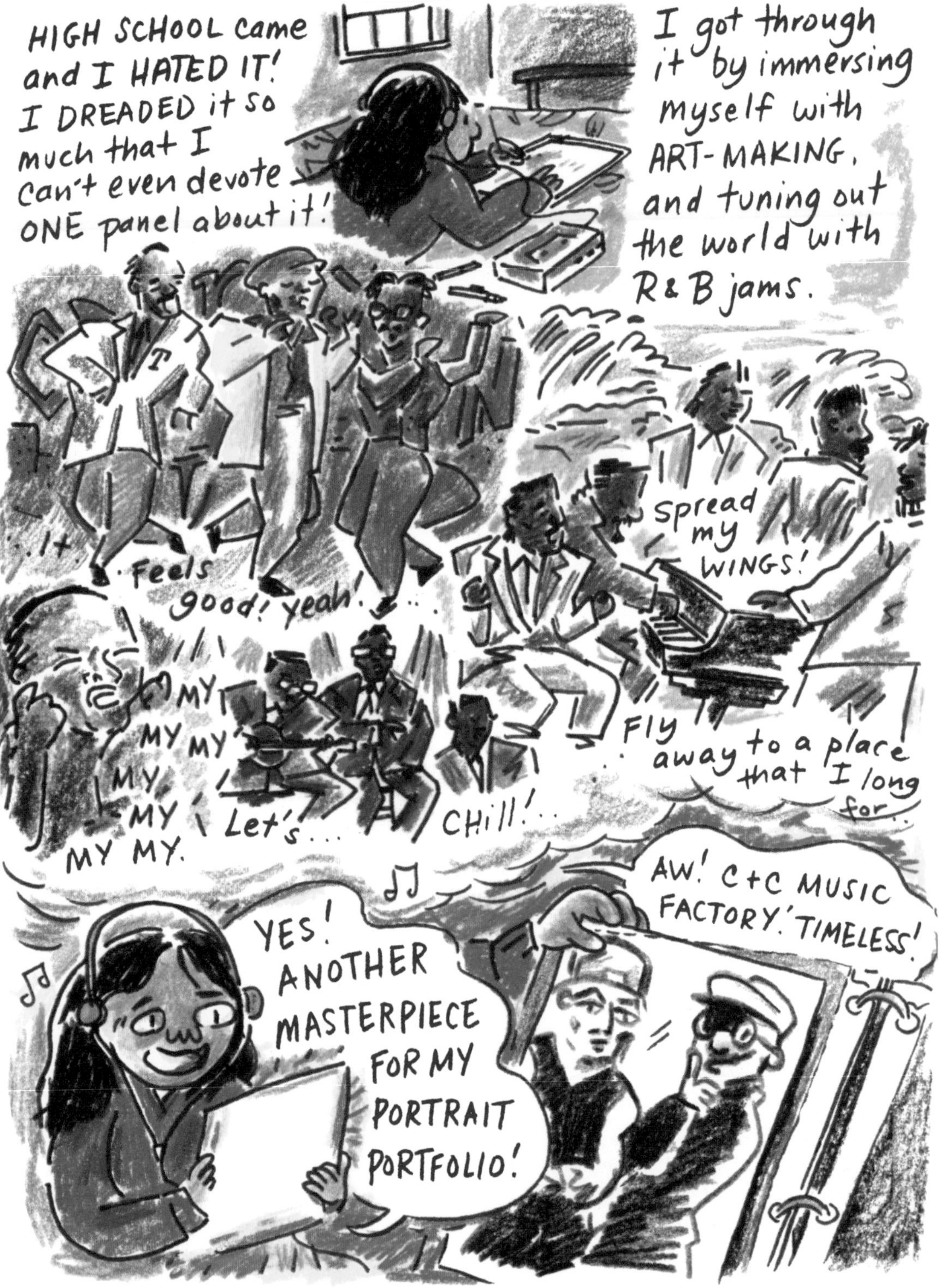
HIGH SCHOOL came and I HATED IT! I DREADED it so much that I can't even devote ONE panel about it!
I got through it by immersing myself with ART-MAKING, and tuning out the world with R&B jams.
...It... Feels good! yeah!...
Spread my WINGS!
MY MY MY MY MY MY MY.
Let's... CHill!...
Fly away to a place that I long for...
YES! ANOTHER MASTERPIECE FOR MY PORTRAIT PORTFOLIO!
AW! C+C MUSIC FACTORY. TIMELESS!

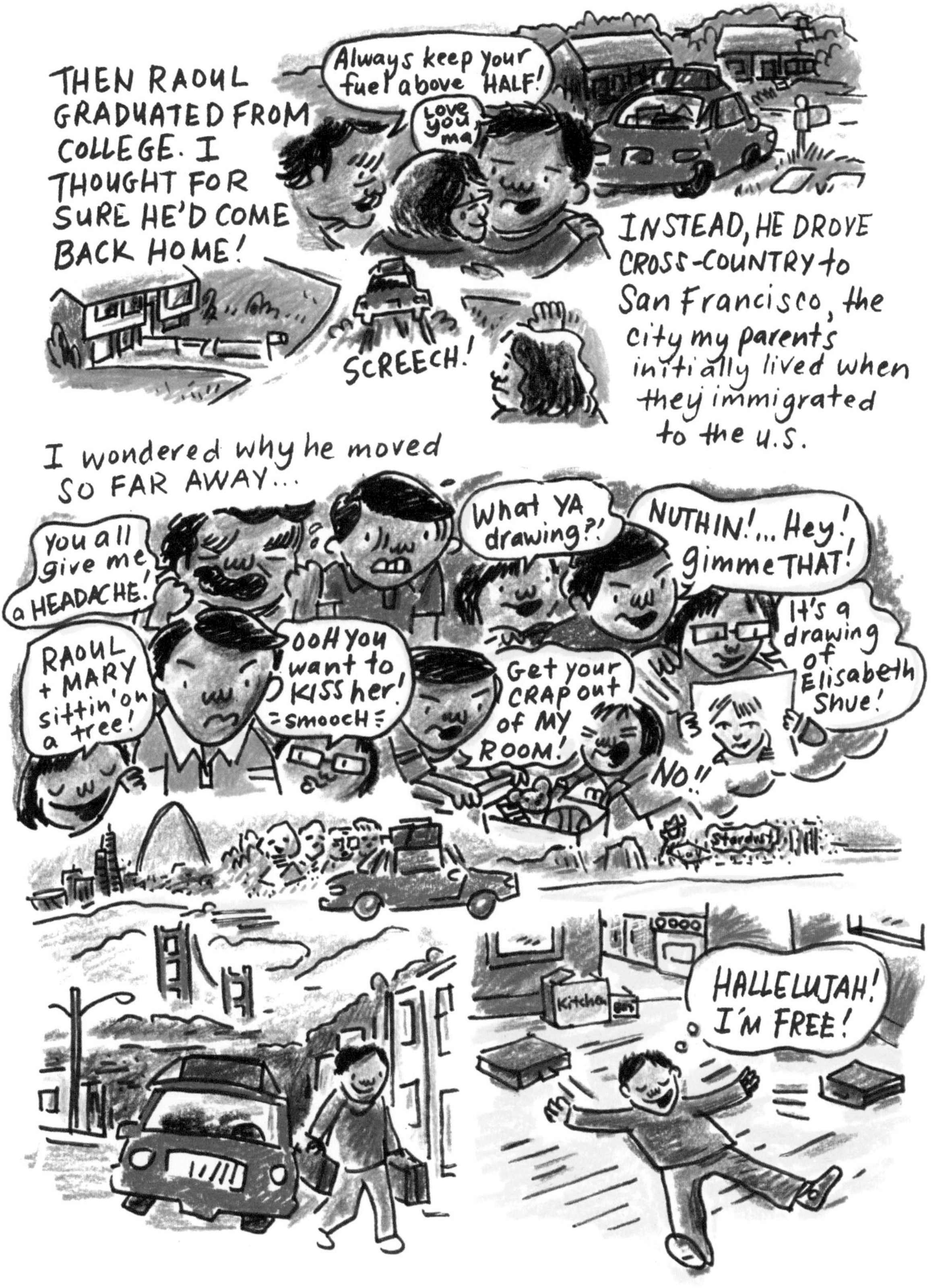
THEN RAOUL GRADUATED FROM COLLEGE. I THOUGHT FOR SURE HE'D COME BACK HOME!
Always keep your fuel above HALF!
Love you, ma
INSTEAD, HE DROVE CROSS-COUNTRY to San Francisco, the city my parents initially lived when they immigrated to the U.S.
SCREECH!
I wondered why he moved SO FAR AWAY...
You all give me a HEADACHE.
What YA drawing?!
NUTHIN!... Hey! gimme THAT!
RAOUL + MARY sittin' on a tree!
OOH you want to KISS her!
smooch
Get your CRAP out of MY ROOM!
It's a drawing of Elisabeth Shue!
NO!!
Stardust
Kitchen
HALLELUJAH! I'M FREE!

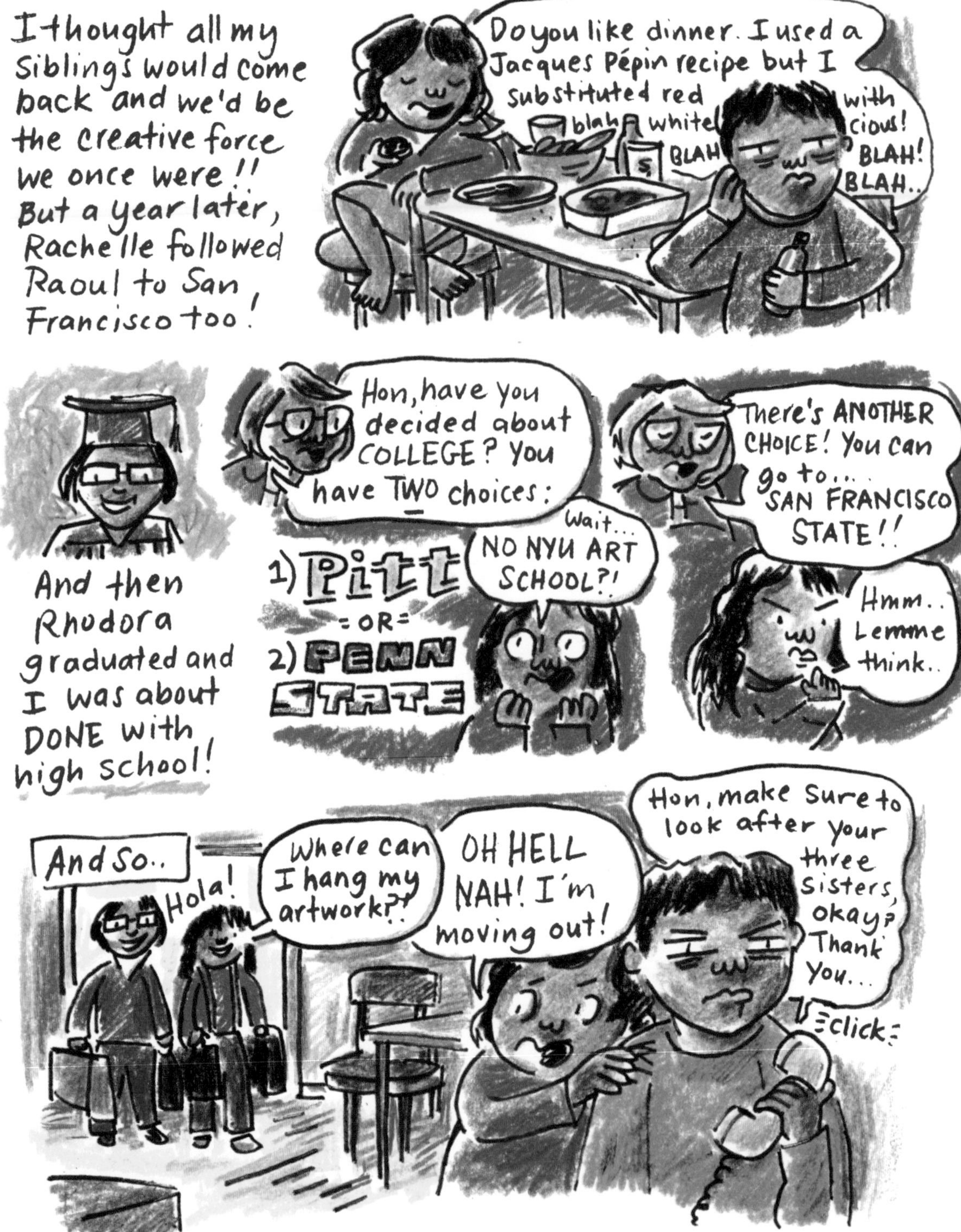
I thought all my siblings would come back and we'd be the creative force we once were!! But a year later, Rachelle followed Raoul to San Francisco too!
Do you like dinner. I used a Jacques Pépin recipe but I substituted red
blah
white
BLAH
with
cious!
BLAH!
BLAH..
And then Rhodora graduated and I was about DONE with high school!
Hon, have you decided about COLLEGE? You have TWO choices:
1) Pitt
= OR =
2) PENN STATE
Wait... NO NYU ART SCHOOL?!
There's ANOTHER CHOICE! You can go to... SAN FRANCISCO STATE!!
Hmm.. Lemme think..
And so..
Hola!
Where can I hang my artwork?!
OH HELL NAH! I'm moving out!
Hon, make sure to look after your three sisters, okay? Thank you...
=click=

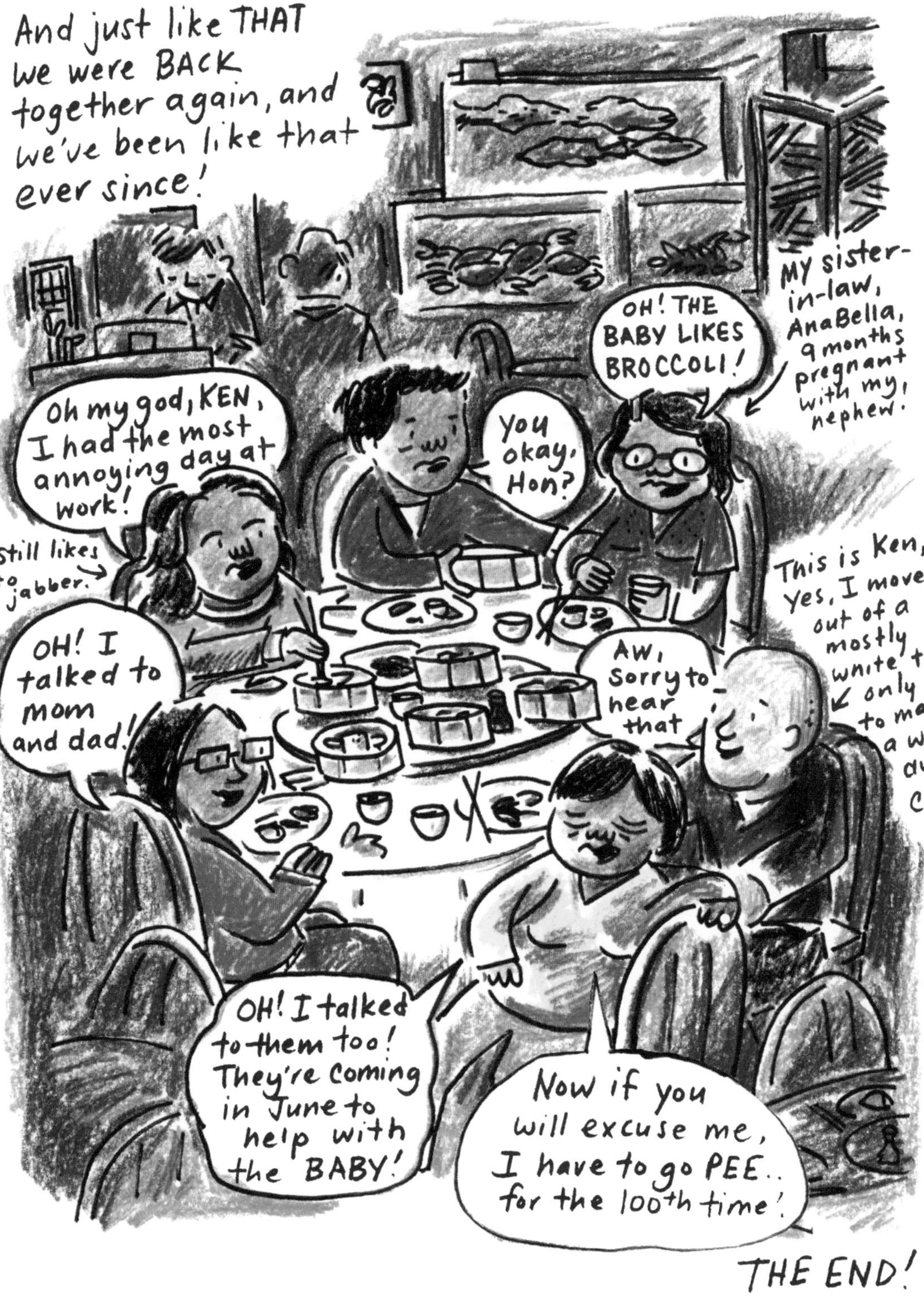
And just like THAT we were BACK together again, and we've been like that ever since!
MY sister-in-law, AnaBella, 9 months pregnant with my nephew!
OH! THE BABY LIKES BROCCOLI!
Oh my god, KEN, I had the most annoying day at work!
Still likes to jabber.
You okay, Hon?
This is Ken, Yes, I moved out of a mostly white town only to marry a white dude! Crazy, huh!
OH! I talked to mom and dad!
Aw, sorry to hear that
OH! I talked to them too! They're coming in June to help with the BABY!
Now if you will excuse me, I have to go PEE.. for the 100th time!
THE END!

LOOK AT ME! I'M 9 Months pregnant and about to debut my first ever graphic novel!! I'm such a SUPERWOMAN!
2009
And it's sooo GLAMOROUS being pregnant! You wear cute sundresses and comfy pants! People open doors for you and give up their seats! It's AMAZING, really!
And I'm SO READY for this baby! We got the crib and the stroller! We washed the baby clothes and bottles! We made a BIRTH PLAN-- I SO GOT THIS!!

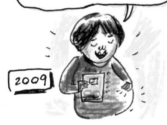

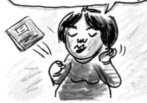

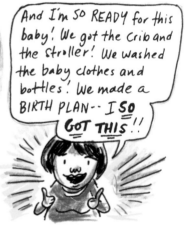

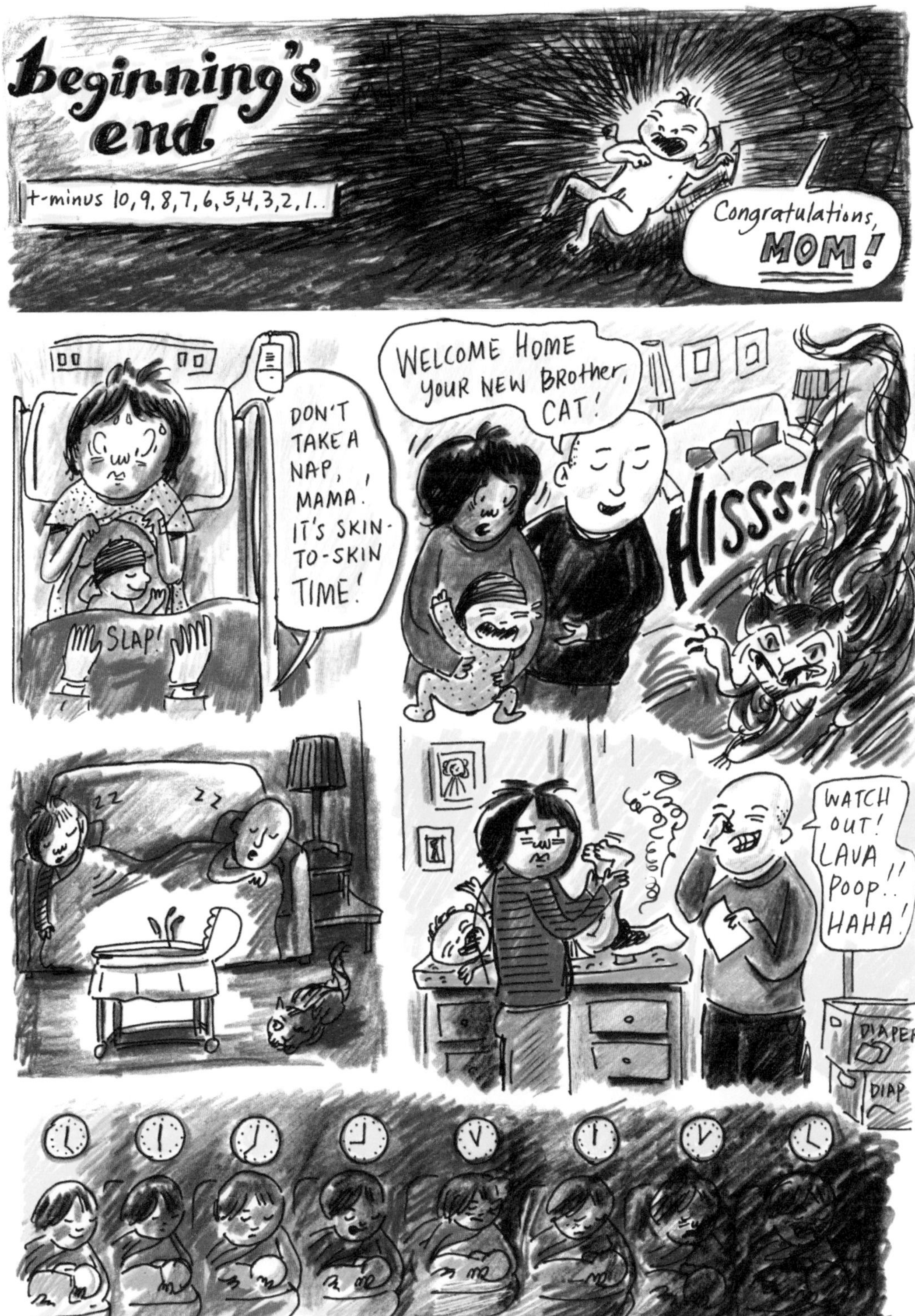
beginning's end
t-minus 10,9,8,7,6,5,4,3,2,1..
Congratulations, MOM!
DON'T TAKE A NAP, MAMA! IT'S SKIN-TO-SKIN TIME!
SLAP!
WELCOME HOME YOUR NEW BROTHER, CAT!
HISSS!
Z Z
Z Z
WATCH OUT! LAVA POOP!! HAHA!
DIAPER
DIAP

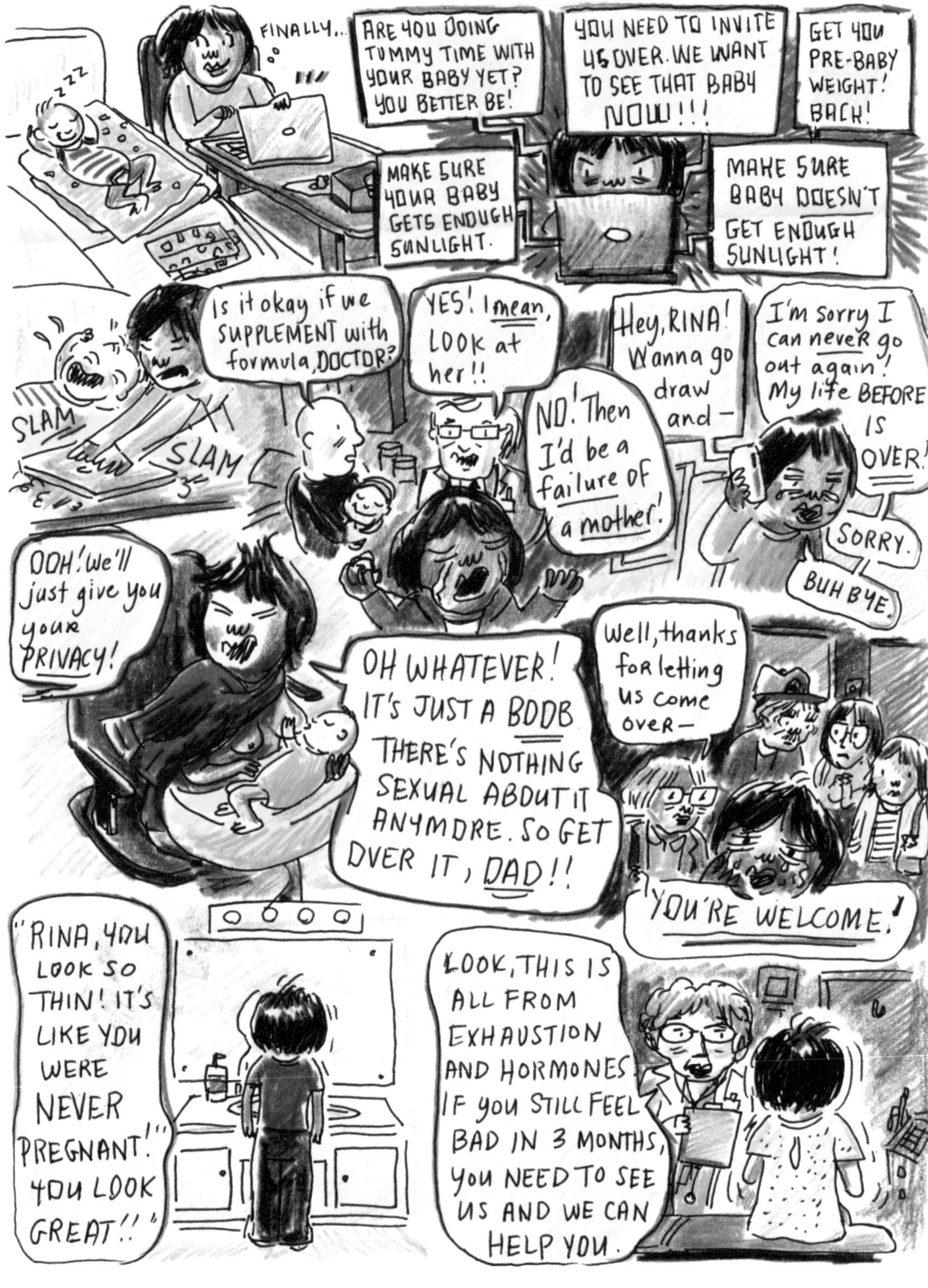

FINALLY...
ARE YOU DOING TUMMY TIME WITH YOUR BABY YET? YOU BETTER BE!
YOU NEED TO INVITE US OVER. WE WANT TO SEE THAT BABY NOW!!!
GET YOU PRE-BABY WEIGHT BACK!
MAKE SURE YOUR BABY GETS ENOUGH SUNLIGHT.
MAKE SURE BABY DOESN'T GET ENOUGH SUNLIGHT!
SLAM
SLAM
Is it okay if we SUPPLEMENT with formula, DOCTOR?
YES! I mean, LOOK at her!!
NO! Then I'd be a failure of a mother!
Hey, RINA! Wanna go draw and—
I'm sorry I can never go out again! My life BEFORE IS OVER!
SORRY.
BUH BYE.
OOH! We'll just give you your PRIVACY!
OH WHATEVER! IT'S JUST A BOOB THERE'S NOTHING SEXUAL ABOUT IT ANYMORE. SO GET OVER IT, DAD!!
Well, thanks for letting us come over—
YOU'RE WELCOME!
"RINA, YOU LOOK SO THIN! IT'S LIKE YOU WERE NEVER PREGNANT!" "YOU LOOK GREAT!!"
LOOK, THIS IS ALL FROM EXHAUSTION AND HORMONES. IF YOU STILL FEEL BAD IN 3 MONTHS, YOU NEED TO SEE US AND WE CAN HELP YOU.

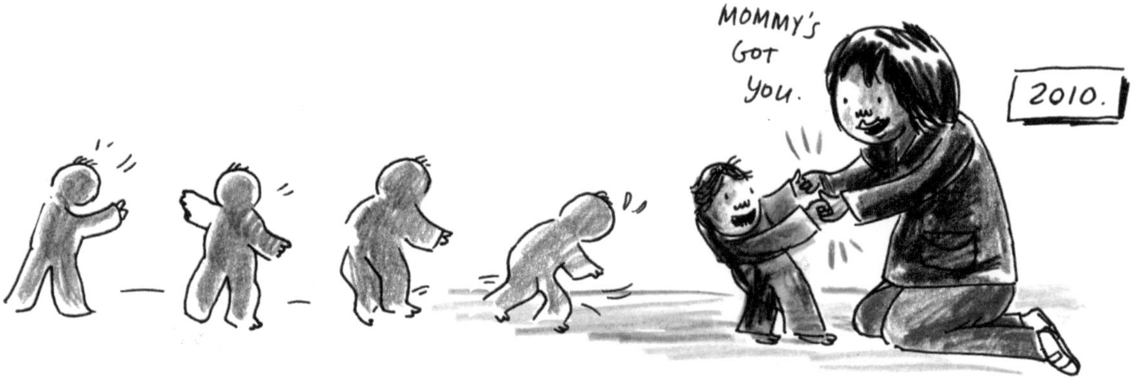
MOMMY'S
GOT
YOU.
2010.

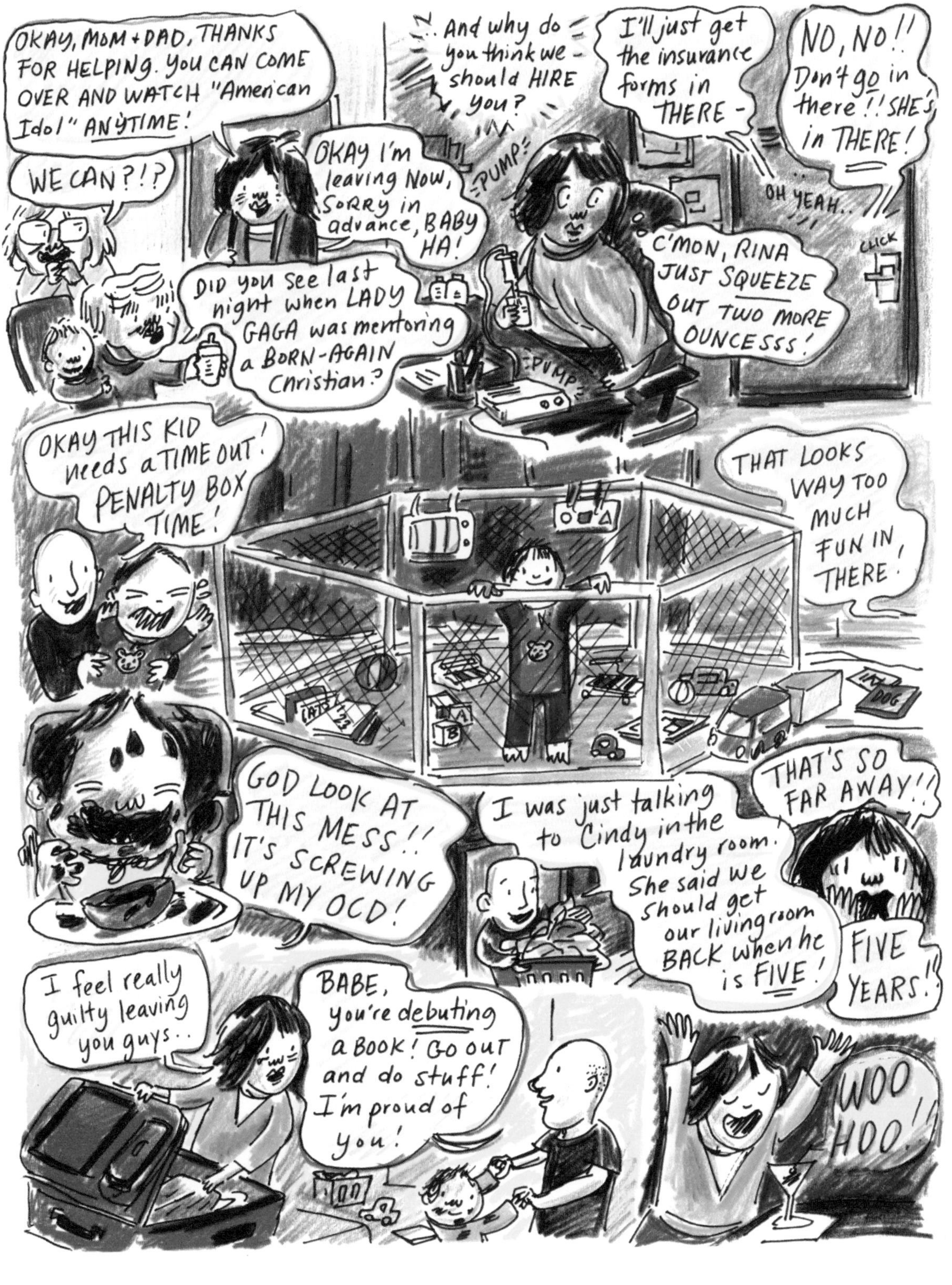
OKAY, MOM + DAD, THANKS FOR HELPING. YOU CAN COME OVER AND WATCH "American Idol" ANYTIME!
WE CAN?!?
OKAY I'm leaving NOW, SORRY in advance, BABY HA!
DID YOU SEE last night when LADY GAGA was mentoring a BORN-AGAIN Christian?
And why do you think we should HIRE you?
PUMP
I'll just get the insurance forms in THERE -
NO, NO!! Don't go in there!! SHE's in THERE!
OH YEAH..
C'MON, RINA JUST SQUEEZE OUT TWO MORE OUNCESSS!
CLICK
PUMP
OKAY THIS KID needs a TIME OUT! PENALTY BOX TIME!
THAT LOOKS WAY TOO MUCH FUN IN THERE!
CATS
DOG
GOD LOOK AT THIS MESS!! IT'S SCREWING UP MY OCD!
I was just talking to Cindy in the laundry room. She said we should get our livingroom BACK when he is FIVE!
THAT'S SO FAR AWAY!!
FIVE YEARS!!
I feel really guilty leaving you guys..
BABE, you're debuting a BOOK! GO OUT and do stuff! I'm proud of you!
WOO HOO!

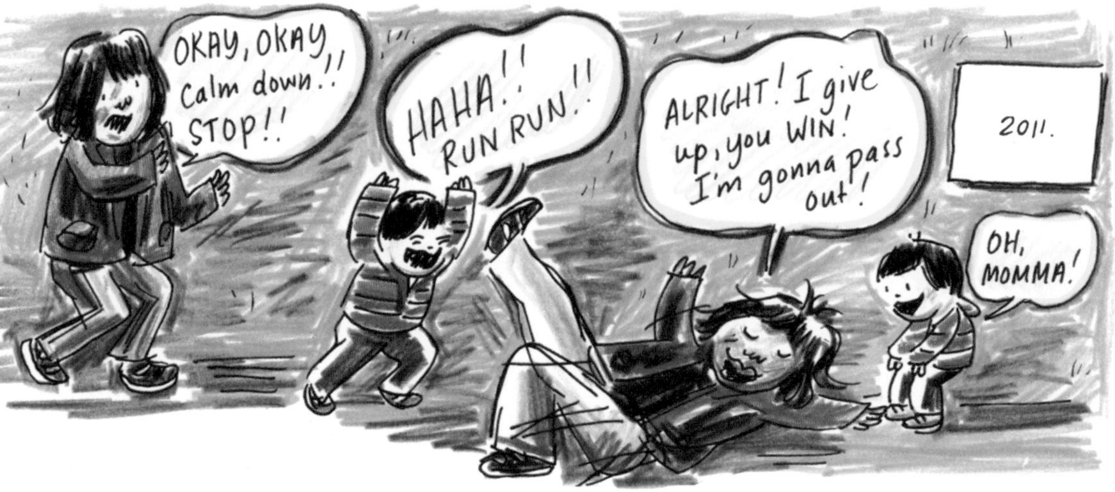
OKAY, OKAY, Calm down!! STOP!!
HAHA!! RUN RUN!!
ALRIGHT! I give up, you WIN! I'm gonna pass out!
2011.
OH, MOMMA!

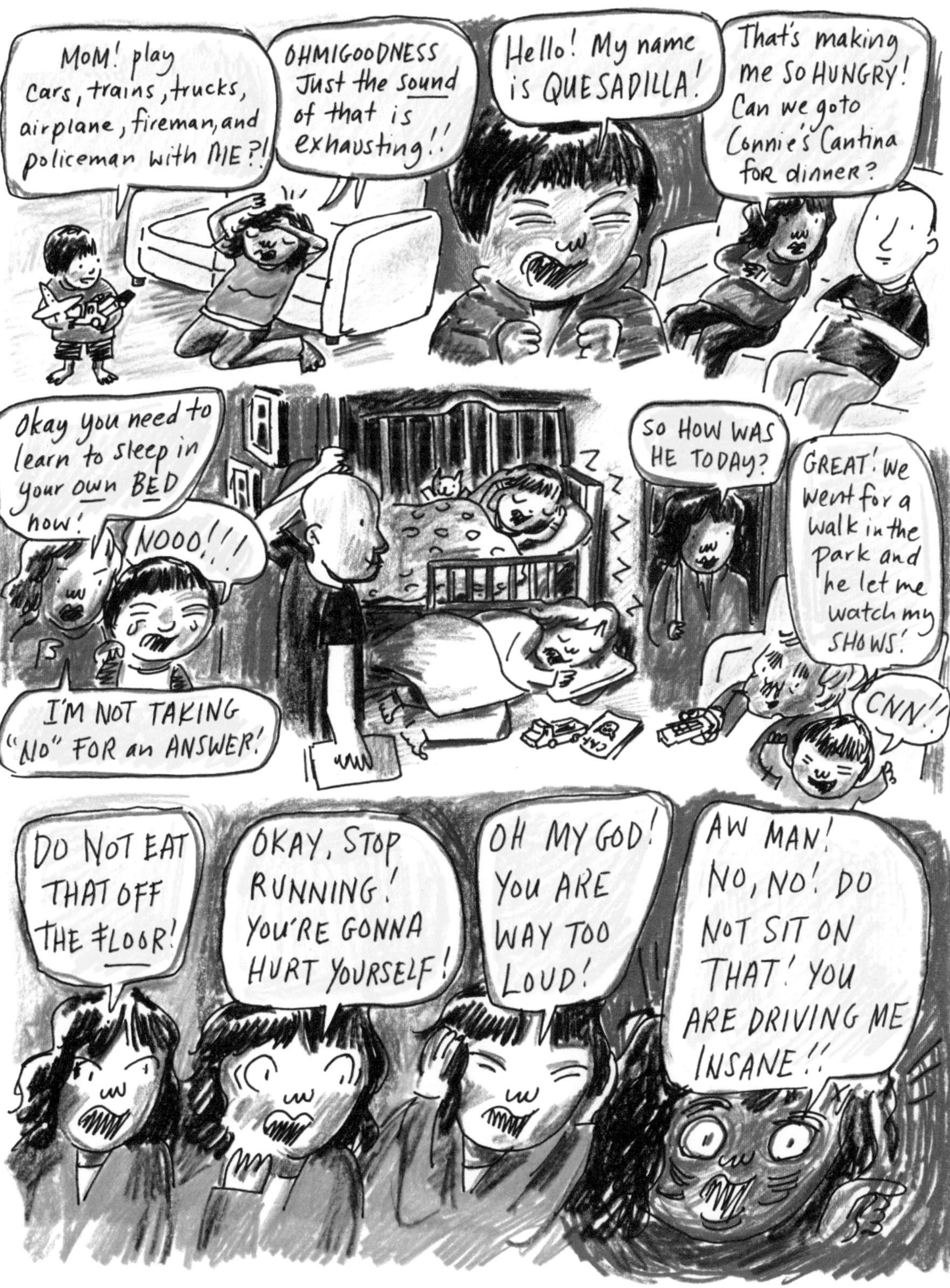
MOM! play cars, trains, trucks, airplane, fireman, and policeman with ME?!
OHMIGOODNESS Just the sound of that is exhausting!!
Hello! My name is QUESADILLA!
That's making me SO HUNGRY! Can we go to Connie's Cantina for dinner?
Okay you need to learn to sleep in your own BED now!
NOOO!!!
I'M NOT TAKING "NO" FOR an ANSWER!
Z Z Z Z Z
SO HOW WAS HE TODAY?
GREAT! We went for a walk in the park and he let me watch my SHOWS!
CNN!
DO NOT EAT THAT OFF THE FLOOR!
OKAY, STOP RUNNING! YOU'RE GONNA HURT YOURSELF!
OH MY GOD! YOU ARE WAY TOO LOUD!
AW MAN! NO, NO! DO NOT SIT ON THAT! YOU ARE DRIVING ME INSANE!!

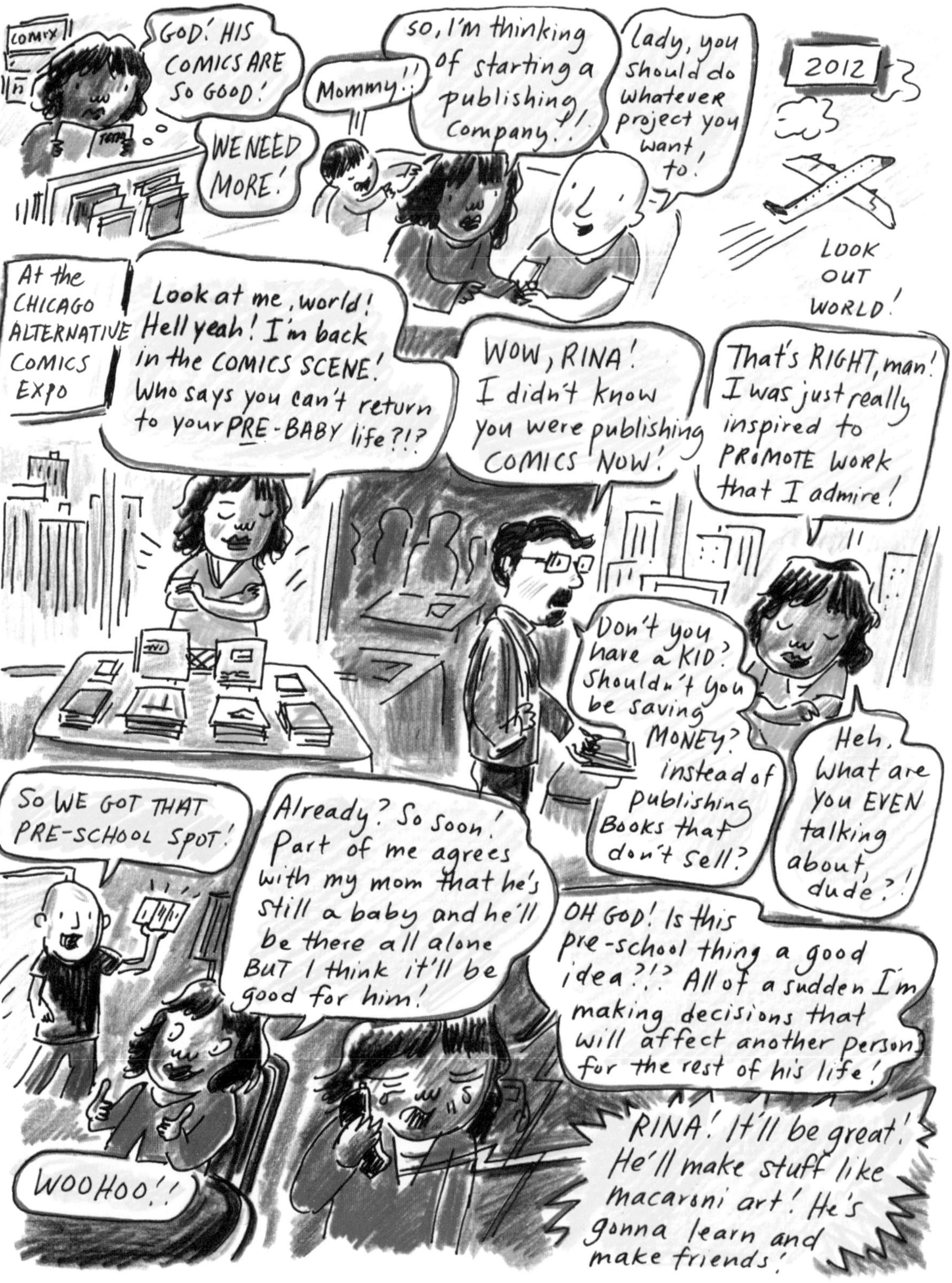
COMIX
GOD! HIS COMICS ARE SO GOOD!
WE NEED MORE!
Mommy!!
So, I'm thinking of starting a publishing company!!
Lady, you should do whatever project you want to!
2012
LOOK OUT WORLD!
At the CHICAGO ALTERNATIVE COMICS EXPO
Look at me, world! Hell yeah! I'm back in the COMICS SCENE! Who says you can't return to your PRE-BABY life?!?
WOW, RINA! I didn't know you were publishing COMICS NOW!
That's RIGHT, man! I was just really inspired to PROMOTE WORK that I admire!
Don't you have a KID? Shouldn't you be saving MONEY? instead of publishing Books that don't sell?
Heh. What are you EVEN talking about, dude?!
So WE GOT THAT PRE-SCHOOL SPOT!
Already? So soon! Part of me agrees with my mom that he's still a baby and he'll be there all alone BUT I think it'll be good for him!
WOOHOO!!
OH GOD! Is this pre-school thing a good idea?!? All of a sudden I'm making decisions that will affect another person for the rest of his life!
RINA! It'll be great! He'll make stuff like macaroni art! He's gonna learn and make friends!

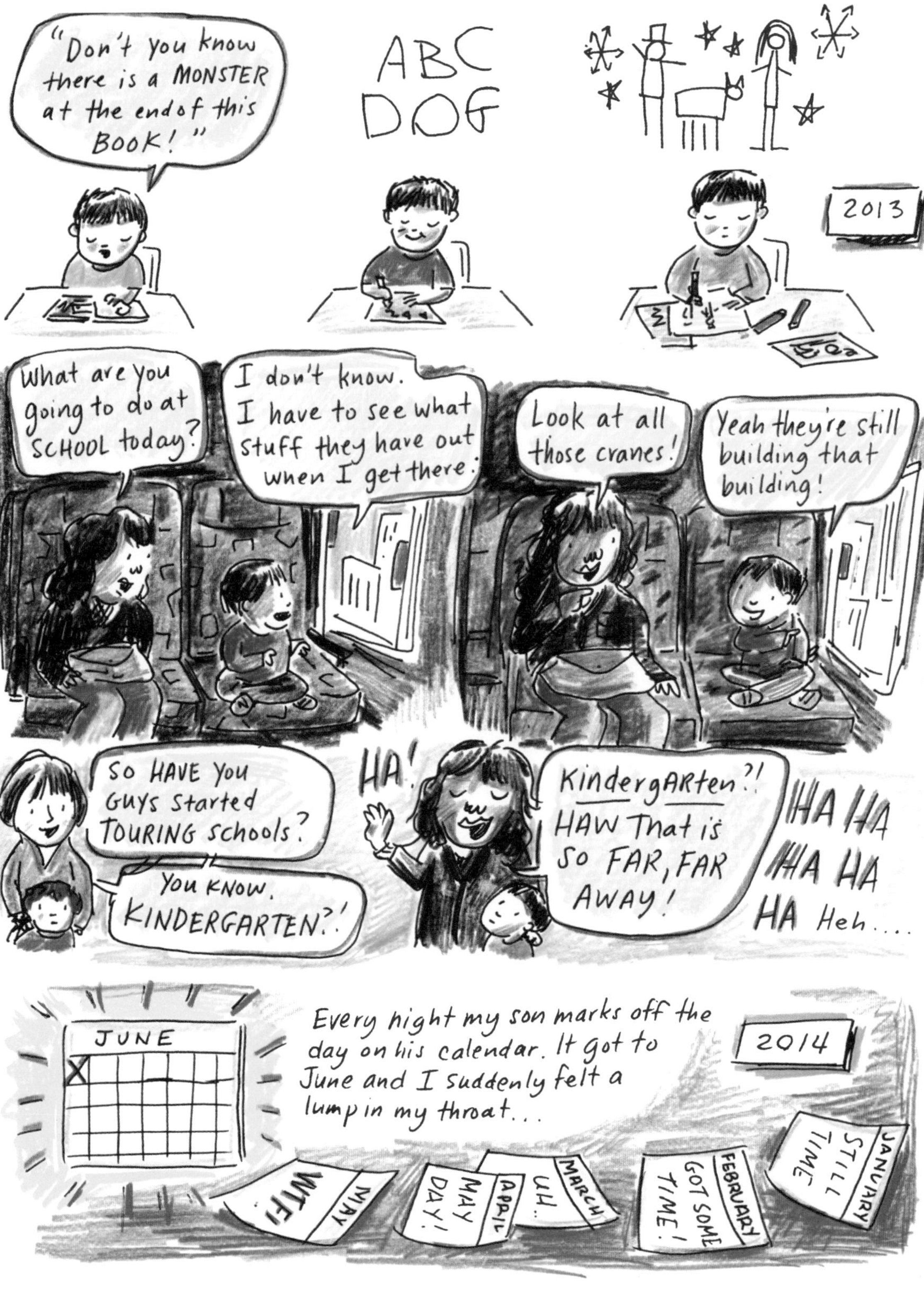

"Don't you know there is a MONSTER at the end of this BOOK!"
ABC DOG
2013
What are you going to do at SCHOOL today?
I don't know. I have to see what stuff they have out when I get there.
Look at all those cranes!
Yeah they're still building that building!
So HAVE you GUYS Started TOURING schools?
You KNOW. KINDERGARTEN?!
HA!
KindergArten?! HAW That is So FAR, FAR AWAY!
HA HA HA HA HA Heh....
JUNE
Every night my son marks off the day on his calendar. It got to June and I suddenly felt a lump in my throat...
2014
MAY WTF!
APRIL MAY DAY!
MARCH UH..
FEBRUARY GOT SOME TIME!
JANUARY STILL TIME

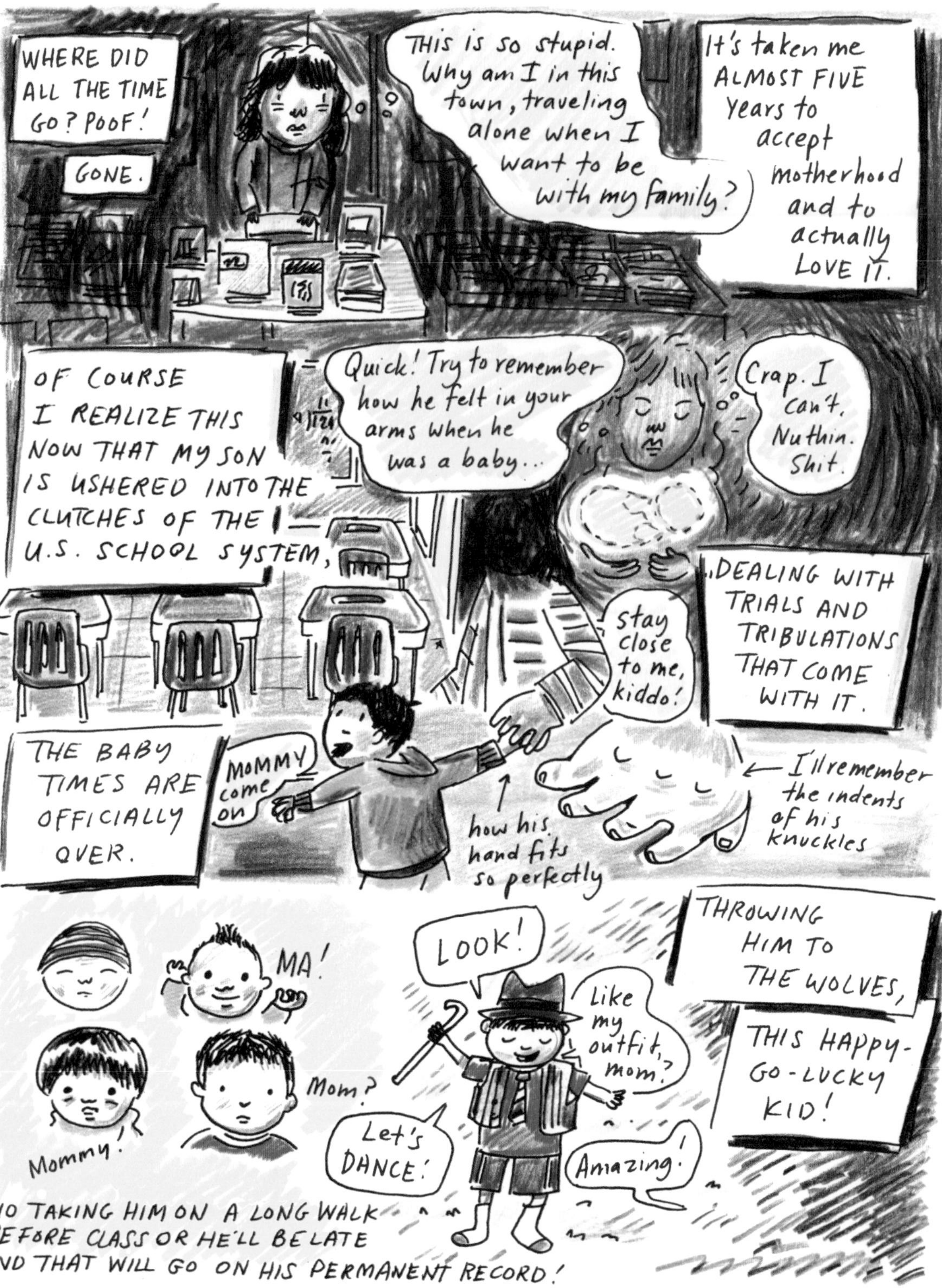
WHERE DID ALL THE TIME GO? POOF!
GONE.
THIS is so stupid. Why am I in this town, traveling alone when I want to be with my family?
It's taken me ALMOST FIVE Years to accept motherhood and to actually LOVE IT.
OF COURSE I REALIZE THIS NOW THAT MY SON IS USHERED INTO THE CLUTCHES OF THE U.S. SCHOOL SYSTEM,
Quick! Try to remember how he felt in your arms when he was a baby...
Crap. I can't. Nuthin. Shit.
DEALING WITH TRIALS AND TRIBULATIONS THAT COME WITH IT.
Stay close to me, kiddo!
THE BABY TIMES ARE OFFICIALLY OVER.
MOMMY come on
how his hand fits so perfectly
I'll remember the indents of his knuckles
MA!
Mom?
Mommy!
LOOK!
Like my outfit, mom?
Let's DANCE!
Amazing!
THROWING HIM TO THE WOLVES,
THIS HAPPY-GO-LUCKY KID!
NO TAKING HIM ON A LONG WALK BEFORE CLASS OR HE'LL BE LATE AND THAT WILL GO ON HIS PERMANENT RECORD!

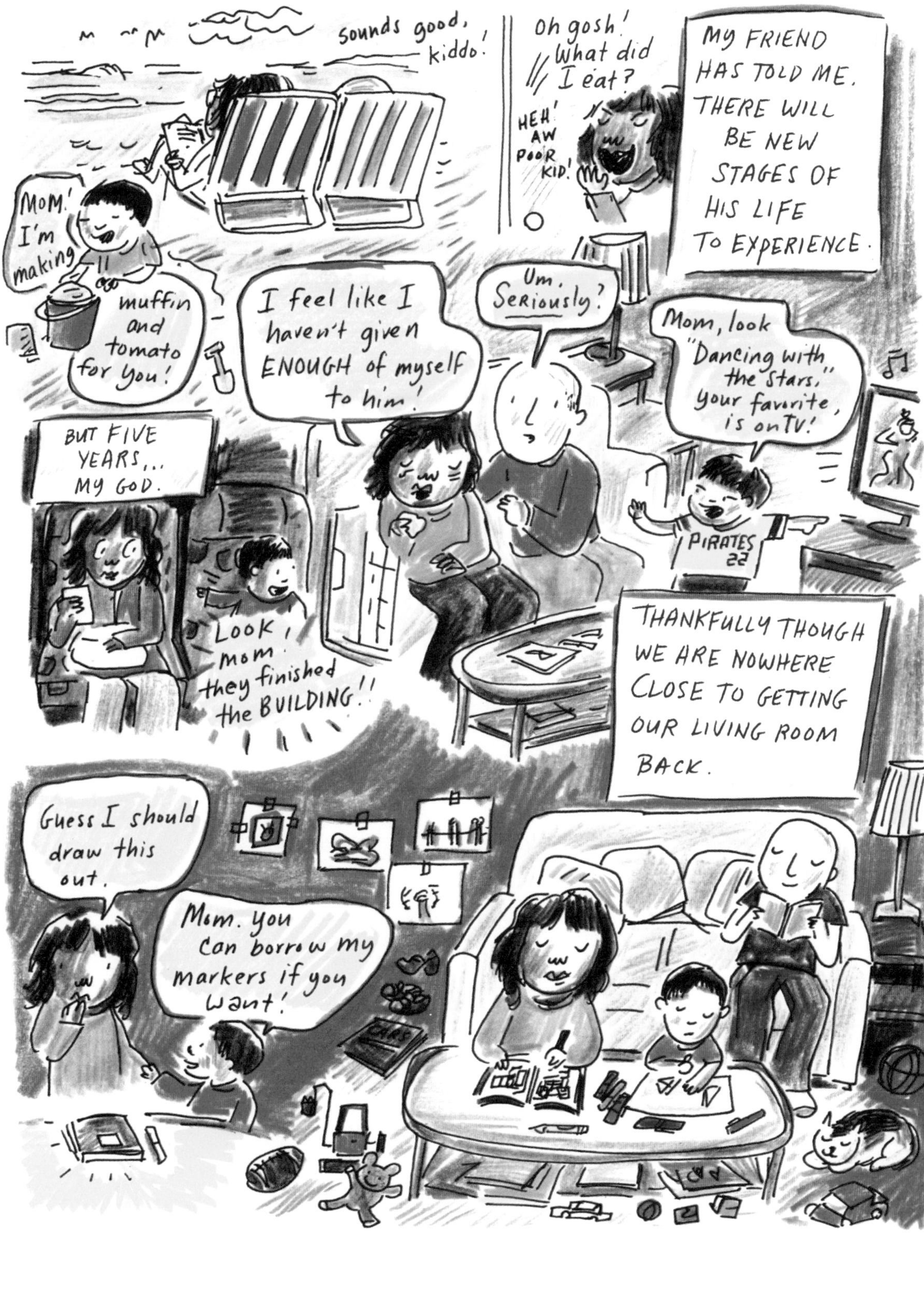
sounds good, kiddo!
MOM! I'm making
muffin and tomato for you!
Oh gosh! What did I eat?
HEH! AW POOR KID!
MY FRIEND HAS TOLD ME. THERE WILL BE NEW STAGES OF HIS LIFE TO EXPERIENCE.
I feel like I haven't given ENOUGH of myself to him!
Um. Seriously?
Mom, look "Dancing with the stars," your favorite, is on TV!
PIRATES 22
BUT FIVE YEARS... MY GOD.
Look, mom! they finished the BUILDING!!
THANKFULLY THOUGH WE ARE NOWHERE CLOSE TO GETTING OUR LIVING ROOM BACK.
Guess I should draw this out.
Mom. you can borrow my markers if you want!
CARS

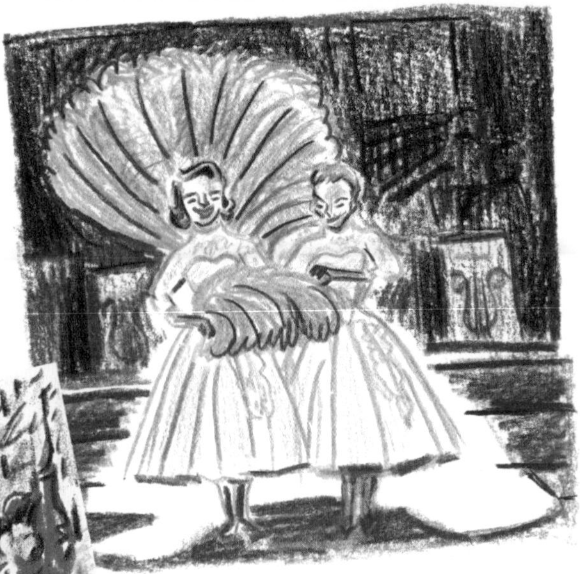

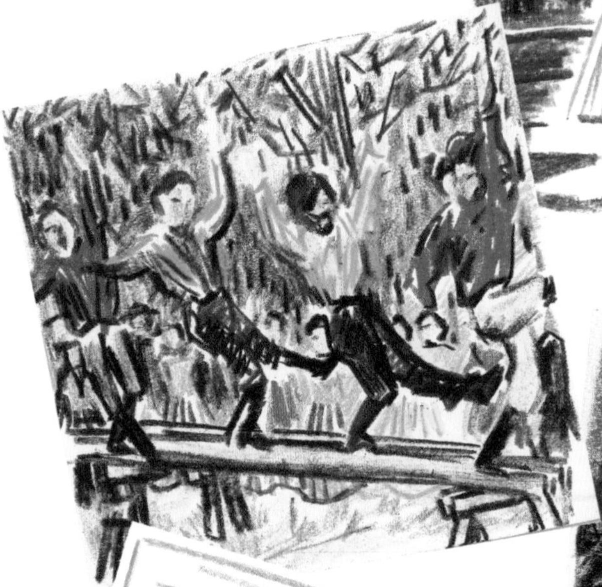

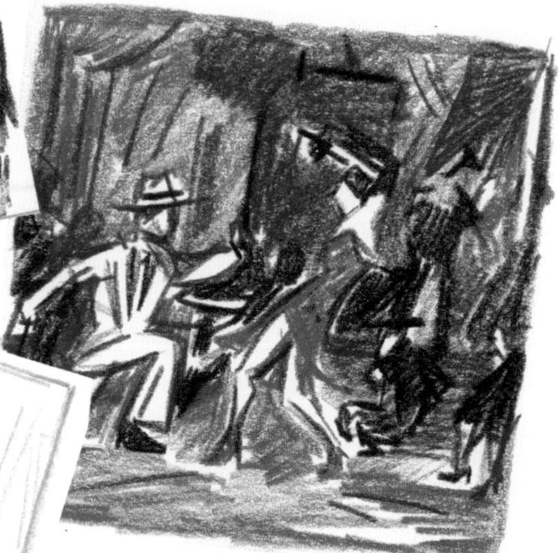

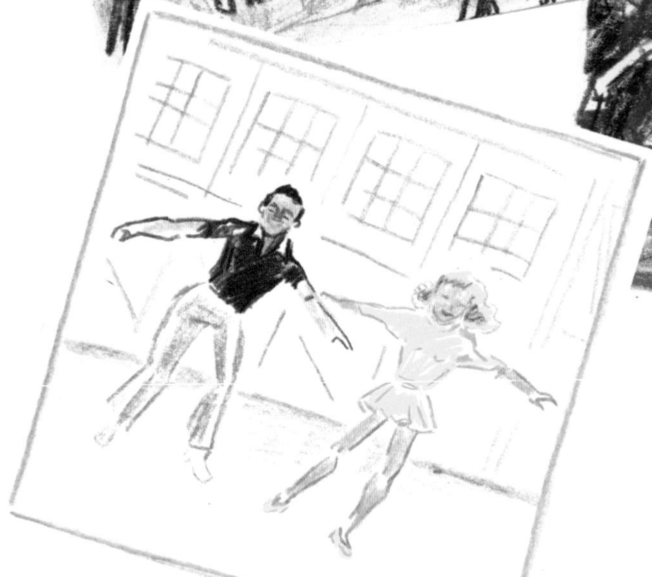

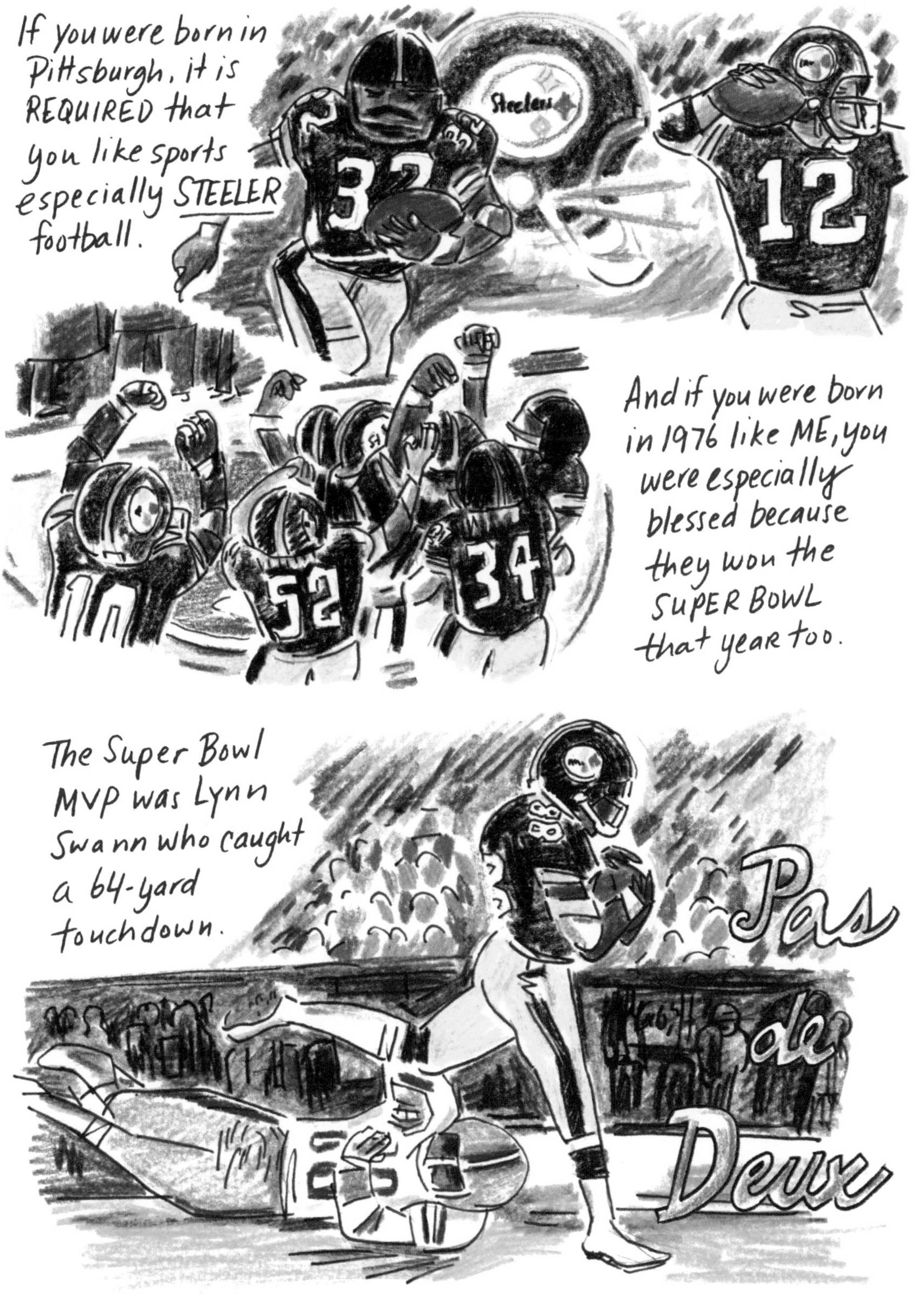
If you were born in Pittsburgh, it is REQUIRED that you like sports especially STEELER football.
Steelers
And if you were born in 1976 like ME, you were especially blessed because they won the SUPER BOWL that year too.
The Super Bowl MVP was Lynn Swann who caught a 64-yard touchdown.
Pas de Deux

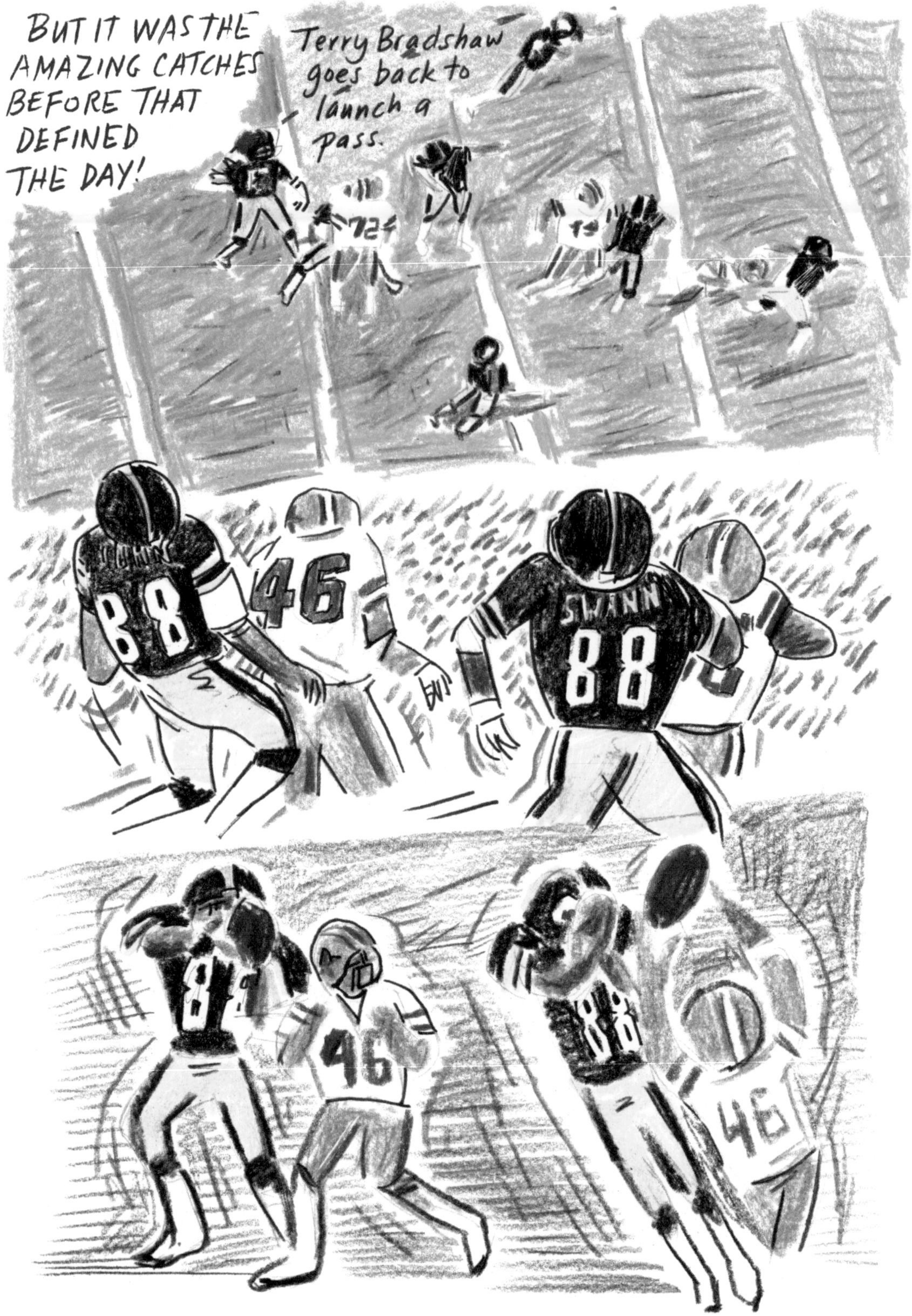
BUT IT WAS THE AMAZING CATCHES BEFORE THAT DEFINED THE DAY!
Terry Bradshaw goes back to launch a pass.
72
46
SWANN
88
88
46
88
46

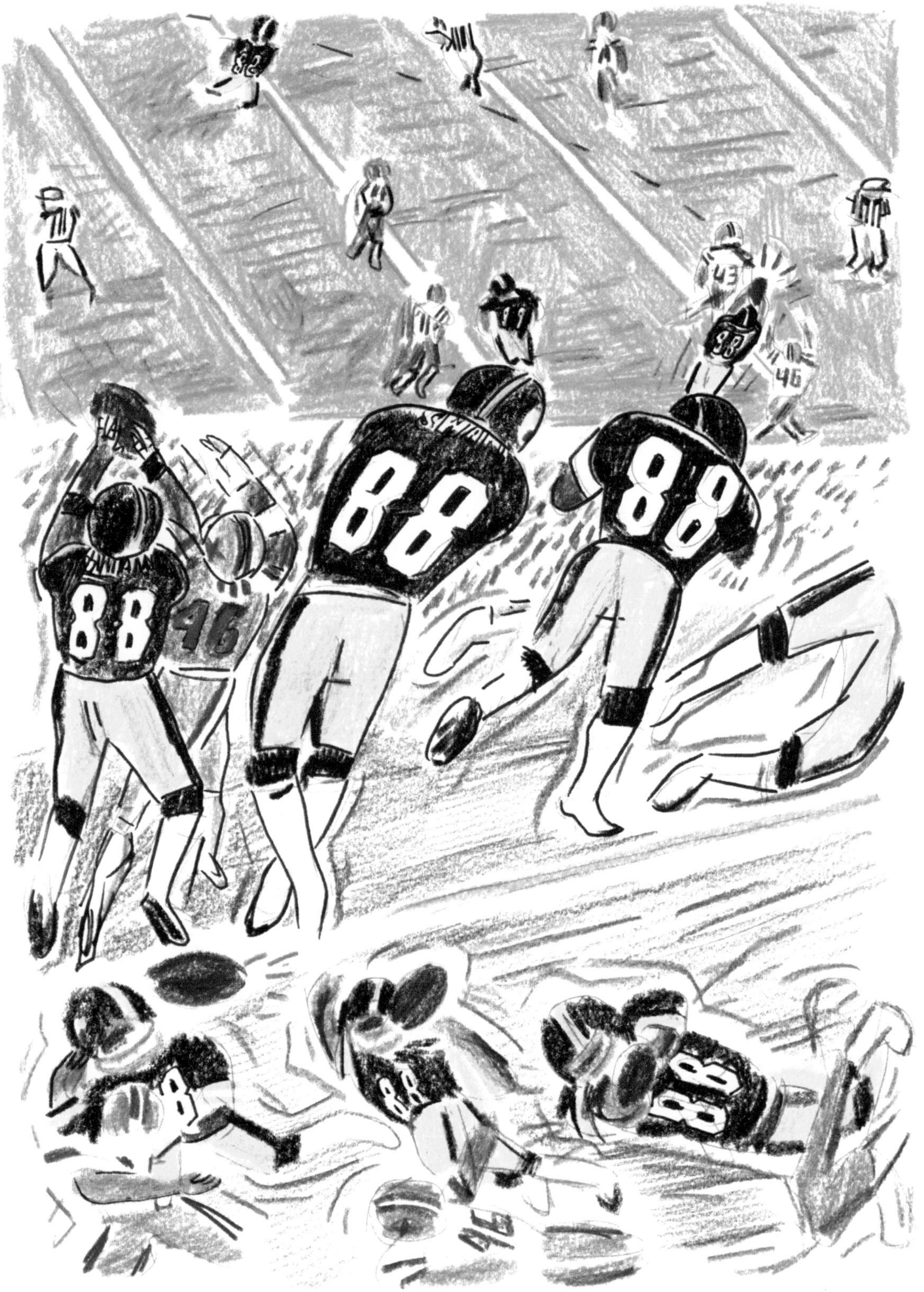
88
46

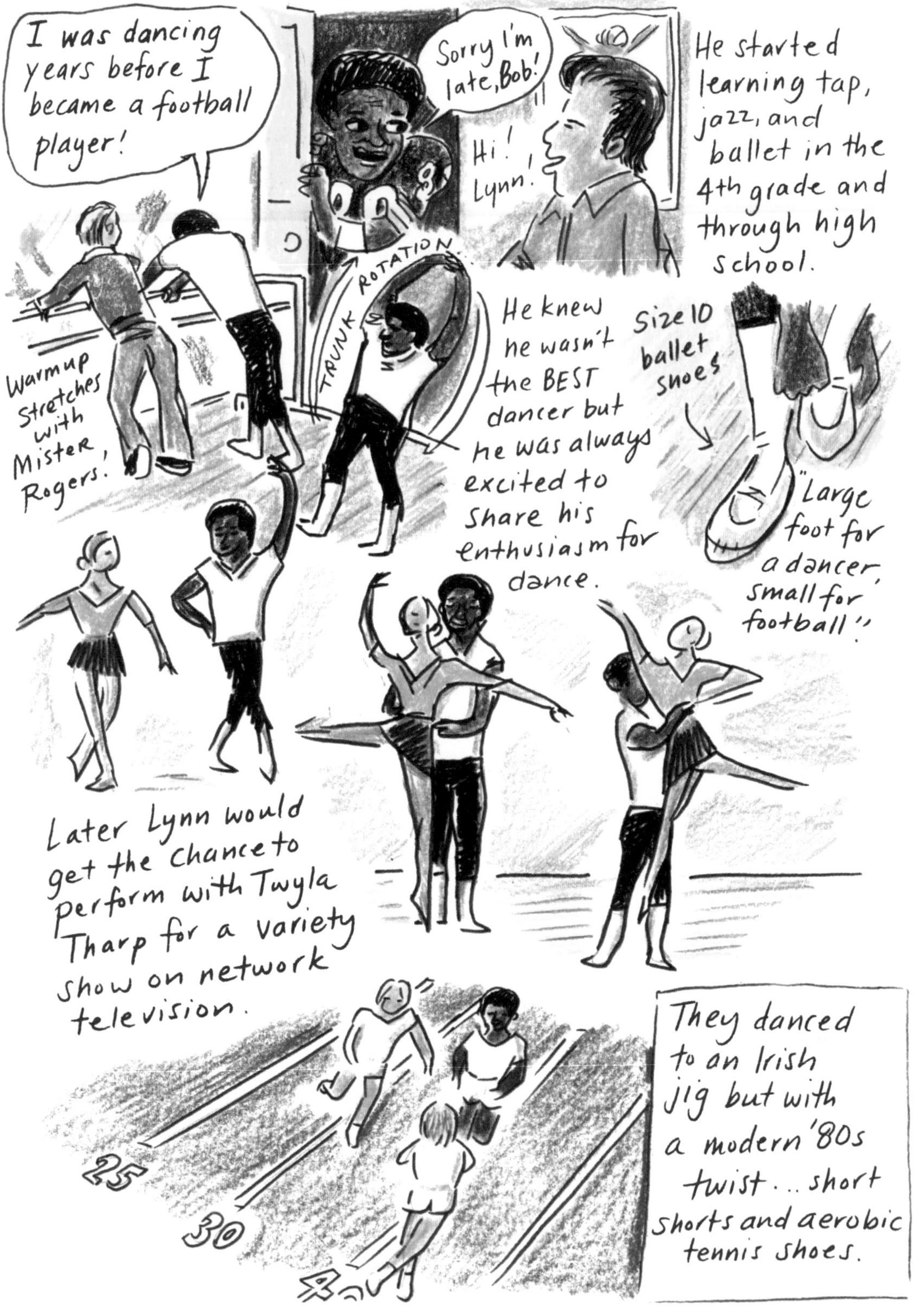
I was dancing years before I became a football player!
Sorry I'm late, Bob!
Hi! Lynn!
He started learning tap, jazz, and ballet in the 4th grade and through high school.
TRUNK ROTATION...
Warmup stretches with Mister Rogers!
He knew he wasn't the BEST dancer but he was always excited to share his enthusiasm for dance.
Size 10 ballet shoes
"Large foot for a dancer, small for football"!
Later Lynn would get the chance to perform with Twyla Tharp for a variety show on network television.
25
30
They danced to an Irish jig but with a modern '80s twist... short shorts and aerobic tennis shoes.

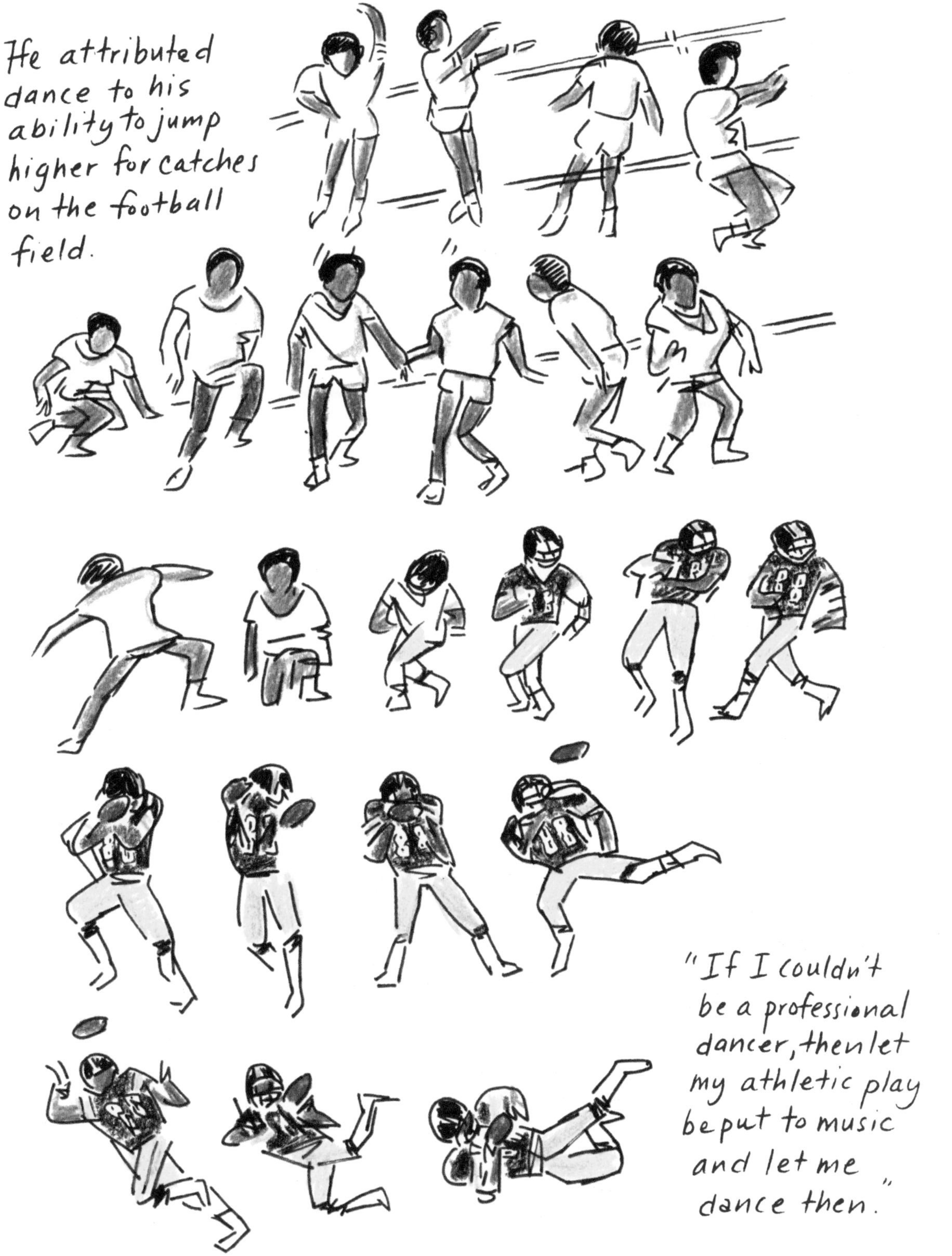
He attributed dance to his ability to jump higher for catches on the football field.
"If I couldn't be a professional dancer, then let my athletic play be put to music and let me dance then."

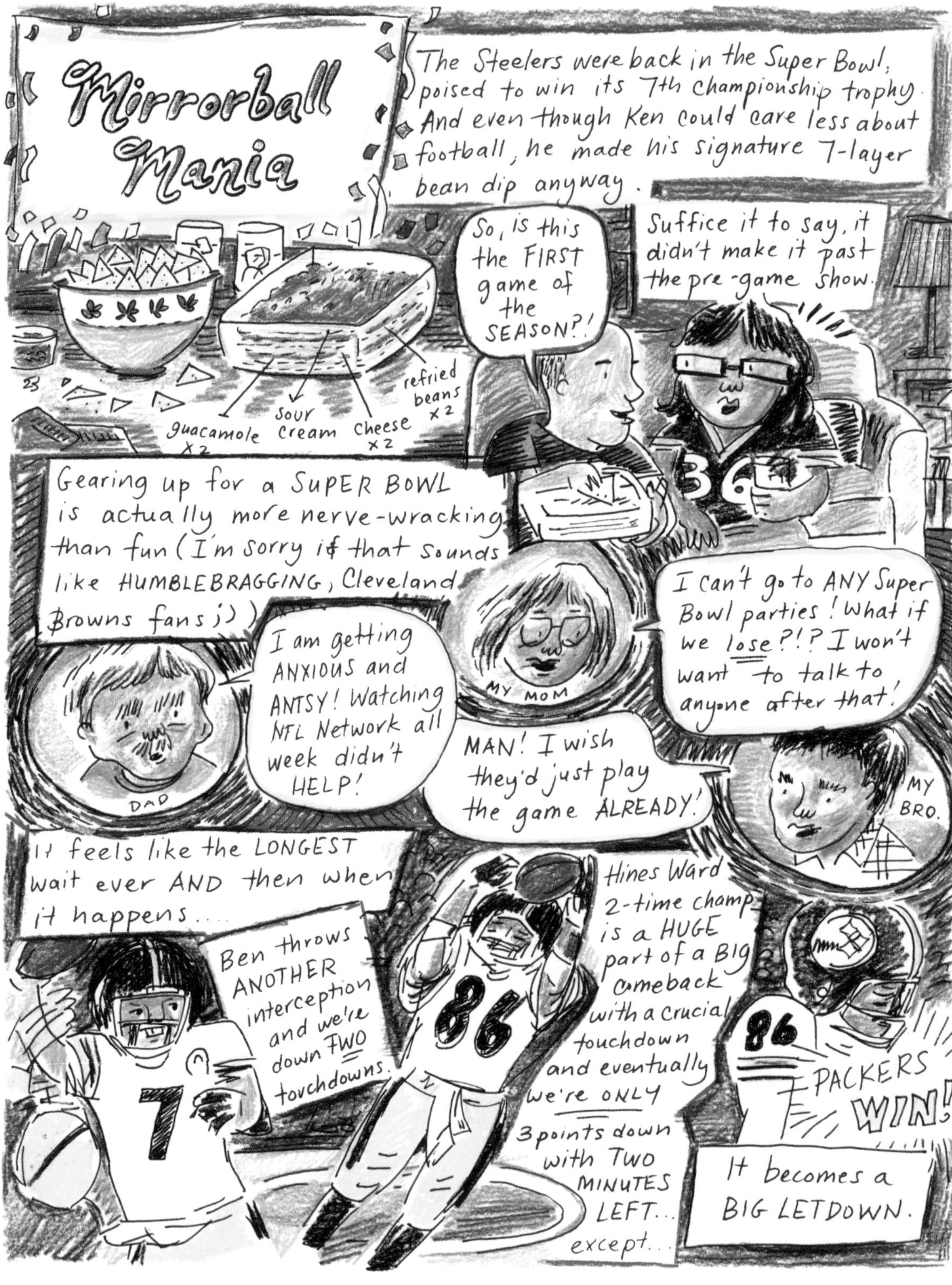
Mirrorball Mania
The Steelers were back in the Super Bowl, poised to win its 7th championship trophy. And even though Ken could care less about football, he made his signature 7-layer bean dip anyway.
guacamole x2
sour cream
cheese x2
refried beans x2
So, is this the FIRST game of the SEASON?!
Suffice it to say, it didn't make it past the pre-game show.
Gearing up for a SUPER BOWL is actually more nerve-wracking than fun (I'm sorry if that sounds like HUMBLEBRAGGING, Cleveland Browns fans ;))
I am getting ANXIOUS and ANTSY! Watching NFL Network all week didn't HELP!
DAD
MY MOM
I can't go to ANY Super Bowl parties! What if we lose?!? I won't want to talk to anyone after that!
MAN! I wish they'd just play the game ALREADY!
MY BRO.
It feels like the LONGEST wait ever AND then when it happens....
Ben throws ANOTHER interception and we're down TWO touchdowns.
Hines Ward 2-time champ is a HUGE part of a BIG comeback with a crucial touchdown and eventually we're ONLY 3 points down with TWO MINUTES LEFT... except...
PACKERS WIN!
It becomes a BIG LETDOWN.

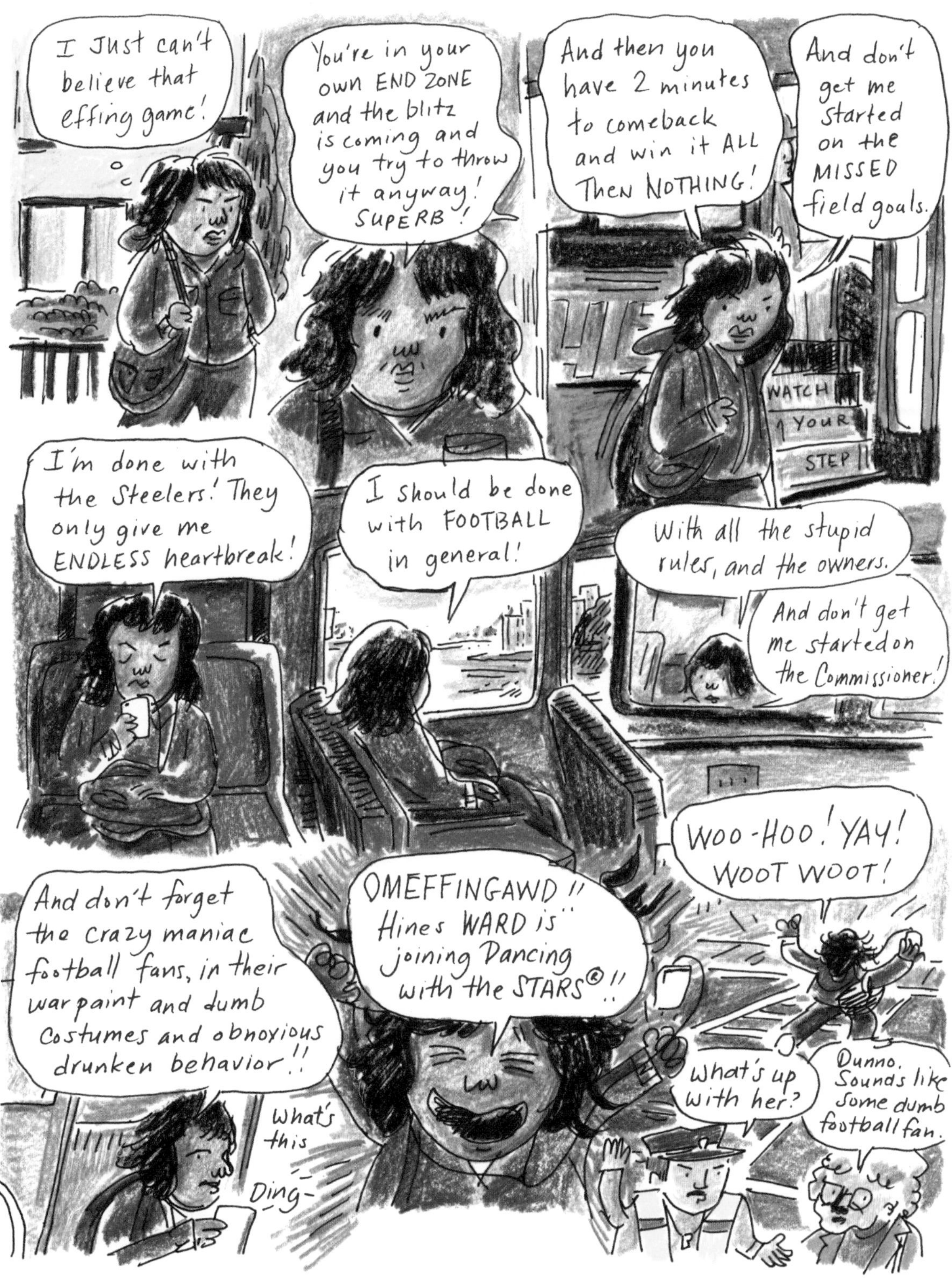
I JUST can't believe that effing game!
You're in your own END ZONE and the blitz is coming and you try to throw it anyway! SUPERB!
And then you have 2 minutes to comeback and win it ALL Then NOTHING!
And don't get me started on the MISSED field goals.
WATCH YOUR STEP
I'm done with the Steelers! They only give me ENDLESS heartbreak!
I should be done with FOOTBALL in general!
With all the stupid rules, and the owners.
And don't get me started on the Commissioner!
And don't forget the crazy maniac football fans, in their warpaint and dumb costumes and obnoxious drunken behavior!!
What's this
Ding-
OMEFFINGAWD!! Hines WARD is joining Dancing with the STARS®!!
WOO-HOO! YAY! WOOT WOOT!
What's up with her?
Dunno. Sounds like some dumb football fan.

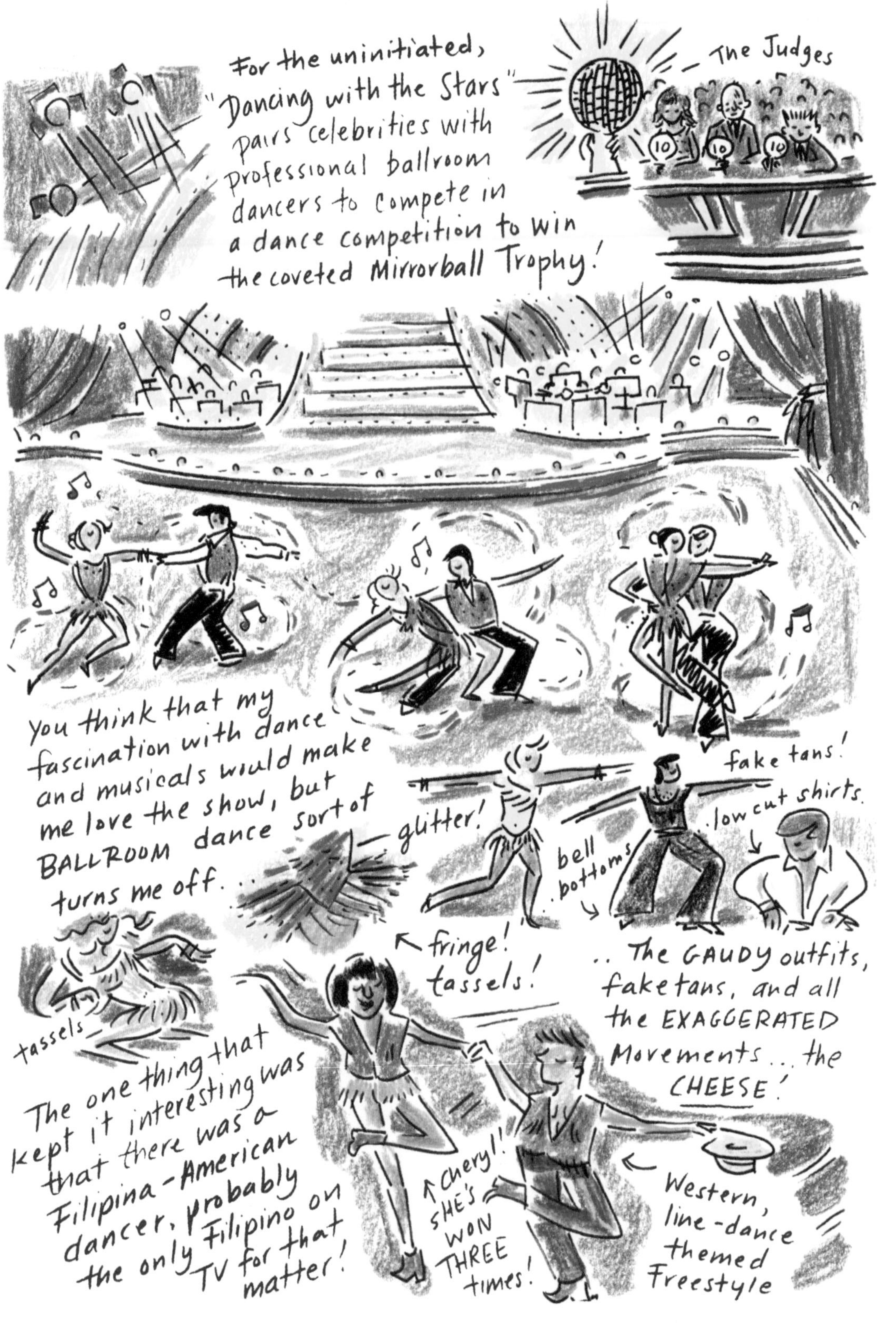
For the uninitiated, "Dancing with the Stars" pairs celebrities with professional ballroom dancers to compete in a dance competition to win the coveted Mirrorball Trophy!
The Judges
10
10
10
you think that my fascination with dance and musicals would make me love the show, but BALLROOM dance sort of turns me off...
glitter!
fake tans!
low cut shirts.
bell bottoms
fringe! tassels!
tassels
.. The GAUDY outfits, fake tans, and all the EXAGGERATED Movements ... the CHEESE!
The one thing that kept it interesting was that there was a Filipina-American dancer, probably the only Filipino on TV for that matter!
Cheryl! SHE'S WON THREE times!
Western, line-dance themed Freestyle

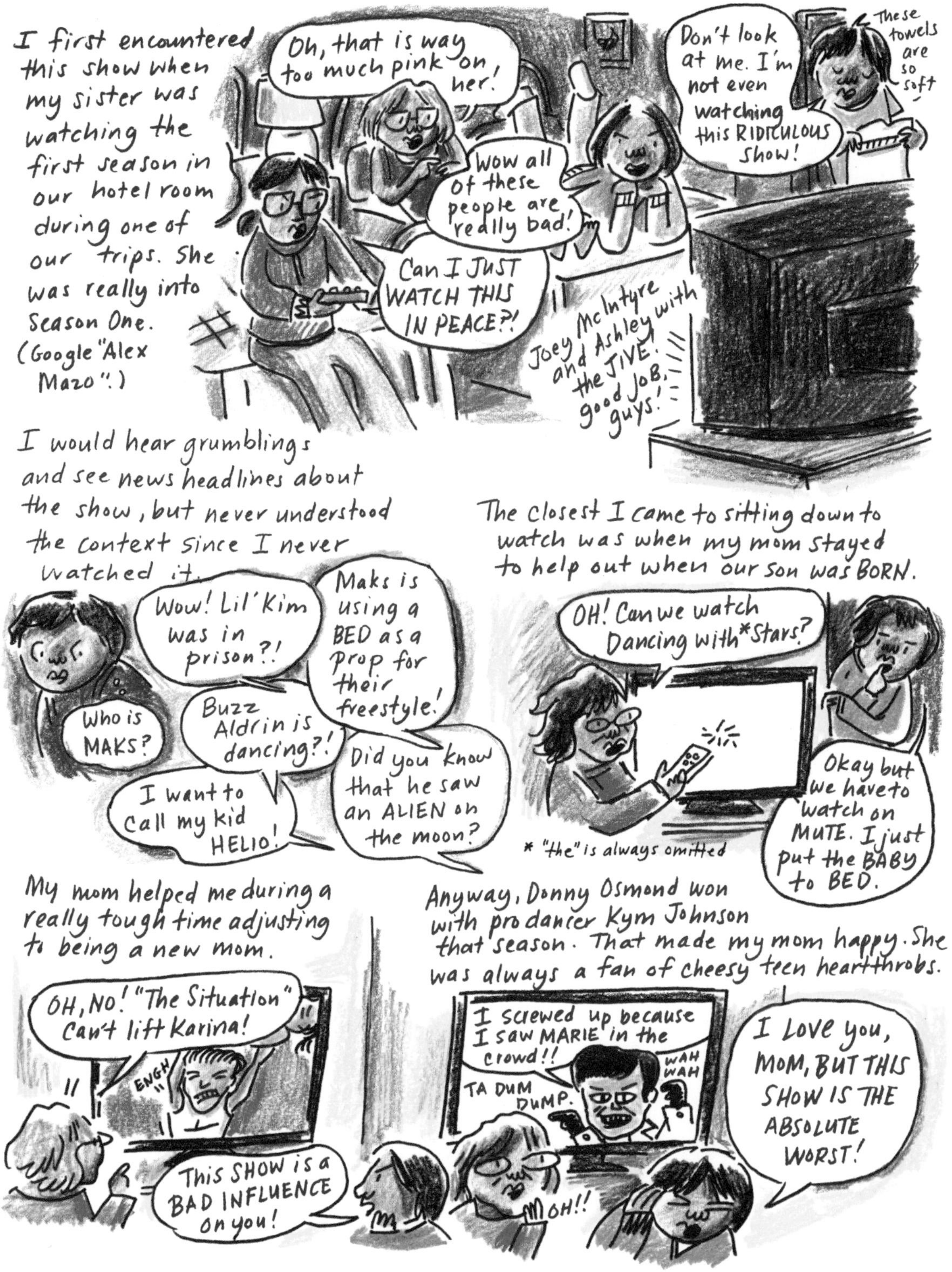
I first encountered this show when my sister was watching the first season in our hotel room during one of our trips. She was really into Season One. (Google "Alex Mazo".)
Oh, that is way too much pink on her!
Wow all of these people are really bad!
Can I JUST WATCH THIS IN PEACE?!
Don't look at me. I'm not even watching this RIDICULOUS show!
These towels are so soft
Joey McIntyre and Ashley with the JIVE! good JOB, guys!
I would hear grumblings and see news headlines about the show, but never understood the context since I never watched it.
Wow! Lil' Kim was in prison?!
Maks is using a BED as a prop for their freestyle!
Who is MAKS?
Buzz Aldrin is dancing?!
I want to call my kid HELIO!
Did you know that he saw an ALIEN on the moon?
The closest I came to sitting down to watch was when my mom stayed to help out when our son was BORN.
OH! Can we watch Dancing with* Stars?
Okay but we have to watch on MUTE. I just put the BABY to BED.
* "the" is always omitted
My mom helped me during a really tough time adjusting to being a new mom.
OH, NO! "The Situation" Can't lift Karina!
ENGH
This SHOW is a BAD INFLUENCE on you!
Anyway, Donny Osmond won with pro dancer Kym Johnson that season. That made my mom happy. She was always a fan of cheesy teen heartthrobs.
I screwed up because I saw MARIE in the crowd!!
WAH WAH
TA DUM DUMP.
OH!!
I Love you, MOM, BUT THIS SHOW IS THE ABSOLUTE WORST!

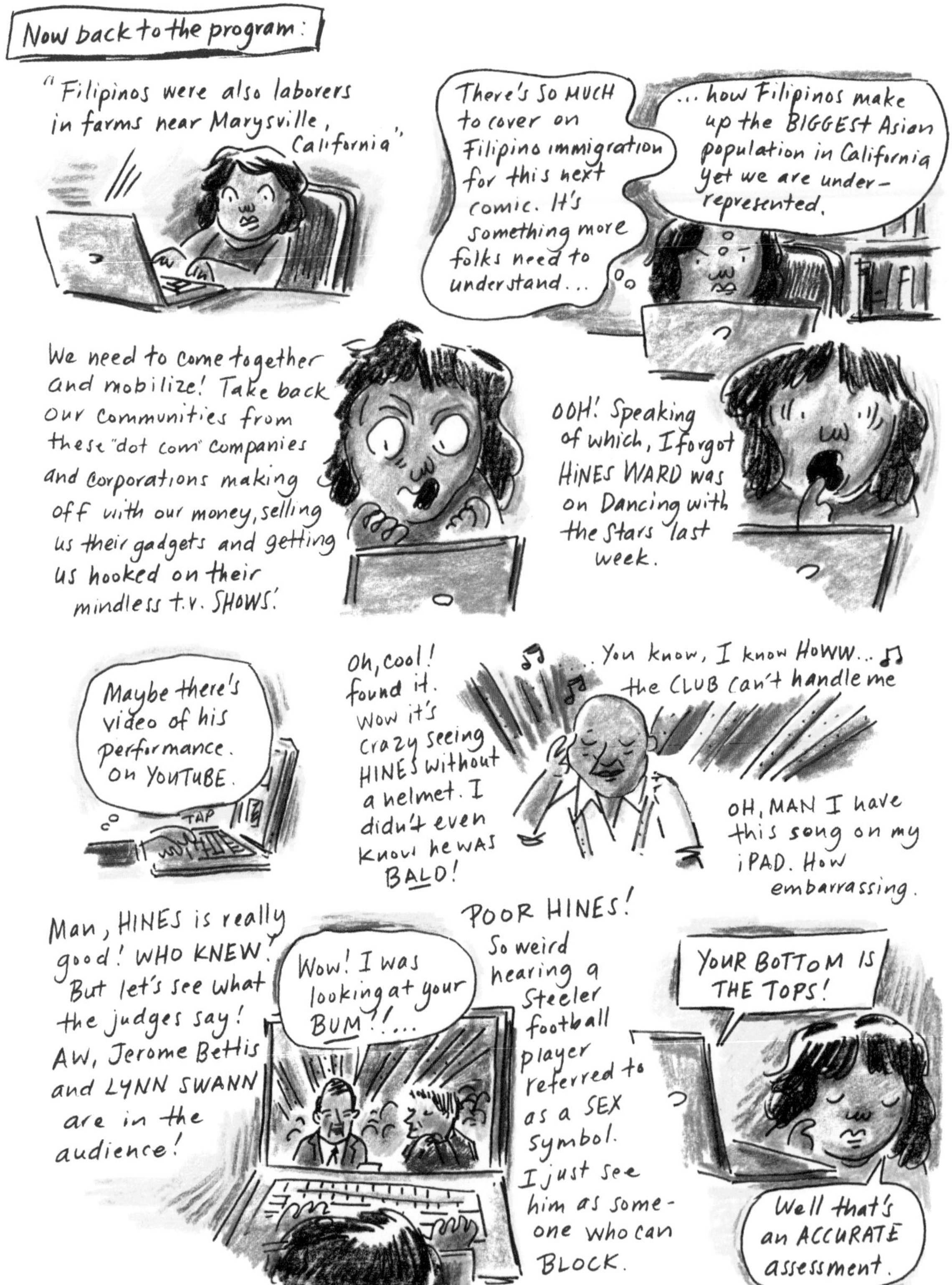
Now back to the program:
"Filipinos were also laborers in farms near Marysville, California"
There's SO MUCH to cover on Filipino immigration for this next comic. It's something more folks need to understand...
...how Filipinos make up the BIGGEST Asian population in California yet we are under-represented.
We need to come together and mobilize! Take back our communities from these "dot com" companies and corporations making off with our money, selling us their gadgets and getting us hooked on their mindless t.v. SHOWS!
OOH! Speaking of which, I forgot HINES WARD was on Dancing with the Stars last week.
Maybe there's video of his performance on YOUTUBE.
TAP
Oh, cool! found it. Wow it's crazy seeing HINES without a helmet. I didn't even know he WAS BALD!
...You know, I know HOWW... the CLUB can't handle me
OH, MAN I have this song on my iPAD. How embarrassing.
Man, HINES is really good! WHO KNEW! But let's see what the judges say! AW, Jerome Bettis and LYNN SWANN are in the audience!
Wow! I was looking at your BUM?!...
POOR HINES! So weird hearing a Steeler football player referred to as a SEX symbol. I just see him as someone who can BLOCK.
YOUR BOTTOM IS THE TOPS!
Well that's an ACCURATE assessment.

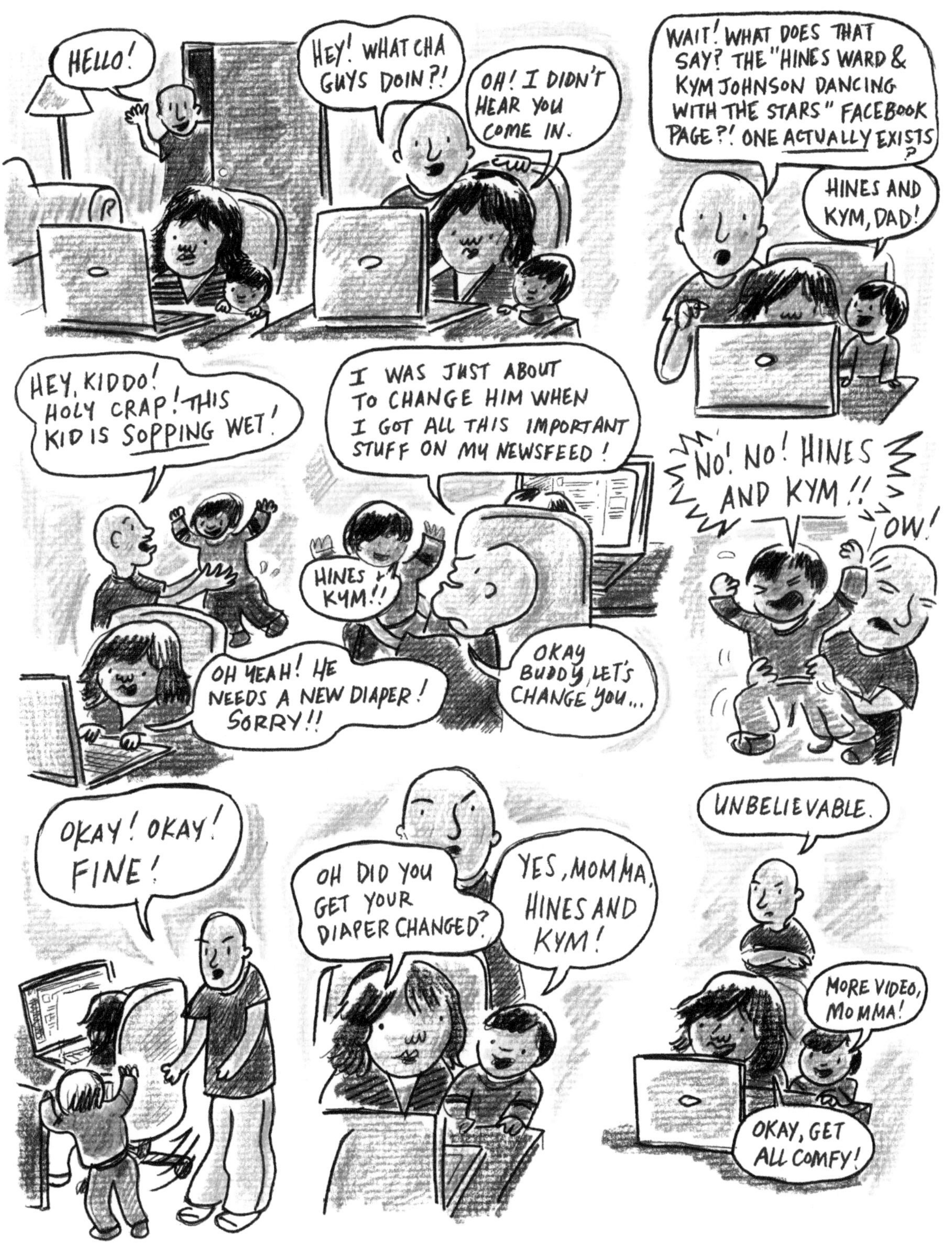
HELLO!
HEY! WHATCHA GUYS DOIN?!
OH! I DIDN'T HEAR YOU COME IN.
WAIT! WHAT DOES THAT SAY? THE "HINES WARD & KYM JOHNSON DANCING WITH THE STARS" FACEBOOK PAGE?! ONE ACTUALLY EXISTS?
HINES AND KYM, DAD!
HEY, KIDDO! HOLY CRAP! THIS KID IS SOPPING WET!
I WAS JUST ABOUT TO CHANGE HIM WHEN I GOT ALL THIS IMPORTANT STUFF ON MY NEWSFEED!
HINES + KYM!!
OH YEAH! HE NEEDS A NEW DIAPER! SORRY!!
OKAY BUDDY, LET'S CHANGE YOU...
NO! NO! HINES AND KYM!!
OW!
OKAY! OKAY! FINE!
OH DID YOU GET YOUR DIAPER CHANGED?
YES, MOMMA, HINES AND KYM!
UNBELIEVABLE.
MORE VIDEO, MOMMA!
OKAY, GET ALL COMFY!

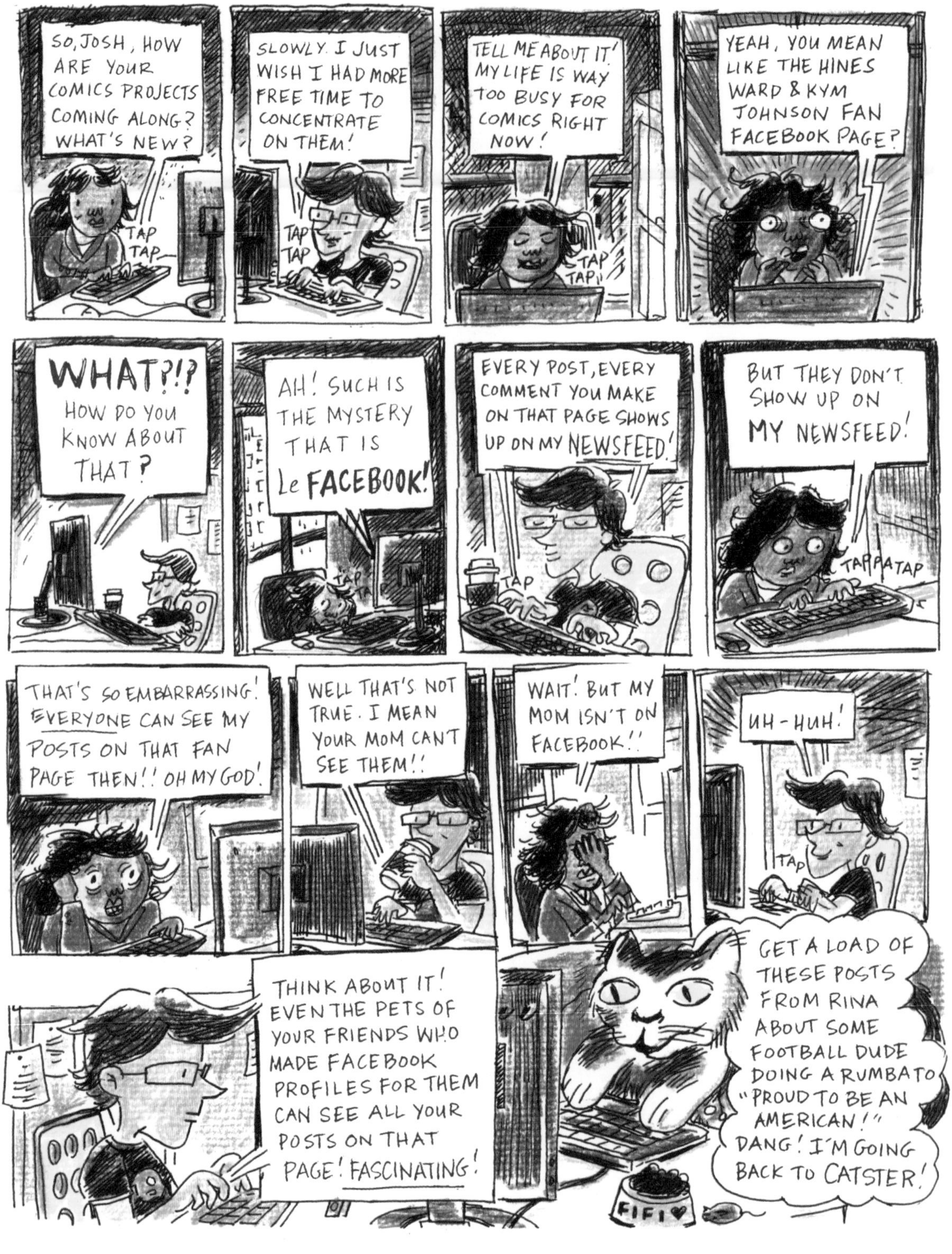

SO, JOSH, HOW ARE YOUR COMICS PROJECTS COMING ALONG? WHAT'S NEW?
TAP TAP
SLOWLY. I JUST WISH I HAD MORE FREE TIME TO CONCENTRATE ON THEM!
TAP TAP
TELL ME ABOUT IT! MY LIFE IS WAY TOO BUSY FOR COMICS RIGHT NOW!
TAP TAP
YEAH, YOU MEAN LIKE THE HINES WARD & KYM JOHNSON FAN FACEBOOK PAGE?
WHAT?!? HOW DO YOU KNOW ABOUT THAT?
AH! SUCH IS THE MYSTERY THAT IS Le FACEBOOK!
EVERY POST, EVERY COMMENT YOU MAKE ON THAT PAGE SHOWS UP ON MY NEWSFEED!
TAP
BUT THEY DON'T SHOW UP ON MY NEWSFEED!
TAPPATAP
THAT'S SO EMBARRASSING! EVERYONE CAN SEE MY POSTS ON THAT FAN PAGE THEN!! OH MY GOD!
WELL THAT'S NOT TRUE. I MEAN YOUR MOM CAN'T SEE THEM!!
WAIT! BUT MY MOM ISN'T ON FACEBOOK!!
UH-HUH!
TAP
THINK ABOUT IT! EVEN THE PETS OF YOUR FRIENDS WHO MADE FACEBOOK PROFILES FOR THEM CAN SEE ALL YOUR POSTS ON THAT PAGE! FASCINATING!
GET A LOAD OF THESE POSTS FROM RINA ABOUT SOME FOOTBALL DUDE DOING A RUMBA TO "PROUD TO BE AN AMERICAN!" DANG! I'M GOING BACK TO CATSTER!
FIFI♥

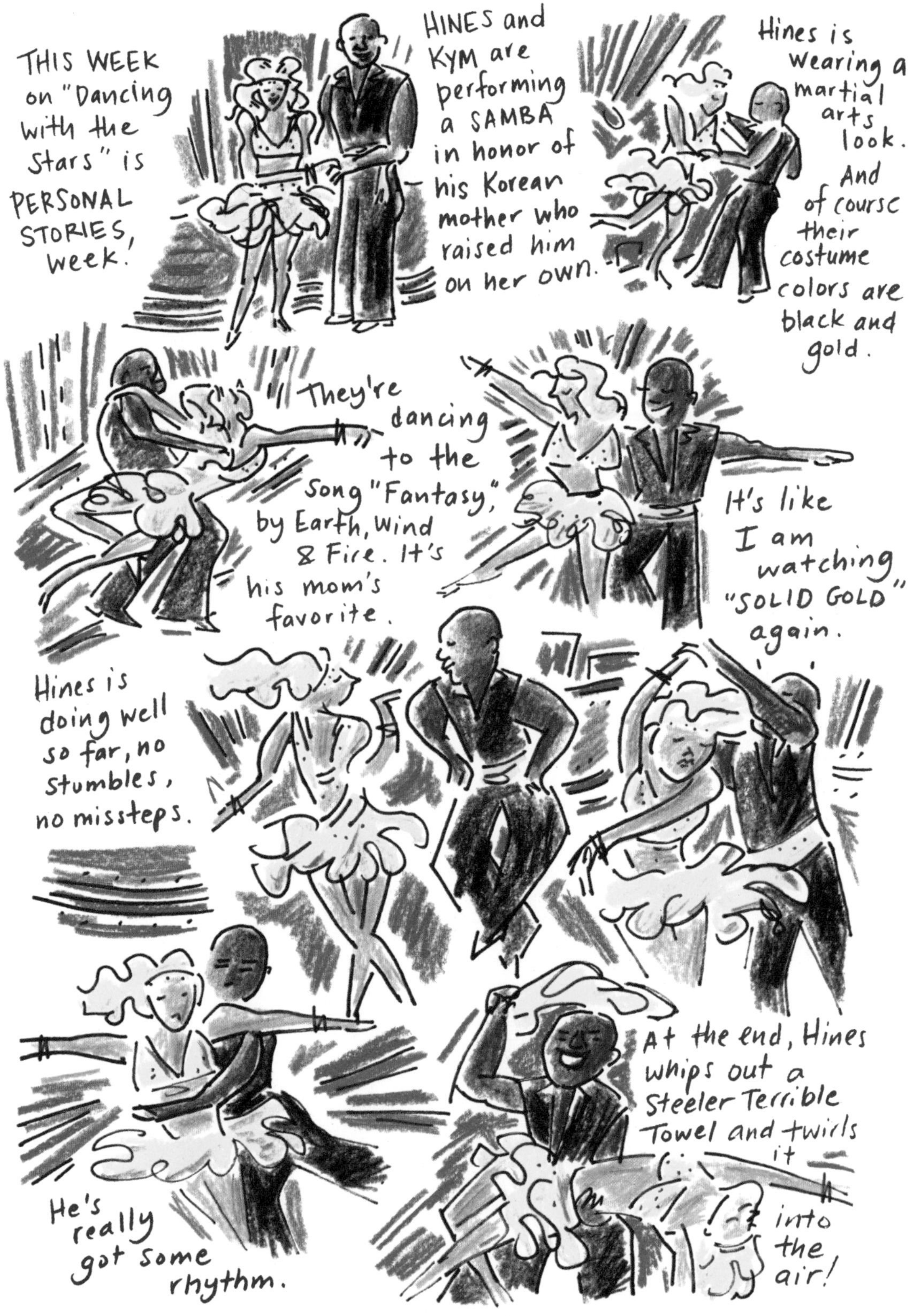
THIS WEEK on "Dancing with the Stars" is PERSONAL STORIES, week!
HINES and KYM are performing a SAMBA in honor of his Korean mother who raised him on her own.
Hines is wearing a martial arts look.
And of course their costume colors are black and gold.
They're dancing to the song "Fantasy," by Earth, Wind & Fire. It's his mom's favorite.
It's like I am watching "SOLID GOLD" again.
Hines is doing well so far, no stumbles, no missteps.
He's really got some rhythm.
At the end, Hines whips out a Steeler Terrible Towel and twirls it
into the air!

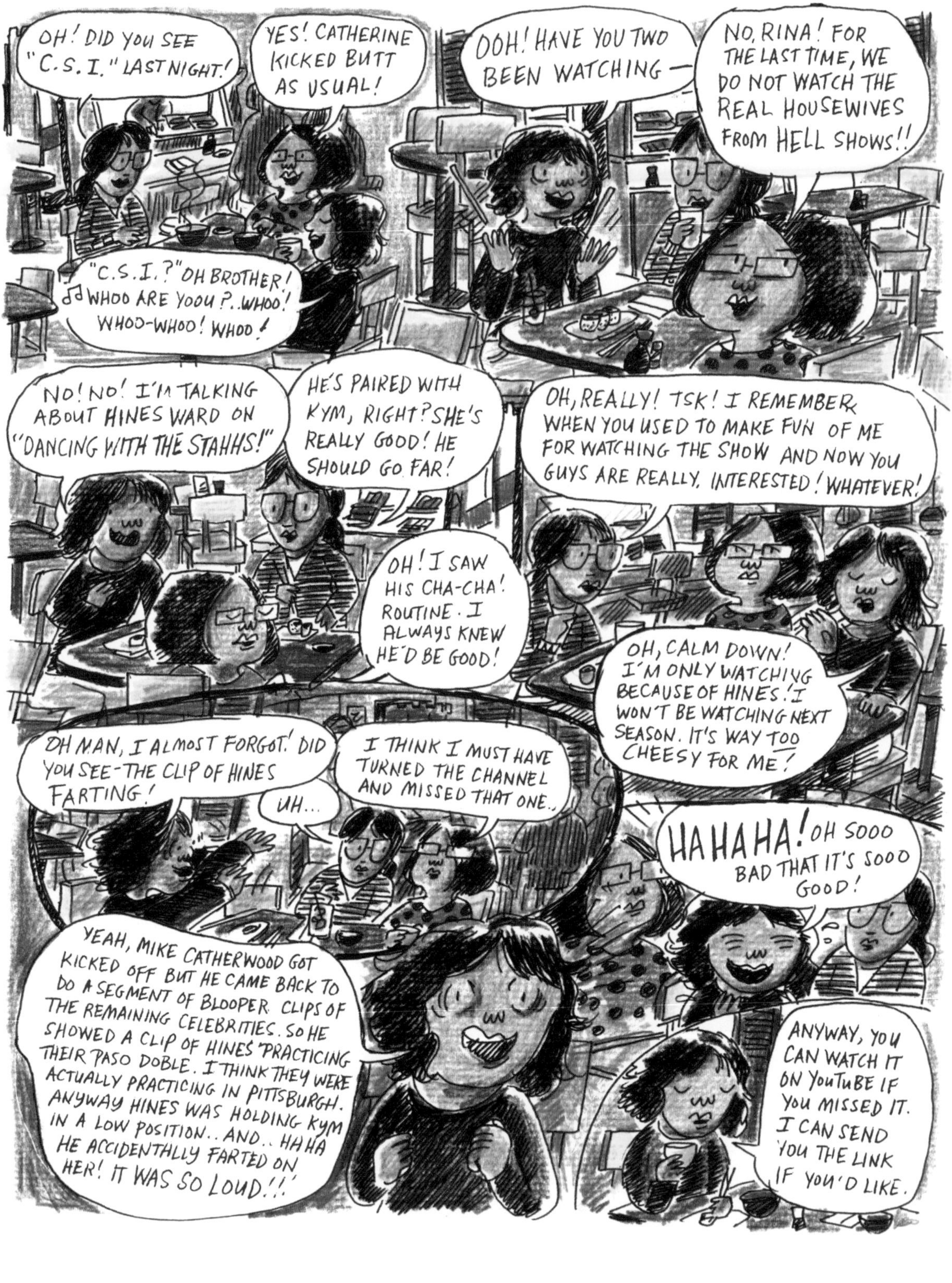

OH! DID YOU SEE "C.S.I." LAST NIGHT!
YES! CATHERINE KICKED BUTT AS USUAL!
"C.S.I.?" OH BROTHER! ♫ WHOO ARE YOOU?.. WHOO! WHOO-WHOO! WHOO!
OOH! HAVE YOU TWO BEEN WATCHING—
NO, RINA! FOR THE LAST TIME, WE DO NOT WATCH THE REAL HOUSEWIVES FROM HELL SHOWS!!
NO! NO! I'M TALKING ABOUT HINES WARD ON "DANCING WITH THE STAHHS!"
HE'S PAIRED WITH KYM, RIGHT? SHE'S REALLY GOOD! HE SHOULD GO FAR!
OH! I SAW HIS CHA-CHA! ROUTINE. I ALWAYS KNEW HE'D BE GOOD!
OH, REALLY! TSK! I REMEMBER WHEN YOU USED TO MAKE FUN OF ME FOR WATCHING THE SHOW AND NOW YOU GUYS ARE REALLY, INTERESTED! WHATEVER!
OH, CALM DOWN! I'M ONLY WATCHING BECAUSE OF HINES! I WON'T BE WATCHING NEXT SEASON. IT'S WAY TOO CHEESY FOR ME!
OH MAN, I ALMOST FORGOT! DID YOU SEE-THE CLIP OF HINES FARTING!
UH...
I THINK I MUST HAVE TURNED THE CHANNEL AND MISSED THAT ONE..
HAHAHA! OH SOOO BAD THAT IT'S SOOO GOOD!
YEAH, MIKE CATHERWOOD GOT KICKED OFF BUT HE CAME BACK TO DO A SEGMENT OF BLOOPER CLIPS OF THE REMAINING CELEBRITIES. SO HE SHOWED A CLIP OF HINES PRACTICING THEIR PASO DOBLE. I THINK THEY WERE ACTUALLY PRACTICING IN PITTSBURGH. ANYWAY HINES WAS HOLDING KYM IN A LOW POSITION.. AND.. HAHA HE ACCIDENTALLY FARTED ON HER! IT WAS SO LOUD!!
ANYWAY, YOU CAN WATCH IT ON YOUTUBE IF YOU MISSED IT. I CAN SEND YOU THE LINK IF YOU'D LIKE.

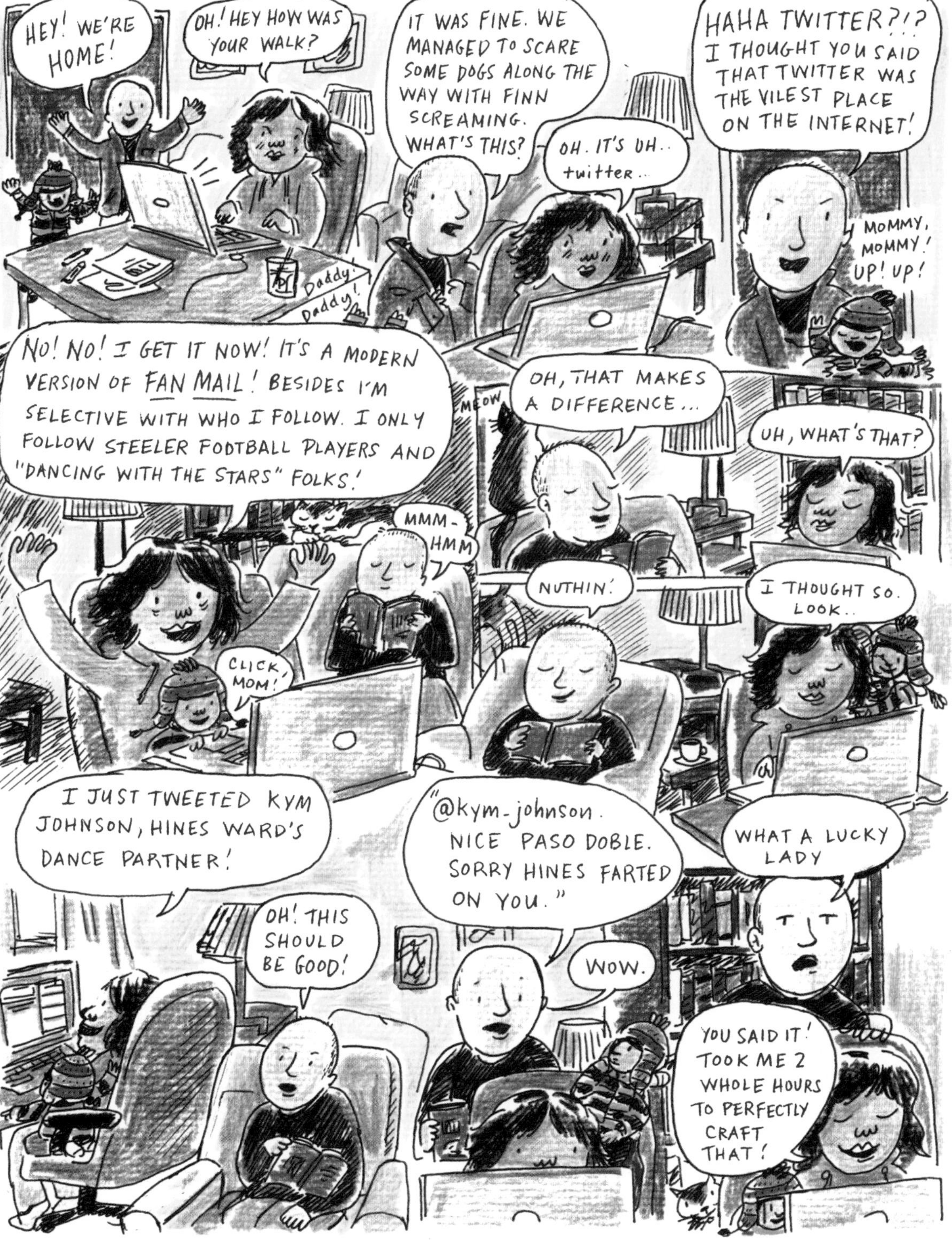
HEY! WE'RE HOME!
OH! HEY HOW WAS YOUR WALK?
Daddy! Daddy!
IT WAS FINE. WE MANAGED TO SCARE SOME DOGS ALONG THE WAY WITH FINN SCREAMING. WHAT'S THIS?
OH. IT'S UH.. twitter...
HAHA TWITTER?!? I THOUGHT YOU SAID THAT TWITTER WAS THE VILEST PLACE ON THE INTERNET!
MOMMY, MOMMY! UP! UP!
NO! NO! I GET IT NOW! IT'S A MODERN VERSION OF FAN MAIL! BESIDES I'M SELECTIVE WITH WHO I FOLLOW. I ONLY FOLLOW STEELER FOOTBALL PLAYERS AND "DANCING WITH THE STARS" FOLKS!
MMM-HMM
CLICK, MOM!
MEOW
OH, THAT MAKES A DIFFERENCE...
UH, WHAT'S THAT?
NUTHIN'
I THOUGHT SO. LOOK..
I JUST TWEETED KYM JOHNSON, HINES WARD'S DANCE PARTNER!
OH! THIS SHOULD BE GOOD!
"@kym_johnson. NICE PASO DOBLE. SORRY HINES FARTED ON YOU."
WOW.
WHAT A LUCKY LADY
YOU SAID IT! TOOK ME 2 WHOLE HOURS TO PERFECTLY CRAFT THAT!

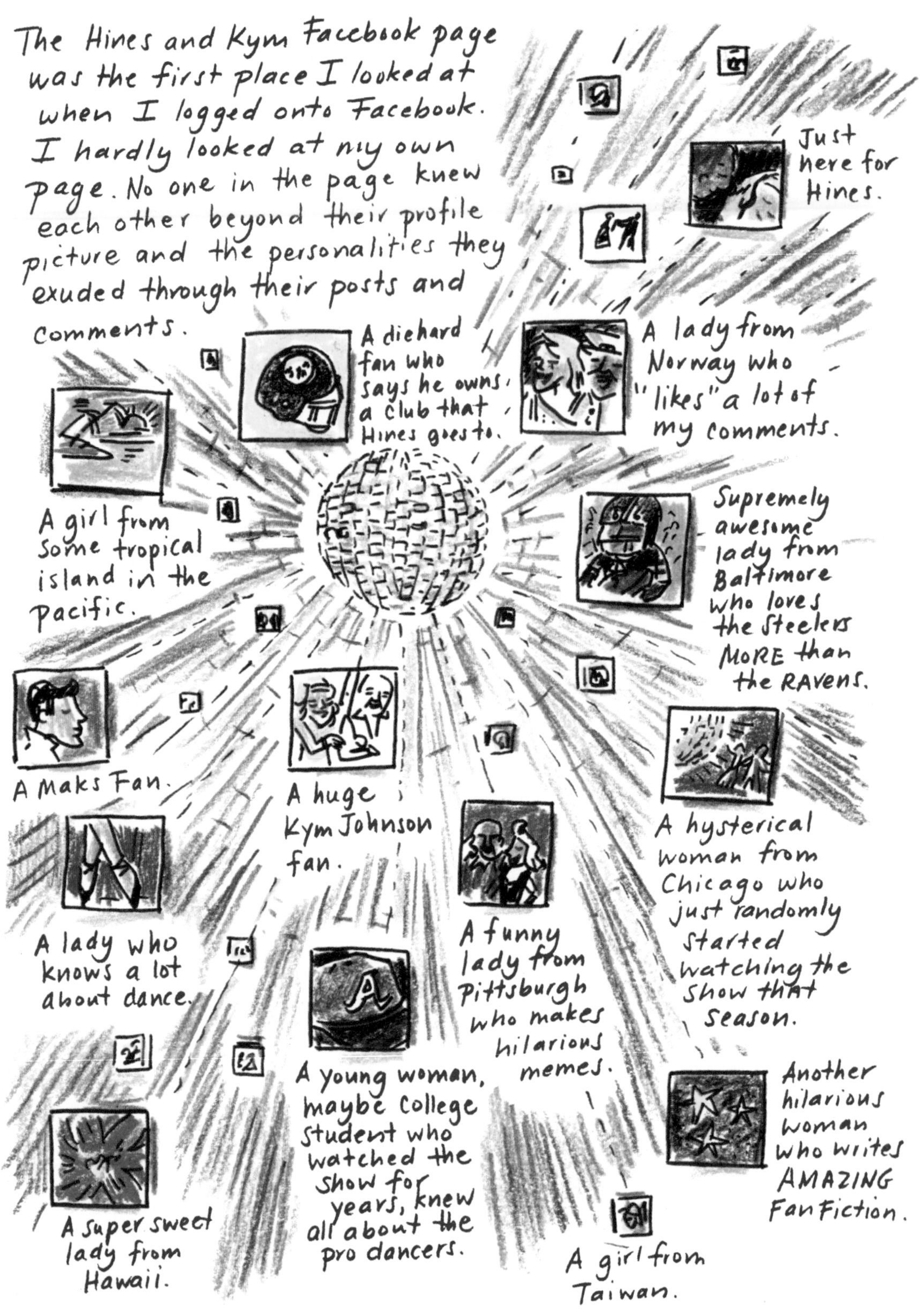
The Hines and Kym Facebook page was the first place I looked at when I logged onto Facebook. I hardly looked at my own page. No one in the page knew each other beyond their profile picture and the personalities they exuded through their posts and comments.
Just here for Hines.
A diehard fan who says he owns a club that Hines goes to.
A lady from Norway who "likes" a lot of my comments.
A girl from some tropical island in the Pacific.
Supremely awesome lady from Baltimore who loves the Steelers MORE than the RAVENS.
A Maks Fan.
A huge Kym Johnson fan.
A hysterical woman from Chicago who just randomly started watching the show that season.
A lady who knows a lot about dance.
A funny lady from Pittsburgh who makes hilarious memes.
A young woman, maybe college student who watched the show for years, knew all about the pro dancers.
Another hilarious woman who writes AMAZING FanFiction.
A super sweet lady from Hawaii.
A girl from Taiwan.

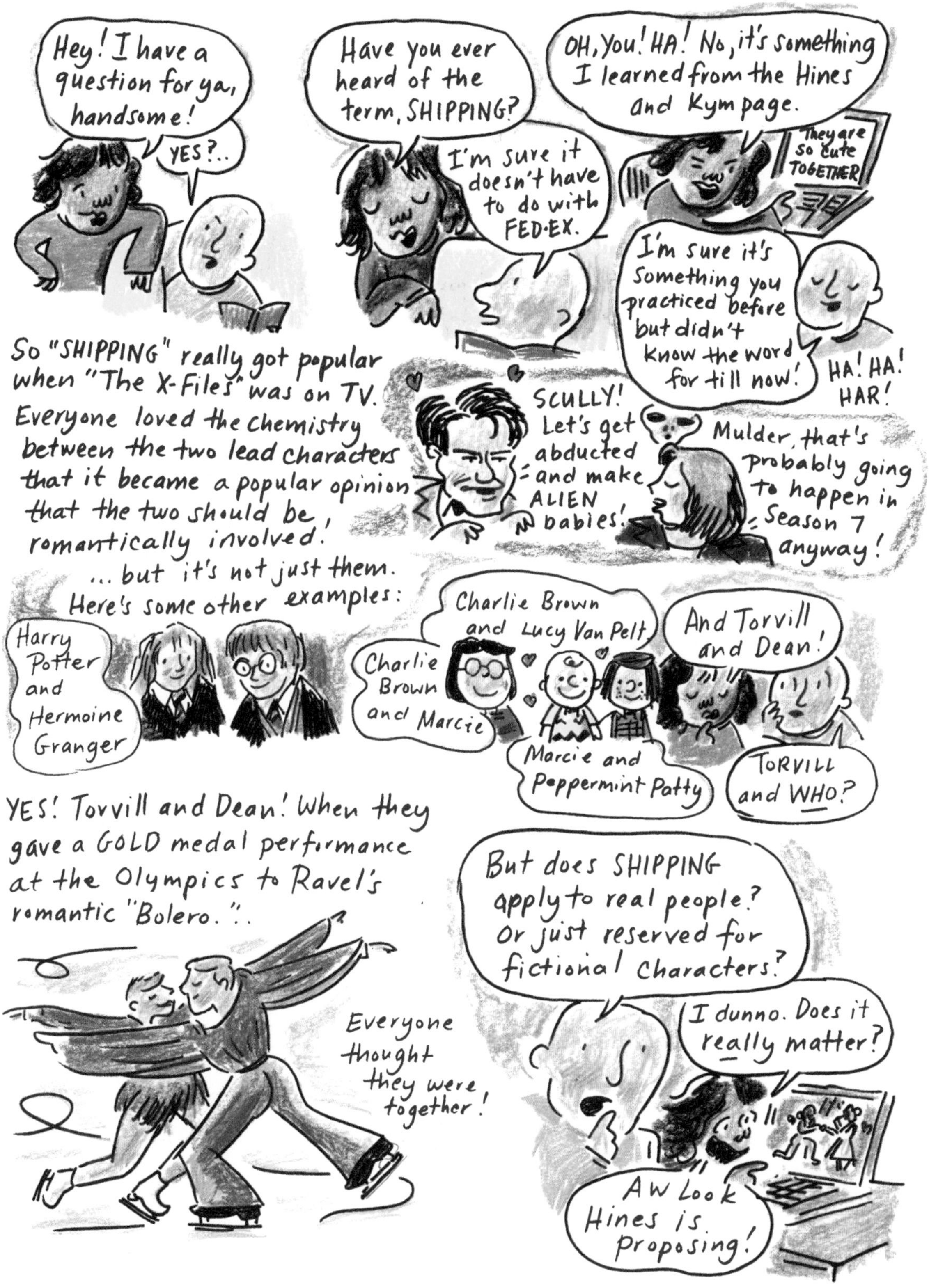
Hey! I have a question for ya, handsome!
YES?..
Have you ever heard of the term, SHIPPING?
I'm sure it doesn't have to do with FED-EX.
OH, YOU! HA! No, it's something I learned from the Hines and Kym page.
They are so cute TOGETHER
I'm sure it's something you practiced before but didn't know the word for till now!
HA! HA! HAR!
So "SHIPPING" really got popular when "The X-Files" was on TV. Everyone loved the chemistry between the two lead characters that it became a popular opinion that the two should be, romantically involved.
SCULLY! Let's get abducted and make ALIEN babies!
Mulder, that's probably going to happen in Season 7 anyway!
...but it's not just them. Here's some other examples:
Harry Potter and Hermoine Granger
Charlie Brown and Lucy Van Pelt
Charlie Brown and Marcie
Marcie and Peppermint Patty
And Torvill and Dean!
TORVILL and WHO?
YES! Torvill and Dean! When they gave a GOLD medal performance at the Olympics to Ravel's romantic "Bolero."..
Everyone thought they were together!
But does SHIPPING apply to real people? Or just reserved for fictional characters?
I dunno. Does it really matter?
AW Look Hines is proposing!

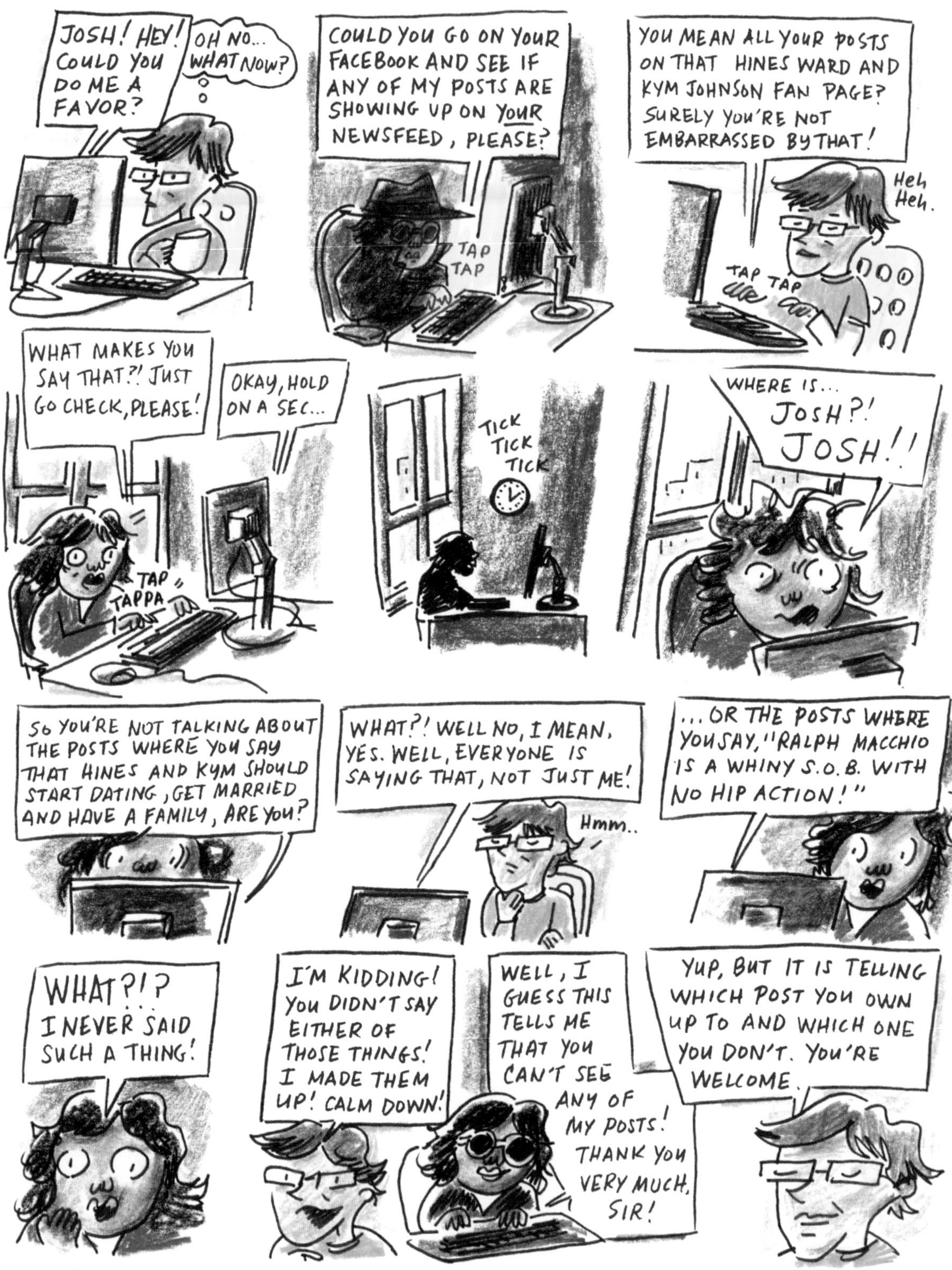
JOSH! HEY! COULD YOU DO ME A FAVOR?
OH NO... WHAT NOW?
COULD YOU GO ON YOUR FACEBOOK AND SEE IF ANY OF MY POSTS ARE SHOWING UP ON YOUR NEWSFEED, PLEASE?
TAP TAP
YOU MEAN ALL YOUR POSTS ON THAT HINES WARD AND KYM JOHNSON FAN PAGE? SURELY YOU'RE NOT EMBARRASSED BY THAT!
Heh Heh.
TAP TAP
WHAT MAKES YOU SAY THAT?! JUST GO CHECK, PLEASE!
OKAY, HOLD ON A SEC...
TAP TAPPA
TICK TICK TICK
WHERE IS... JOSH?! JOSH!!
SO YOU'RE NOT TALKING ABOUT THE POSTS WHERE YOU SAY THAT HINES AND KYM SHOULD START DATING, GET MARRIED AND HAVE A FAMILY, ARE YOU?
WHAT?! WELL NO, I MEAN, YES. WELL, EVERYONE IS SAYING THAT, NOT JUST ME!
Hmm..
...OR THE POSTS WHERE YOU SAY, "RALPH MACCHIO IS A WHINY S.O.B. WITH NO HIP ACTION!"
WHAT?!? I NEVER SAID SUCH A THING!
I'M KIDDING! YOU DIDN'T SAY EITHER OF THOSE THINGS! I MADE THEM UP! CALM DOWN!
WELL, I GUESS THIS TELLS ME THAT YOU CAN'T SEE ANY OF MY POSTS! THANK YOU VERY MUCH, SIR!
YUP, BUT IT IS TELLING WHICH POST YOU OWN UP TO AND WHICH ONE YOU DON'T. YOU'RE WELCOME.

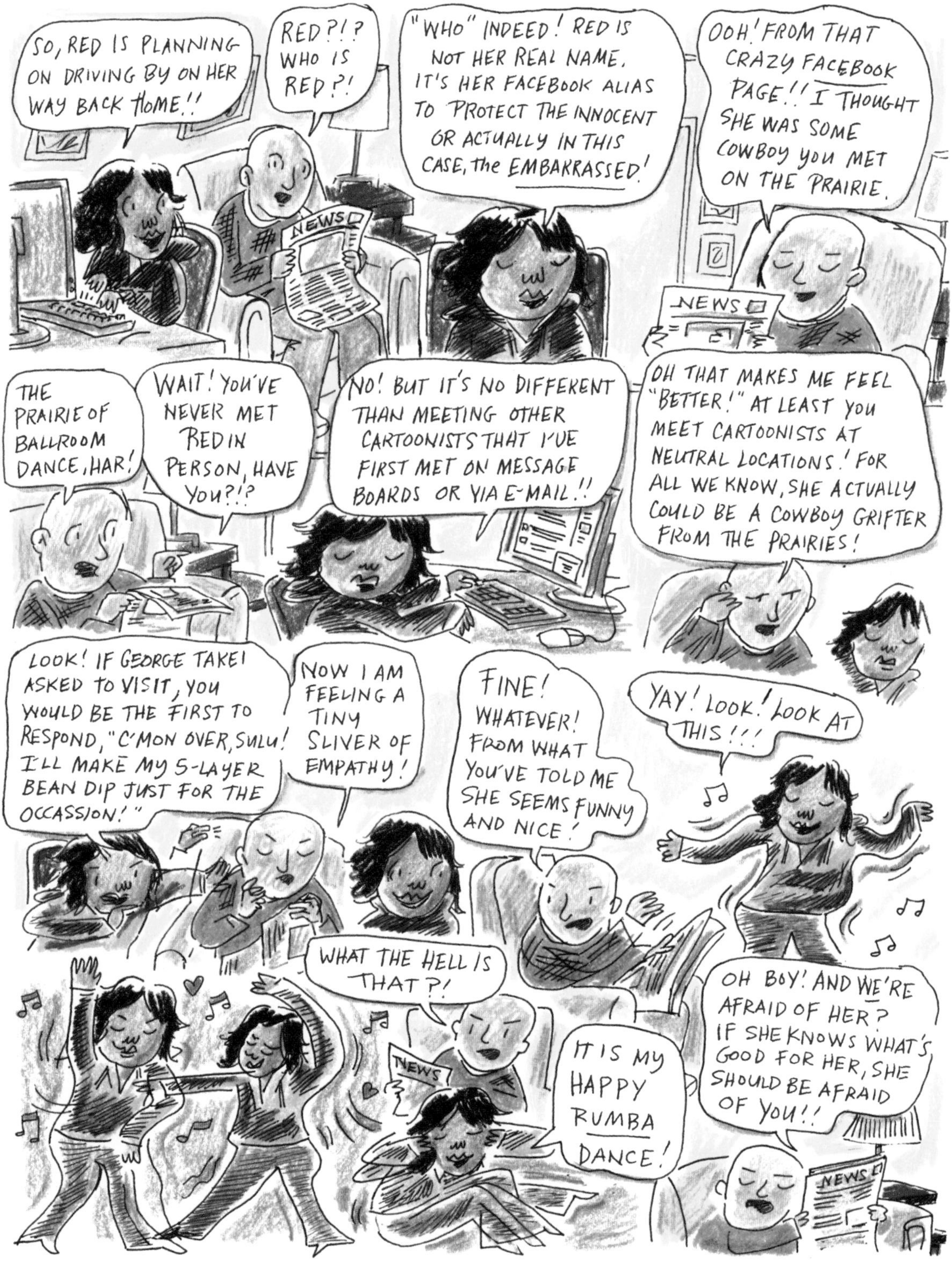
SO, RED IS PLANNING ON DRIVING BY ON HER WAY BACK HOME!!
RED?!? WHO IS RED?!
"WHO" INDEED! RED IS NOT HER REAL NAME. IT'S HER FACEBOOK ALIAS TO PROTECT THE INNOCENT OR ACTUALLY IN THIS CASE, the EMBARRASSED!
OOH! FROM THAT CRAZY FACEBOOK PAGE!! I THOUGHT SHE WAS SOME COWBOY YOU MET ON THE PRAIRIE.
NEWS
NEWS
THE PRAIRIE OF BALLROOM DANCE, HAR!
WAIT! YOU'VE NEVER MET RED IN PERSON, HAVE YOU?!?
NO! BUT IT'S NO DIFFERENT THAN MEETING OTHER CARTOONISTS THAT I'VE FIRST MET ON MESSAGE BOARDS OR VIA E-MAIL!!
OH THAT MAKES ME FEEL "BETTER!" AT LEAST YOU MEET CARTOONISTS AT NEUTRAL LOCATIONS! FOR ALL WE KNOW, SHE ACTUALLY COULD BE A COWBOY GRIFTER FROM THE PRAIRIES!
LOOK! IF GEORGE TAKEI ASKED TO VISIT, YOU WOULD BE THE FIRST TO RESPOND, "C'MON OVER, SULU! I'LL MAKE MY 5-LAYER BEAN DIP JUST FOR THE OCCASSION!"
NOW I AM FEELING A TINY SLIVER OF EMPATHY!
FINE! WHATEVER! FROM WHAT YOU'VE TOLD ME SHE SEEMS FUNNY AND NICE!
YAY! LOOK! LOOK AT THIS!!!
WHAT THE HELL IS THAT?!
NEWS
IT IS MY HAPPY RUMBA DANCE!
OH BOY! AND WE'RE AFRAID OF HER? IF SHE KNOWS WHAT'S GOOD FOR HER, SHE SHOULD BE AFRAID OF YOU!!
NEWS

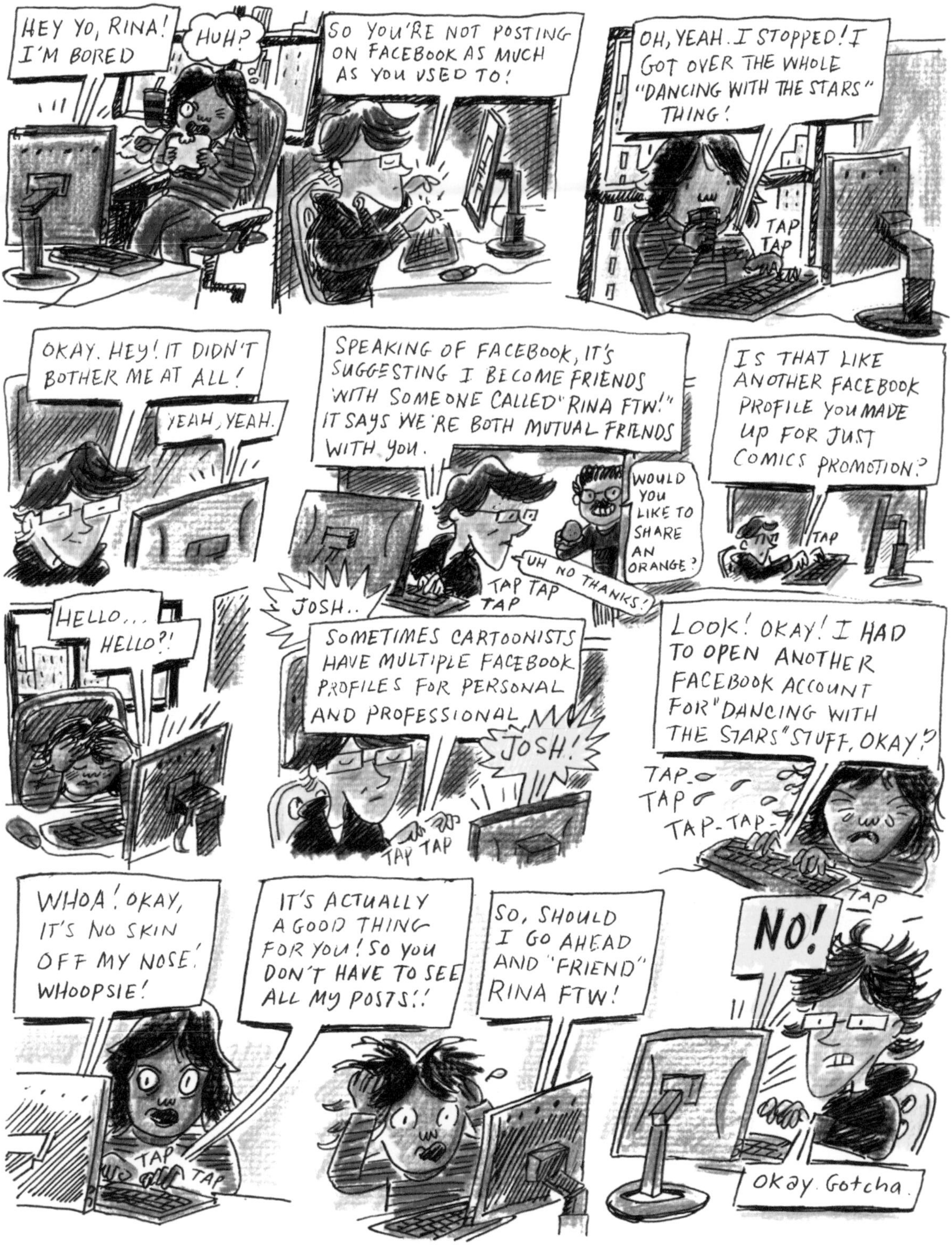
HEY YO, RINA! I'M BORED
HUH?
SO YOU'RE NOT POSTING ON FACEBOOK AS MUCH AS YOU USED TO!
OH, YEAH. I STOPPED! I GOT OVER THE WHOLE "DANCING WITH THE STARS" THING!
TAP TAP
OKAY. HEY! IT DIDN'T BOTHER ME AT ALL!
YEAH, YEAH.
SPEAKING OF FACEBOOK, IT'S SUGGESTING I BECOME FRIENDS WITH SOMEONE CALLED "RINA FTW!" IT SAYS WE'RE BOTH MUTUAL FRIENDS WITH YOU.
WOULD YOU LIKE TO SHARE AN ORANGE?
UH NO THANKS!
TAP TAP TAP
IS THAT LIKE ANOTHER FACEBOOK PROFILE YOU MADE UP FOR JUST COMICS PROMOTION?
TAP
HELLO... HELLO?!
JOSH..
SOMETIMES CARTOONISTS HAVE MULTIPLE FACEBOOK PROFILES FOR PERSONAL AND PROFESSIONAL
JOSH!
TAP TAP
LOOK! OKAY! I HAD TO OPEN ANOTHER FACEBOOK ACCOUNT FOR "DANCING WITH THE STARS" STUFF, OKAY?
TAP TAP TAP-TAP
TAP
WHOA! OKAY, IT'S NO SKIN OFF MY NOSE! WHOOPSIE!
TAP TAP
IT'S ACTUALLY A GOOD THING FOR YOU! SO YOU DON'T HAVE TO SEE ALL MY POSTS!!
SO, SHOULD I GO AHEAD AND "FRIEND" RINA FTW!
NO!
Okay. Gotcha.

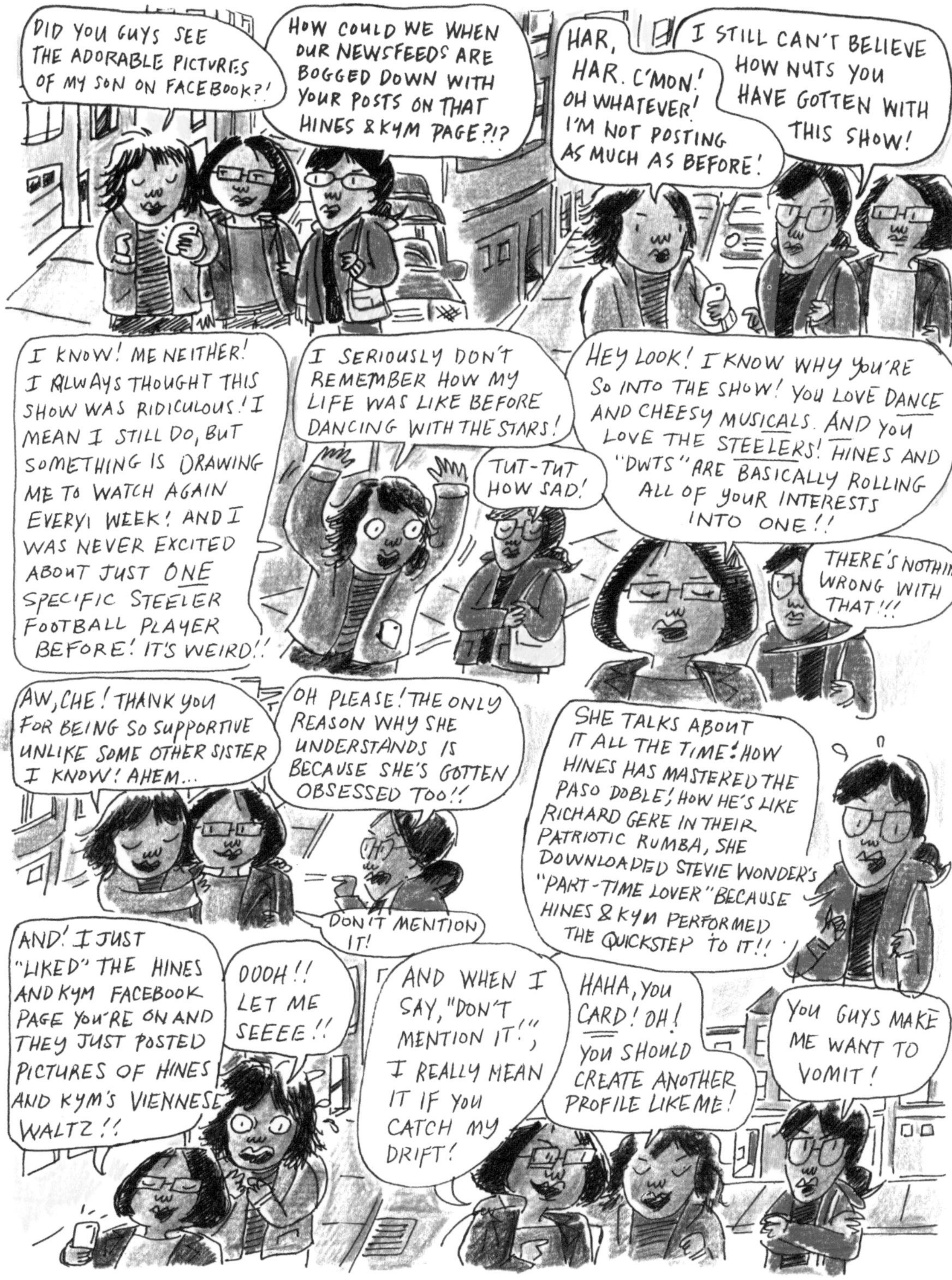

DID YOU GUYS SEE THE ADORABLE PICTURES OF MY SON ON FACEBOOK?!
HOW COULD WE WHEN OUR NEWSFEEDS ARE BOGGED DOWN WITH YOUR POSTS ON THAT HINES & KYM PAGE?!?
HAR, HAR. C'MON! OH WHATEVER! I'M NOT POSTING AS MUCH AS BEFORE!
I STILL CAN'T BELIEVE HOW NUTS YOU HAVE GOTTEN WITH THIS SHOW!
I KNOW! ME NEITHER! I ALWAYS THOUGHT THIS SHOW WAS RIDICULOUS! I MEAN I STILL DO, BUT SOMETHING IS DRAWING ME TO WATCH AGAIN EVERY WEEK! AND I WAS NEVER EXCITED ABOUT JUST ONE SPECIFIC STEELER FOOTBALL PLAYER BEFORE! IT'S WEIRD!!
I SERIOUSLY DON'T REMEMBER HOW MY LIFE WAS LIKE BEFORE DANCING WITH THE STARS!
TUT-TUT HOW SAD!
HEY LOOK! I KNOW WHY YOU'RE SO INTO THE SHOW! YOU LOVE DANCE AND CHEESY MUSICALS. AND YOU LOVE THE STEELERS! HINES AND "DWTS" ARE BASICALLY ROLLING ALL OF YOUR INTERESTS INTO ONE!!
THERE'S NOTHIN WRONG WITH THAT!!!
AW, CHE! THANK YOU FOR BEING SO SUPPORTIVE UNLIKE SOME OTHER SISTER I KNOW! AHEM...
OH PLEASE! THE ONLY REASON WHY SHE UNDERSTANDS IS BECAUSE SHE'S GOTTEN OBSESSED TOO!!
DON'T MENTION IT!
SHE TALKS ABOUT IT ALL THE TIME! HOW HINES HAS MASTERED THE PASO DOBLE! HOW HE'S LIKE RICHARD GERE IN THEIR PATRIOTIC RUMBA, SHE DOWNLOADED STEVIE WONDER'S "PART-TIME LOVER" BECAUSE HINES & KYM PERFORMED THE QUICKSTEP TO IT!!
AND! I JUST "LIKED" THE HINES AND KYM FACEBOOK PAGE YOU'RE ON AND THEY JUST POSTED PICTURES OF HINES AND KYM'S VIENNESE WALTZ!!
OOOH!! LET ME SEEEE!!
AND WHEN I SAY, "DON'T MENTION IT!", I REALLY MEAN IT IF YOU CATCH MY DRIFT!
HAHA, YOU CARD! OH! YOU SHOULD CREATE ANOTHER PROFILE LIKE ME!
YOU GUYS MAKE ME WANT TO VOMIT!

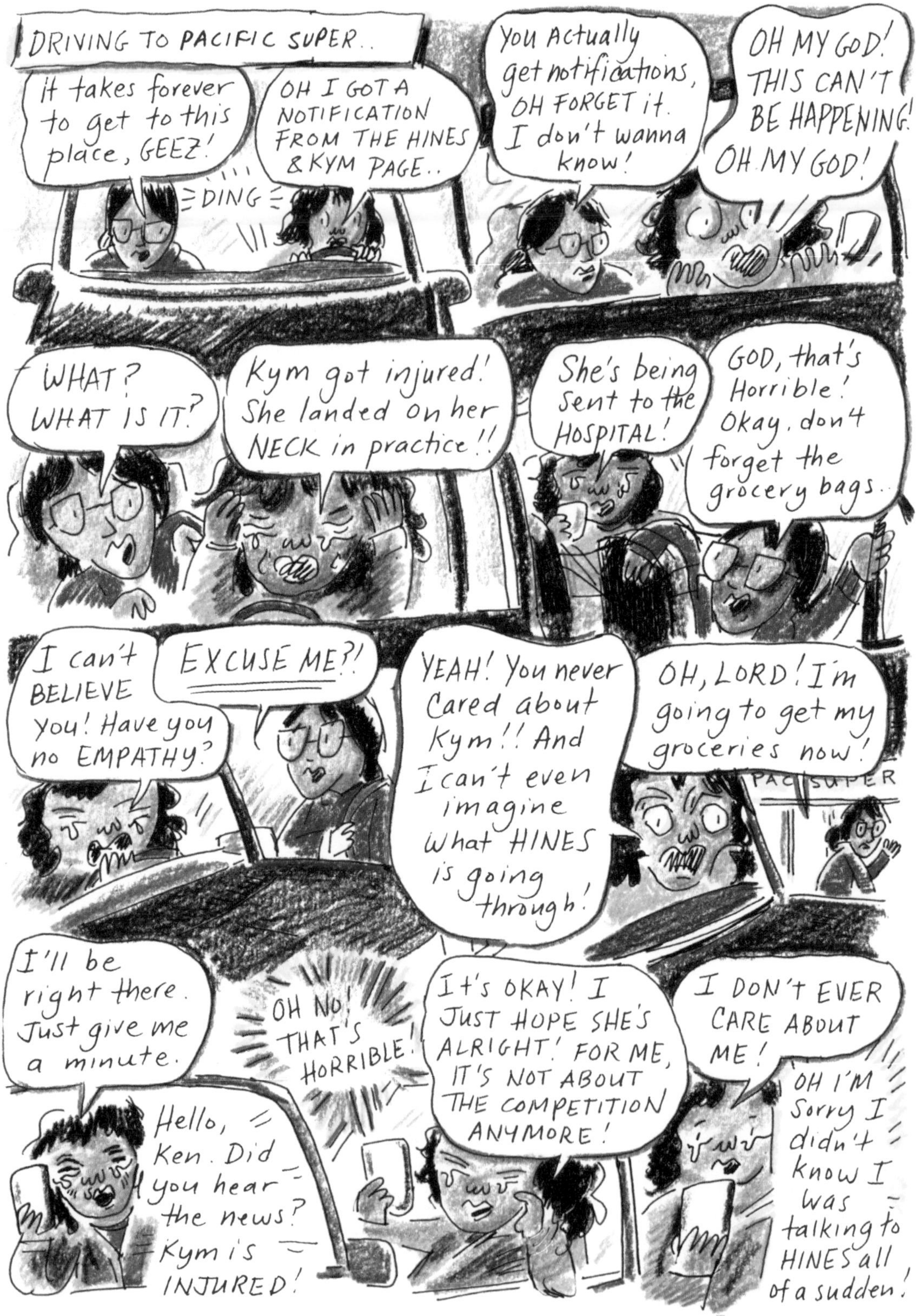
DRIVING TO PACIFIC SUPER..
it takes forever to get to this place, GEEZ!
DING
OH I GOT A NOTIFICATION FROM THE HINES & KYM PAGE..
You Actually get notifications, OH FORGET it. I don't wanna know!
OH MY GOD! THIS CAN'T BE HAPPENING! OH MY GOD!
WHAT? WHAT IS IT?
Kym got injured! She landed on her NECK in practice!!
She's being sent to the HOSPITAL!
GOD, that's Horrible! Okay. don't forget the grocery bags..
I can't BELIEVE you! Have you no EMPATHY?
EXCUSE ME?!
YEAH! You never Cared about Kym!! And I can't even imagine what HINES is going through!
OH, LORD! I'm going to get my groceries now!
PAC SUPER
I'll be right there. Just give me a minute.
Hello, Ken. Did you hear the news? Kym is INJURED!
OH NO! THAT'S HORRIBLE!
It's OKAY! I JUST HOPE SHE'S ALRIGHT! FOR ME, IT'S NOT ABOUT THE COMPETITION ANYMORE!
I DON'T EVER CARE ABOUT ME!
OH I'M Sorry I didn't know I was talking to HINES all of a sudden!

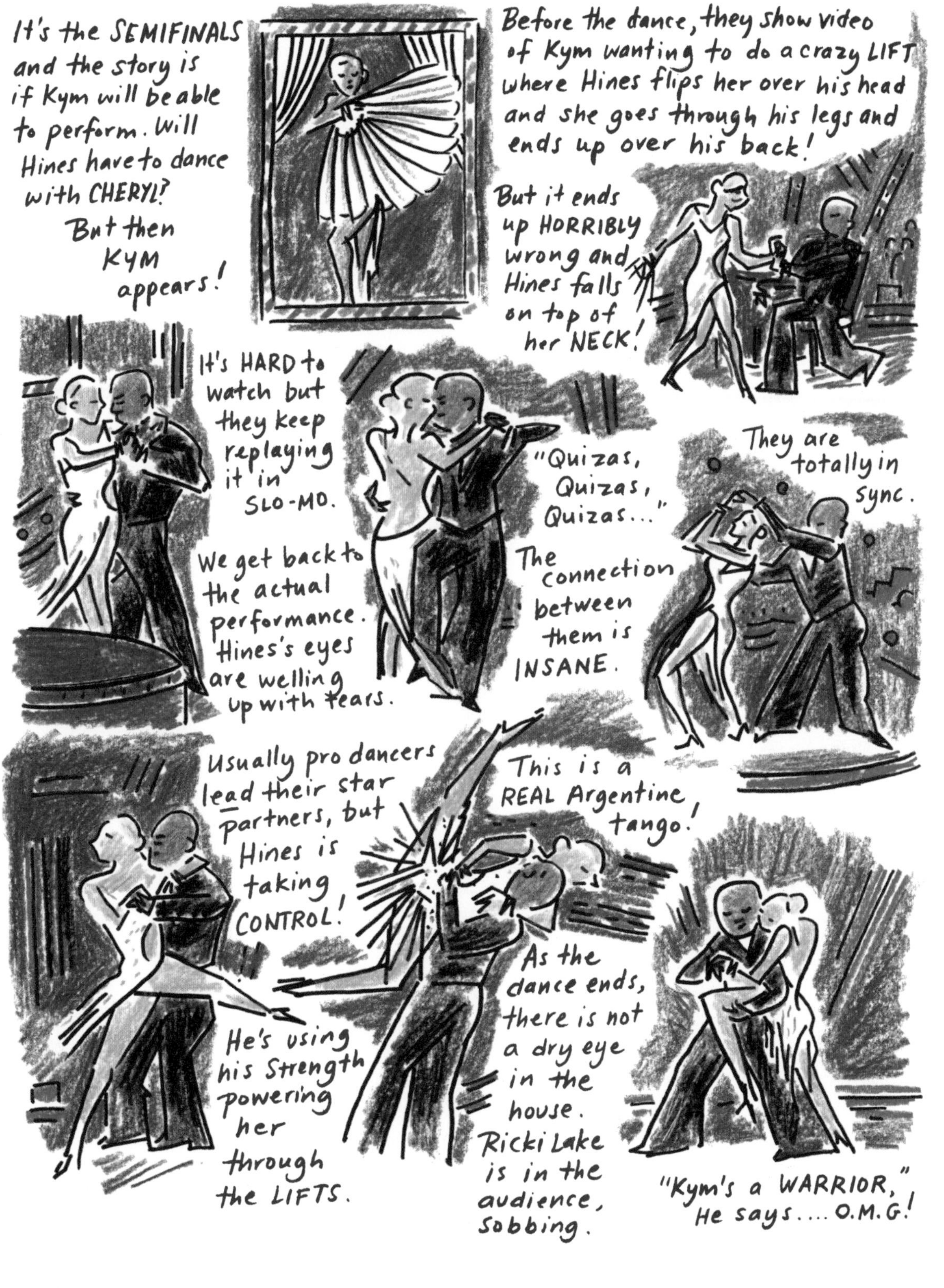
It's the SEMIFINALS and the story is if Kym will be able to perform. Will Hines have to dance with CHERYL?
But then KYM appears!
Before the dance, they show video of Kym wanting to do a crazy LIFT where Hines flips her over his head and she goes through his legs and ends up over his back!
But it ends up HORRIBLY wrong and Hines falls on top of her NECK!
It's HARD to watch but they keep replaying it in SLO-MO.
We get back to the actual performance. Hines's eyes are welling up with tears.
"Quizas, Quizas, Quizas..."
The connection between them is INSANE.
They are totally in sync.
Usually pro dancers lead their star partners, but Hines is taking CONTROL!
He's using his Strength powering her through the LIFTS.
This is a REAL Argentine tango!
As the dance ends, there is not a dry eye in the house.
Ricki Lake is in the audience, sobbing.
"Kym's a WARRIOR," He says.... O.M.G!

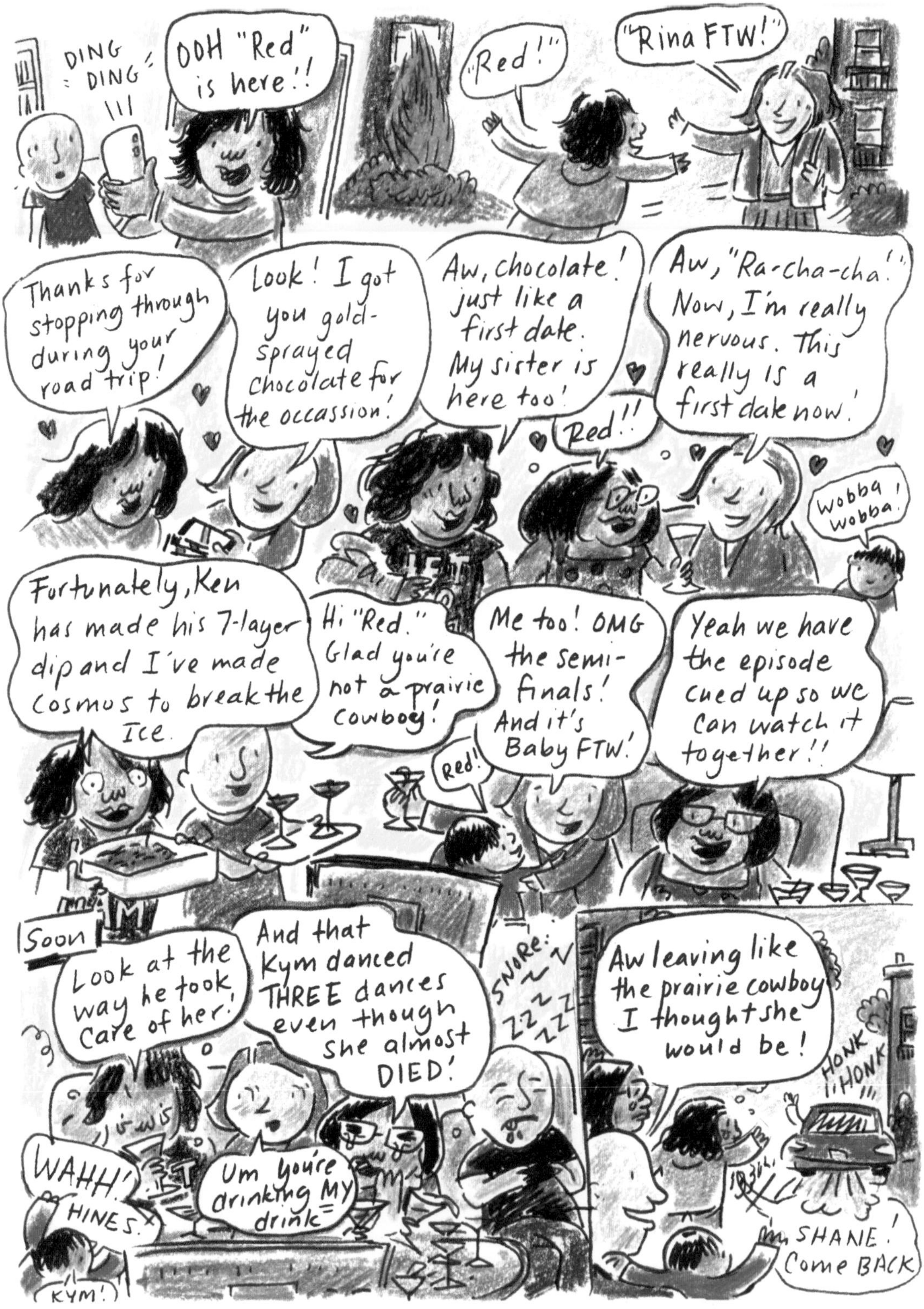
DING DING
OOH "Red" is here!!
"Red!"
"Rina FTW!"
Thanks for stopping through during your road trip!
Look! I got you gold-sprayed chocolate for the occassion!
Aw, chocolate! just like a first date. My sister is here too!
Red!!
Aw, "Ra-cha-cha!" Now, I'm really nervous. This really is a first date now!
wobba! wobba!
Fortunately, Ken has made his 7-layer dip and I've made cosmos to break the ice.
Hi "Red." Glad you're not a prairie cowboy!
Red!
Me too! OMG the semi-finals! And it's Baby FTW!
Yeah we have the episode cued up so we can watch it together!!
Soon
Look at the way he took care of her!
And that Kym danced THREE dances even though she almost DIED!
SNORE: Z Z Z Z Z
WAHH!
HINES.
KYM!
Um you're drinking MY drink
Aw leaving like the prairie cowboy I thought she would be!
HONK HONK
SHANE! Come BACK

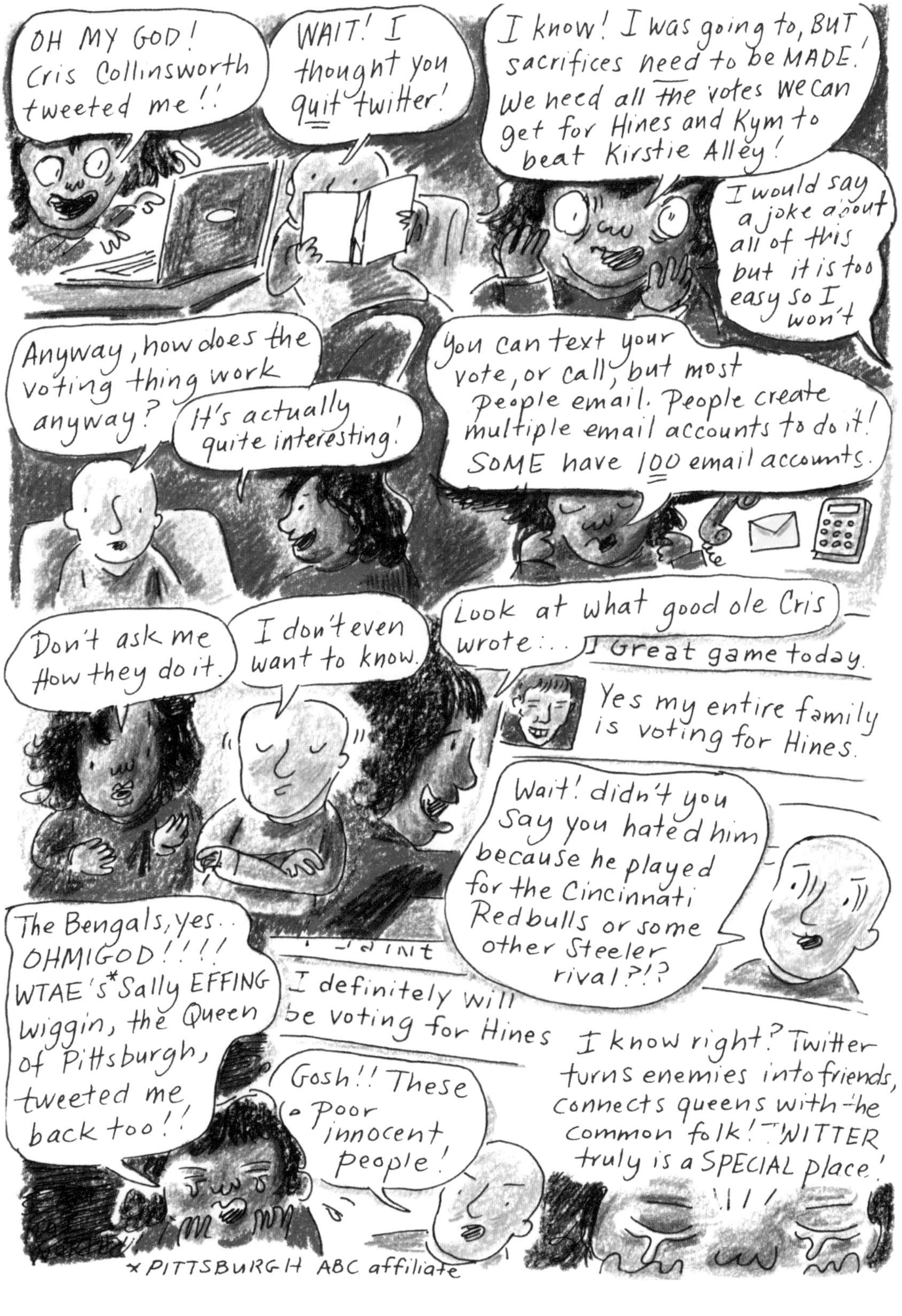
OH MY GOD! Cris Collinsworth tweeted me!!
WAIT! I thought you quit twitter!
I know! I was going to, BUT sacrifices need to be MADE! We need all the votes we can get for Hines and Kym to beat Kirstie Alley!
I would say a joke about all of this but it is too easy so I won't
Anyway, how does the voting thing work anyway?
It's actually quite interesting!
You can text your vote, or call, but most people email. People create multiple email accounts to do it! SOME have 100 email accounts.
Don't ask me How they do it.
I don't even want to know.
Look at what good ole Cris wrote...
Great game today.
Yes my entire family is voting for Hines.
Wait! didn't you say you hated him because he played for the Cincinnati Redbulls or some other Steeler rival?!?
The Bengals, yes... OHMIGOD!!!! WTAE's* Sally EFFING wiggin, the Queen of Pittsburgh, tweeted me back too!!
I definitely will be voting for Hines
Gosh!! These poor innocent people!
I know right? Twitter turns enemies into friends, connects queens with the common folk! TWITTER truly is a SPECIAL place!
*PITTSBURGH ABC affiliate

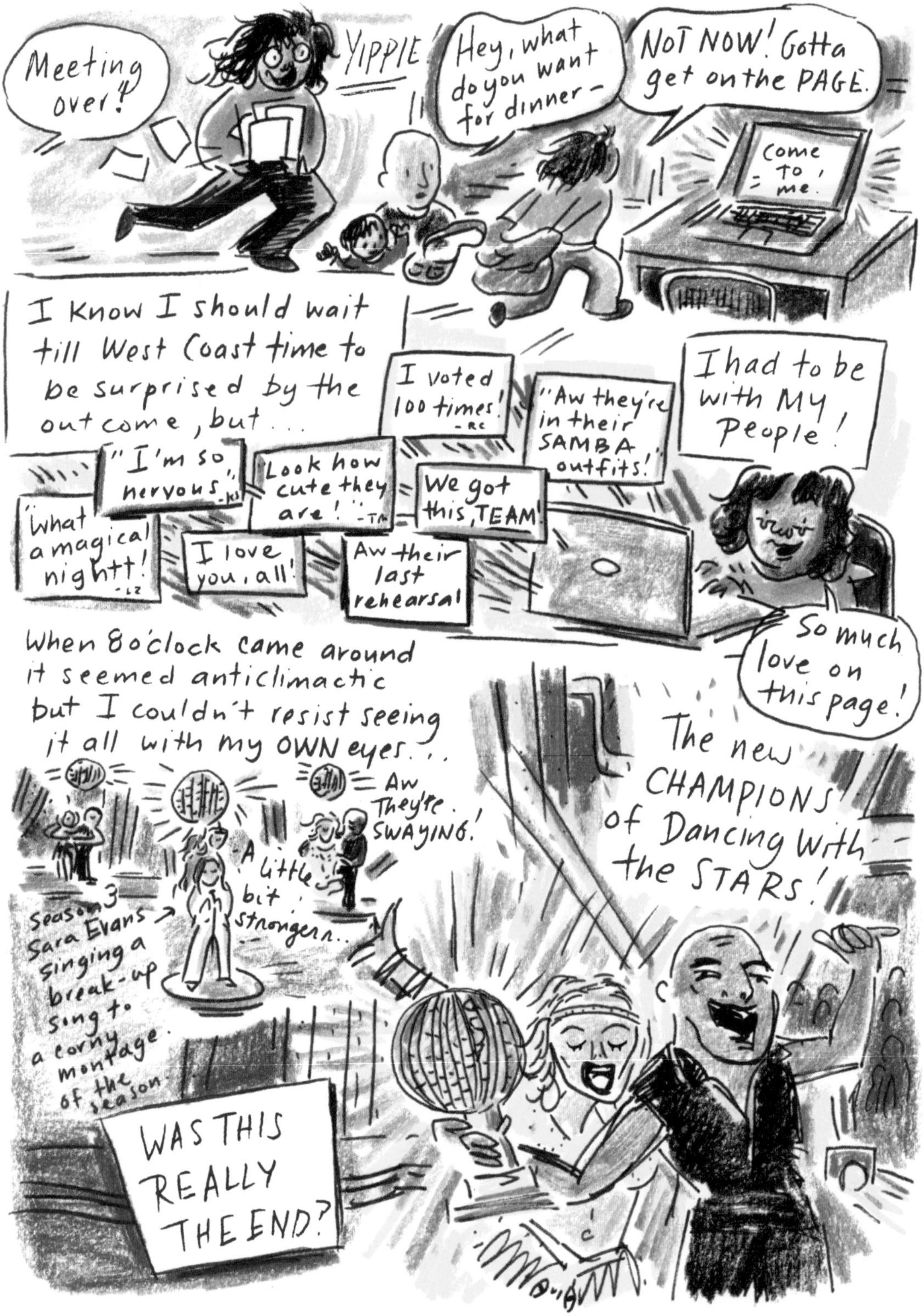

Meeting over!
YIPPIE
Hey, what do you want for dinner –
NOT NOW! Gotta get on the PAGE.
come to me.
I know I should wait till West Coast time to be surprised by the outcome, but...
"I'm so nervous" -KS
"What a magical nightt!" -LZ
Look how cute they are!" -TM
I love you, all!
I voted 100 times! -RC
We got this, TEAM!
Aw their last rehearsal
"Aw they're in their SAMBA outfits!"
I had to be with MY people!
So much love on this page!
When 8 o'clock came around it seemed anticlimactic but I couldn't resist seeing it all with my OWN eyes...
Aw They're SWAYING!
A little bit strongerrr...
Season 3 Sara Evans singing a break-up song to a corny montage of the season.
The new CHAMPIONS of Dancing with the STARS!
WAS THIS REALLY THE END?

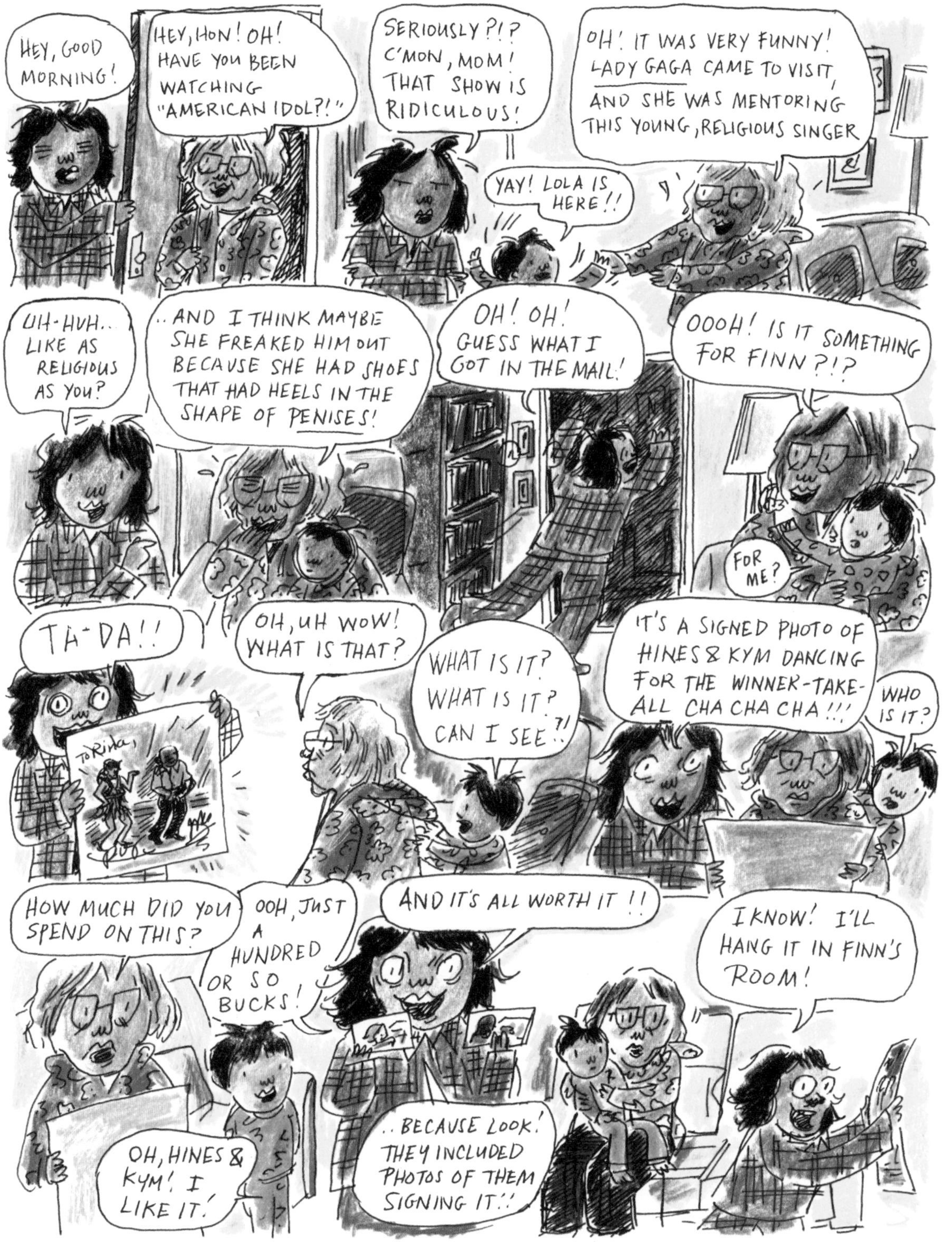
HEY, GOOD MORNING!
HEY, HON! OH! HAVE YOU BEEN WATCHING "AMERICAN IDOL?!"
SERIOUSLY?!? C'MON, MOM! THAT SHOW IS RIDICULOUS!
OH! IT WAS VERY FUNNY! LADY GAGA CAME TO VISIT, AND SHE WAS MENTORING THIS YOUNG, RELIGIOUS SINGER
YAY! LOLA IS HERE!!
UH-HUH.. LIKE AS RELIGIOUS AS YOU?
..AND I THINK MAYBE SHE FREAKED HIM OUT BECAUSE SHE HAD SHOES THAT HAD HEELS IN THE SHAPE OF PENISES!
OH! OH! GUESS WHAT I GOT IN THE MAIL!
OOOH! IS IT SOMETHING FOR FINN?!?
FOR ME?
TA-DA!!
TO RINA,
OH, UH WOW! WHAT IS THAT?
WHAT IS IT? WHAT IS IT? CAN I SEE?!
IT'S A SIGNED PHOTO OF HINES & KYM DANCING FOR THE WINNER-TAKE-ALL CHA CHA CHA!!!
WHO IS IT?
HOW MUCH DID YOU SPEND ON THIS?
OOH, JUST A HUNDRED OR SO BUCKS!
OH, HINES & KYM! I LIKE IT!
AND IT'S ALL WORTH IT!!
..BECAUSE LOOK! THEY INCLUDED PHOTOS OF THEM SIGNING IT!!
I KNOW! I'LL HANG IT IN FINN'S ROOM!

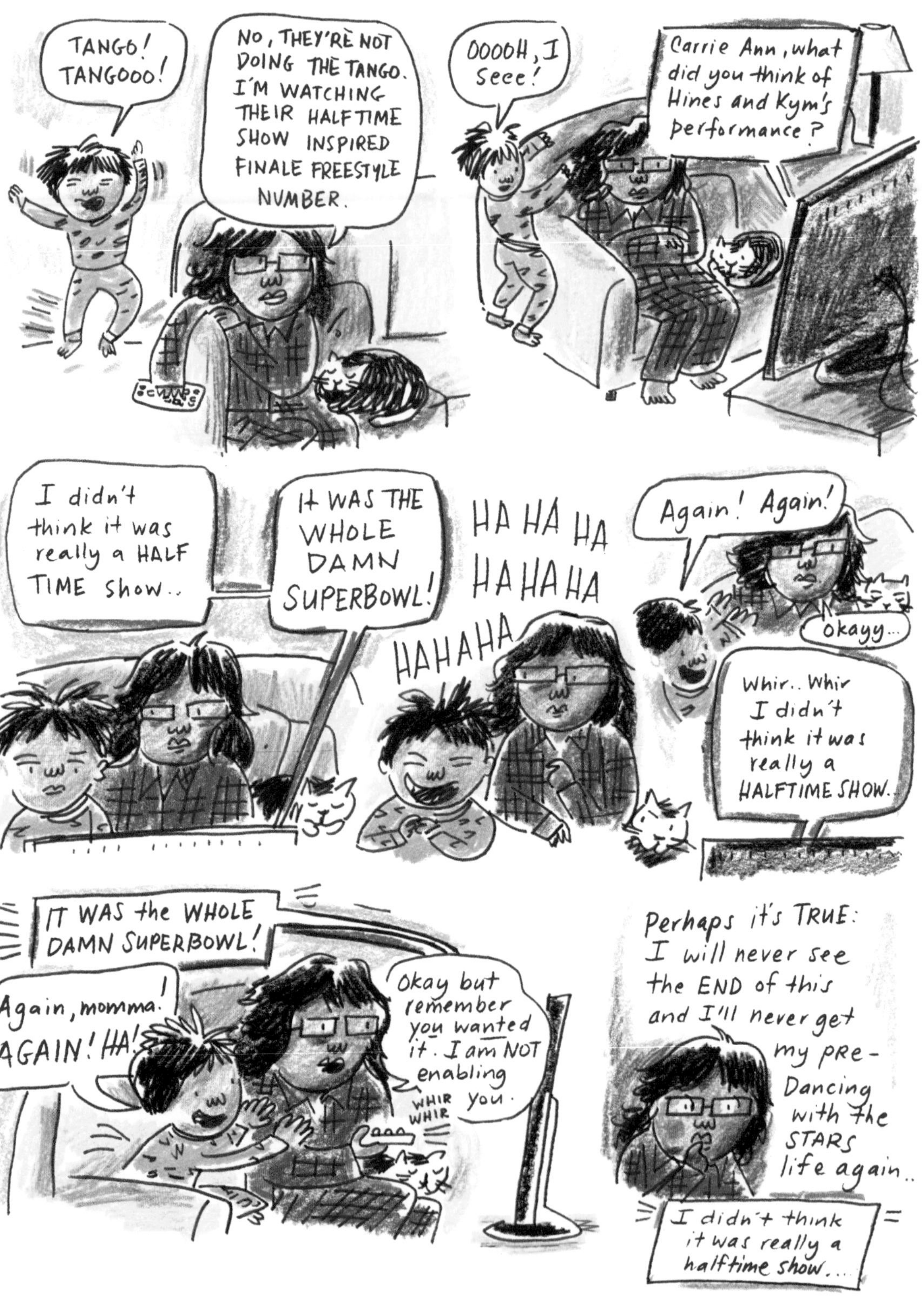
TANGO! TANGOOO!
NO, THEY'RE NOT DOING THE TANGO. I'M WATCHING THEIR HALFTIME SHOW INSPIRED FINALE FREESTYLE NUMBER.
OOOOH, I Seee!
Carrie Ann, what did you think of Hines and Kym's performance?
I didn't think it was really a HALF TIME show..
It WAS THE WHOLE DAMN SUPERBOWL!
HA HA HA HAHAHA HAHAHA
Again! Again!
okayy...
Whir.. Whir I didn't think it was really a HALFTIME SHOW..
IT WAS the WHOLE DAMN SUPERBOWL!
Again, momma! AGAIN! HA!
Okay but remember you wanted it. I am NOT enabling you.
WHIR WHIR
Perhaps it's TRUE: I will never see the END of this and I'll never get my pre-Dancing with the STARS life again..
I didn't think it was really a halftime show...

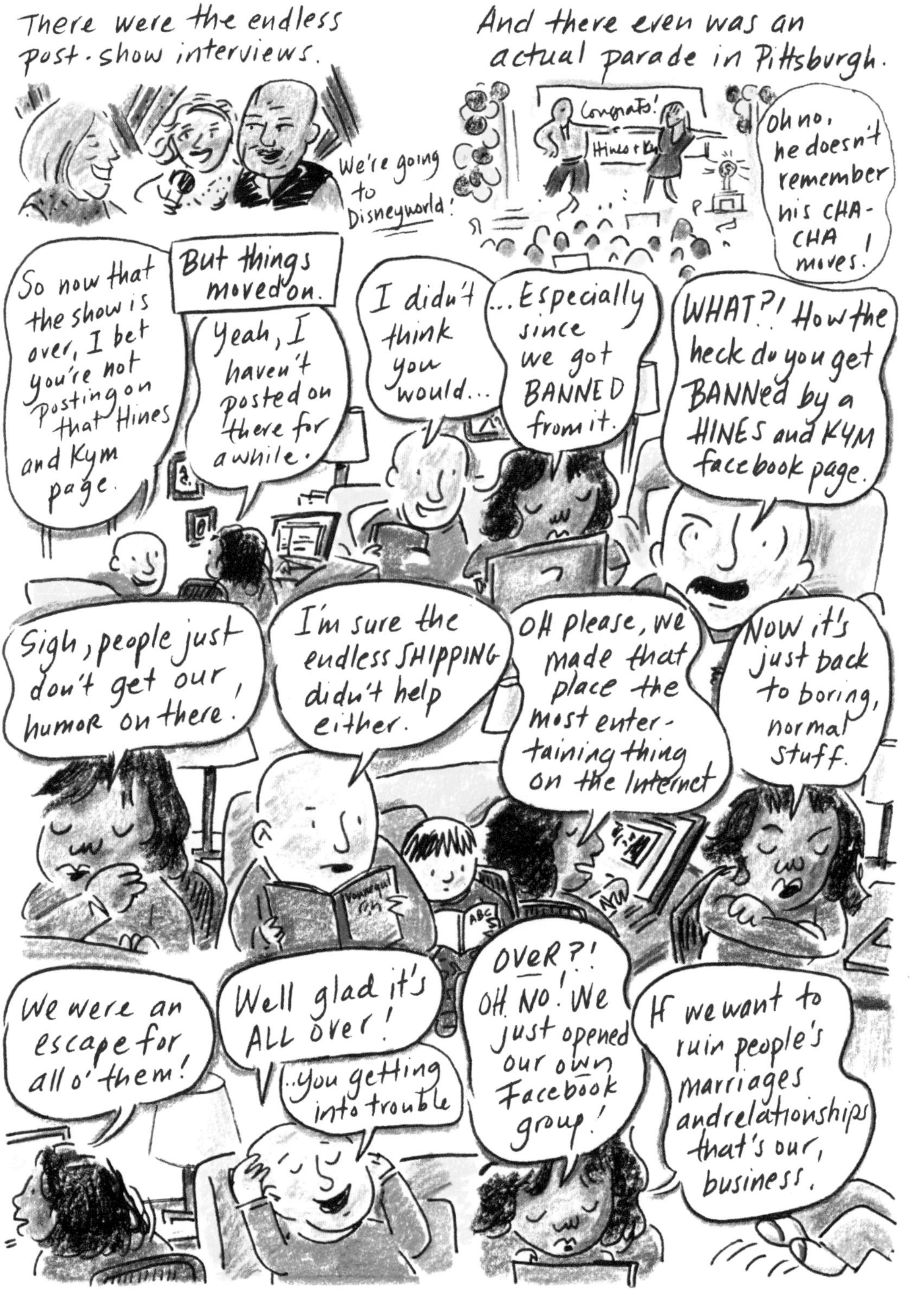
There were the endless post-show interviews.
We're going to Disneyworld!
And there even was an actual parade in Pittsburgh.
Congrats!
Oh no, he doesn't remember his CHA-CHA moves!
So now that the show is over, I bet you're not posting on that Hines and Kym page.
But things moved on.
Yeah, I haven't posted on there for a while.
I didn't think you would...
...Especially since we got BANNED from it.
WHAT?! How the heck do you get BANNED by a HINES and KYM facebook page.
Sigh, people just don't get our humor on there!
I'm sure the endless SHIPPING didn't help either.
OH please, we made that place the most entertaining thing on the Internet
Now it's just back to boring, normal stuff.
ABC
We were an escape for all o' them!
Well glad it's ALL over!
..You getting into trouble
OVER?! OH NO! We just opened our own Facebook group!
If we want to ruin people's marriages and relationships that's our business.

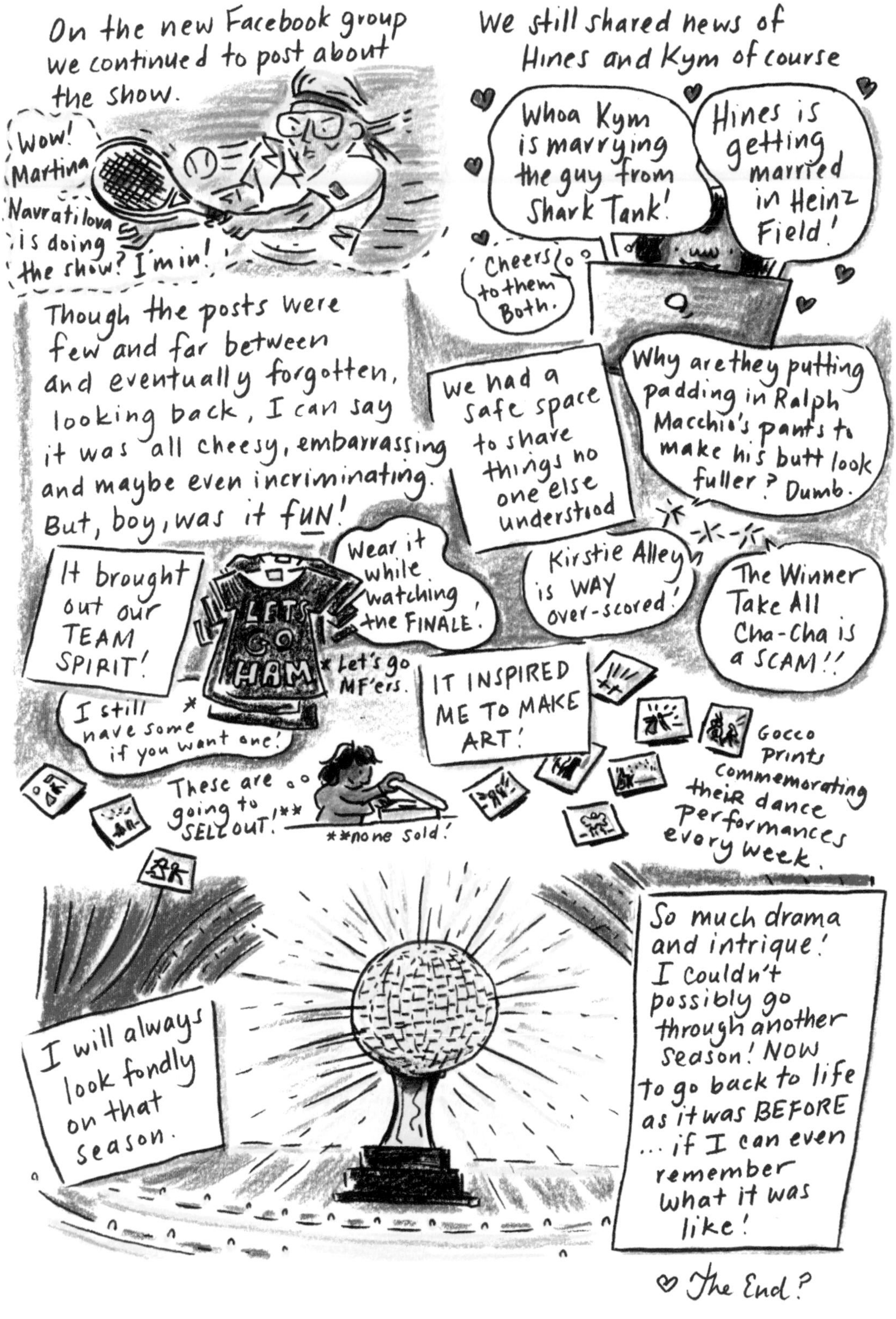
On the new Facebook group we continued to post about the show.
Wow! Martina Navratilova is doing the show? I'm in!
We still shared news of Hines and Kym of course
Whoa Kym is marrying the guy from Shark Tank!
Hines is getting married in Heinz Field!
Cheers to them Both.
Though the posts were few and far between and eventually forgotten, looking back, I can say it was all cheesy, embarrassing and maybe even incriminating. But, boy, was it FUN!
We had a safe space to share things no one else understood
Why are they putting padding in Ralph Macchio's pants to make his butt look fuller? Dumb.
Kirstie Alley is WAY over-scored!
The Winner Take All Cha-Cha is a SCAM!!
It brought out our TEAM SPIRIT!
LETS GO HAM
*Let's go MF'ers.
Wear it while watching the FINALE!
I still have some if you want one!
IT INSPIRED ME TO MAKE ART!
These are going to SELL OUT!**
**none sold!
Gocco Prints commemorating their dance performances every week.
I will always look fondly on that season.
So much drama and intrigue! I couldn't possibly go through another season! NOW to go back to life as it was BEFORE ... if I can even remember what it was like!
The End?

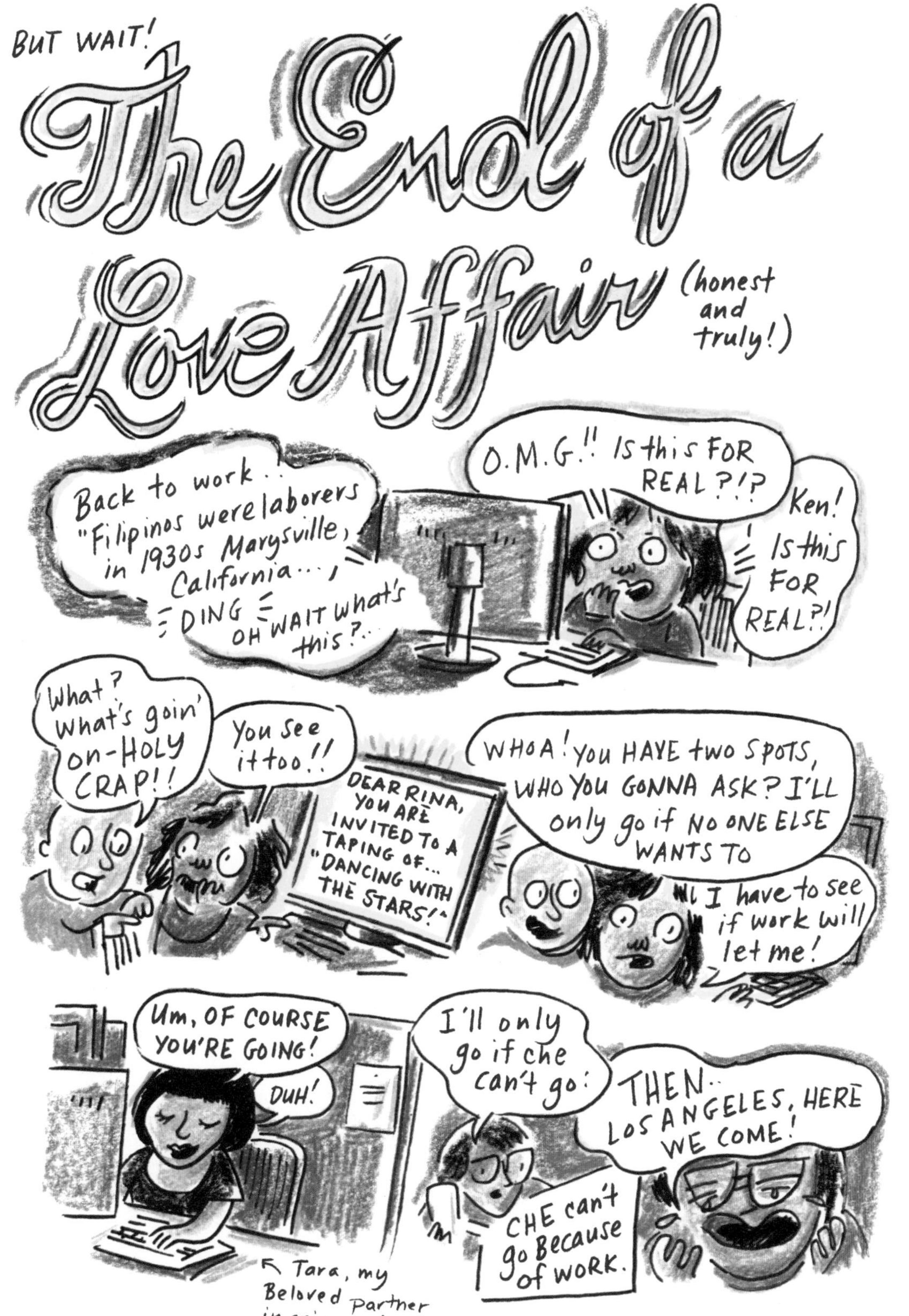
BUT WAIT!
The End of a Love Affair
(honest and truly!)
Back to work.. "Filipinos were laborers in 1930s Marysville, California...,
DING
OH WAIT what's this?..
O.M.G!! Is this FOR REAL?!?
Ken! Is this FOR REAL?!
What? What's goin' on-HOLY CRAP!!
You see it too!!
DEAR RINA, YOU ARE INVITED TO A TAPING OF... "DANCING WITH THE STARS!"
WHOA! You HAVE two SPOTS, WHO YOU GONNA ASK? I'LL only go if NO ONE ELSE WANTS TO
I have to see if work will let me!
Um, OF COURSE YOU'RE GOING!
DUH!
Tara, my Beloved partner in crime at work.
I'll only go if Che can't go.
THEN.. LOS ANGELES, HERE WE COME!
CHE can't go Because of WORK.

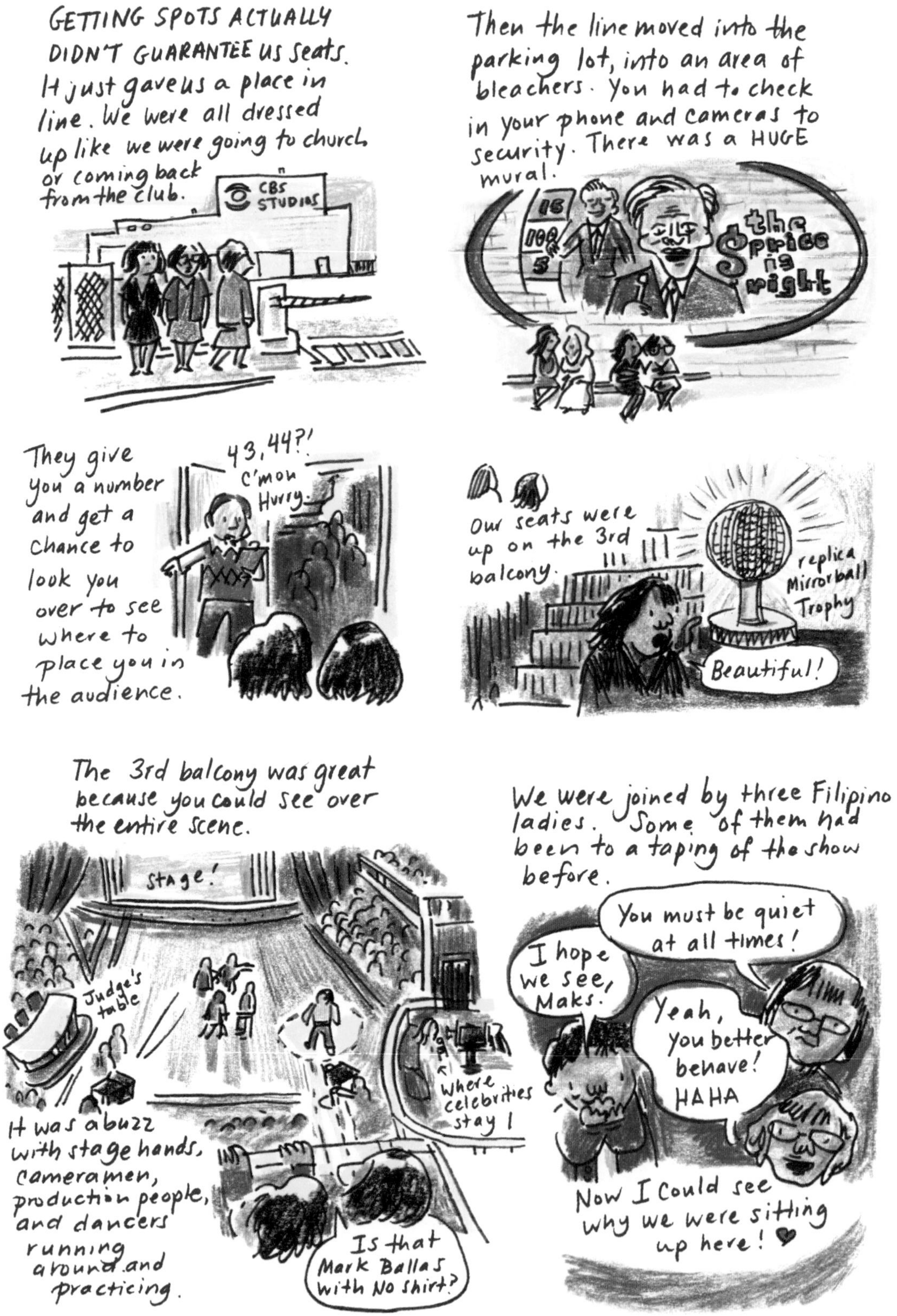
GETTING SPOTS ACTUALLY DIDN'T GUARANTEE US Seats. It just gave us a place in line. We were all dressed up like we were going to church or coming back from the club.
CBS STUDIOS
Then the line moved into the parking lot, into an area of bleachers. You had to check in your phone and cameras to security. There was a HUGE mural.
the price is right
They give you a number and get a chance to look you over to see where to place you in the audience.
43, 44?! C'mon Hurry.
Our seats were up on the 3rd balcony.
replica Mirrorball Trophy
Beautiful!
The 3rd balcony was great because you could see over the entire scene.
stage!
Judge's table
where celebrities stay!
It was abuzz with stage hands, cameramen, production people, and dancers running around and practicing.
Is that Mark Ballas with No shirt?
We were joined by three Filipino ladies. Some of them had been to a taping of the show before.
You must be quiet at all times!
I hope we see, Maks.
Yeah, you better behave! HAHA
Now I could see why we were sitting up here!

Then a guy came out for final instructions and to work the crowd, and then the countdown began. It became silent.

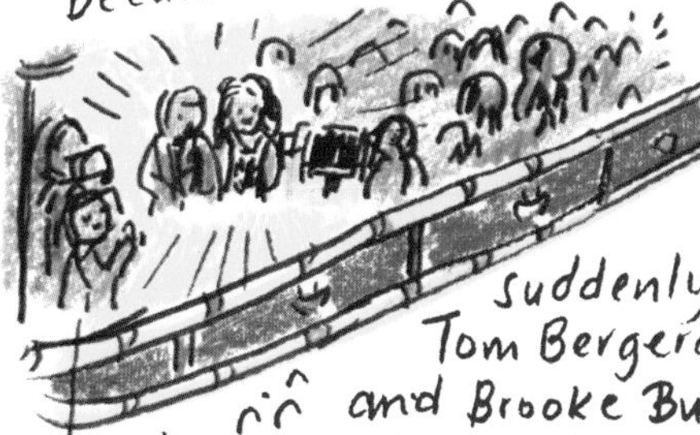

suddenly Tom Bergeron and Brooke Burke are on the 1st balcony, but you can't hear what they're saying

don't look directly into the camera.

The 3 judges come out to "Sexy and I know it." Carrie Ann waves to crowd, Len glides across the floor and Bruno, of course, is hamming it up.

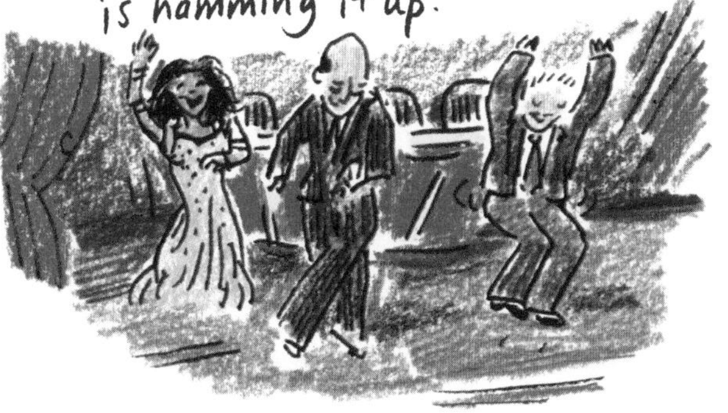

We can only really hear the music, No dialogue because it's on another audio track to better control for flubs or accidental curse words.

The dance troupe is practicing the intro dance. Sasha Farber stretches his legs, does one last pirouette then leaves the stage! Amazing!

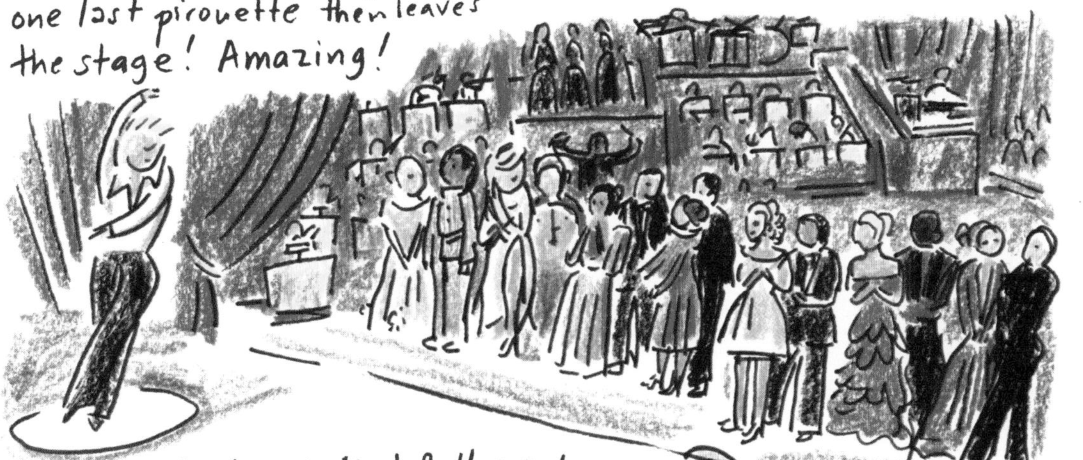

First up is Mark Ballos and opera singer Katherine Jenkins. I feel bad for them because they had to wait an awful long time to perform. They are dancing to Pachelbel's Canon in D Major.

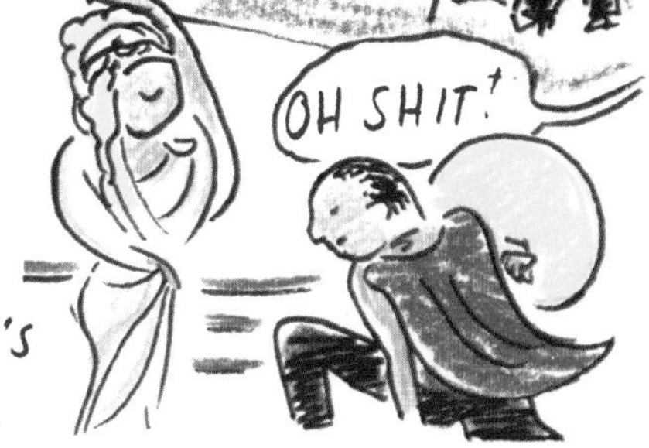
OH SHIT!

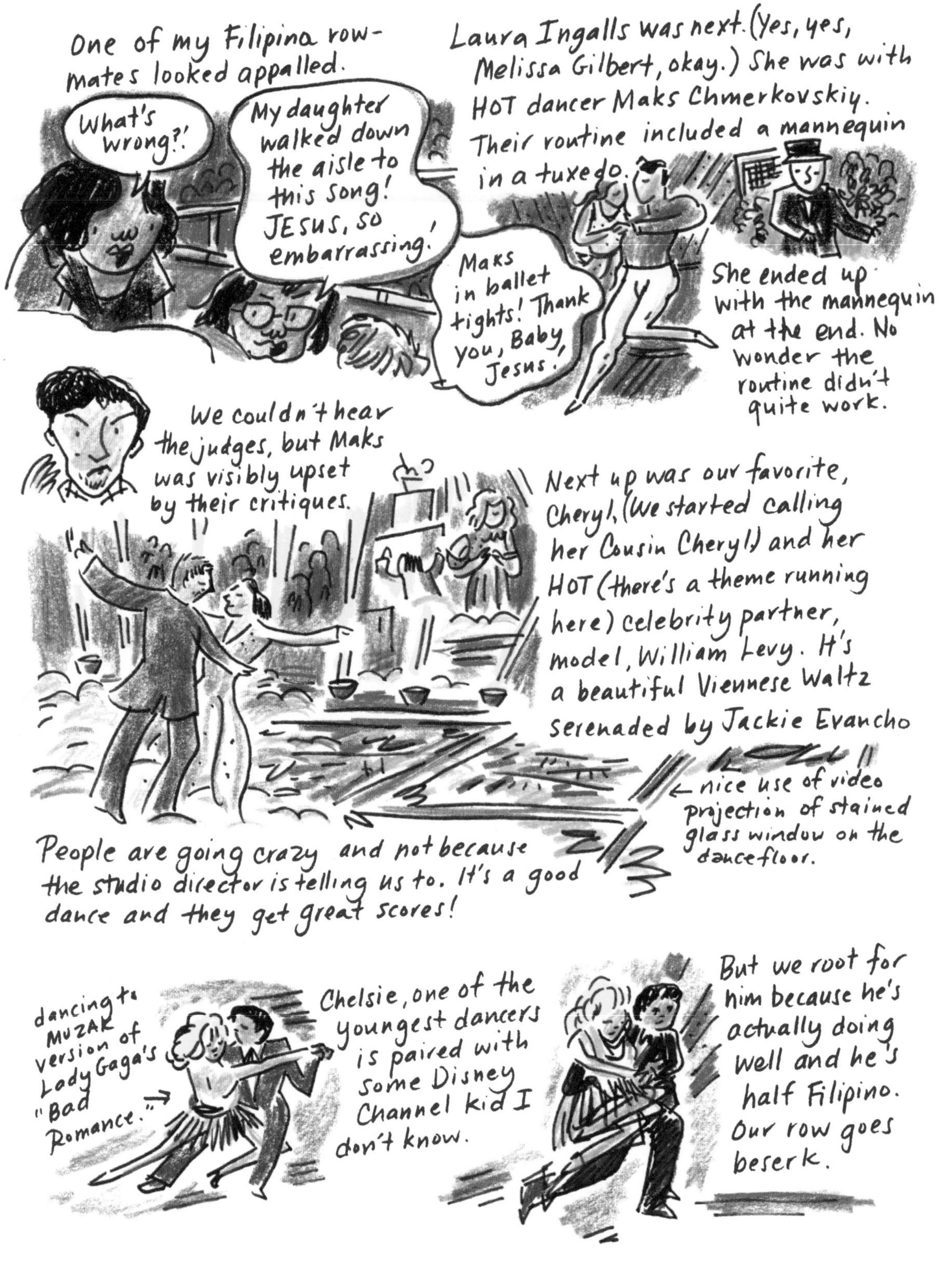
One of my Filipina row-mates looked appalled.
What's wrong?!
My daughter walked down the aisle to this song! JESUS, so embarrassing!
Laura Ingalls was next. (Yes, yes, Melissa Gilbert, okay.) She was with HOT dancer Maks Chmerkovskiy. Their routine included a mannequin in a tuxedo.
Maks in ballet tights! Thank you, Baby Jesus!
She ended up with the mannequin at the end. No wonder the routine didn't quite work.
We couldn't hear the judges, but Maks was visibly upset by their critiques.
Next up was our favorite, Cheryl, (We started calling her Cousin Cheryl) and her HOT (there's a theme running here) celebrity partner, model, William Levy. It's a beautiful Viennese Waltz serenaded by Jackie Evancho
← nice use of video projection of stained glass window on the dancefloor.
People are going crazy and not because the studio director is telling us to. It's a good dance and they get great scores!
dancing to MUZAK version of Lady Gaga's "Bad Romance." →
Chelsie, one of the youngest dancers is paired with some Disney Channel kid I don't know.
But we root for him because he's actually doing well and he's half Filipino. Our row goes beserk.

Between each dance, the remaining couples would practice. You could see the "Skybox" where all the couples are interviewed and can see all the dances. You also get to see backstage drama LIVE!

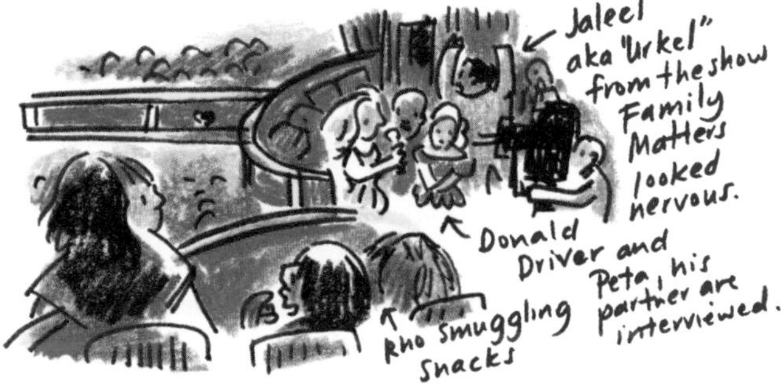
Jaleel aka "Urkel" from the show Family Matters looked nervous.
Donald Driver and Peta, his partner are interviewed.
Rho smuggling snacks

Eventually it's our awesome Kym Johnson and Urkel's turn with a Viennese Waltz. He's not as great as her and Hines's but it still looks amazing to me!

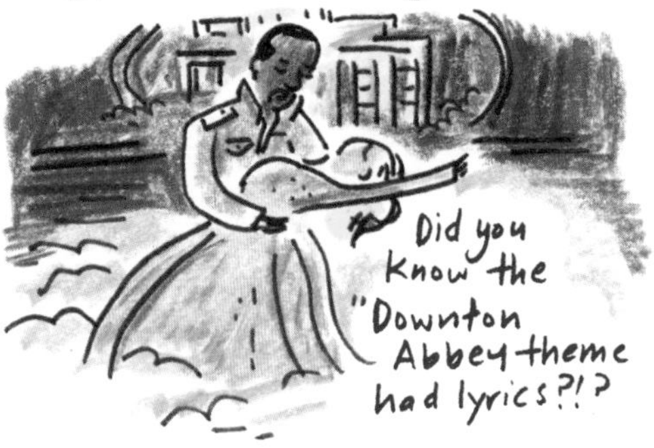
Did you know the "Downton Abbey theme had lyrics?!?

During the breaks, you see all the pro dancers and celebs trying to be relaxed. One time heartthrob Derek Hough, who is my sister's favorite, looked toward our general direction so naturally I had to take advantage of that.

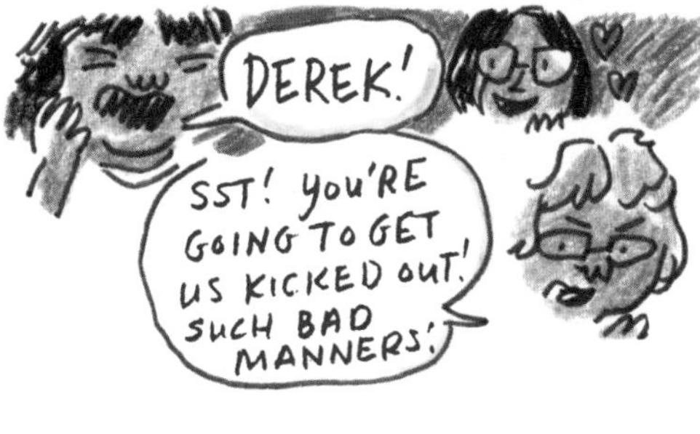
DEREK!
SST! YOU'RE GOING TO GET US KICKED OUT! SUCH BAD MANNERS!

The Filipina aunties' tune changed when Derek pointed at us professing his love for us back!

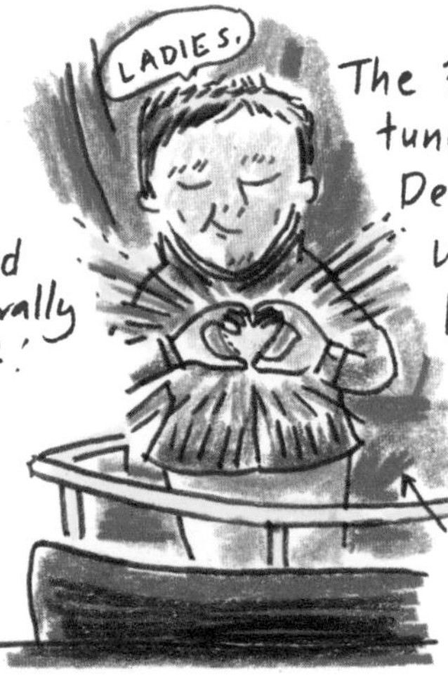
LADIES.
OOH! DEREK WE LOVE YOUU!!
in full Gothic costume for their vampire tango.

After all the main performances there was a team challenge. The team with the three guys with the most enormous pecs WON of course!

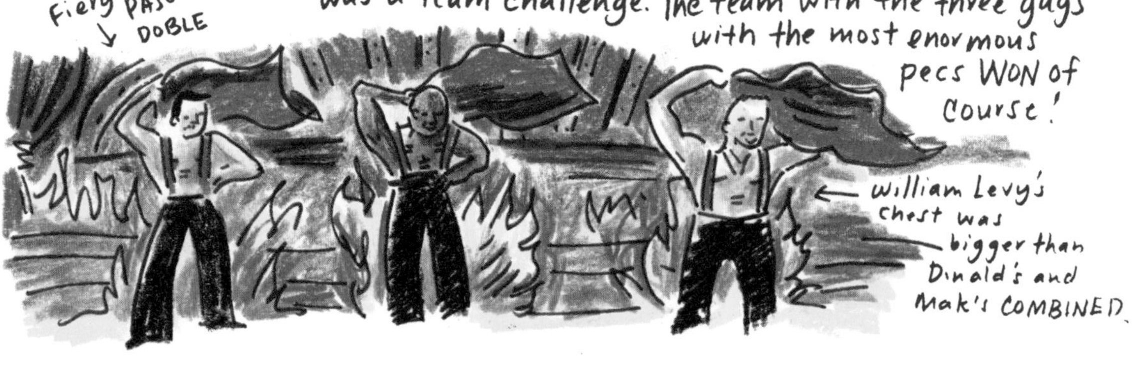
Fiery PASO DOBLE
William Levy's chest was bigger than Donald's and Mak's COMBINED.

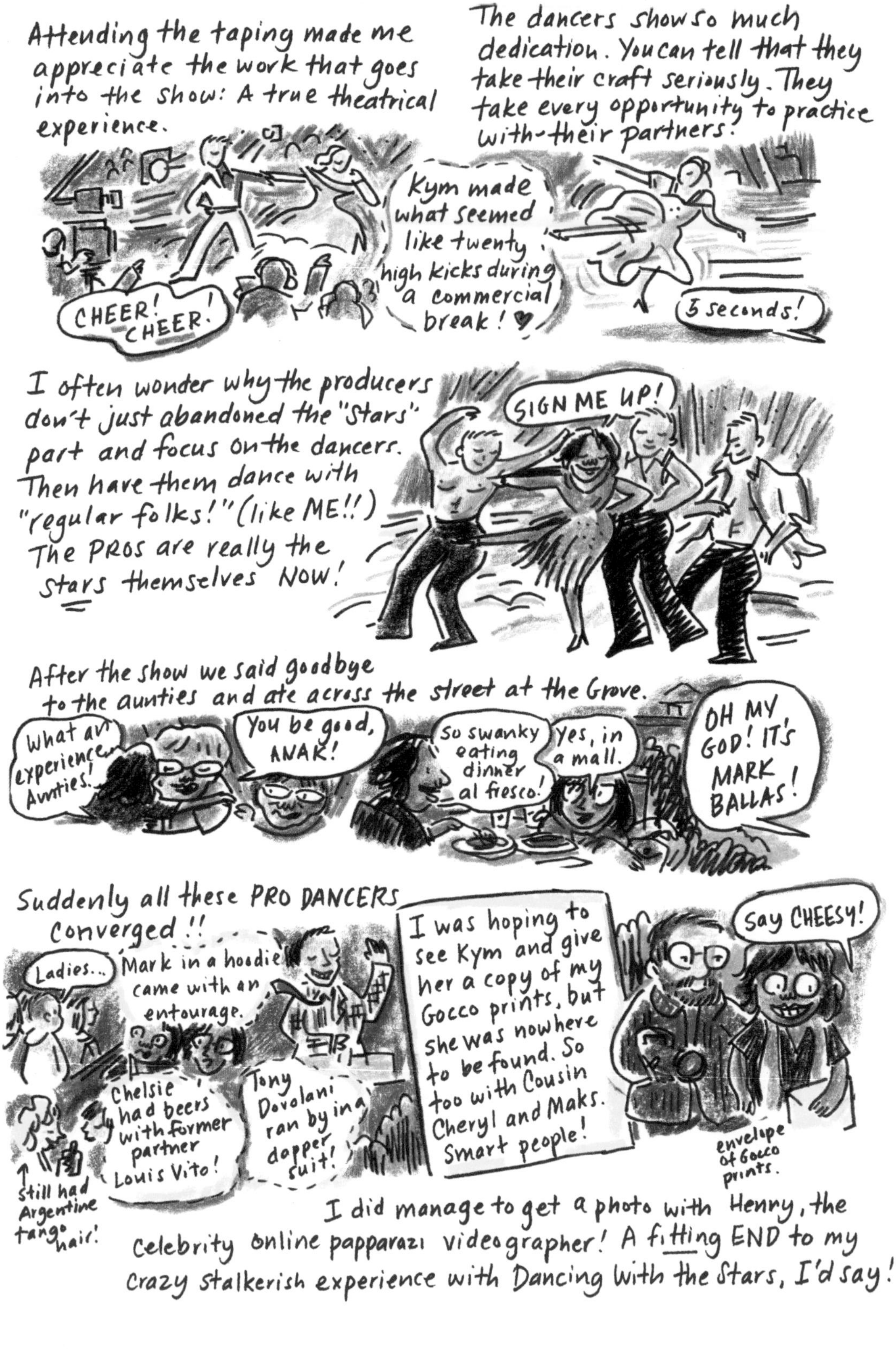
Attending the taping made me appreciate the work that goes into the show: A true theatrical experience.
CHEER! CHEER!
Kym made what seemed like twenty high kicks during a commercial break! ♥
The dancers show so much dedication. You can tell that they take their craft seriously. They take every opportunity to practice with their partners.
5 seconds!
I often wonder why the producers don't just abandoned the "Stars" part and focus on the dancers. Then have them dance with "regular folks!" (like ME!!) The PROs are really the stars themselves NOW!
SIGN ME UP!
After the show we said goodbye to the aunties and ate across the street at the Grove.
What an experience, Aunties!
You be good, ANAK!
So swanky eating dinner al fresco!
Yes, in a mall.
OH MY GOD! IT'S MARK BALLAS!
Suddenly all these PRO DANCERS converged!!
Ladies...
Mark in a hoodie came with an entourage.
still had Argentine tango hair!
Chelsie had beers with former partner Louis Vito!
Tony Dovolani ran by in a dapper suit!
I was hoping to see Kym and give her a copy of my Gocco prints, but she was nowhere to be found. So too with Cousin Cheryl and Maks. Smart people!
Say CHEESY!
envelope of Gocco prints.
I did manage to get a photo with Henry, the celebrity online papparazi videographer! A fitting END to my crazy stalkerish experience with Dancing with the Stars, I'd say!

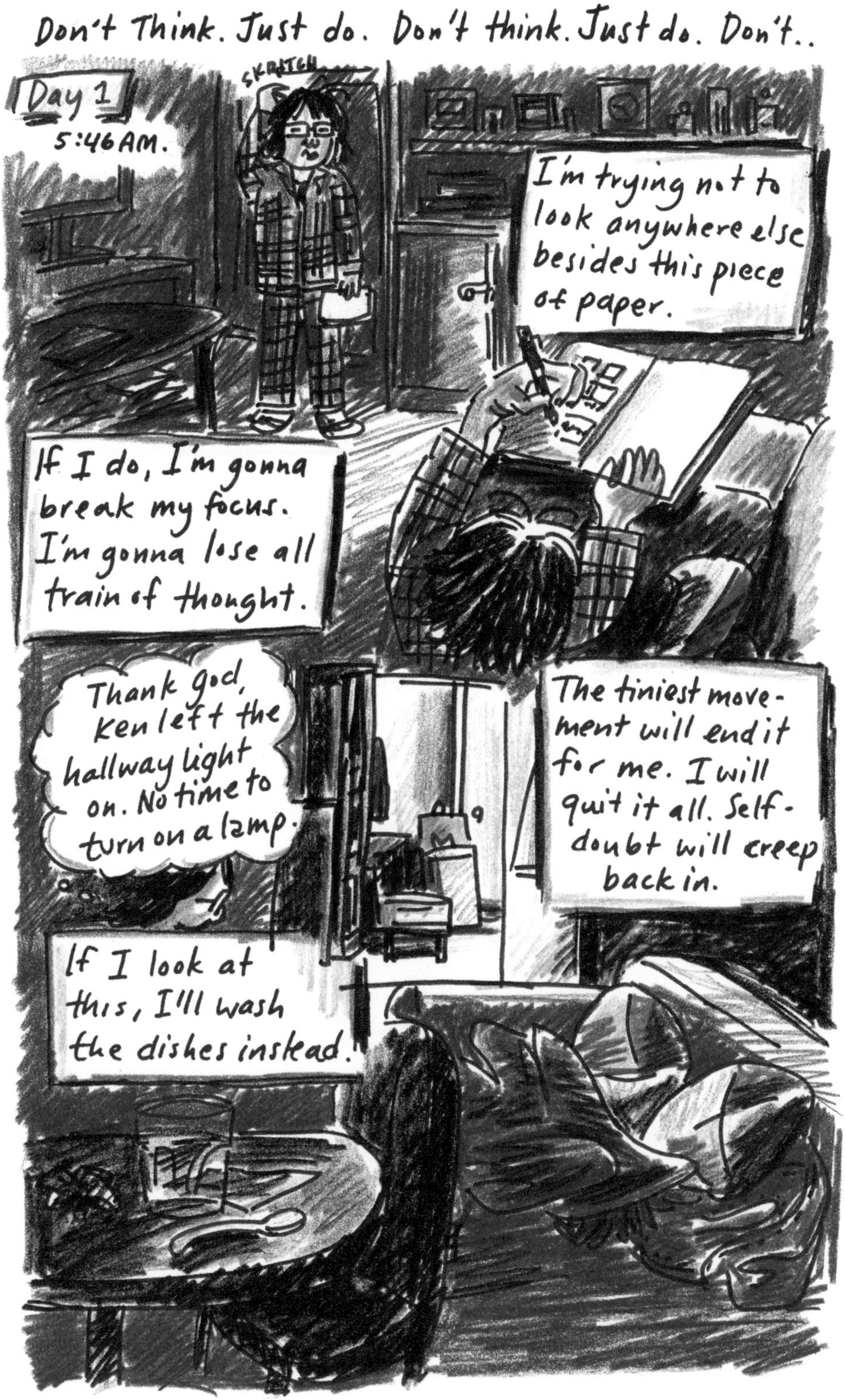
Don't Think. Just do. Don't think. Just do. Don't..
Day 1
5:46AM.
SKRATCH
I'm trying not to look anywhere else besides this piece of paper.
If I do, I'm gonna break my focus. I'm gonna lose all train of thought.
Thank god, Ken left the hallway light on. No time to turn on a lamp.
The tiniest movement will end it for me. I will quit it all. Self-doubt will creep back in.
If I look at this, I'll wash the dishes instead.

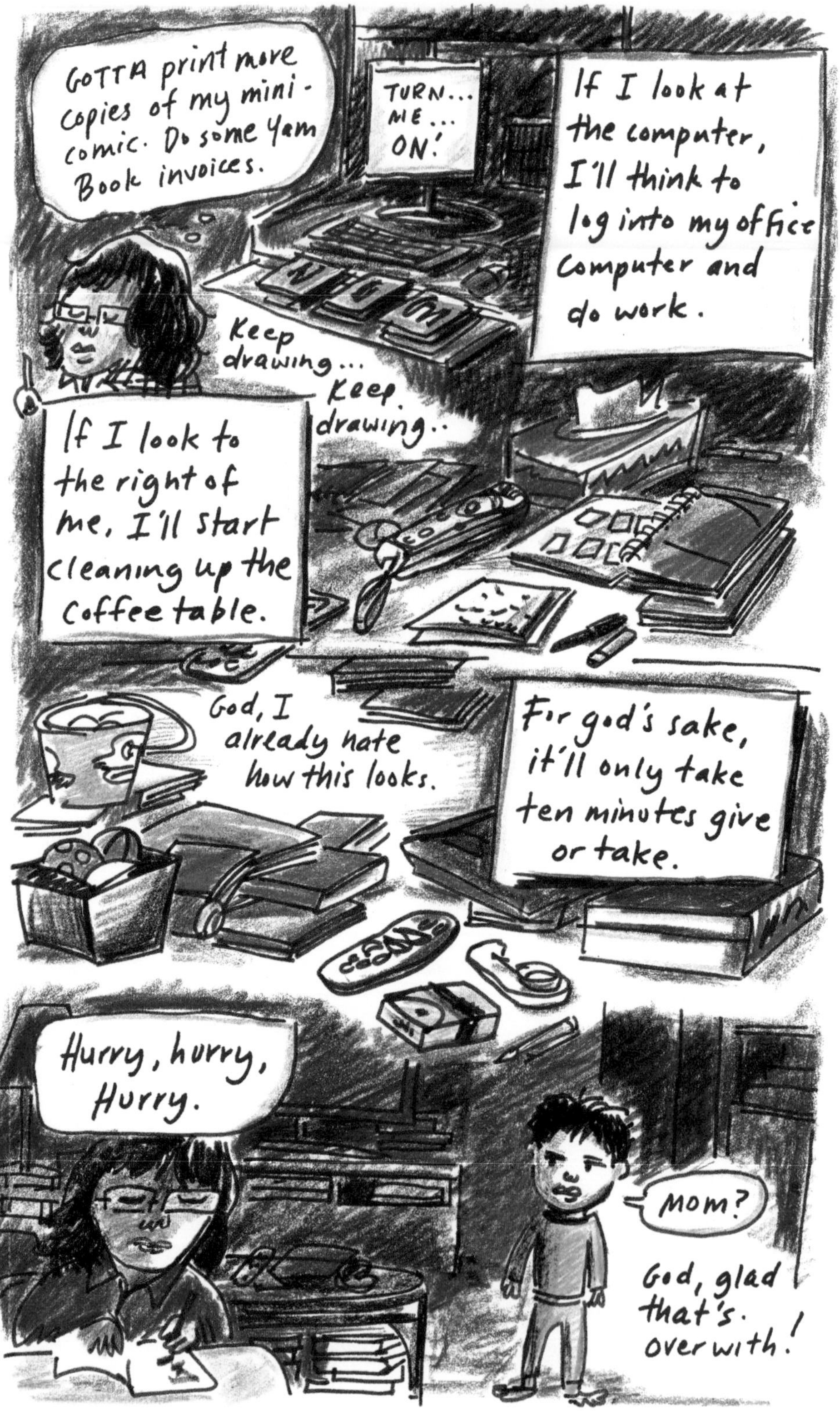
GOTTA print more copies of my mini-comic. Do some Yam Book invoices.
TURN... ME... ON!
If I look at the computer, I'll think to log into my office computer and do work.
Keep drawing...
Keep drawing..
If I look to the right of me, I'll start cleaning up the coffee table.
God, I already hate how this looks.
For god's sake, it'll only take ten minutes give or take.
Hurry, hurry, Hurry.
MOM?
God, glad that's over with!

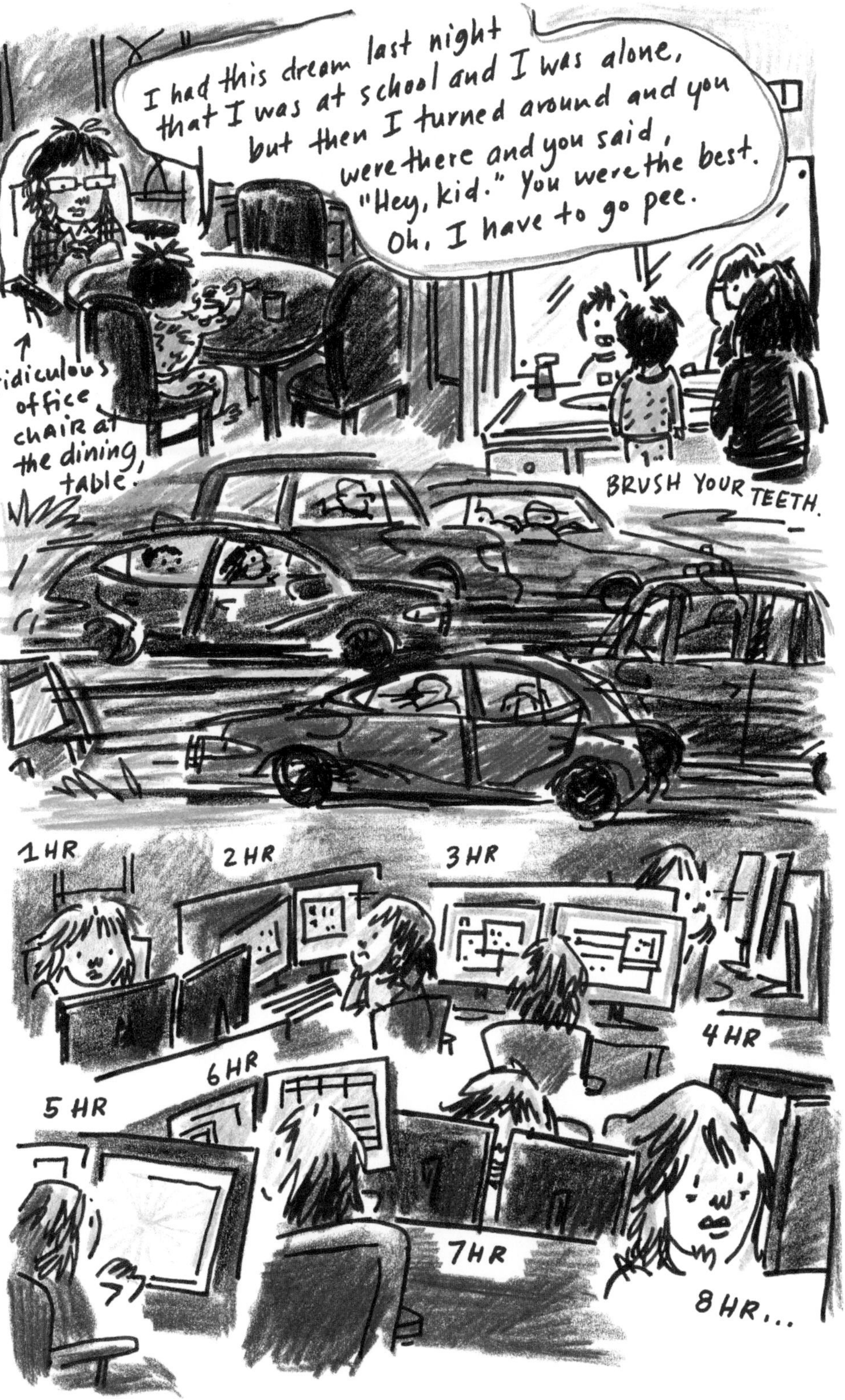
I had this dream last night that I was at school and I was alone, but then I turned around and you were there and you said, "Hey, kid." You were the best. Oh, I have to go pee.
ridiculous office chair at the dining table.
BRUSH YOUR TEETH.
1 HR
2 HR
3 HR
4 HR
5 HR
6 HR
7 HR
8 HR...

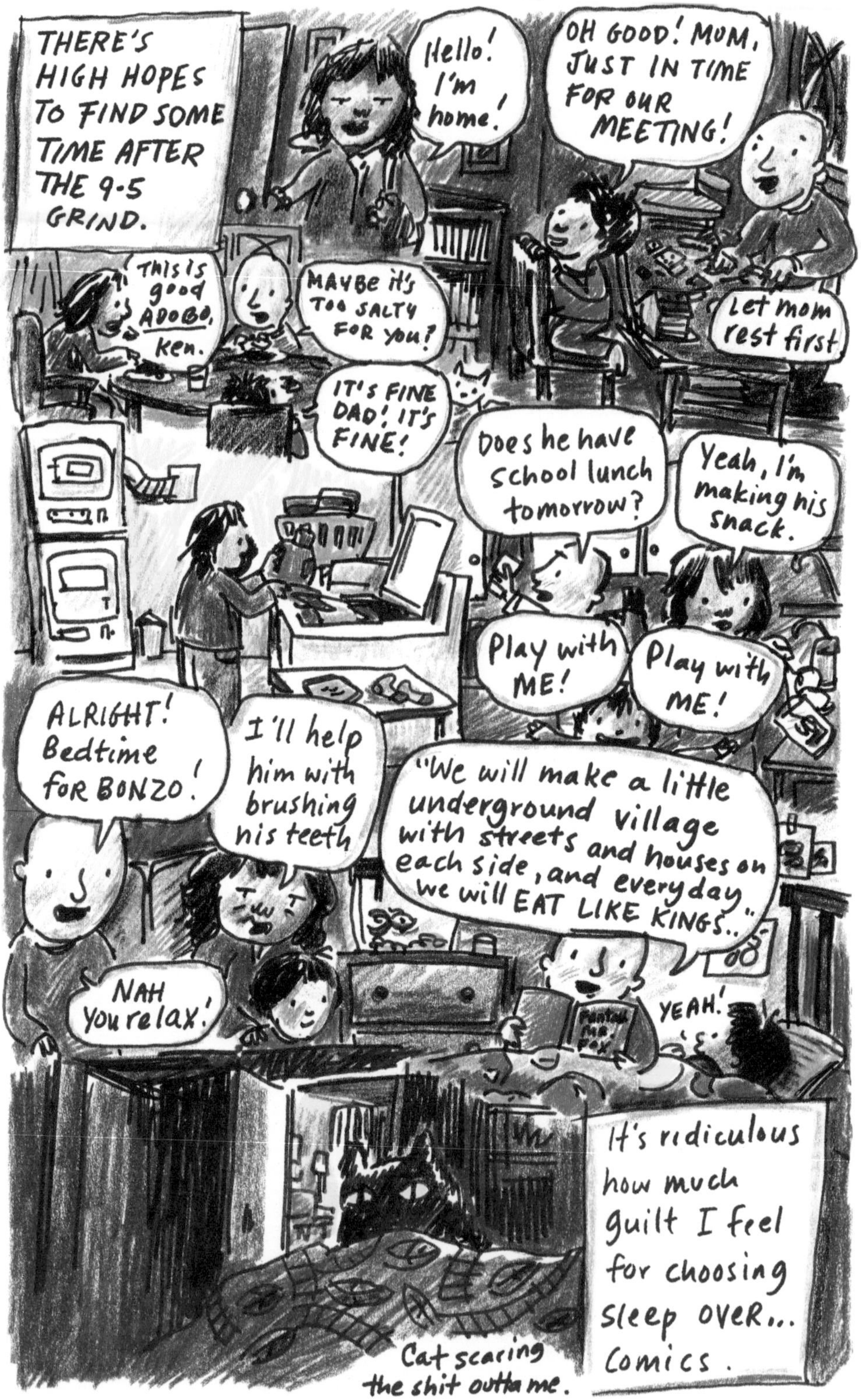

THERE'S HIGH HOPES TO FIND SOME TIME AFTER THE 9-5 GRIND.
Hello! I'm home!
OH GOOD! MUM, JUST IN TIME FOR OUR MEETING!
Let mom rest first
This is good ADOBO, Ken.
MAYBE it's TOO SALTY FOR you?
IT'S FINE DAD! IT'S FINE!
Does he have school lunch tomorrow?
Yeah, I'm making his snack.
Play with ME!
Play with ME!
ALRIGHT! Bedtime FOR BONZO!
I'll help him with brushing his teeth
NAH you relax!
"We will make a little underground village with streets and houses on each side, and everyday we will EAT LIKE KINGS..."
YEAH!
Cat scaring the shit outta me.
It's ridiculous how much guilt I feel for choosing sleep over... comics.

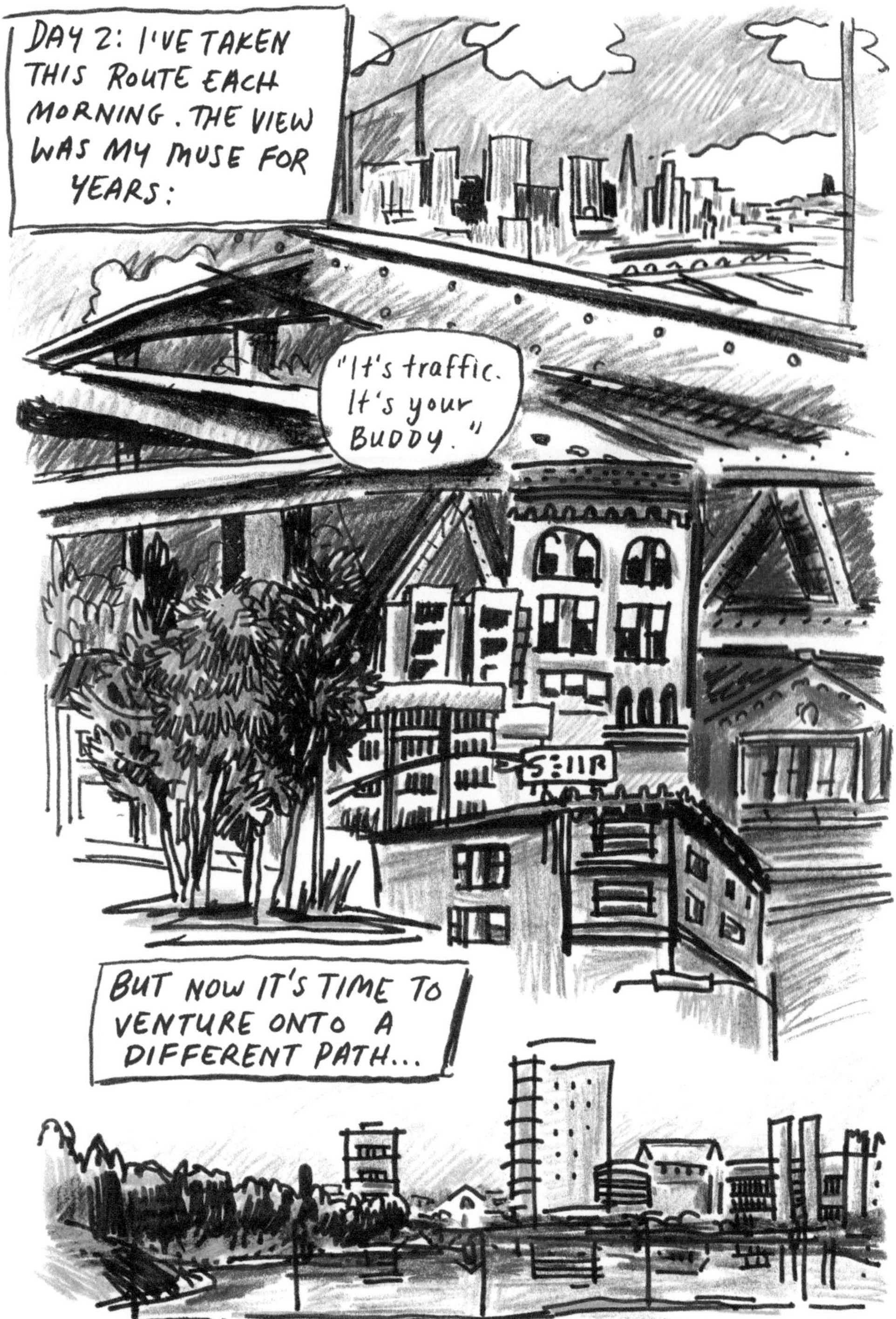
DAY 2: I'VE TAKEN THIS ROUTE EACH MORNING. THE VIEW WAS MY MUSE FOR YEARS:
"It's traffic. It's your BUDDY."
BUT NOW IT'S TIME TO VENTURE ONTO A DIFFERENT PATH...

TO FIND INSPIRATION IN NEW PLACES.

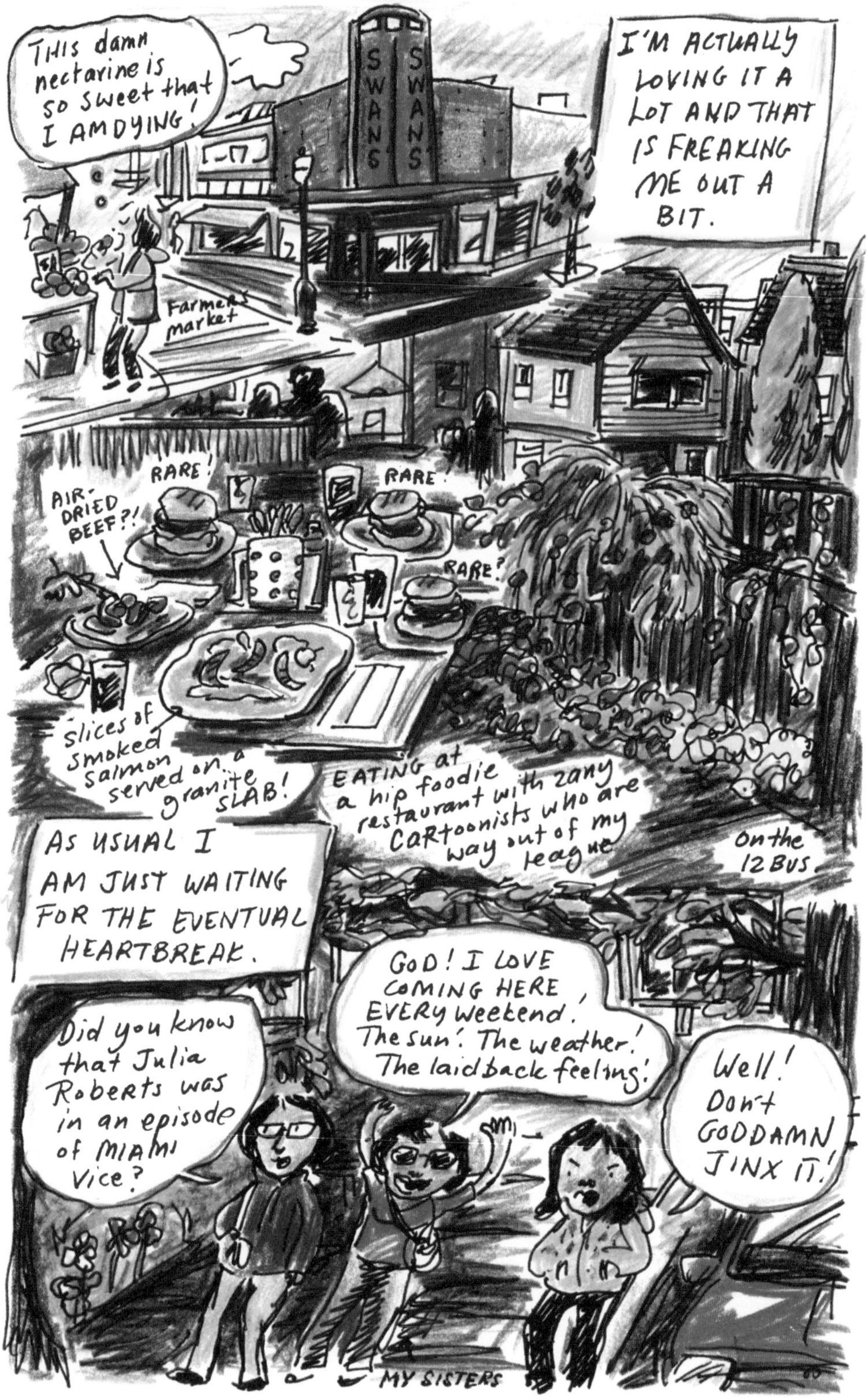
THIS damn nectarine is so sweet that I AMDYING!
SWANS
SWANS
I'M ACTUALLY LOVING IT A LOT AND THAT IS FREAKING ME OUT A BIT.
Farmers market
AIR-DRIED BEEF?!
RARE!
RARE
RARE?
slices of smoked salmon served on a granite SLAB!
EATING at a hip foodie restaurant with zany CARtoonists who are way out of my league
AS USUAL I AM JUST WAITING FOR THE EVENTUAL HEARTBREAK.
On the 12 BUS
Did you know that Julia Roberts was in an episode of MIAMI Vice?
GOD! I LOVE COMING HERE, EVERY weekend! The sun! The weather! The laidback feeling!
Well! Don't GODDAMN JINX IT!
MY SISTERS

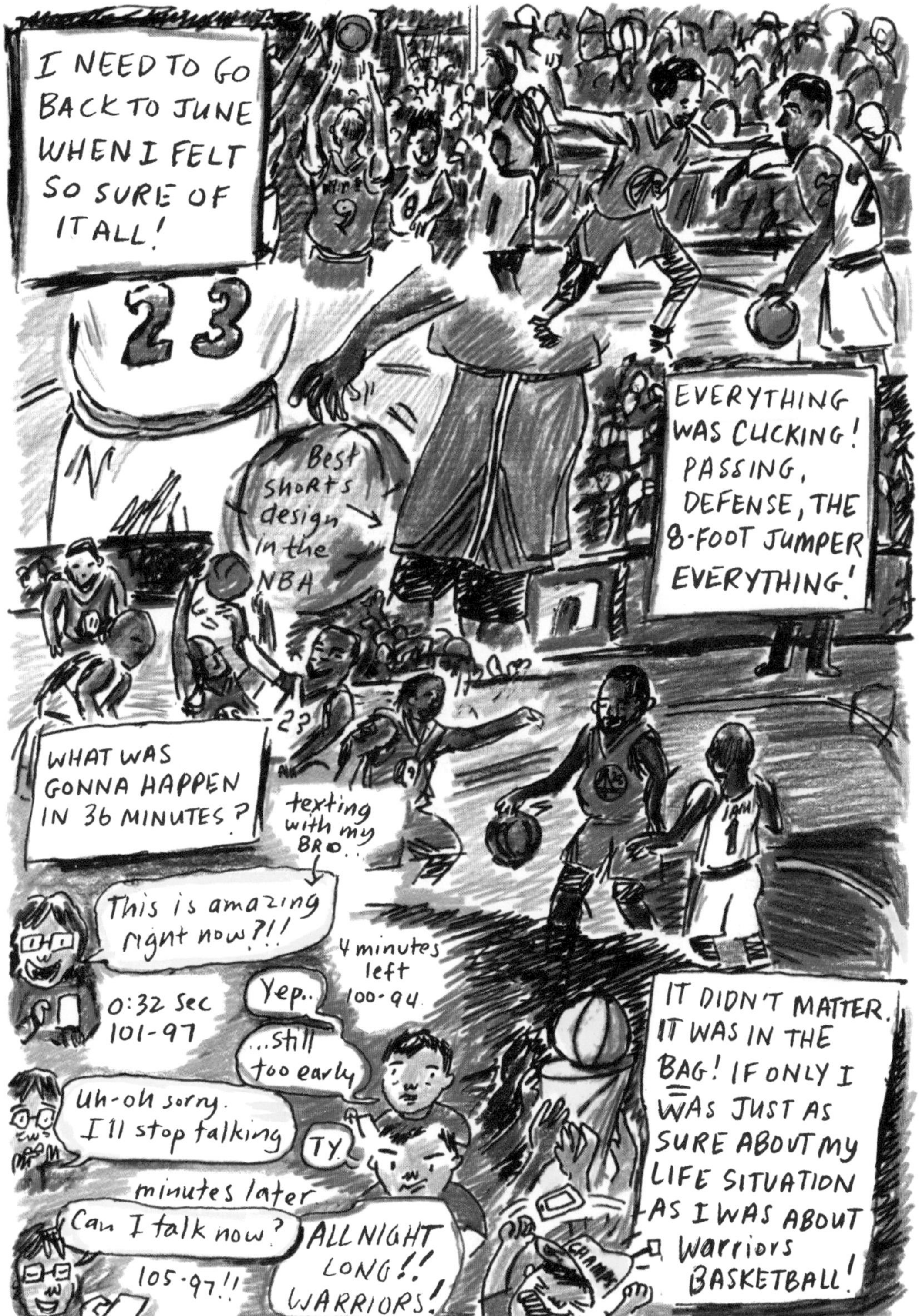

I NEED TO GO BACK TO JUNE WHEN I FELT SO SURE OF IT ALL!
23
Best shorts design in the NBA
EVERYTHING WAS CLICKING! PASSING, DEFENSE, THE 8-FOOT JUMPER EVERYTHING!
WHAT WAS GONNA HAPPEN IN 36 MINUTES?
texting with my BRO..
This is amazing right now?!!
4 minutes left 100-94
0:32 sec 101-97
Yep..
...still too early
Uh-oh sorry. I'll stop talking
TY.
minutes later
Can I talk now?
105-97!!
ALL NIGHT LONG!! WARRIORS!
IT DIDN'T MATTER. IT WAS IN THE BAG! IF ONLY I WAS JUST AS SURE ABOUT MY LIFE SITUATION AS I WAS ABOUT Warriors BASKETBALL!

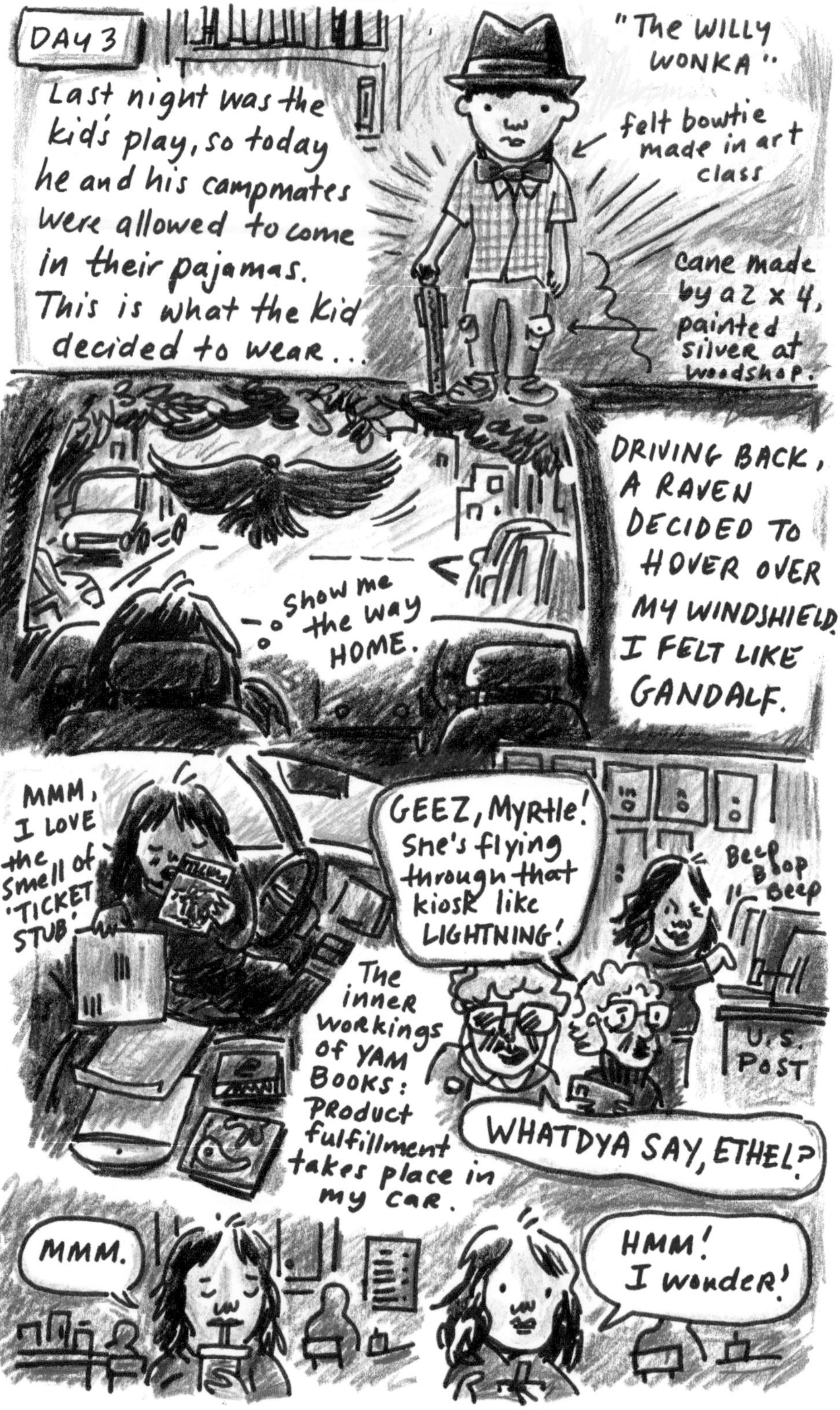
DAY 3
Last night was the kid's play, so today he and his campmates were allowed to come in their pajamas. This is what the kid decided to wear...
"The WILLY WONKA"
felt bowtie made in art class
cane made by a 2 x 4, painted silver at woodshop.
DRIVING BACK, A RAVEN DECIDED TO HOVER OVER MY WINDSHIELD. I FELT LIKE GANDALF.
Show me the way HOME.
MMM, I LOVE the smell of 'TICKET STUB'!
GEEZ, Myrtle! She's flying through that kiosk like LIGHTNING!
Beep Boop Beep
The inner workings of YAM BOOKS: Product fulfillment takes place in my car.
U.S. POST
WHATDYA SAY, ETHEL?
MMM.
HMM! I wonder!

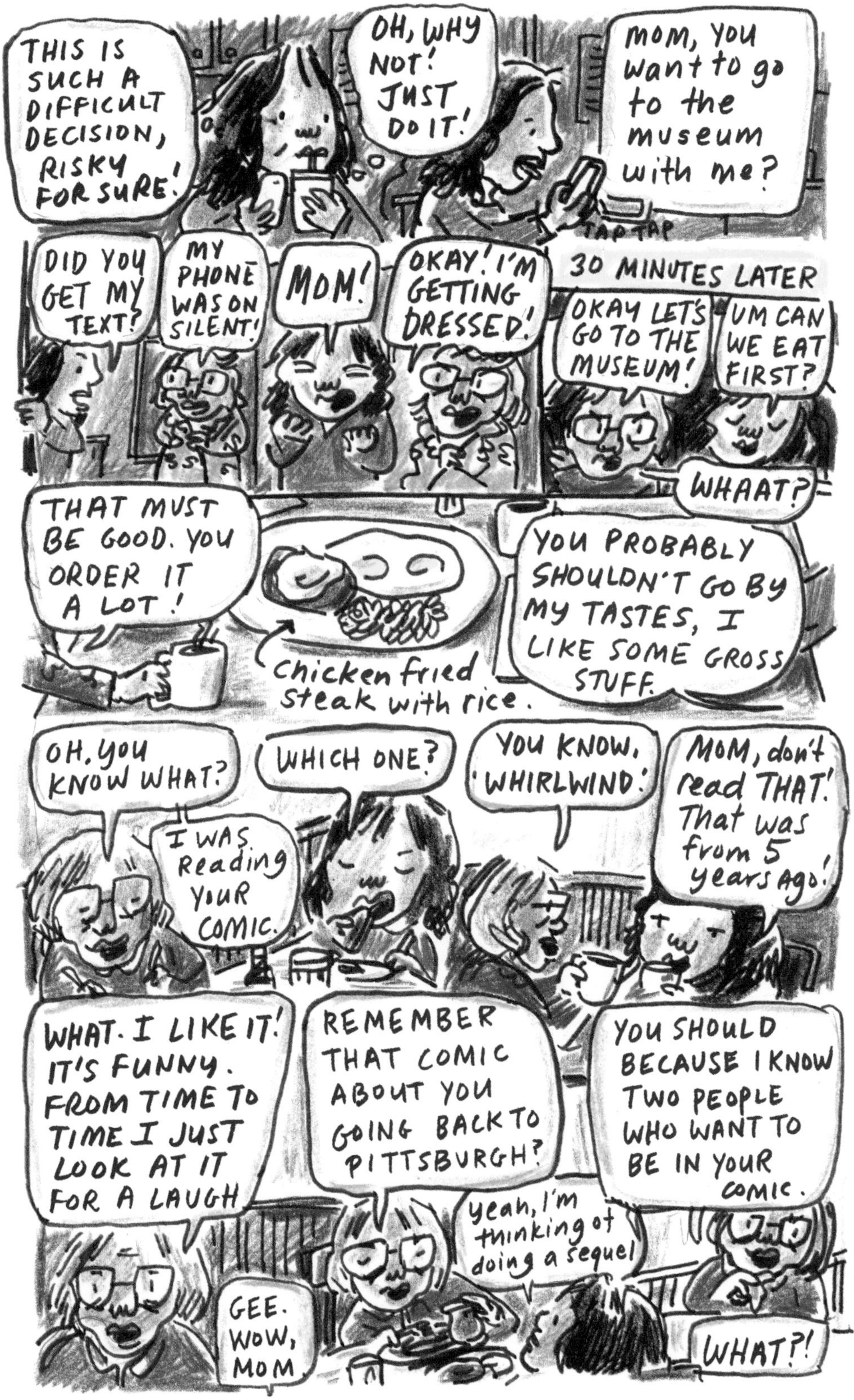
THIS IS SUCH A DIFFICULT DECISION, RISKY FOR SURE!
OH, WHY NOT! JUST DO IT!
MOM, YOU want to go to the museum with me?
TAP TAP
DID YOU GET MY TEXT?
MY PHONE WAS ON SILENT!
MOM!
OKAY! I'M GETTING DRESSED!
30 MINUTES LATER
OKAY LET'S GO TO THE MUSEUM!
UM CAN WE EAT FIRST?
WHAAT?
THAT MUST BE GOOD. YOU ORDER IT A LOT!
Chicken fried steak with rice.
YOU PROBABLY SHOULDN'T GO BY MY TASTES, I LIKE SOME GROSS STUFF.
OH, YOU KNOW WHAT?
I WAS Reading YOUR COMIC.
WHICH ONE?
YOU KNOW. 'WHIRLWIND.'
MOM, don't read THAT! That was from 5 years ago!
WHAT. I LIKE IT! IT'S FUNNY. FROM TIME TO TIME I JUST LOOK AT IT FOR A LAUGH
GEE. WOW, MOM
REMEMBER THAT COMIC ABOUT YOU GOING BACK TO PITTSBURGH?
yeah, I'm thinking of doing a sequel
YOU SHOULD BECAUSE I KNOW TWO PEOPLE WHO WANT TO BE IN YOUR COMIC.
WHAT?!

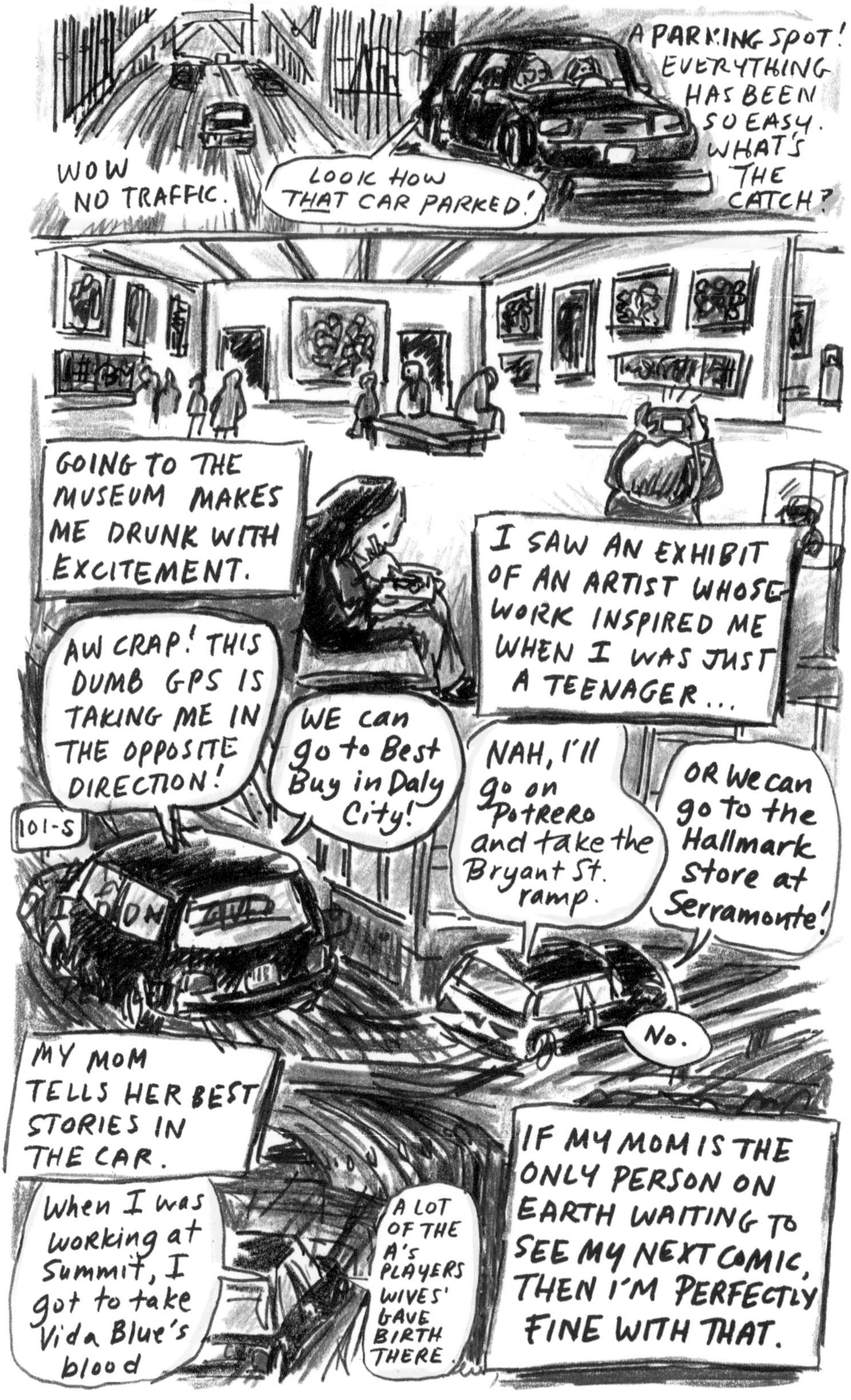
WOW NO TRAFFIC.
LOOK HOW THAT CAR PARKED!
A PARKING SPOT! EVERYTHING HAS BEEN SO EASY. WHAT'S THE CATCH?
GOING TO THE MUSEUM MAKES ME DRUNK WITH EXCITEMENT.
I SAW AN EXHIBIT OF AN ARTIST WHOSE WORK INSPIRED ME WHEN I WAS JUST A TEENAGER...
AW CRAP! THIS DUMB GPS IS TAKING ME IN THE OPPOSITE DIRECTION!
WE can go to Best Buy in Daly City!
NAH, I'll go on Potrero and take the Bryant St. ramp.
OR We can go to the Hallmark store at Serramonte!
101-S
No.
MY MOM TELLS HER BEST STORIES IN THE CAR.
When I was working at Summit, I got to take Vida Blue's blood
A LOT OF THE A's PLAYERS WIVES' GAVE BIRTH THERE.
IF MY MOM IS THE ONLY PERSON ON EARTH WAITING TO SEE MY NEXT COMIC, THEN I'M PERFECTLY FINE WITH THAT.

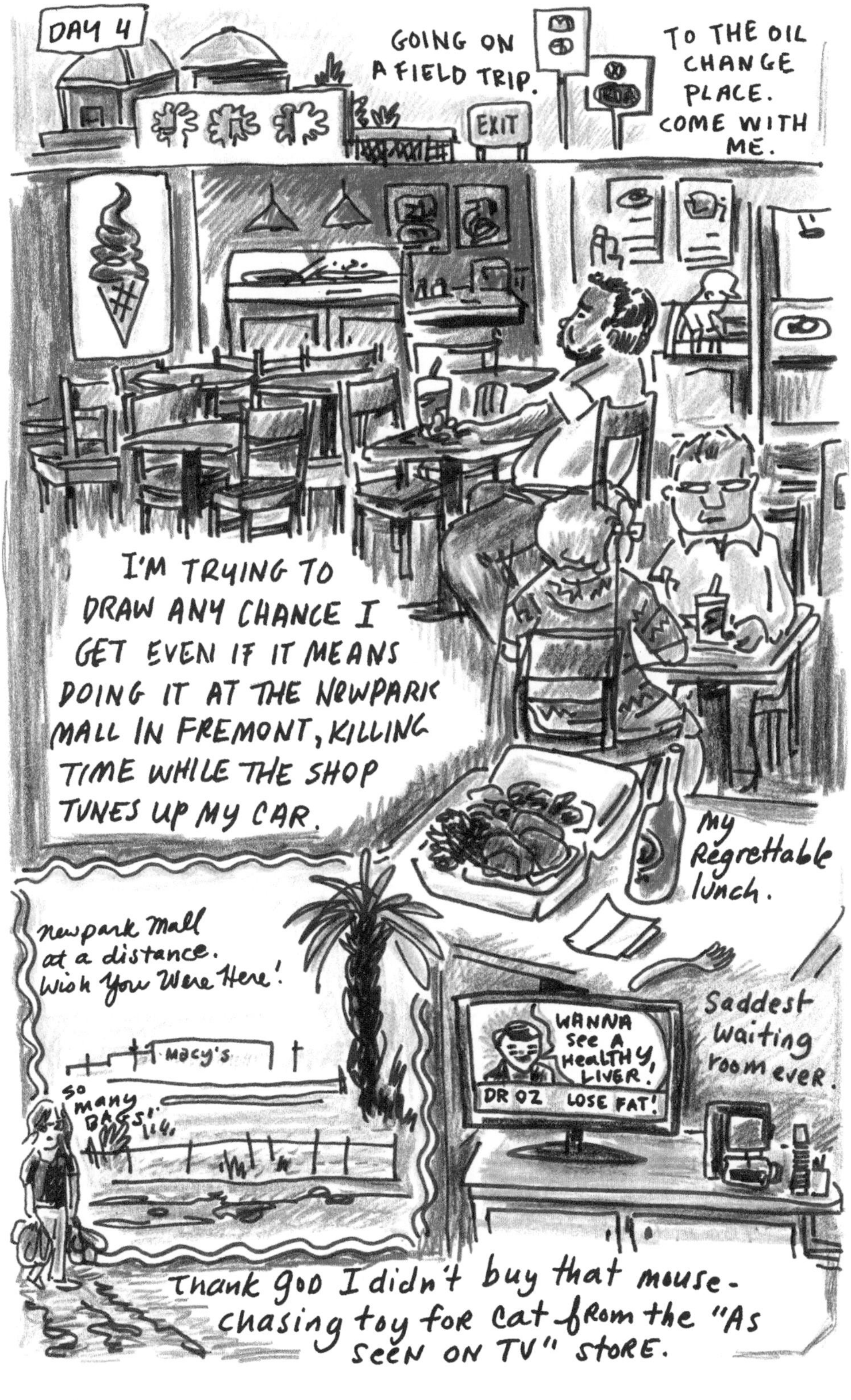
DAY 4
GOING ON A FIELD TRIP. TO THE OIL CHANGE PLACE. COME WITH ME.
EXIT
I'M TRYING TO DRAW ANY CHANCE I GET EVEN IF IT MEANS DOING IT AT THE NEWPARK MALL IN FREMONT, KILLING TIME WHILE THE SHOP TUNES UP MY CAR.
My Regrettable lunch.
newpark Mall at a distance. Wish You Were Here!
macy's
so many BAGS!
Saddest waiting room ever.
WANNA see A HEALTHY LIVER!
DR OZ
LOSE FAT!
Thank god I didn't buy that mouse-chasing toy for cat from the "As seen on TV" store.

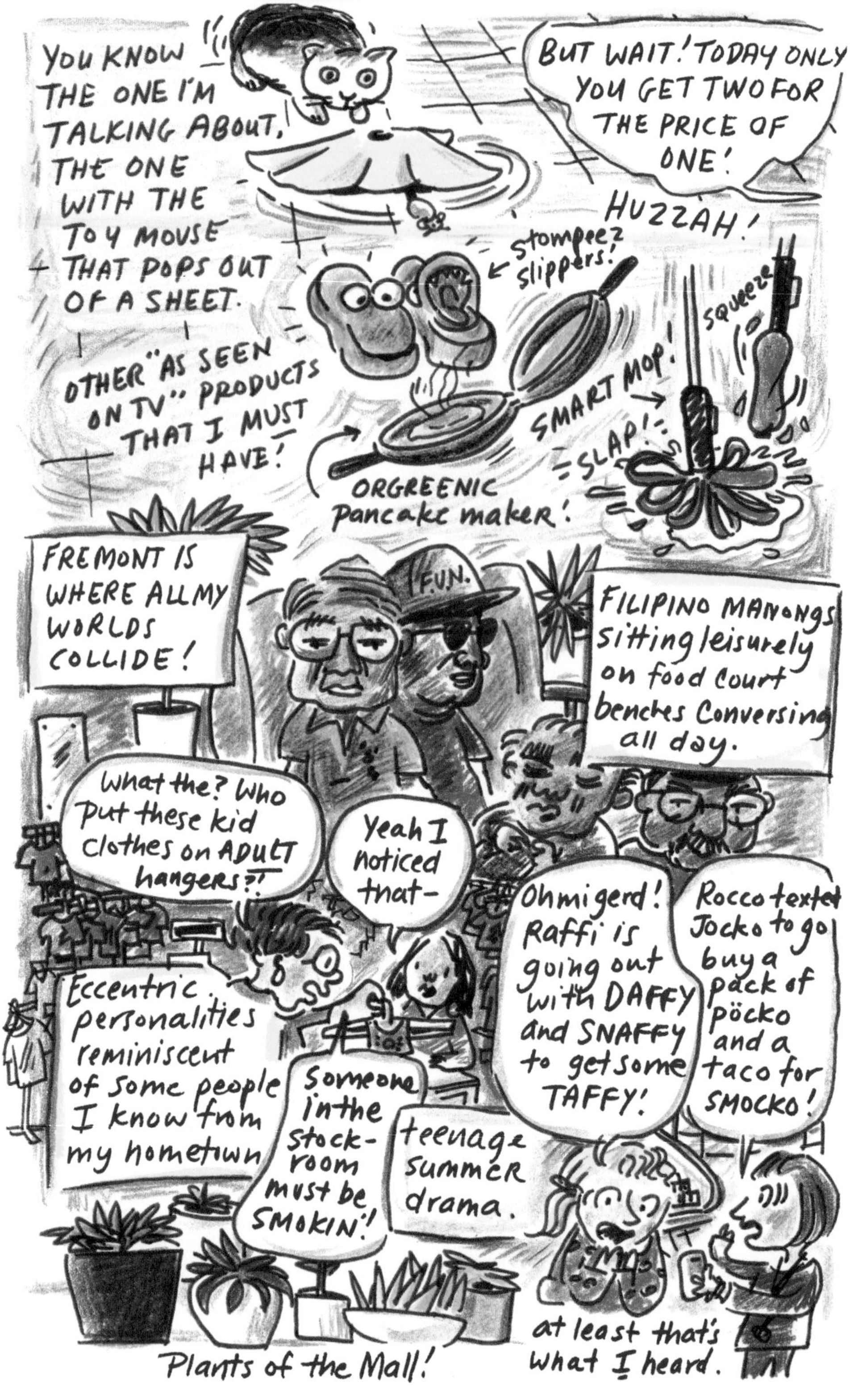
YOU KNOW THE ONE I'M TALKING ABOUT, THE ONE WITH THE TOY MOUSE THAT POPS OUT OF A SHEET.
BUT WAIT! TODAY ONLY YOU GET TWO FOR THE PRICE OF ONE!
HUZZAH!
stompeez slippers!
OTHER "AS SEEN ON TV" PRODUCTS THAT I MUST HAVE!
SMART MOP!
squeeze
SLAP!
ORGREENIC pancake maker!
FREMONT IS WHERE ALL MY WORLDS COLLIDE!
F.U.N.
FILIPINO MANONGS sitting leisurely on food court benches conversing all day.
What the? Who put these kid clothes on ADULT hangers?!
Yeah I noticed that-
Ohmigerd! Raffi is going out with DAFFY and SNAFFY to get some TAFFY!
Rocco texted Jocko to go buy a pack of pöcko and a taco for SMOCKO!
Eccentric personalities reminiscent of some people I know from my hometown
Someone in the stock-room must be SMOKIN'!
teenage summer drama.
Plants of the Mall!
at least that's what I heard.

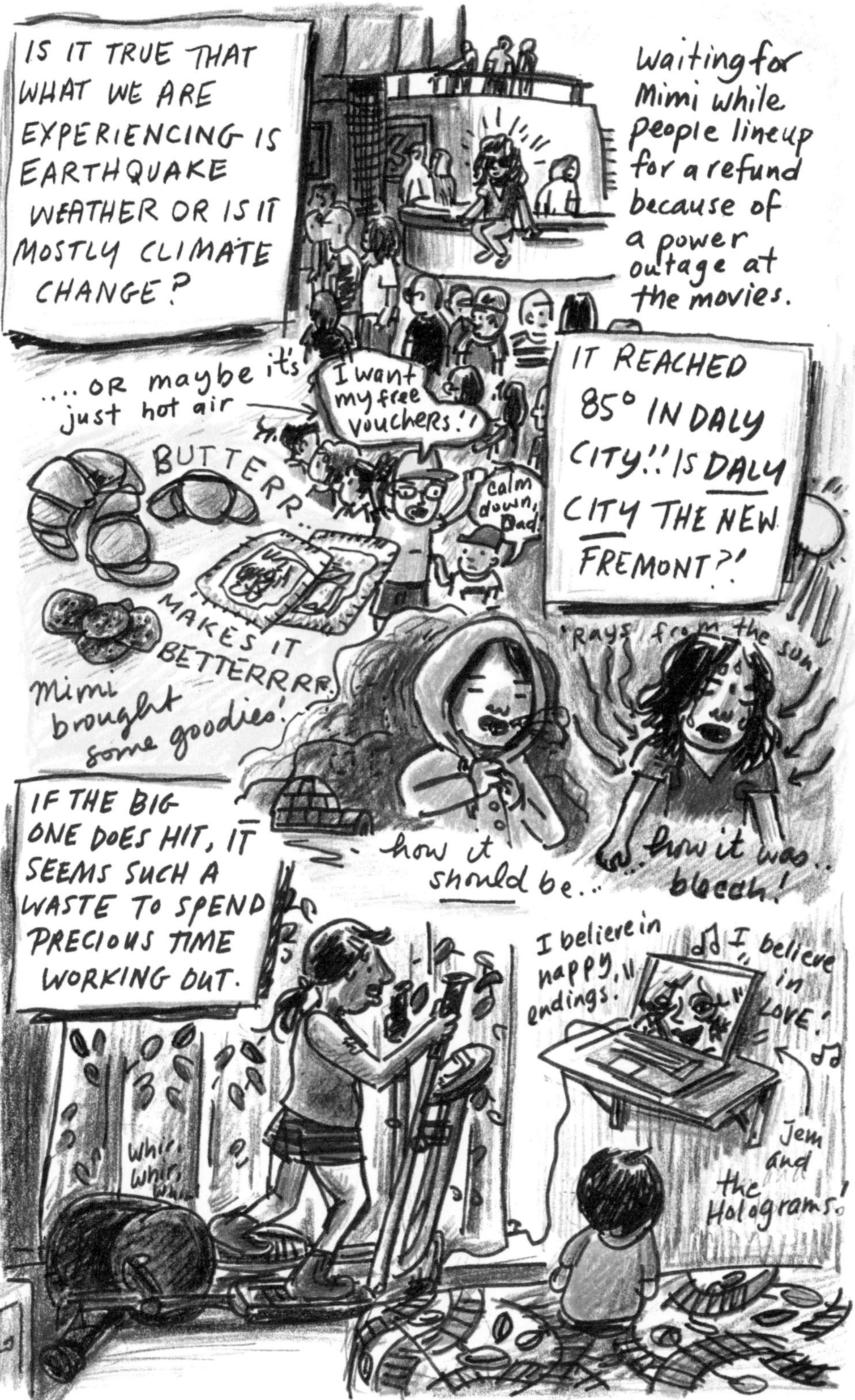
IS IT TRUE THAT WHAT WE ARE EXPERIENCING IS EARTHQUAKE WEATHER OR IS IT MOSTLY CLIMATE CHANGE?
Waiting for Mimi while people line up for a refund because of a power outage at the movies.
....or maybe it's just hot air
I want my free vouchers!
calm down, Dad!
IT REACHED 85° IN DALY CITY!! IS DALY CITY THE NEW FREMONT?!
BUTTERRR...
MAKES IT BETTERRRR.
Mimi brought some goodies!
Rays from the sun
how it should be...
how it was... blecch!
IF THE BIG ONE DOES HIT, IT SEEMS SUCH A WASTE TO SPEND PRECIOUS TIME WORKING OUT.
I believe in happy endings.
I believe in LOVE!
Jem and the Holograms!
whir, whir,

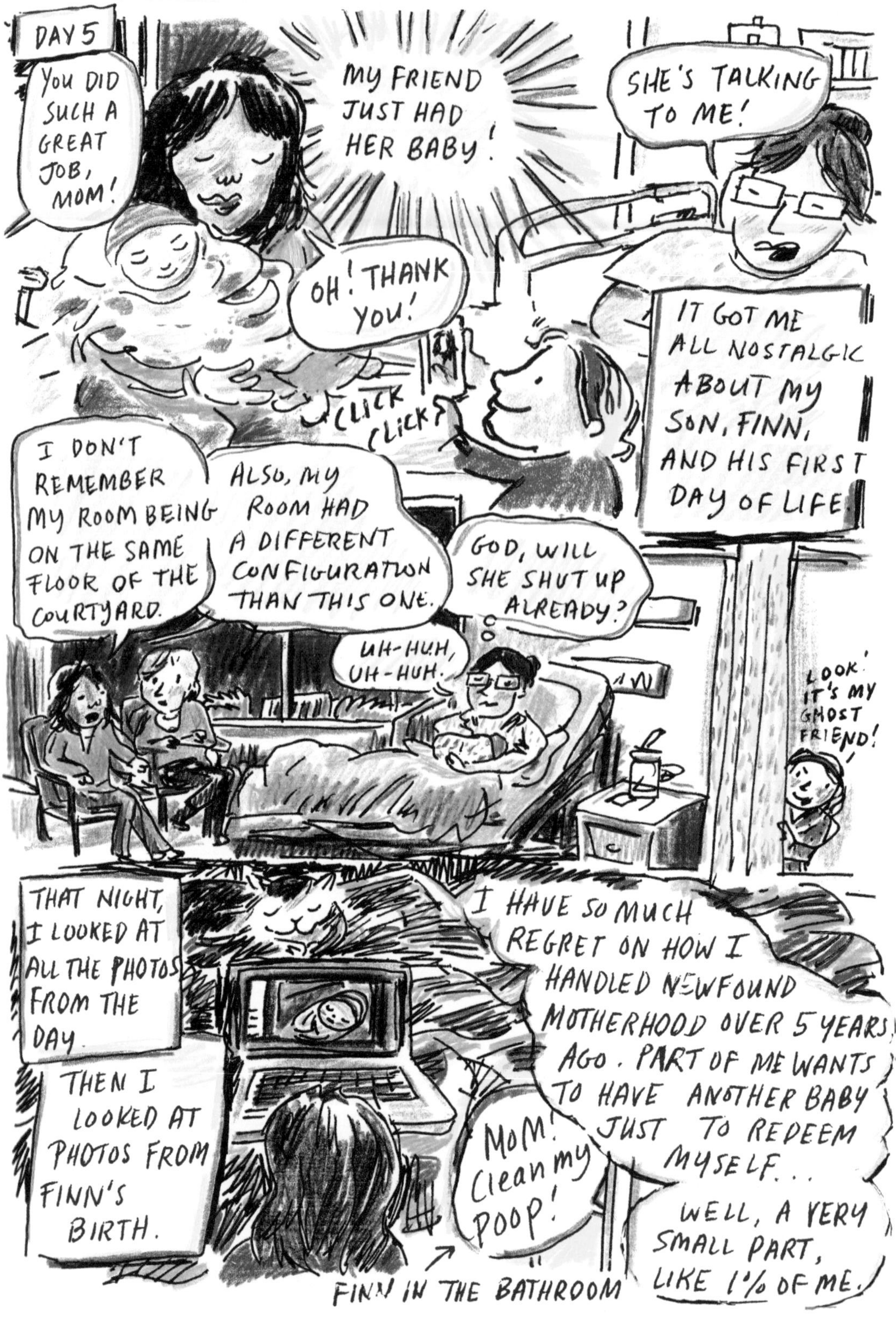
DAY 5
YOU DID SUCH A GREAT JOB, MOM!
MY FRIEND JUST HAD HER BABY!
SHE'S TALKING TO ME!
OH! THANK YOU!
CLICK CLICK
IT GOT ME ALL NOSTALGIC ABOUT MY SON, FINN, AND HIS FIRST DAY OF LIFE.
I DON'T REMEMBER MY ROOM BEING ON THE SAME FLOOR OF THE COURTYARD.
ALSO, MY ROOM HAD A DIFFERENT CONFIGURATION THAN THIS ONE.
GOD, WILL SHE SHUT UP ALREADY?
UH-HUH, UH-HUH.
LOOK! IT'S MY GHOST FRIEND!
THAT NIGHT, I LOOKED AT ALL THE PHOTOS FROM THE DAY.
I HAVE SO MUCH REGRET ON HOW I HANDLED NEWFOUND MOTHERHOOD OVER 5 YEARS AGO. PART OF ME WANTS TO HAVE ANOTHER BABY JUST TO REDEEM MYSELF...
THEN I LOOKED AT PHOTOS FROM FINN'S BIRTH.
MOM! Clean my POOP!
WELL, A VERY SMALL PART, LIKE 1% OF ME.
FINN IN THE BATHROOM

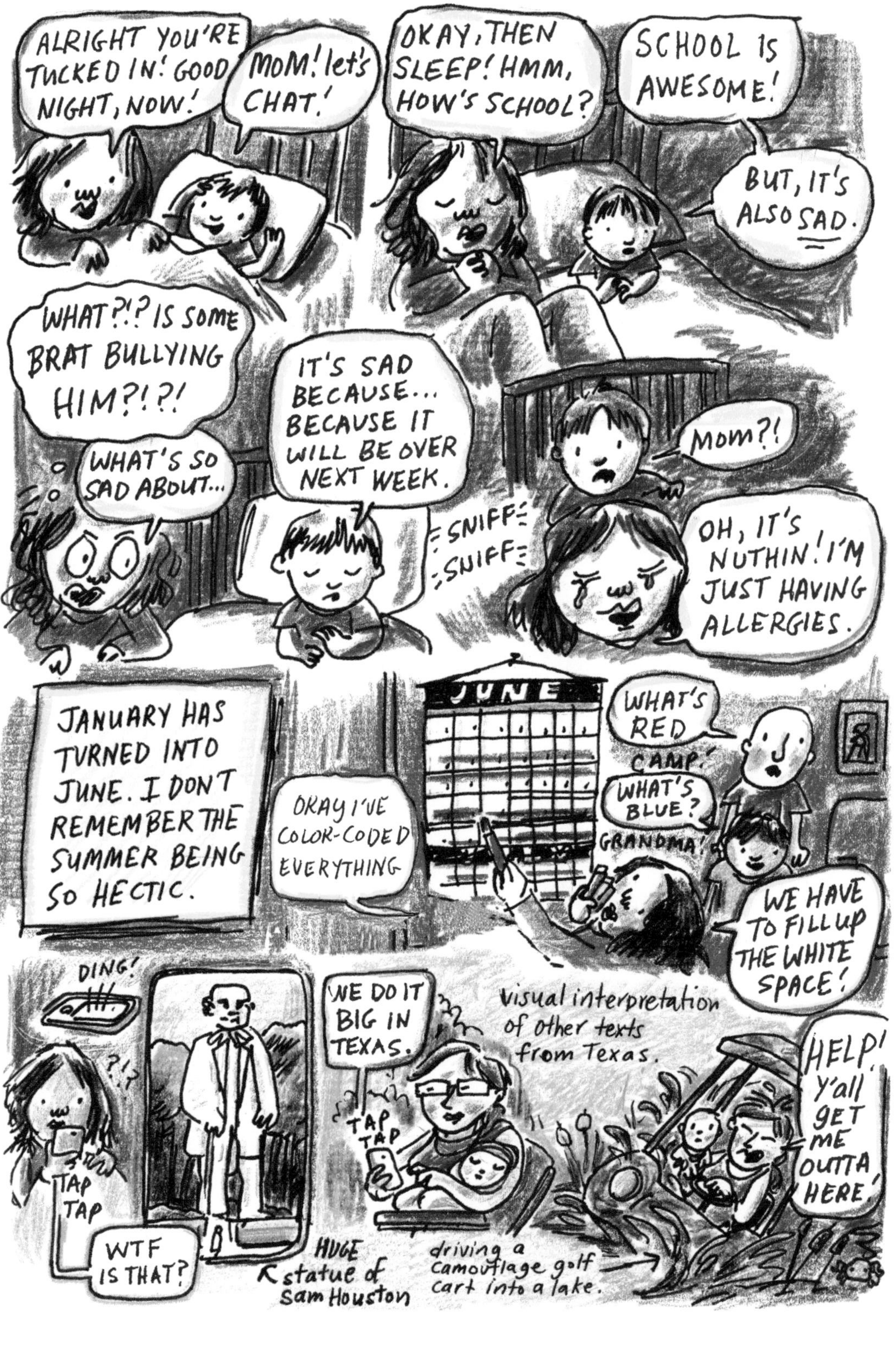
ALRIGHT YOU'RE TUCKED IN! GOOD NIGHT, NOW!
MOM! let's CHAT!
OKAY, THEN SLEEP! HMM, HOW'S SCHOOL?
SCHOOL IS AWESOME!
BUT, IT'S ALSO SAD.
WHAT?!?! IS SOME BRAT BULLYING HIM?!?!
WHAT'S SO SAD ABOUT...
IT'S SAD BECAUSE... BECAUSE IT WILL BE OVER NEXT WEEK.
SNIFF
SNIFF
MOM?!
OH, IT'S NUTHIN! I'M JUST HAVING ALLERGIES.
JANUARY HAS TURNED INTO JUNE. I DON'T REMEMBER THE SUMMER BEING SO HECTIC.
JUNE
OKAY I'VE COLOR-CODED EVERYTHING
WHAT'S RED
CAMP!
WHAT'S BLUE?
GRANDMA!
WE HAVE TO FILL UP THE WHITE SPACE!
DING!
?!?
TAP TAP
WTF IS THAT?
HUGE statue of Sam Houston
WE DO IT BIG IN TEXAS.
TAP TAP
visual interpretation of other texts from Texas.
driving a camouflage golf cart into a lake.
HELP! Y'all GET ME OUTTA HERE!

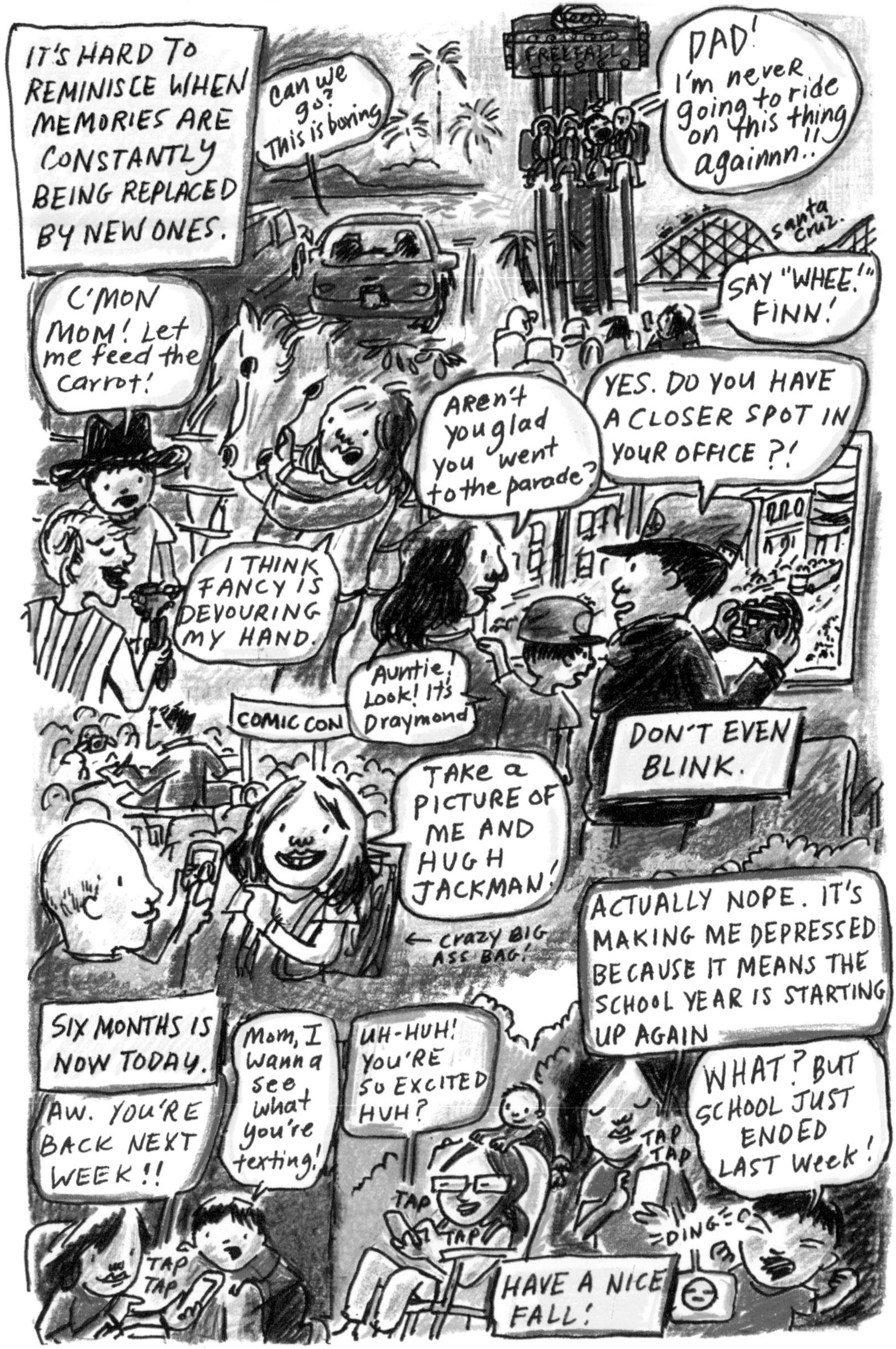
IT'S HARD TO REMINISCE WHEN MEMORIES ARE CONSTANTLY BEING REPLACED BY NEW ONES.
Can we go? This is boring
FREEFALL
DAD! I'm never going to ride on this thing againnn..!!
santa cruz.
SAY "WHEE!" FINN!
C'MON MOM! Let me feed the carrot!
Aren't you glad you went to the parade?
YES. DO YOU HAVE A CLOSER SPOT IN YOUR OFFICE?!
I THINK FANCY IS DEVOURING MY HAND.
Auntie! Look! It's Draymond
COMIC CON
DON'T EVEN BLINK.
Take a PICTURE OF ME AND HUGH JACKMAN!
← crazy BIG ASS BAG!
ACTUALLY NOPE. IT'S MAKING ME DEPRESSED BECAUSE IT MEANS THE SCHOOL YEAR IS STARTING UP AGAIN
SIX MONTHS IS NOW TODAY.
AW. YOU'RE BACK NEXT WEEK!!
Mom, I wanna see what you're texting!
UH-HUH! YOU'RE SO EXCITED HUH?
WHAT? BUT SCHOOL JUST ENDED LAST Week!
TAP TAP
TAP TAP
TAP TAP
DING
HAVE A NICE FALL!

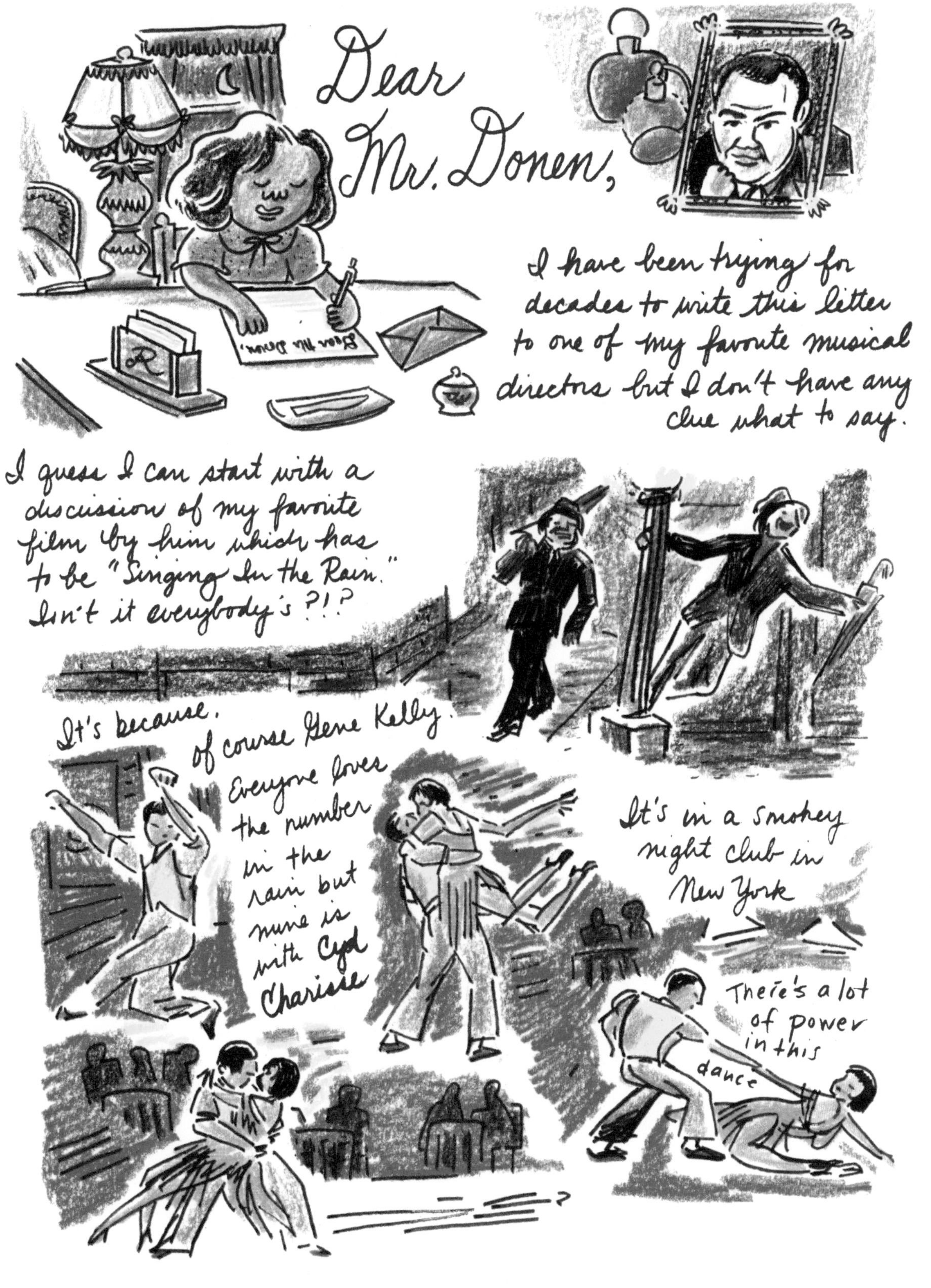
Dear Mr. Donen,
Dear Mr. Donen,
I have been trying for decades to write this letter to one of my favorite musical directors but I don't have any clue what to say.
I guess I can start with a discussion of my favorite film by him which has to be "Singing In the Rain." Isn't it everybody's ?!?
It's because.
of course Gene Kelly.
Everyone loves the number in the rain but mine is with Cyd Charisse
It's in a smokey night club in New York
There's a lot of power in this dance

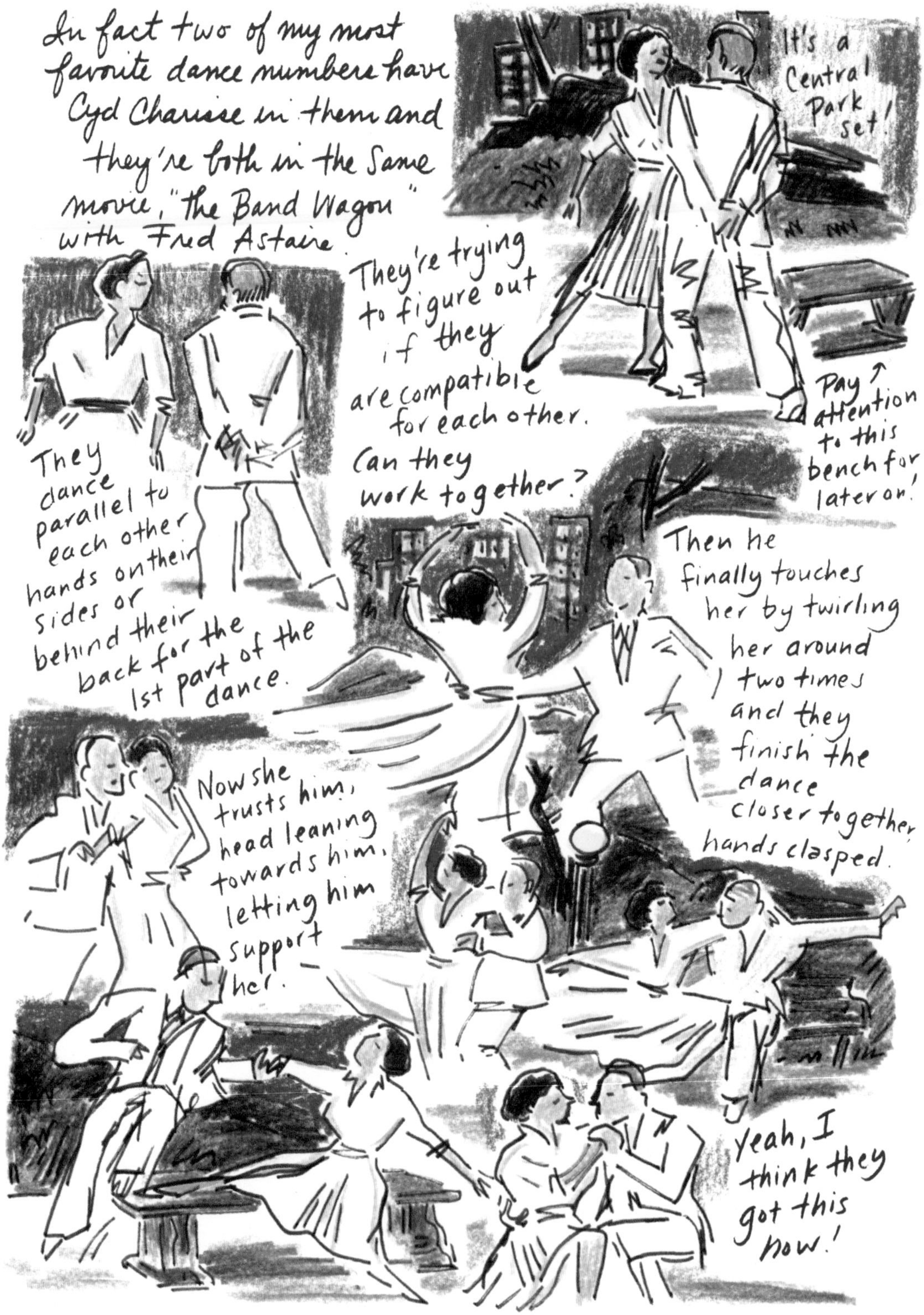
In fact two of my most favorite dance numbers have Cyd Charisse in them and they're both in the Same movie, "the Band Wagon" with Fred Astaire.
It's a Central Park set!
Pay attention to this bench for later on!
They're trying to figure out if they are compatible for each other.
Can they work together?
They dance parallel to each other hands on their sides or behind their back for the 1st part of the dance.
Then he finally touches her by twirling her around two times and they finish the dance closer together, hands clasped.
Now she trusts him, head leaning towards him, letting him support her.
Yeah, I think they got this now!

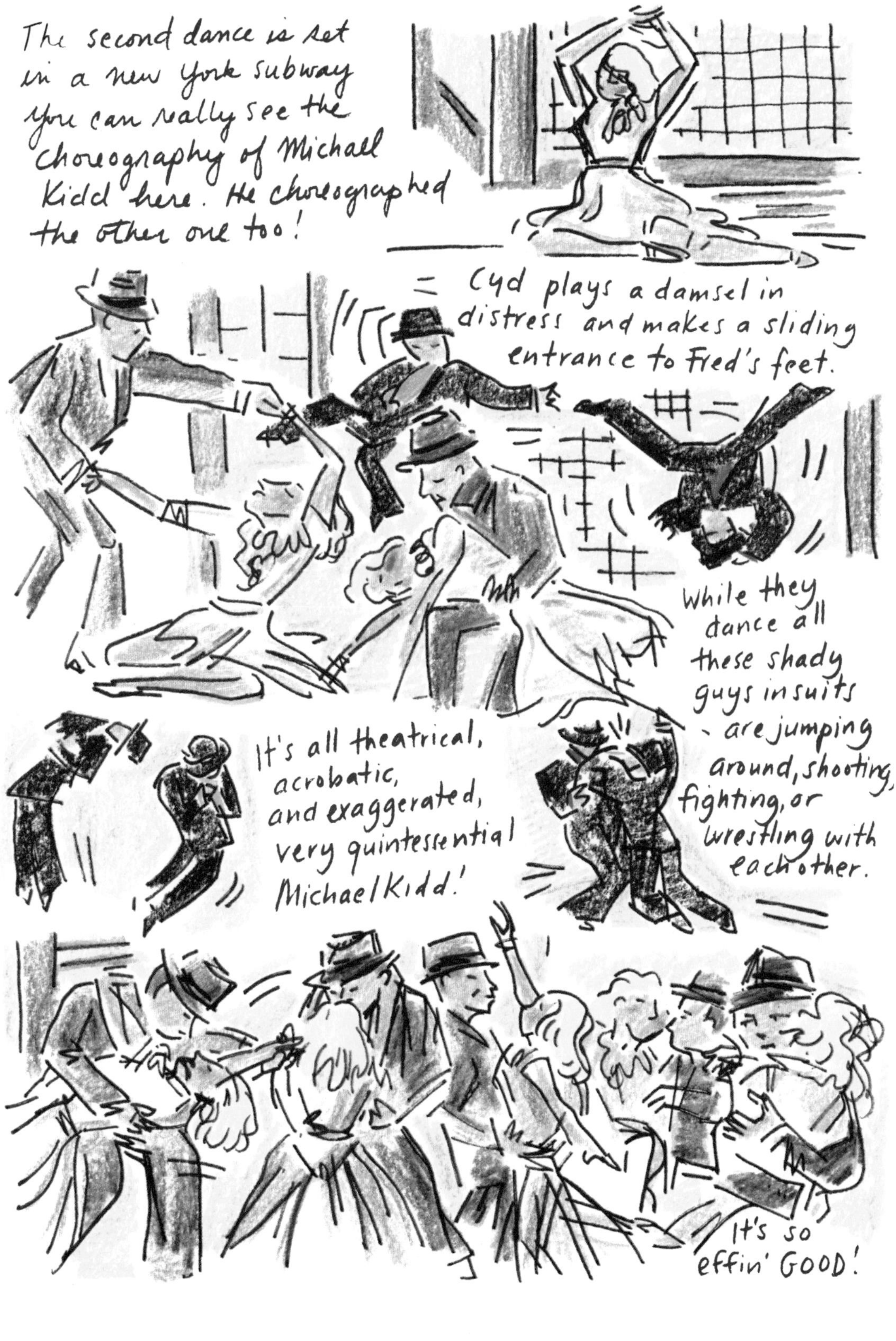
The second dance is set in a New York subway you can really see the choreography of Michael Kidd here. He choreographed the other one too!
Cyd plays a damsel in distress and makes a sliding entrance to Fred's feet.
While they dance all these shady guys in suits are jumping around, shooting, fighting, or wrestling with each other.
It's all theatrical, acrobatic, and exaggerated, very quintessential Michael Kidd!
It's so effin' GOOD!

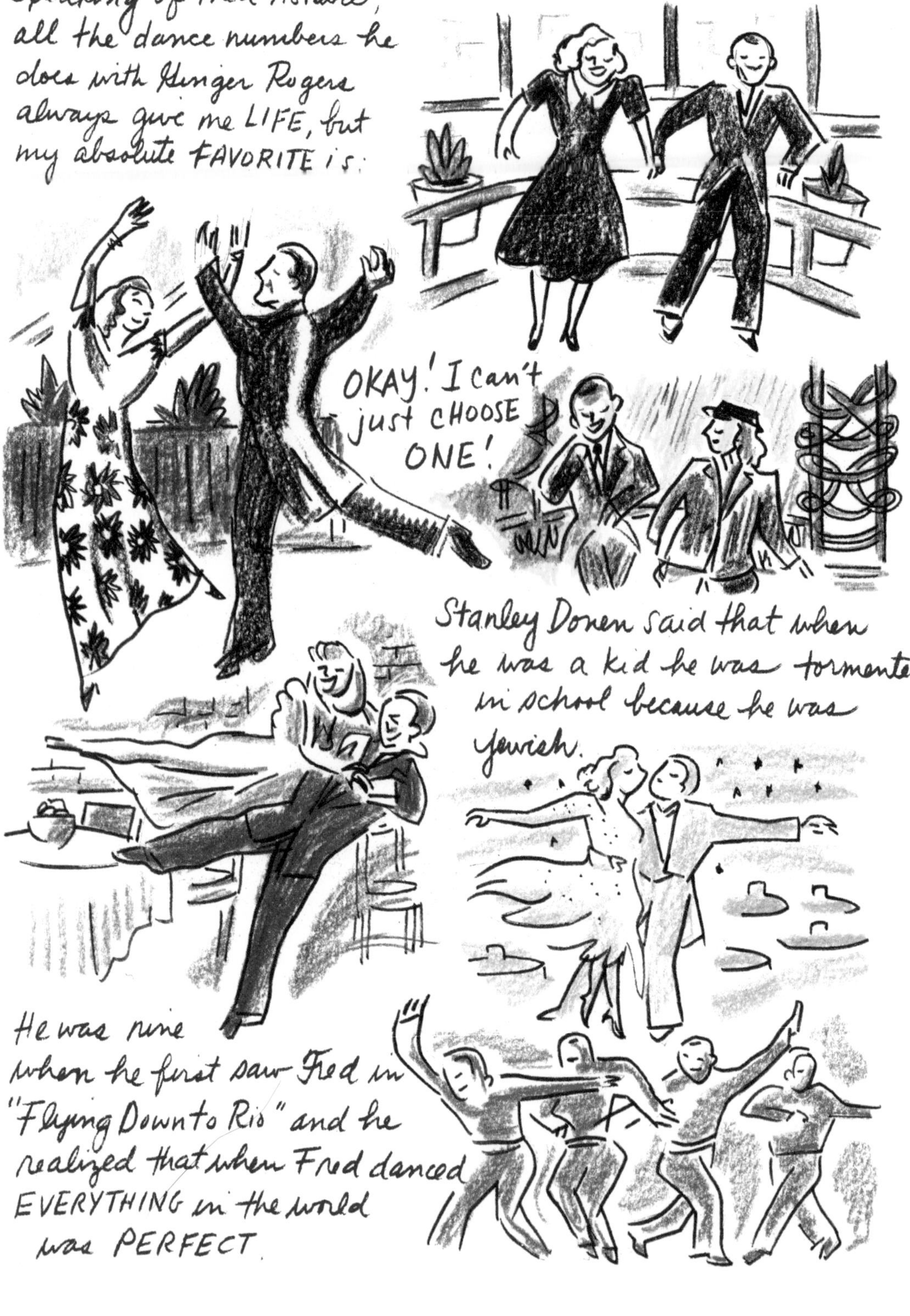
Speaking of Fred Astaire, all the dance numbers he does with Ginger Rogers always give me LIFE, but my absolute FAVORITE is:
OKAY! I can't just CHOOSE ONE!
Stanley Donen said that when he was a kid he was tormented in school because he was Jewish.
He was nine when he first saw Fred in "Flying Down to Rio" and he realized that when Fred danced EVERYTHING in the world was PERFECT.

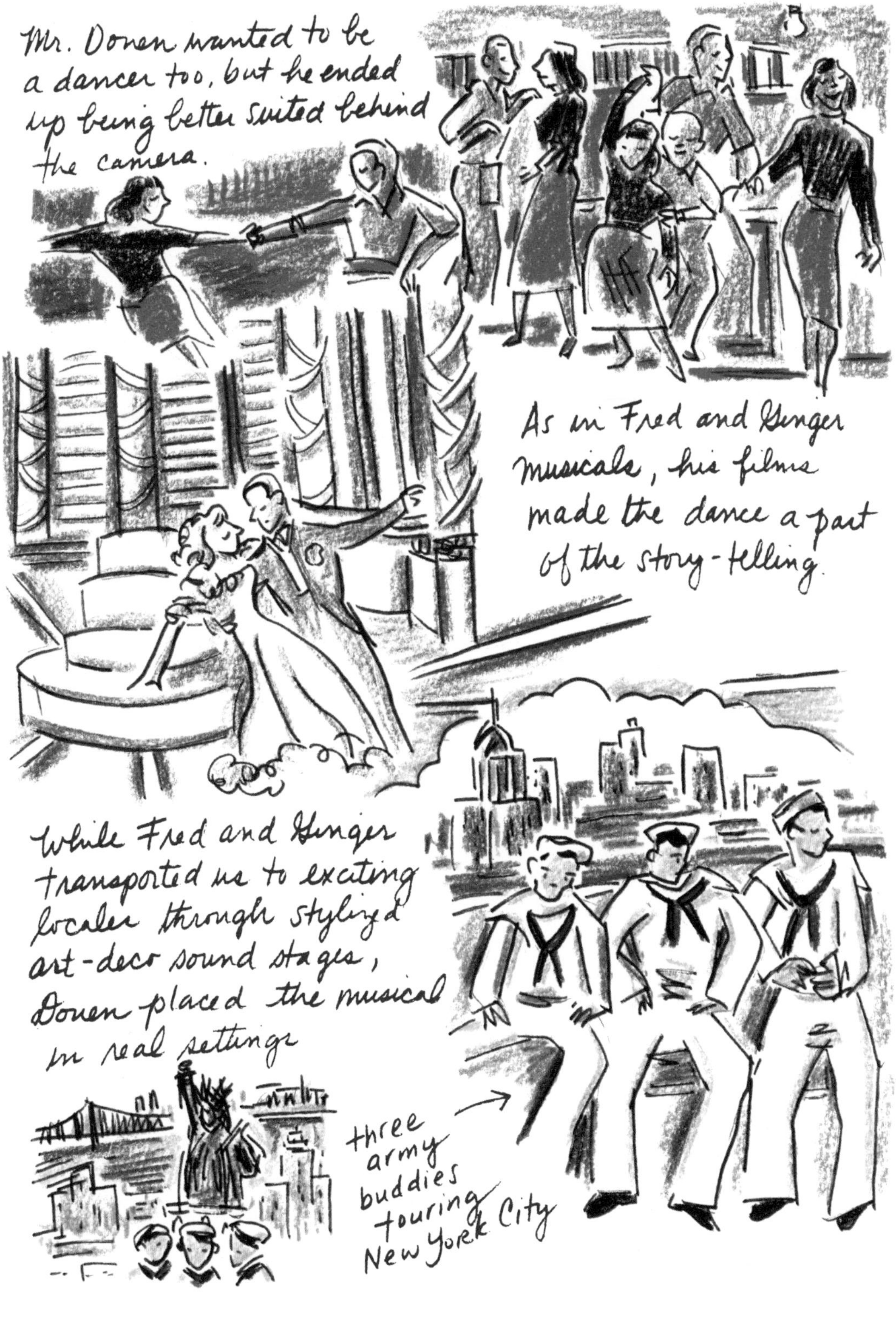
Mr. Donen wanted to be a dancer too, but he ended up being better suited behind the camera.
As in Fred and Ginger musicals, his films made the dance a part of the story-telling.
While Fred and Ginger transported us to exciting locales through stylized art-deco sound stages, Donen placed the musical in real settings
three army buddies touring New York City

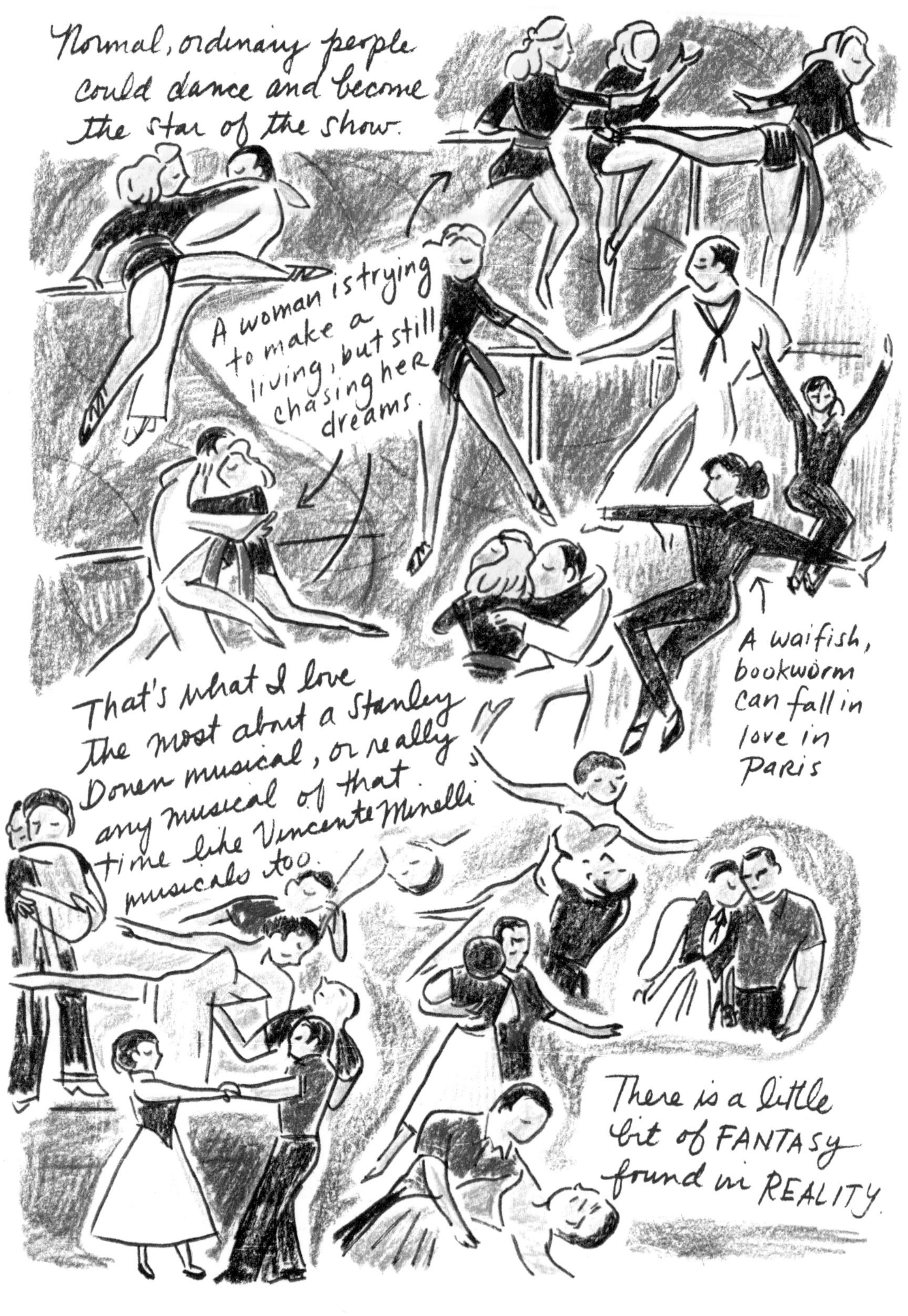
Normal, ordinary people could dance and become the star of the show.
A woman is trying to make a living, but still chasing her dreams.
A waifish, bookworm can fall in love in Paris
That's what I love the most about a Stanley Donen musical, or really any musical of that time like Vincente Minelli musicals too.
There is a little bit of FANTASY found in REALITY.

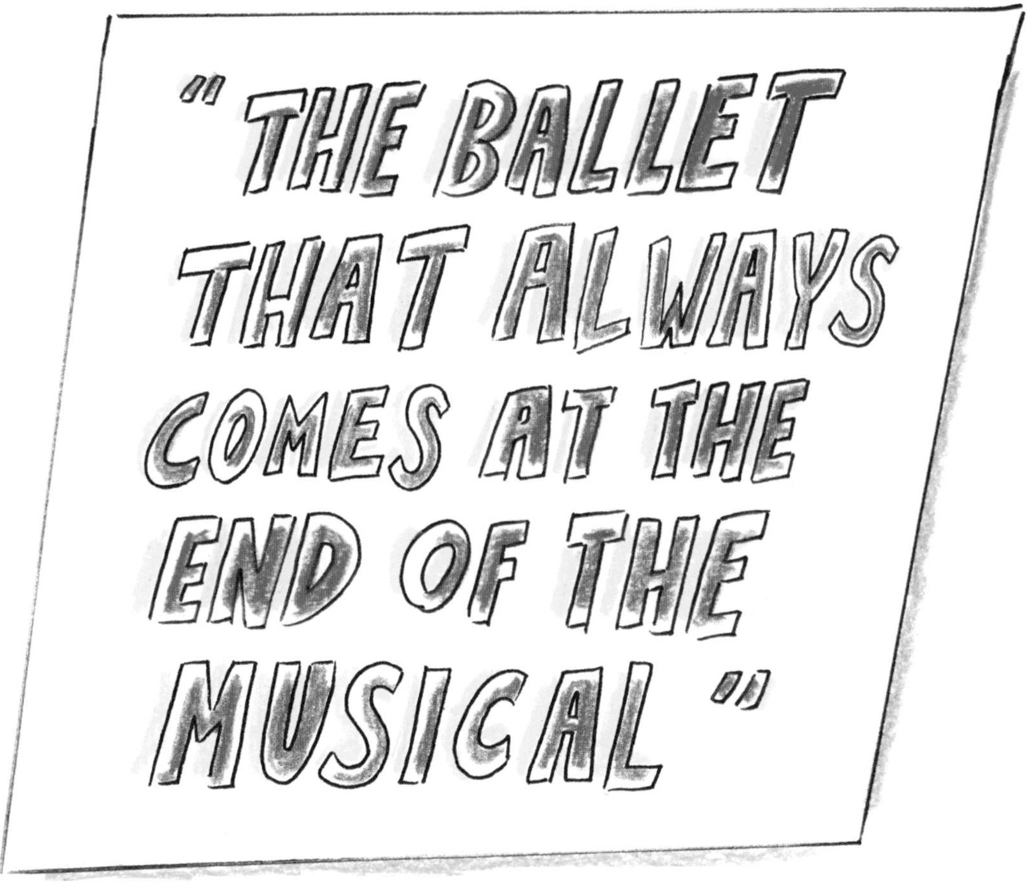
"THE BALLET THAT ALWAYS COMES AT THE END OF THE MUSICAL"

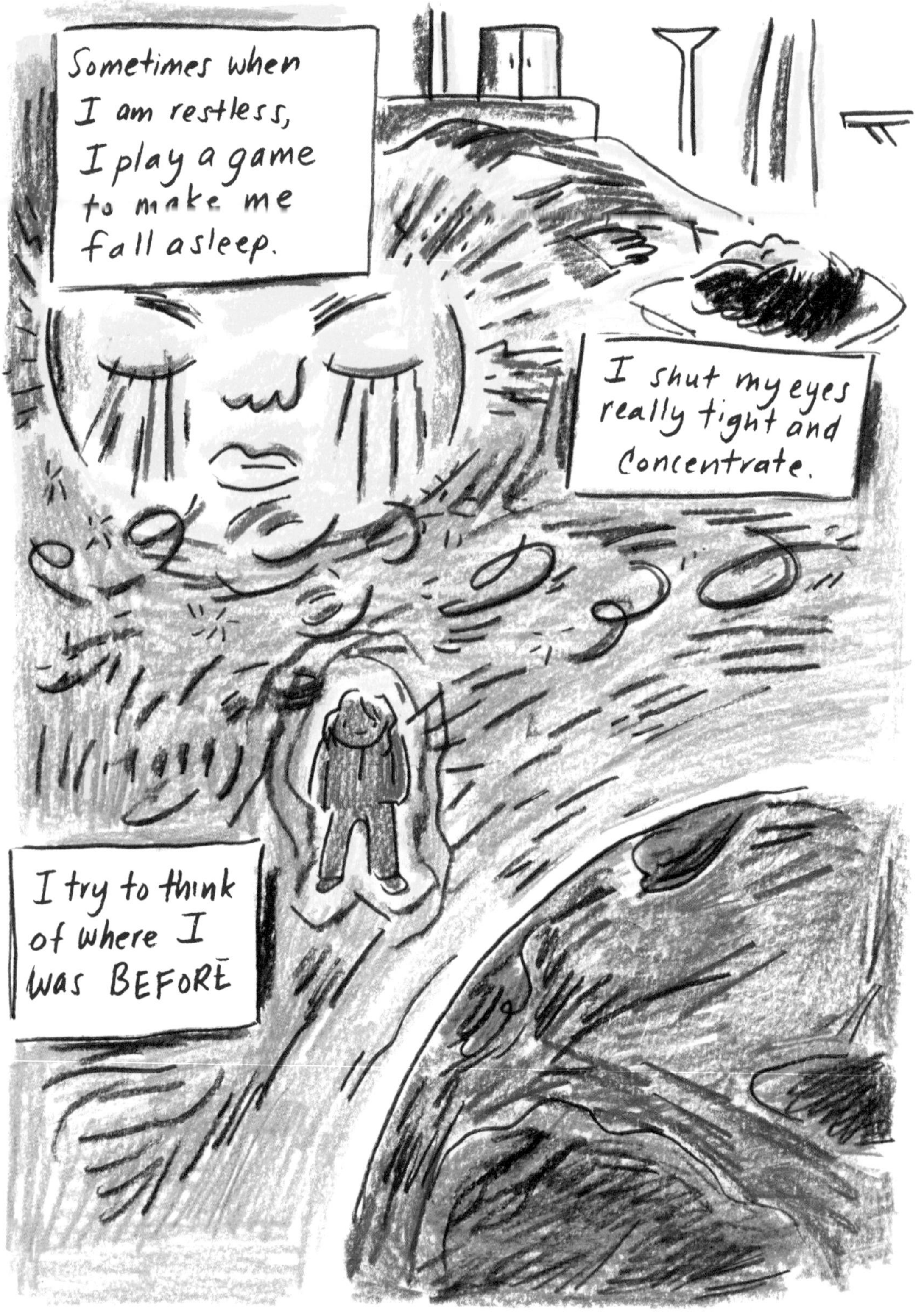
Sometimes when I am restless, I play a game to make me fall asleep.
I shut my eyes really tight and Concentrate.
I try to think of where I was BEFORE

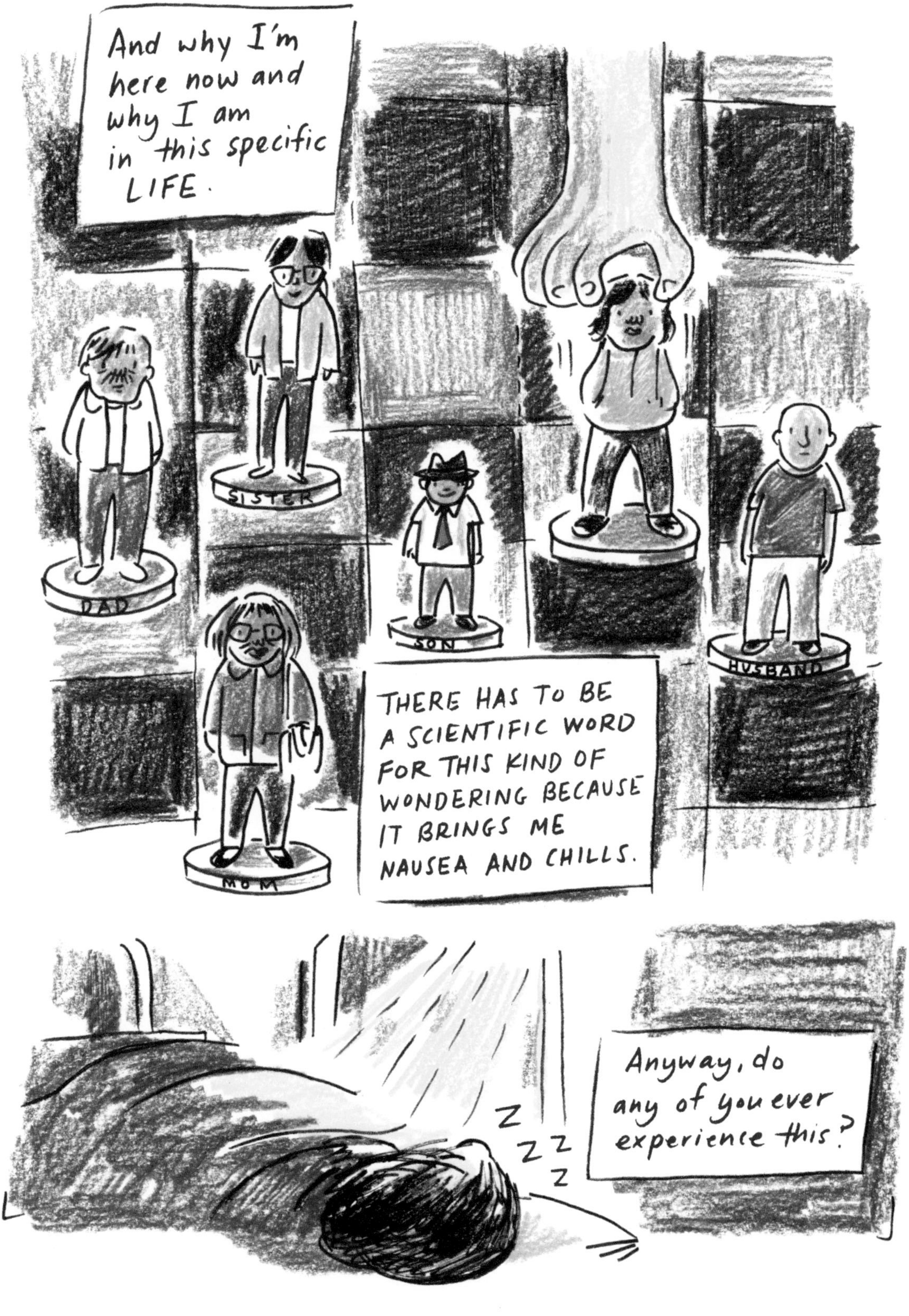
And why I'm here now and why I am in this specific LIFE.
SISTER
DAD
SON
HUSBAND
MOM
THERE HAS TO BE A SCIENTIFIC WORD FOR THIS KIND OF WONDERING BECAUSE IT BRINGS ME NAUSEA AND CHILLS.
Z Z Z Z
Anyway, do any of you ever experience this?

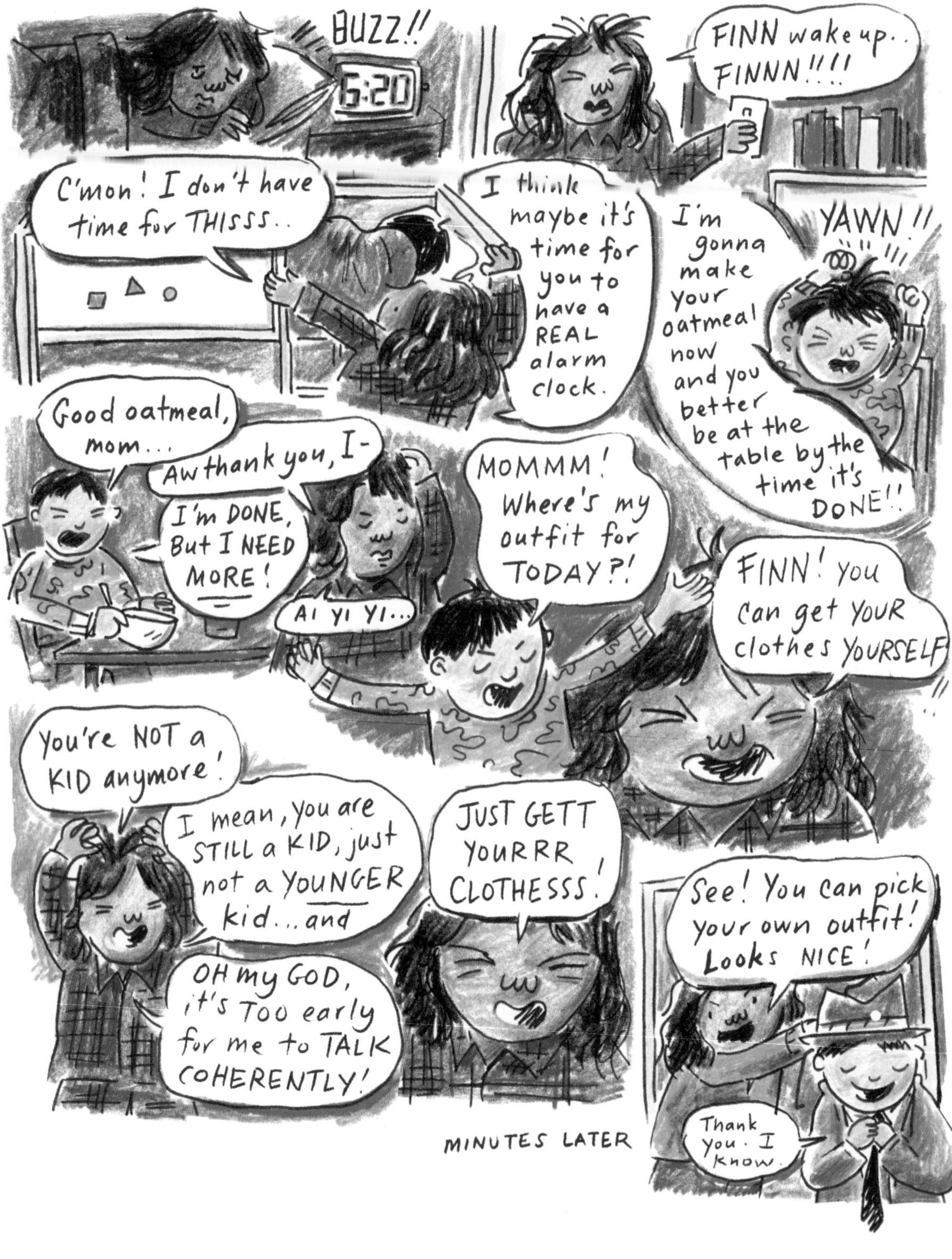
BUZZ!!
6:20
FINN wake up.. FINNN!!!!
C'mon! I don't have time for THISSS..
I think maybe it's time for you to have a REAL alarm clock.
YAWN!!
I'm gonna make your oatmeal now and you better be at the table by the time it's DONE!!
Good oatmeal, mom...
Aw thank you, I-
I'm DONE, But I NEED MORE!
AI YI YI...
MOMMM! Where's my outfit for TODAY?!
FINN! You can get YOUR clothes YOURSELF
You're NOT a KID anymore!
I mean, you are STILL a KID, just not a YOUNGER kid...and
OH my GOD, it's TOO early for me to TALK COHERENTLY!
JUST GETT YOURRR CLOTHESSS!
MINUTES LATER
See! You can pick your own outfit! Looks NICE!
Thank you. I know.

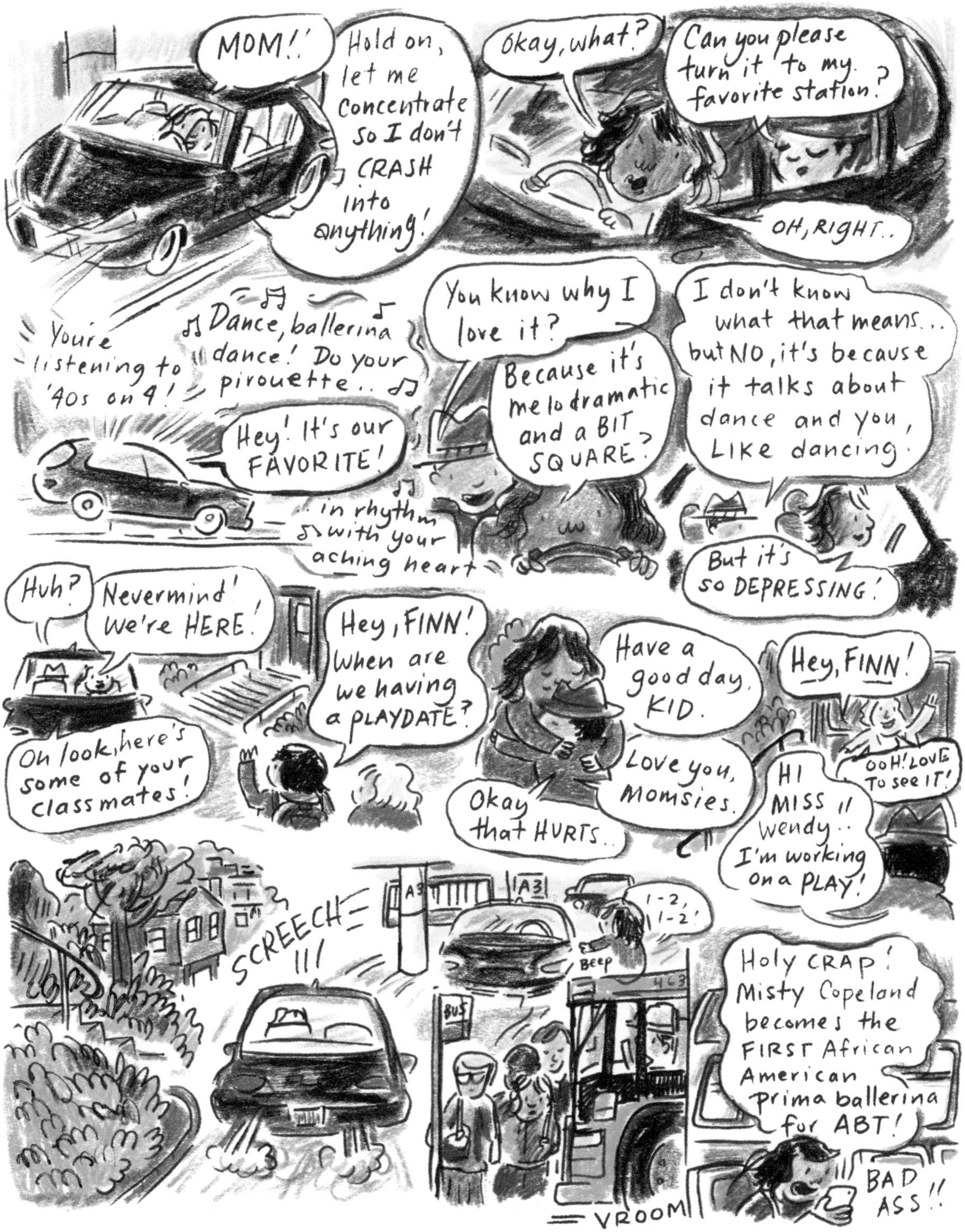
MOM!!
Hold on, let me concentrate so I don't CRASH into anything!
Okay, what?
Can you please turn it to my favorite station?
OH, RIGHT..
You're listening to '40s on 4!
Dance, ballerina dance! Do your pirouette..
in rhythm with your aching heart
Hey! It's our FAVORITE!
You know why I love it?
Because it's melodramatic and a BIT SQUARE?
I don't know what that means... but NO, it's because it talks about dance and you, LIKE dancing!
But it's so DEPRESSING!
Huh?
Nevermind! We're HERE!
Oh look, here's some of your classmates!
Hey, FINN! When are we having a PLAYDATE?
Have a good day, KID.
Love you, Momsies.
Okay that HURTS.
Hey, FINN!
HI MISS Wendy!! I'm working on a PLAY!
OOH! LOVE TO see IT!
SCREECH!!!
A3
A3
1-2, 1-2!
Beep
BUS
Holy CRAP! Misty Copeland becomes the FIRST African American prima ballerina for ABT!
BAD ASS!!
VROOM

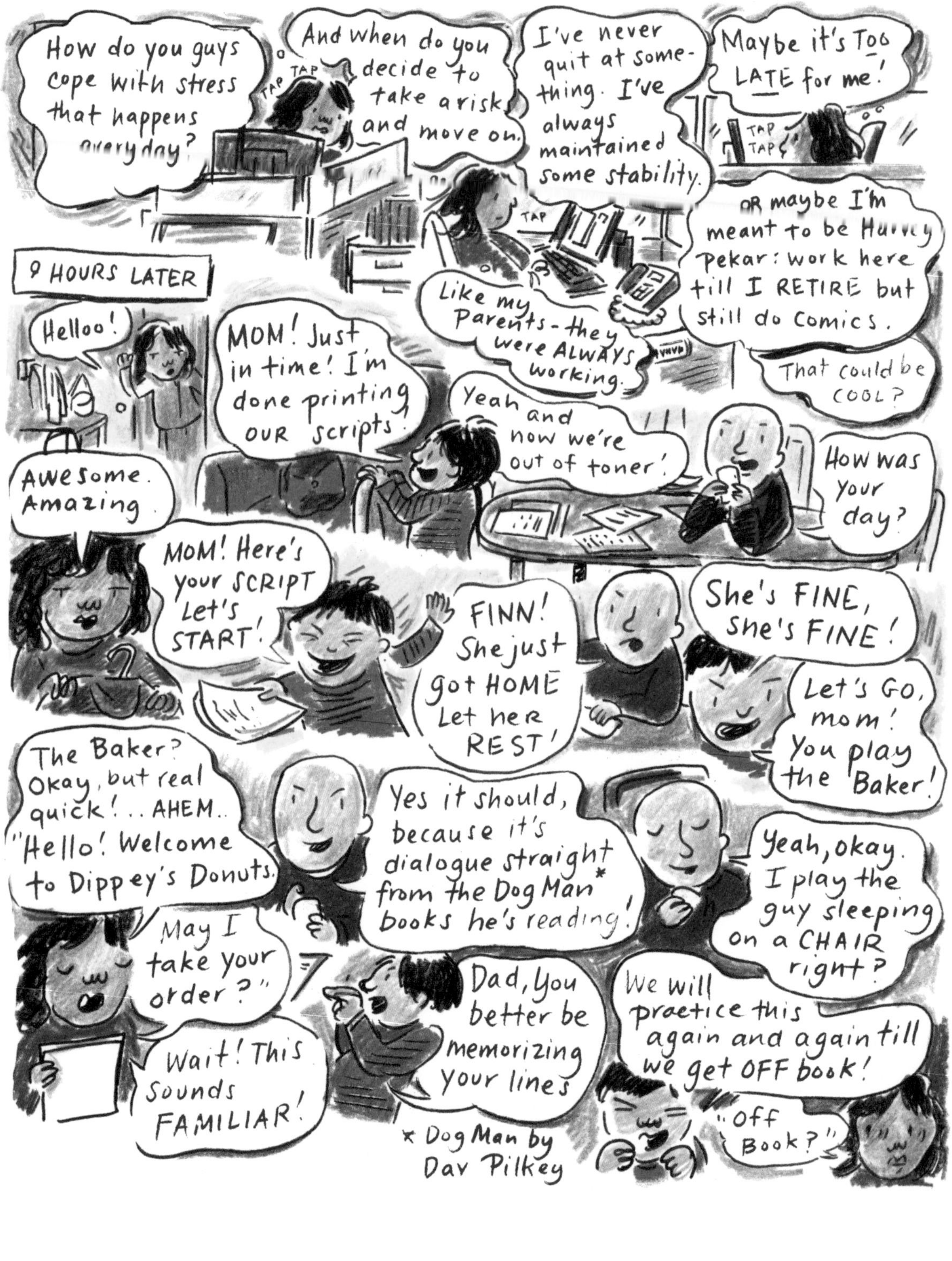
How do you guys cope with stress that happens everyday?
TAP TAP
And when do you decide to take a risk and move on.
I've never quit at something. I've always maintained some stability.
TAP
Like my Parents - they were ALWAYS working.
Maybe it's TOO LATE for me!
TAP TAP
OR maybe I'm meant to be Harvey Pekar: work here till I RETIRE but still do comics.
That could be COOL?
9 HOURS LATER
Helloo!
MOM! Just in time! I'm done printing our scripts!
Yeah and now we're out of toner!
How was your day?
Awesome. Amazing.
MOM! Here's your SCRIPT Let's START!
FINN! She just got HOME Let her REST!
She's FINE, She's FINE!
Let's GO, mom! You play the Baker!
The Baker? Okay, but real quick! .. AHEM.. "Hello! Welcome to Dippey's Donuts.
May I take your order?"
Yes it should, because it's dialogue straight from the Dog Man* books he's reading!
Yeah, okay. I play the guy sleeping on a CHAIR right?
Wait! This sounds FAMILIAR!
Dad, You better be memorizing your lines
We will practice this again and again till we get OFF book!
"Off Book?"
* Dog Man by Dav Pilkey

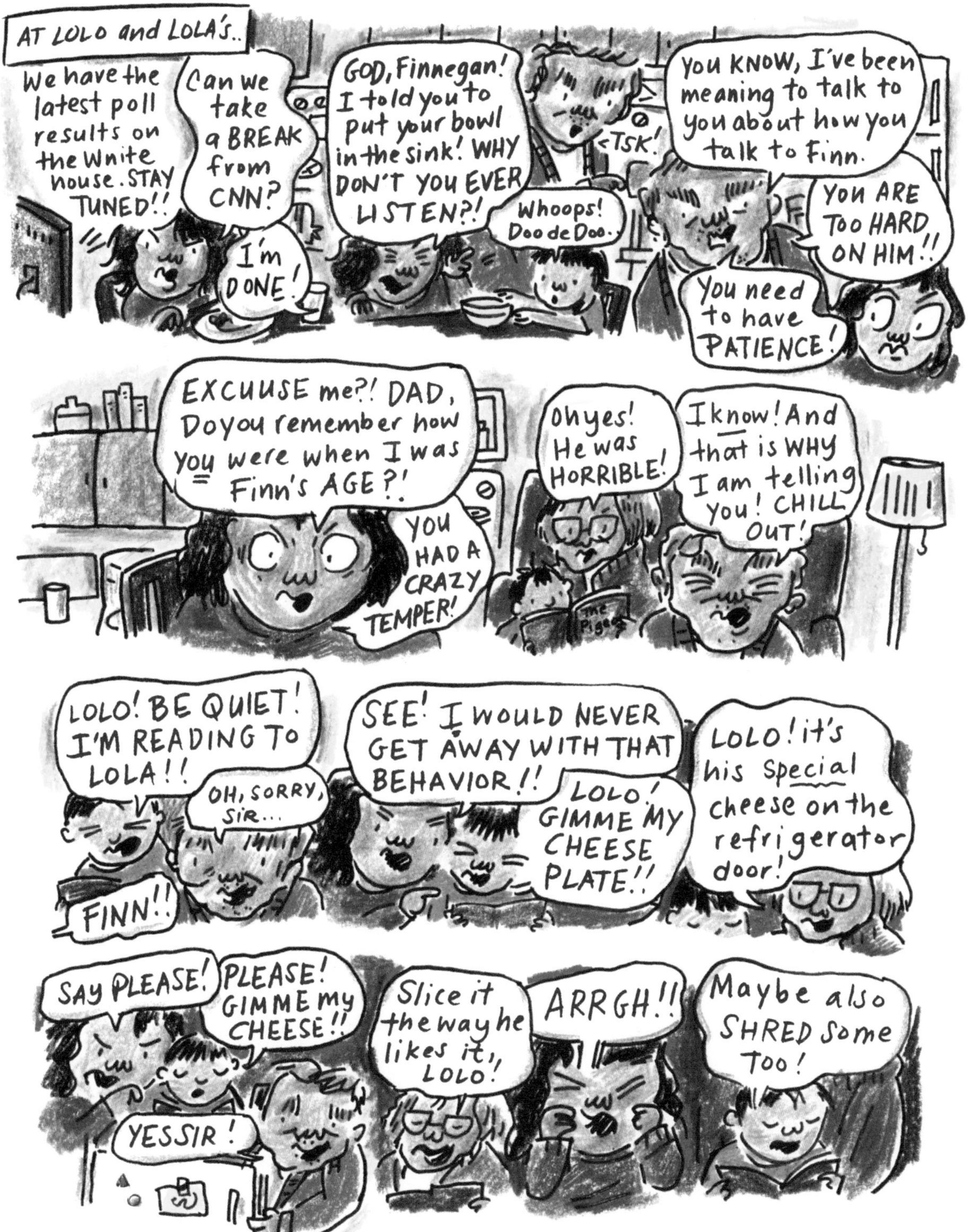
AT LOLO and LOLA'S..
We have the latest poll results on the White house. STAY TUNED!!
Can we take a BREAK from CNN?
I'm DONE!
GOD, Finnegan! I told you to put your bowl in the sink! WHY DON'T YOU EVER LISTEN?!
Whoops! Doo de Doo..
<TSK!
You KNOW, I've been meaning to talk to you about how you talk to Finn.
You ARE TOO HARD ON HIM!!
You need to have PATIENCE!
EXCUUSE me?! DAD, Do you remember how you were when I was Finn's AGE?!
YOU HAD A CRAZY TEMPER!
Oh yes! He was HORRIBLE!
I know! And that is WHY I am telling you! CHILL OUT!
THE Pigeon
LOLO! BE QUIET! I'M READING TO LOLA!!
OH, SORRY, SIR...
FINN!!
SEE! I WOULD NEVER GET AWAY WITH THAT BEHAVIOR!!
LOLO! GIMME MY CHEESE PLATE!!
LOLO! it's his special cheese on the refrigerator door!
SAY PLEASE!
PLEASE! GIMME my CHEESE!!
YESSIR!
Slice it the way he likes it, LOLO!
ARRGH!!
Maybe also SHRED some too!

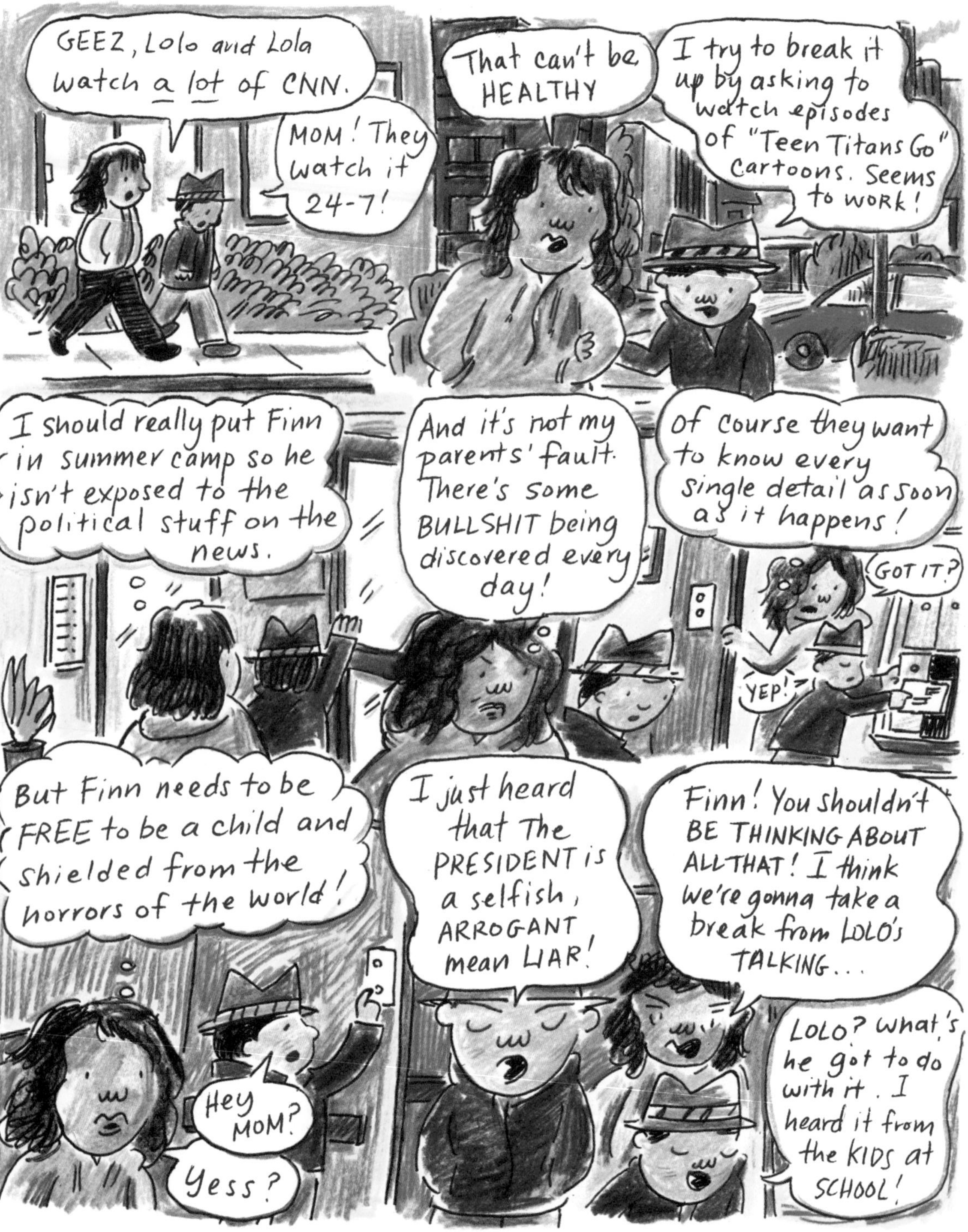
GEEZ, Lolo and Lola watch a lot of CNN.
MOM! They watch it 24-7!
That can't be HEALTHY
I try to break it up by asking to watch episodes of "Teen Titans Go" cartoons. Seems to work!
I should really put Finn in summer camp so he isn't exposed to the political stuff on the news.
And it's not my parents' fault. There's some BULLSHIT being discovered every day!
Of course they want to know every single detail as soon as it happens!
GOT IT?
YEP!
But Finn needs to be FREE to be a child and shielded from the horrors of the world!
Hey MOM?
Yess?
I just heard that The PRESIDENT is a selfish, ARROGANT mean LIAR!
Finn! You shouldn't BE THINKING ABOUT ALL THAT! I think we're gonna take a break from LOLO's TALKING...
LOLO? What's he got to do with it. I heard it from the KIDS at SCHOOL!

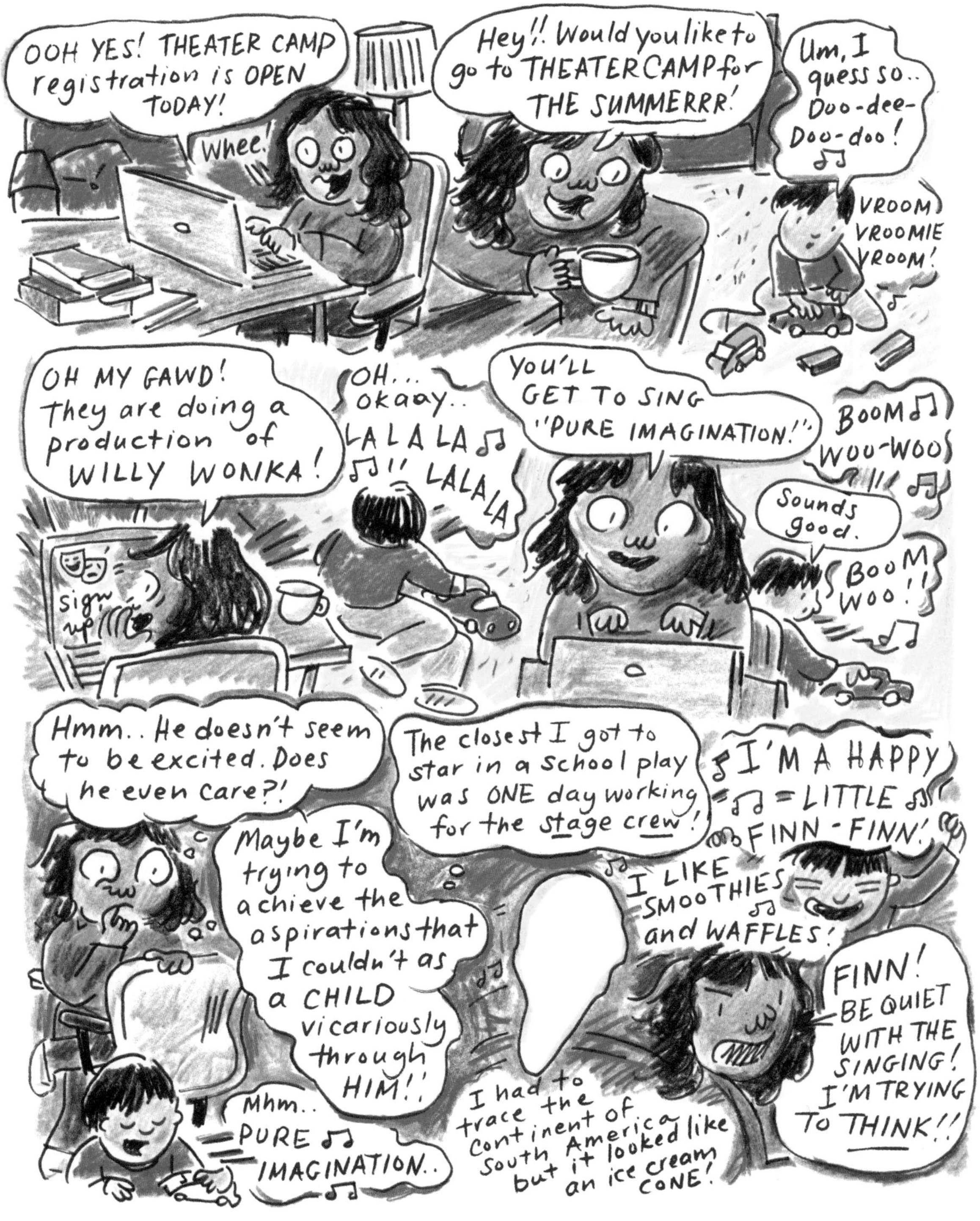
OOH YES! THEATER CAMP registration is OPEN TODAY!
Whee!
Hey!! Would you like to go to THEATER CAMP for THE SUMMERRR!
Um, I guess so.. Doo-dee-Doo-doo!
VROOM VROOMIE VROOM!
OH MY GAWD! They are doing a production of WILLY WONKA!
sign up
OH... okaay.. LALALA LALALA
YOU'LL GET TO SING "PURE IMAGINATION!"
BOOM WOO-WOO
Sounds good.
BOOM WOO!!
Hmm.. He doesn't seem to be excited. Does he even care?!
Maybe I'm trying to achieve the aspirations that I couldn't as a CHILD vicariously through HIM!
Mhm.. PURE IMAGINATION..
The closest I got to star in a school play was ONE day working for the stage crew!
I had to trace the continent of South America but it looked like an ice cream CONE!
I'M A HAPPY LITTLE FINN-FINN!
I LIKE SMOOTHIES and WAFFLES!
FINN! BE QUIET WITH THE SINGING! I'M TRYING TO THINK!!

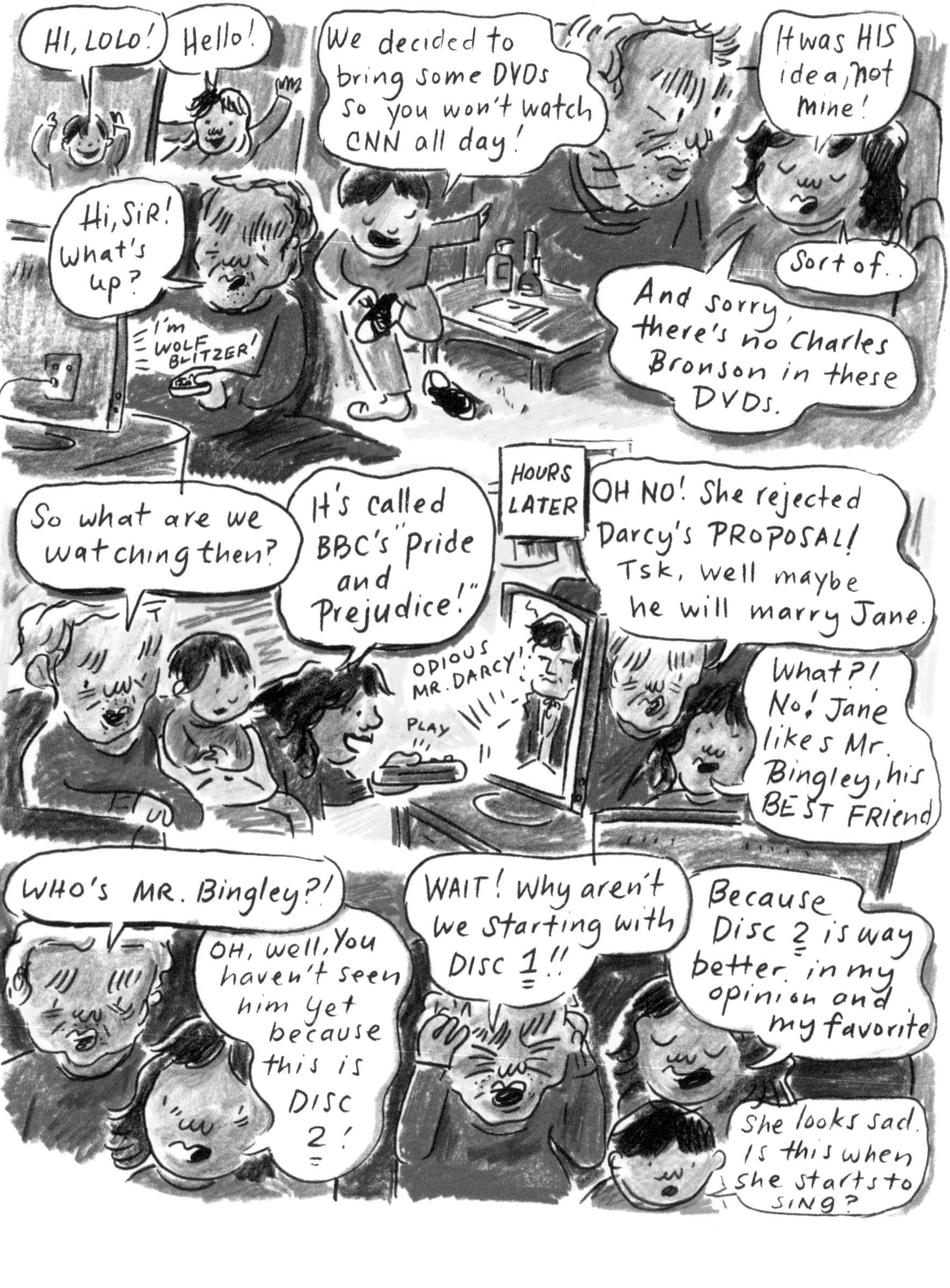
HI, LOLO!
Hello!
We decided to bring some DVDs so you won't watch CNN all day!
It was HIS idea, not mine!
Hi, SIR! What's up?
I'm WOLF BLITZER!
Sort of..
And sorry, there's no Charles Bronson in these DVDs.
So what are we watching then?
It's called BBC's "Pride and Prejudice!"
ODIOUS MR. DARCY!
PLAY
HOURS LATER
OH NO! She rejected Darcy's PROPOSAL! Tsk, well maybe he will marry Jane.
What?! No! Jane likes Mr. Bingley, his BEST FRIEND
WHO's MR. Bingley?!
OH, well, You haven't seen him yet because this is DISC 2!
WAIT! Why aren't we starting with DISC 1!!
Because Disc 2 is way better in my opinion and my favorite
She looks sad. Is this when she starts to SING?

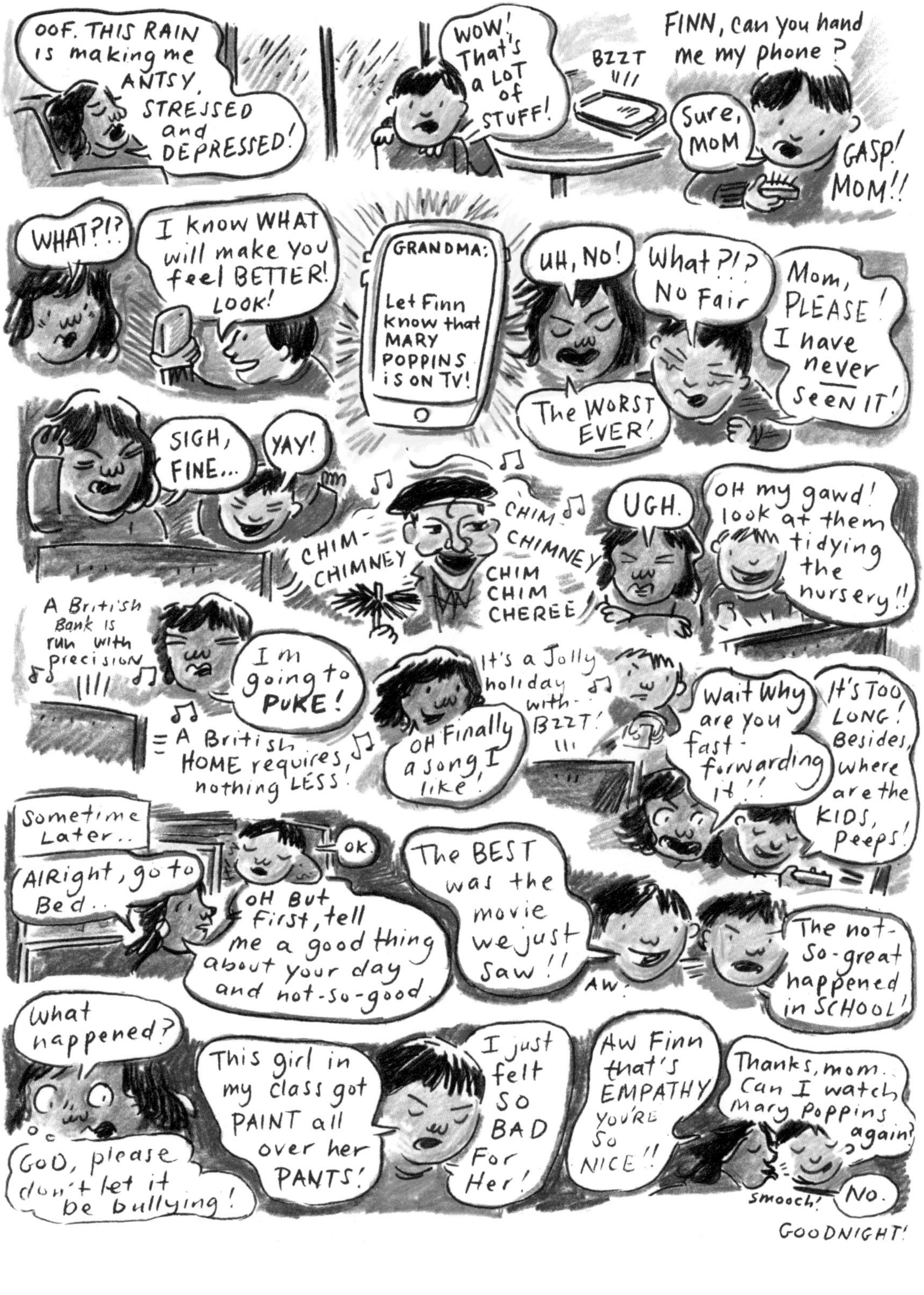
OOF. THIS RAIN is making me ANTSY, STRESSED and DEPRESSED!
WOW! That's a LOT of STUFF!
BZZT
FINN, can you hand me my phone?
Sure, MOM
GASP! MOM!!
WHAT?!?
I know WHAT will make you feel BETTER! LOOK!
GRANDMA:
Let Finn know that MARY POPPINS is ON TV!
UH, NO!
What?!? No Fair
Mom, PLEASE! I have never seen it!
The WORST EVER!
SIGH, FINE...
YAY!
CHIM-CHIMNEY
CHIM-CHIMNEY
CHIM CHIM CHEREE
UGH.
OH my gawd! look at them tidying the nursery!!
A British Bank is run with precision
I'm going to PUKE!
A British HOME requires nothing LESS!
It's a Jolly holiday with- BZZT!
OH Finally a song I like!
Wait Why are you fast-forwarding it!!
It's TOO LONG! Besides, where are the KIDS, Peeps!
Sometime Later..
AlRight, go to Bed..
OK.
OH But First, tell me a good thing about your day and not-so-good
The BEST was the movie we just saw!!
AW.
The not-so-great happened in SCHOOL!
What happened?
GOD, please don't let it be bullying!
This girl in my class got PAINT all over her PANTS!
I just felt SO BAD For Her!
Aw Finn that's EMPATHY You're So NICE!!
Thanks, mom. Can I watch Mary Poppins again?
smooch!
No.
GOODNIGHT!

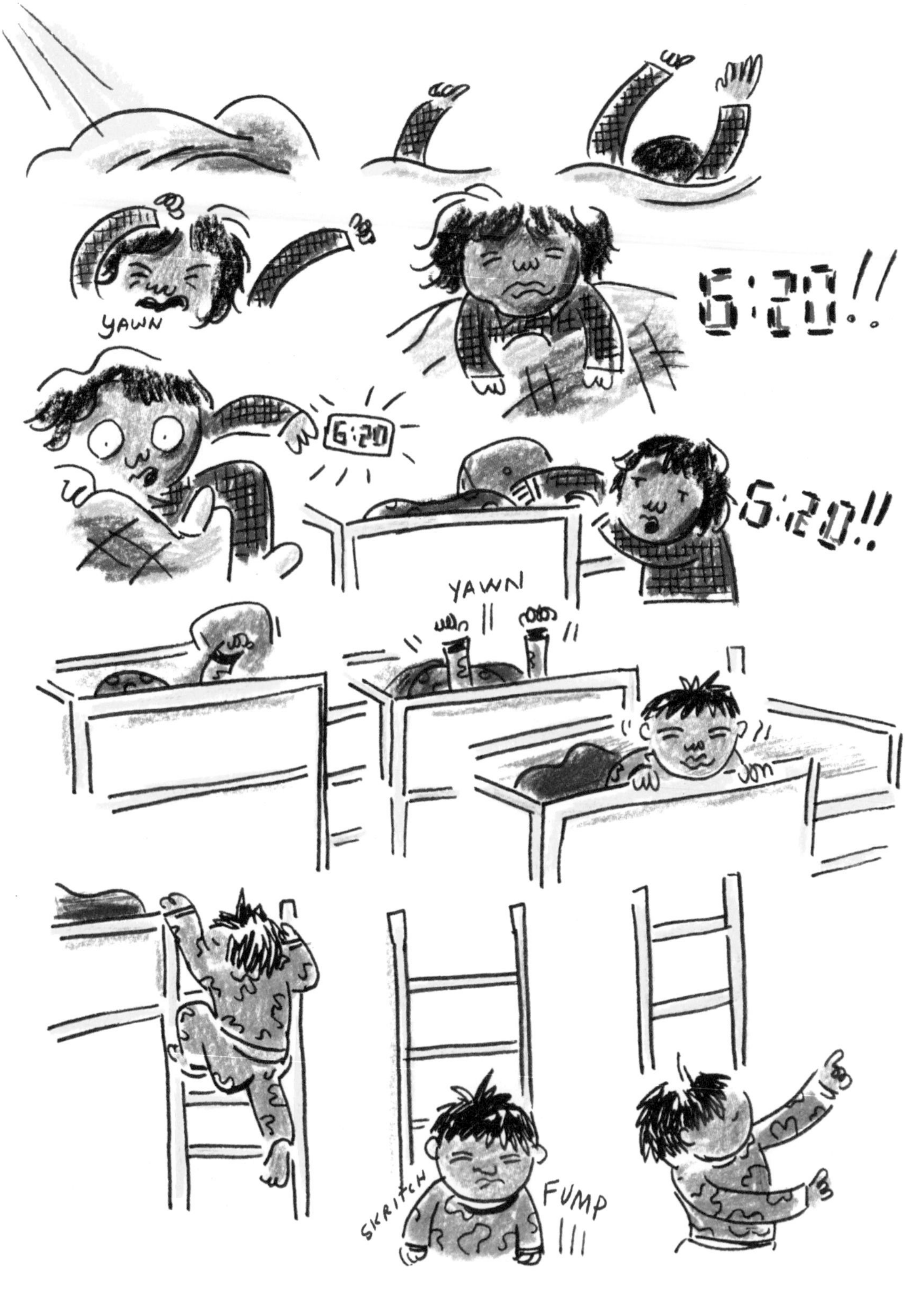
YAWN
6:20!!
6:20
6:20!!
YAWN
SKRITCH
FUMP

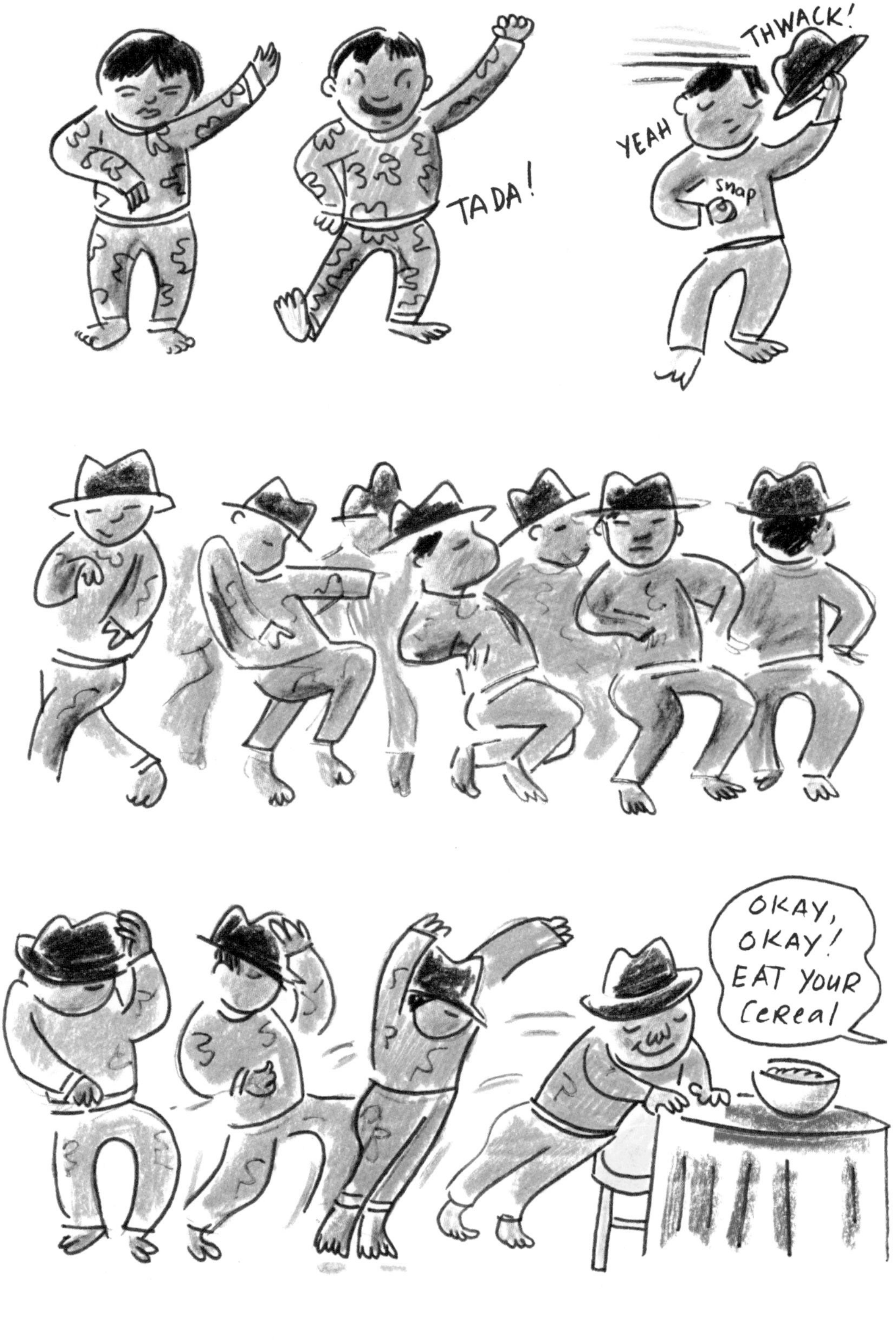
TADA!
THWACK!
YEAH
snap
OKAY, OKAY! EAT YOUR Cereal

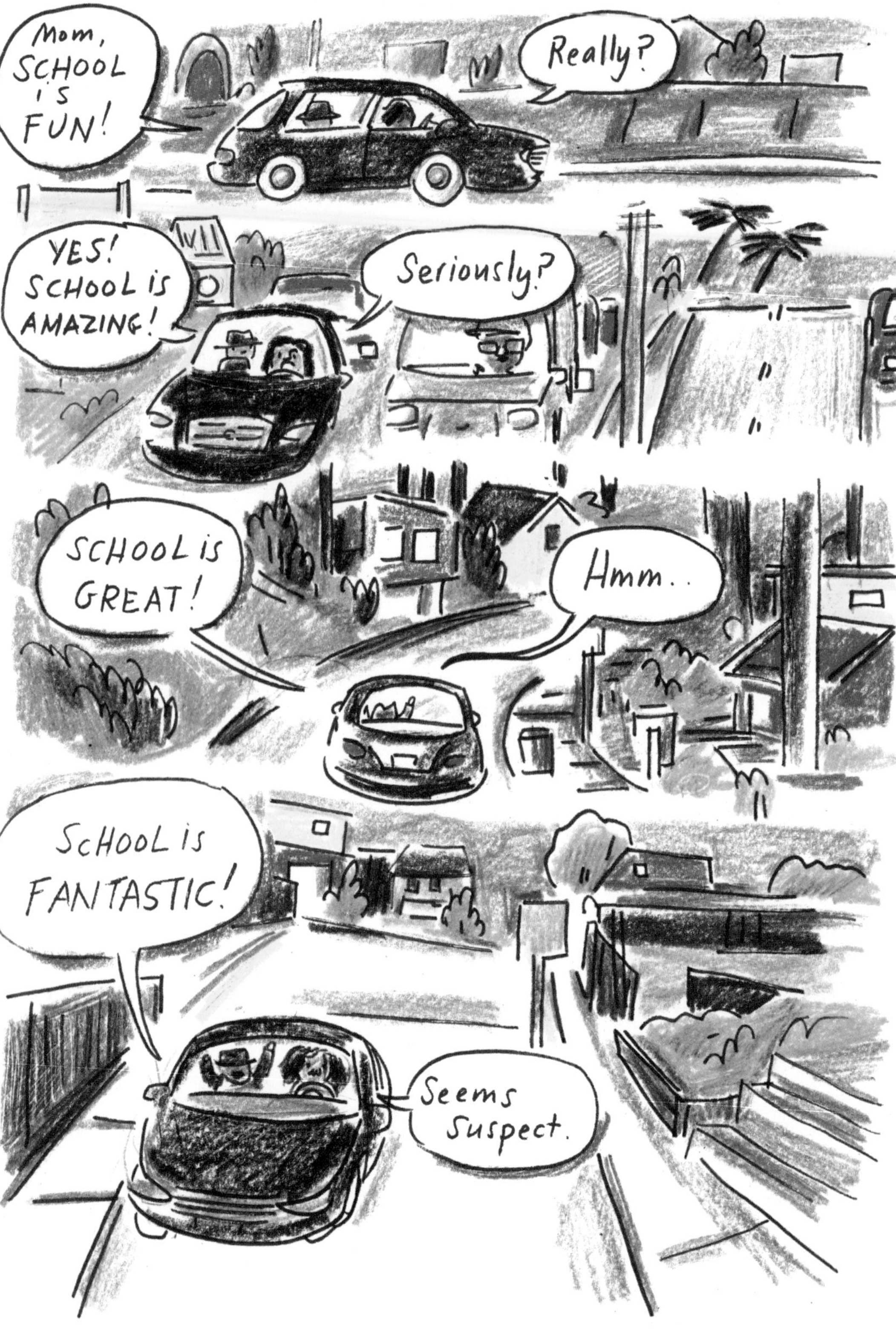

Mom, SCHOOL is FUN!
Really?
YES! SCHOOL is AMAZING!
Seriously?
SCHOOL is GREAT!
Hmm..
SCHOOL is FANTASTIC!
Seems suspect.

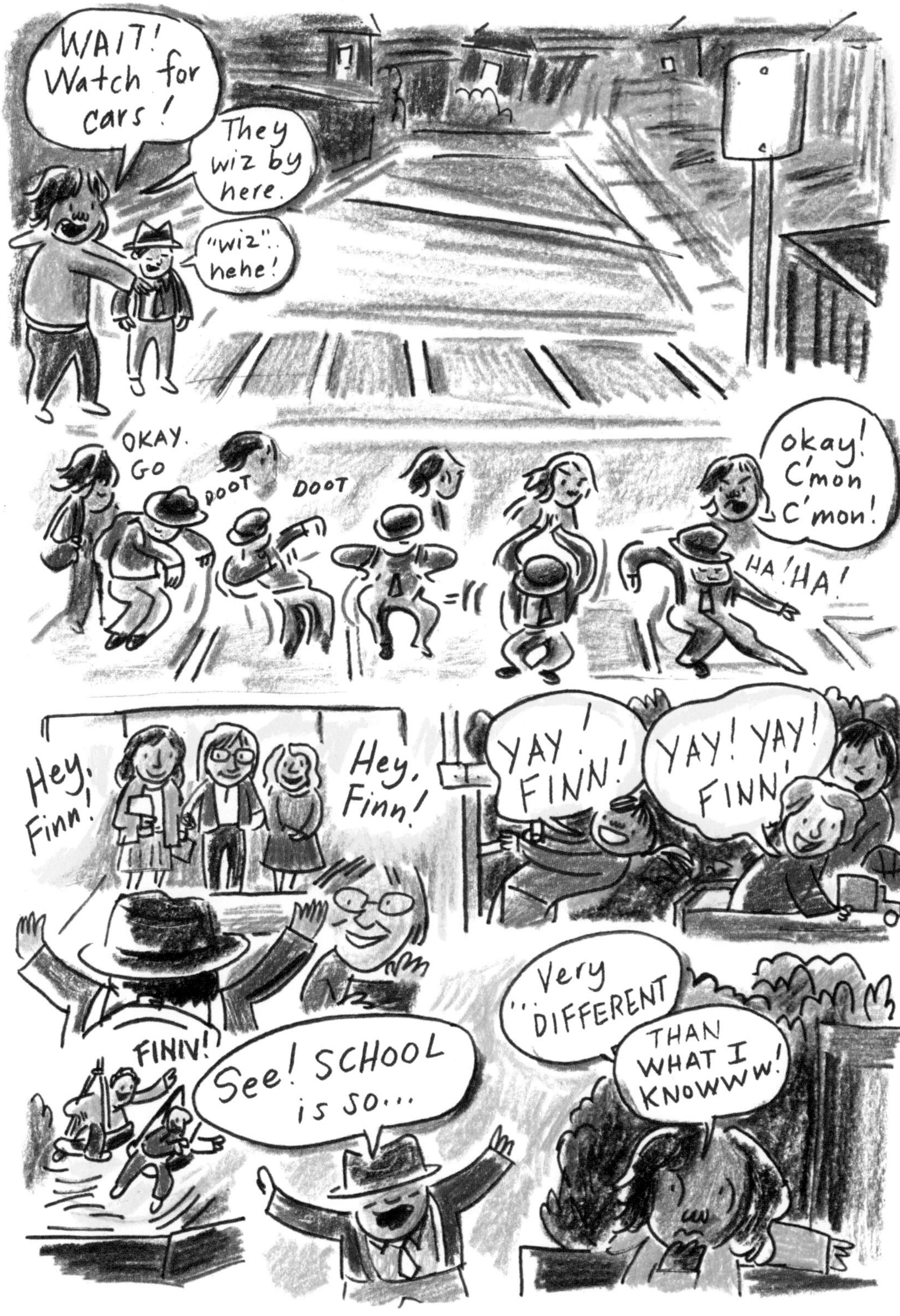
WAIT! Watch for cars!
They wiz by here.
"wiz"... hehe!
OKAY. GO
DOOT
DOOT
okay! C'mon C'mon!
HA! HA!
Hey, Finn!
Hey, Finn!
YAY! FINN!
YAY! YAY! FINN!
FINN!
See! SCHOOL is so...
...Very DIFFERENT
THAN WHAT I KNOWWW!

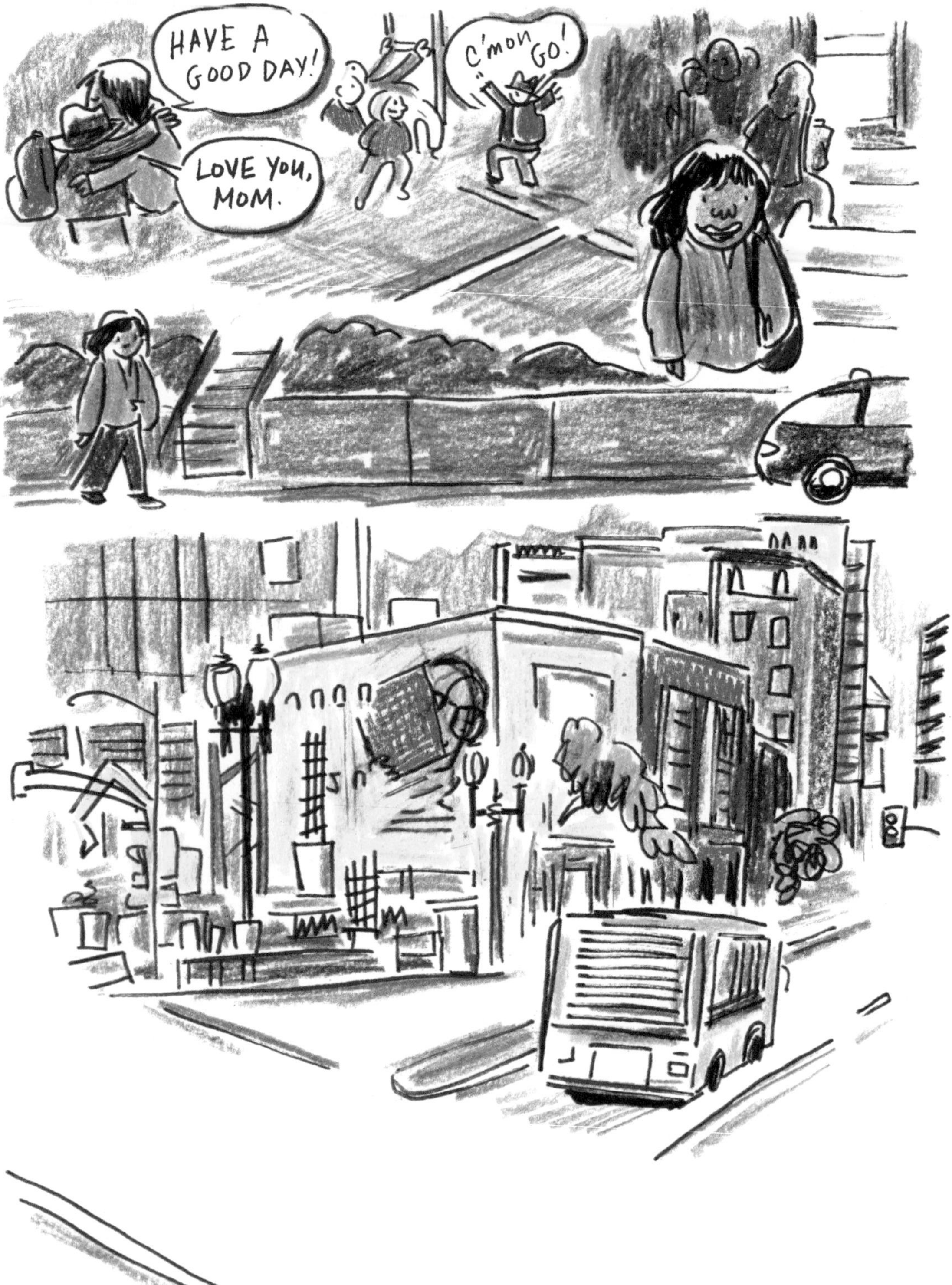
HAVE A GOOD DAY!
LOVE YOU, MOM.
C'MON GO!

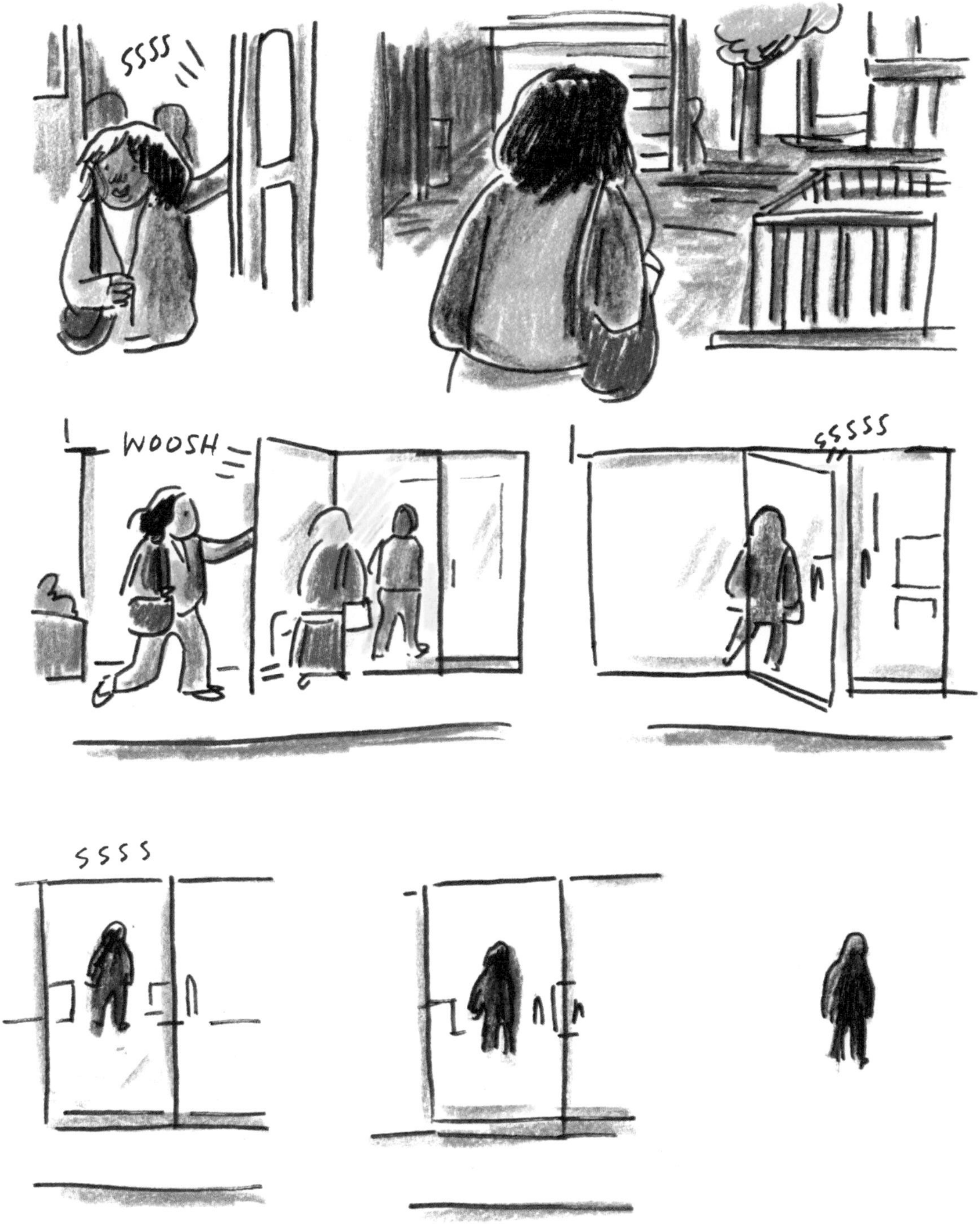
SSSS
WOOSH
SSSSS
SSSS

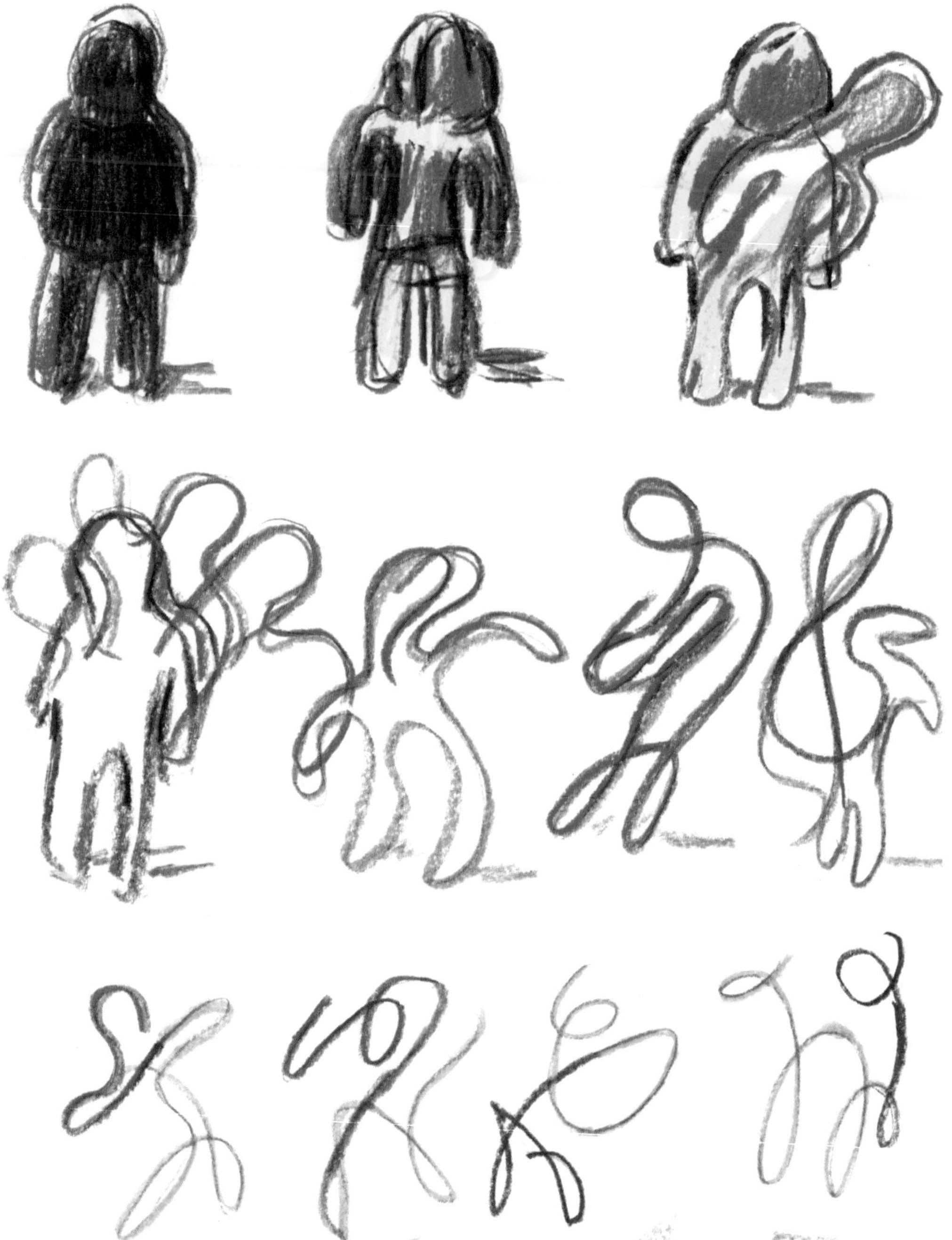

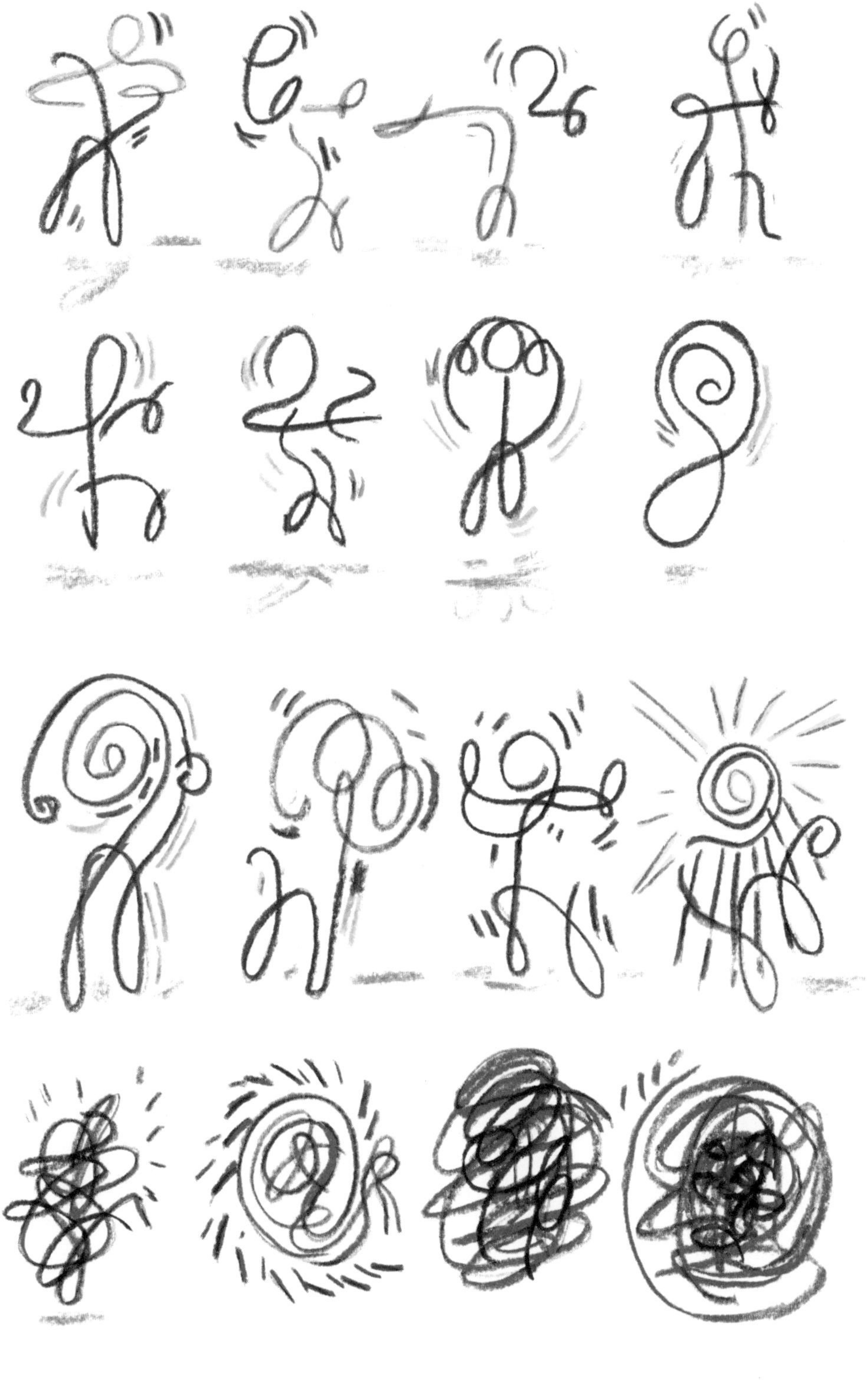

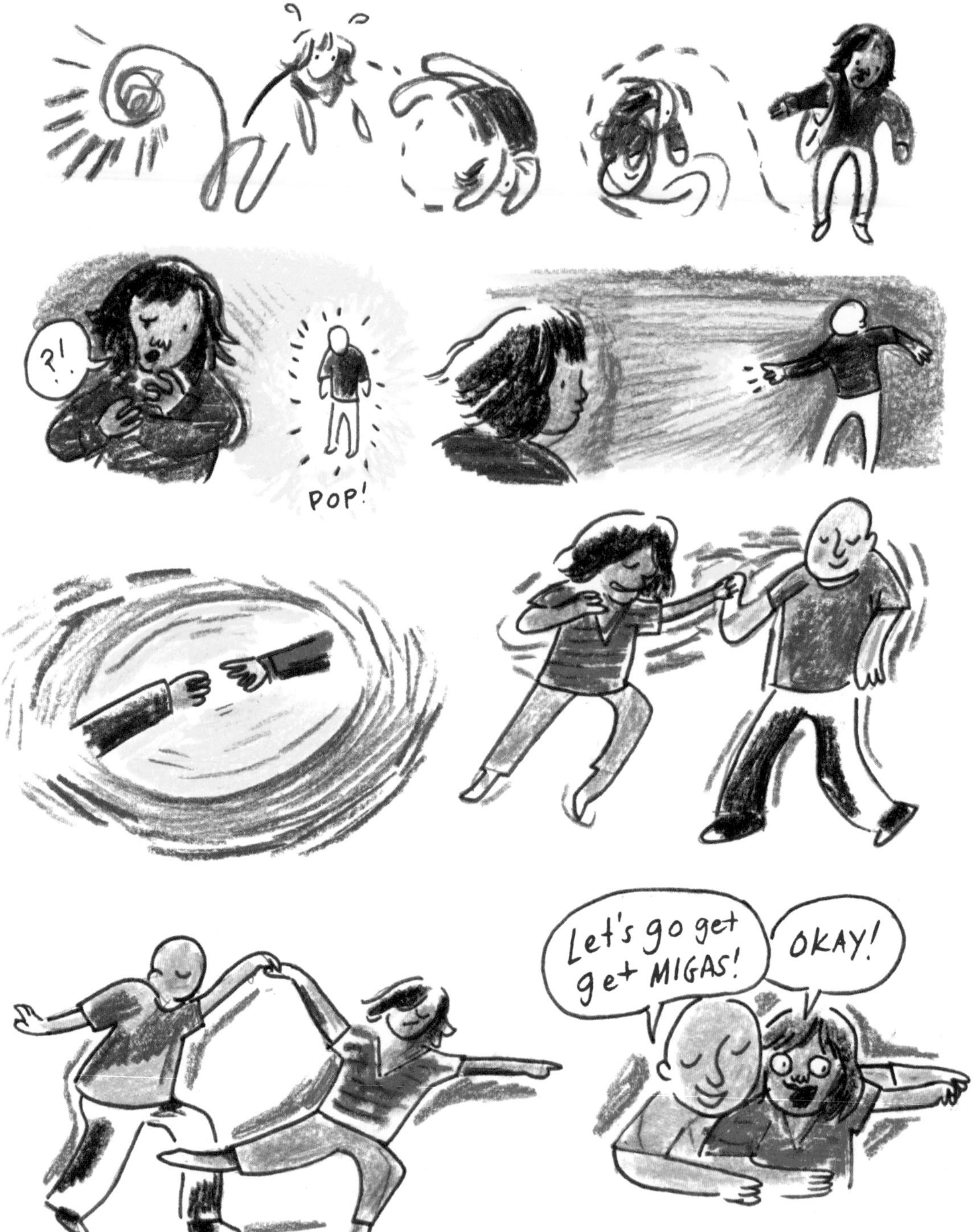
?!
POP!
Let's go get get MIGAS!
OKAY!

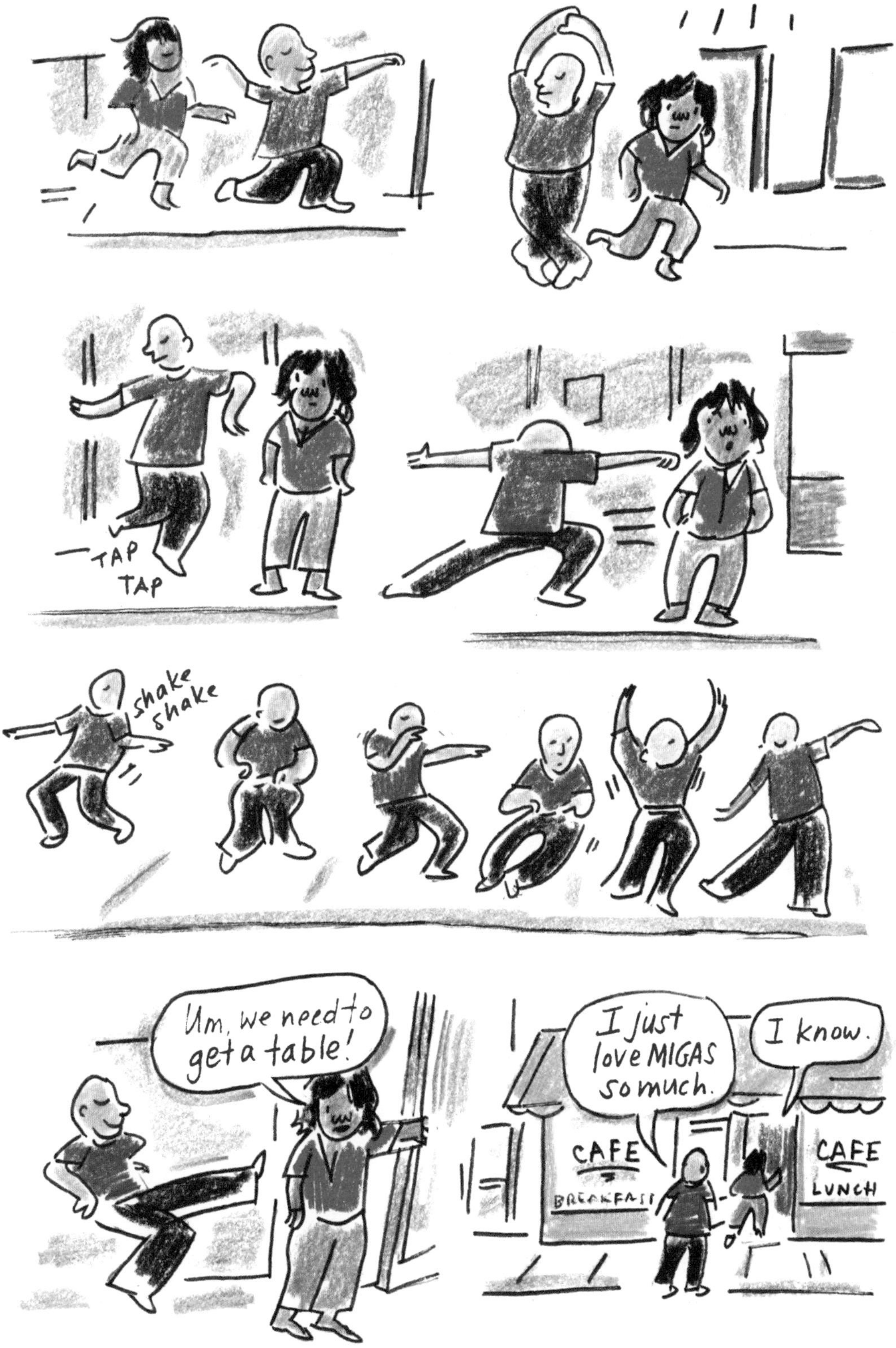
TAP
TAP
shake shake
Um, we need to get a table!
I just love MIGAS so much.
I know.
CAFE
BREAKFAST
CAFE
LUNCH

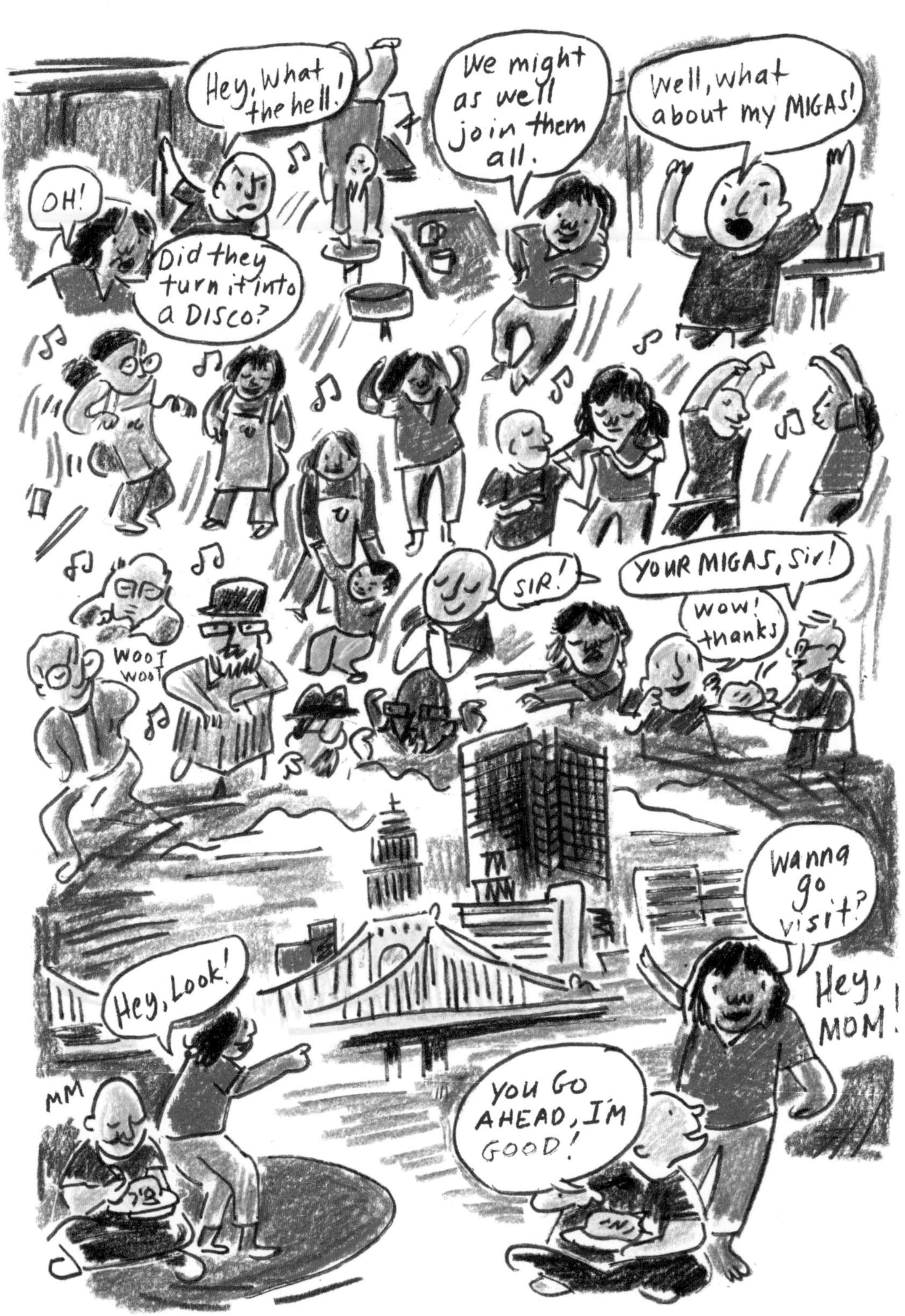

OH!
Hey, What the hell!
Did they turn it into a DISCO?
We might as well join them all.
Well, what about my MIGAS!
WOOT WOOT
SIR!
YOUR MIGAS, Sir!
WOW! thanks
Hey, Look!
MM
Wanna go visit?
Hey, MOM!
YOU GO AHEAD, I'M GOOD!

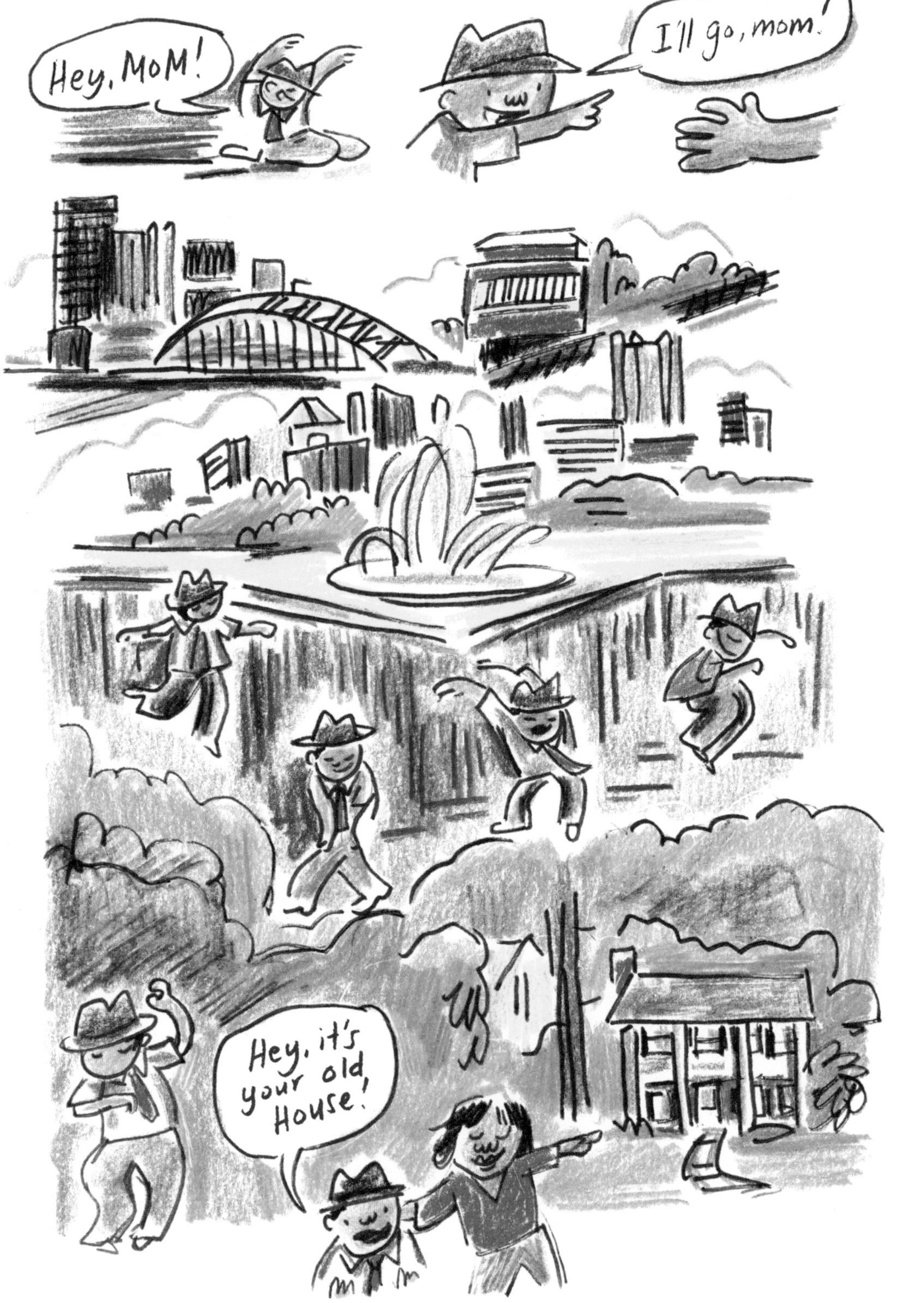
Hey, MOM!
I'll go, mom!
Hey, it's your old House!

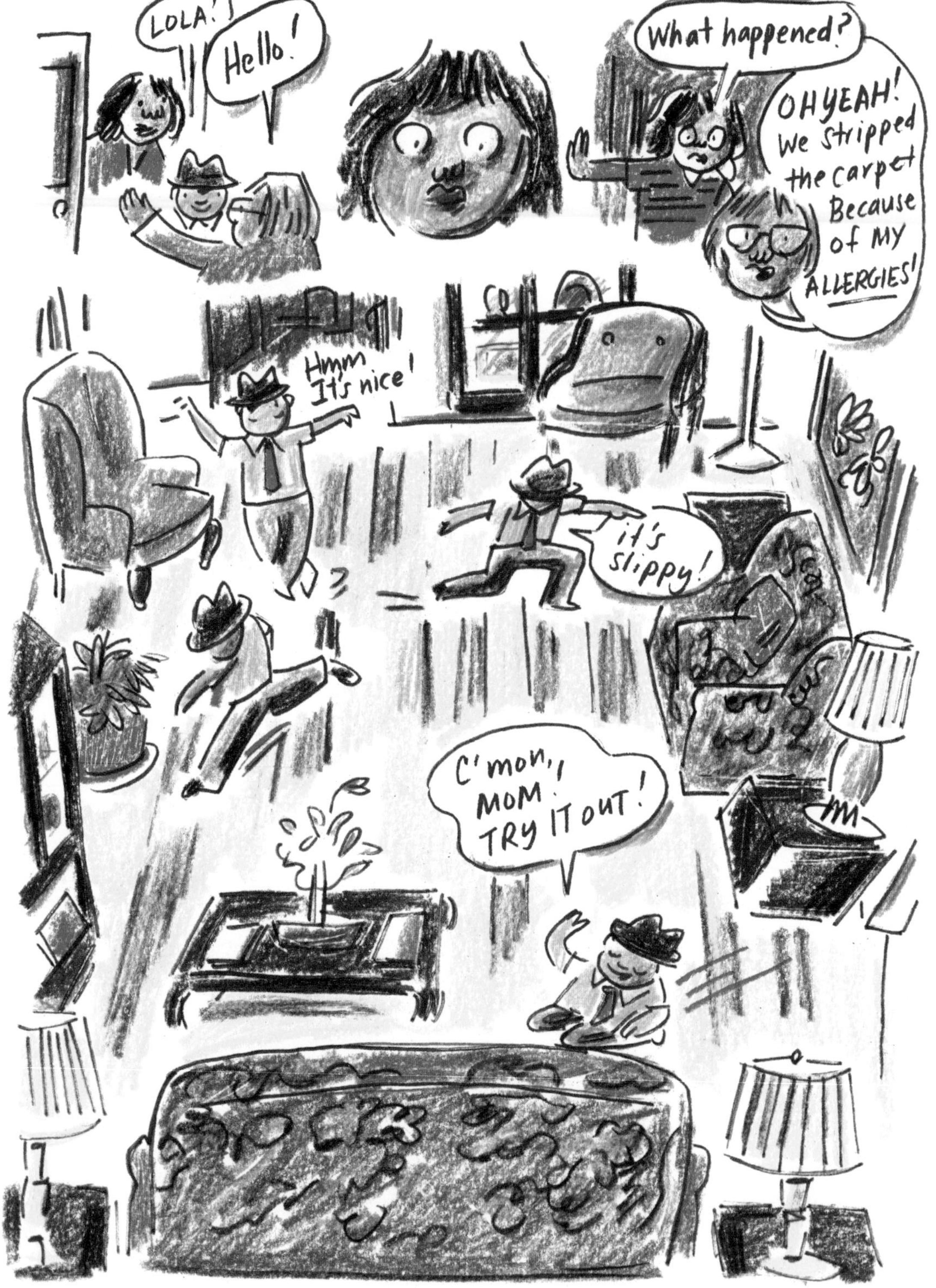
LOLA!
Hello!
What happened?
OH YEAH! We stripped the carpet Because of MY ALLERGIES!
Hmm It's nice!
it's slippy!
C'mon, MOM! TRY IT OUT!

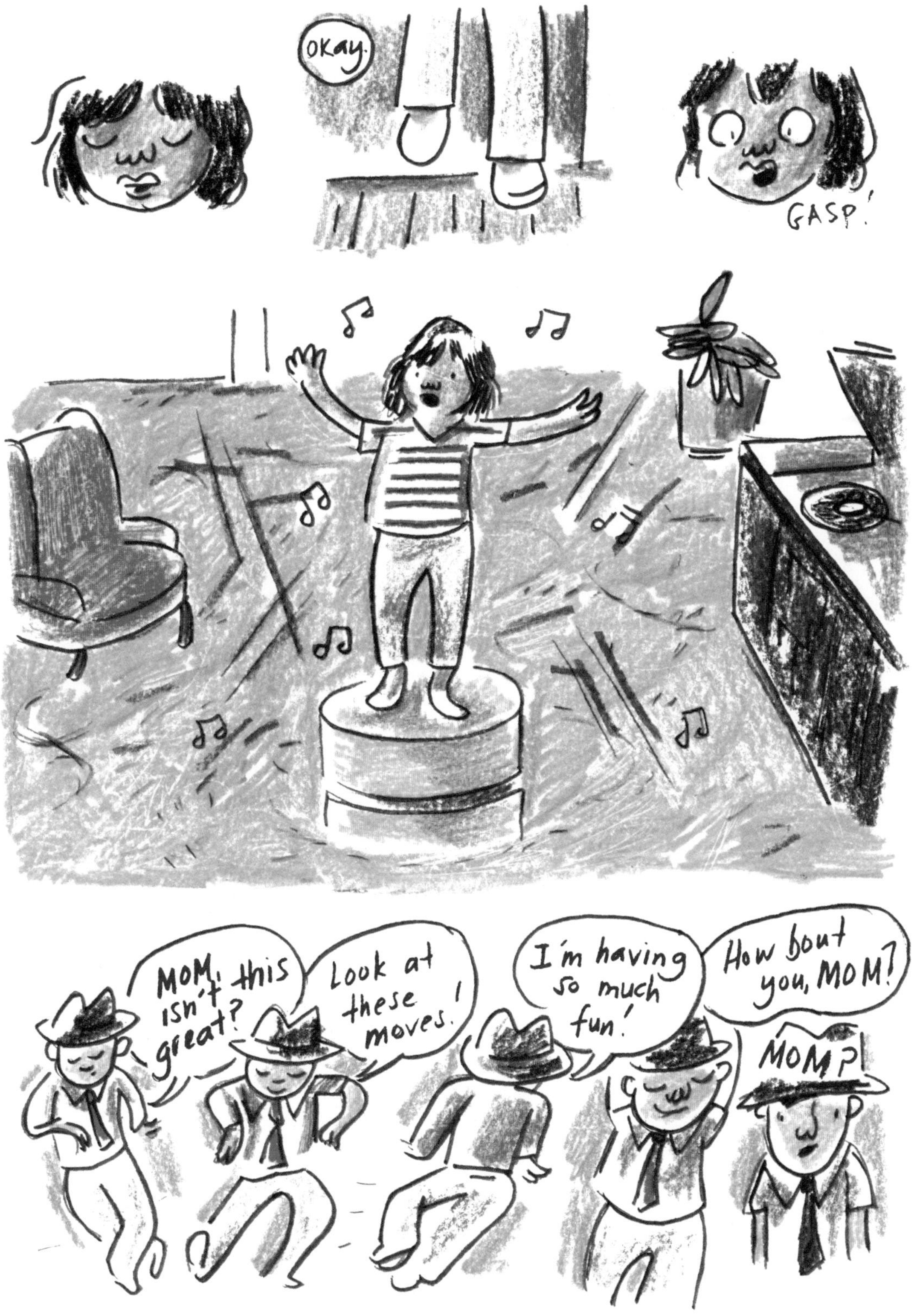

Okay.
GASP!
MOM, isn't this great?
Look at these moves!
I'm having so much fun!
How bout you, MOM?
MOM?

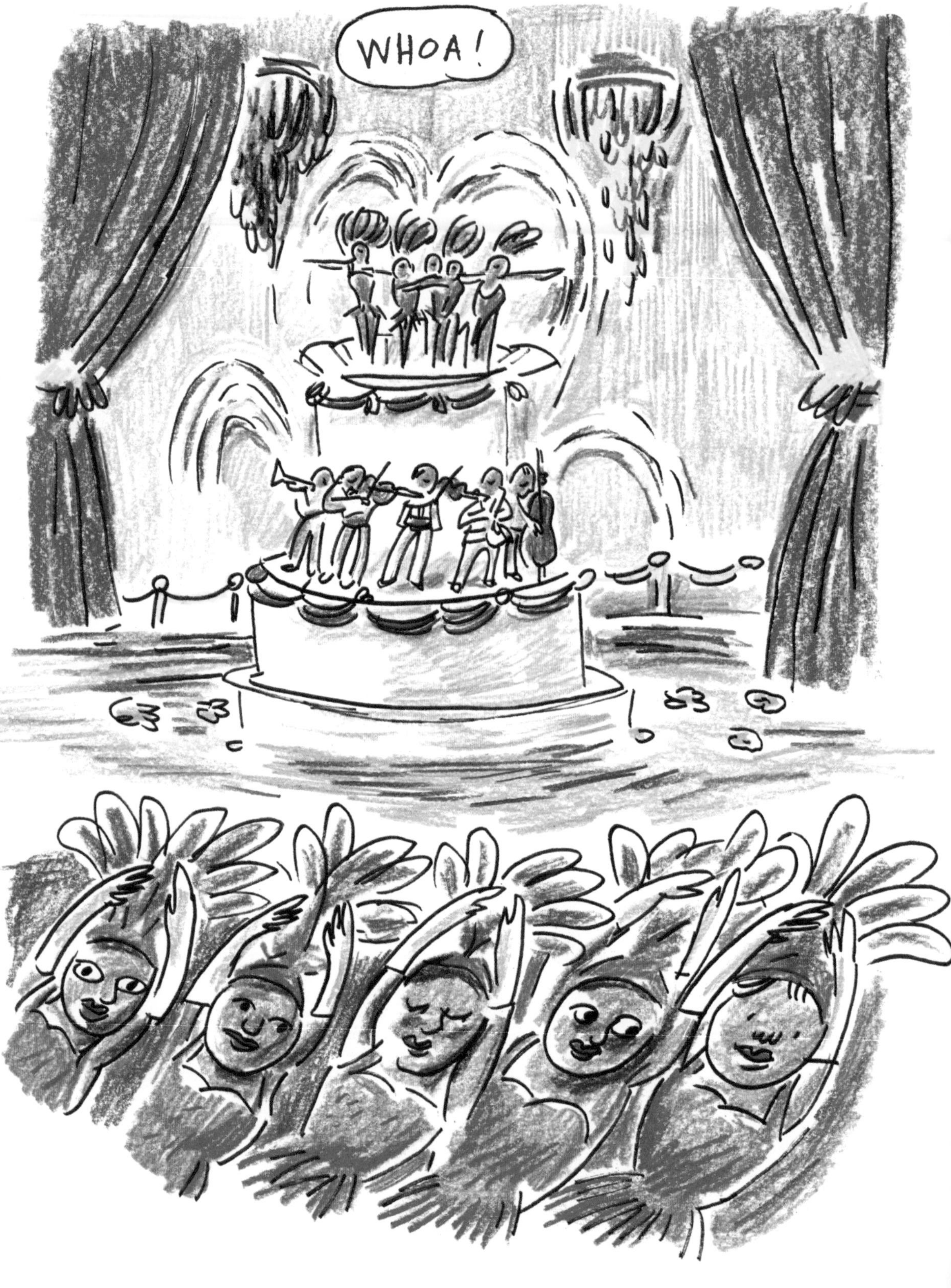
WHOA!

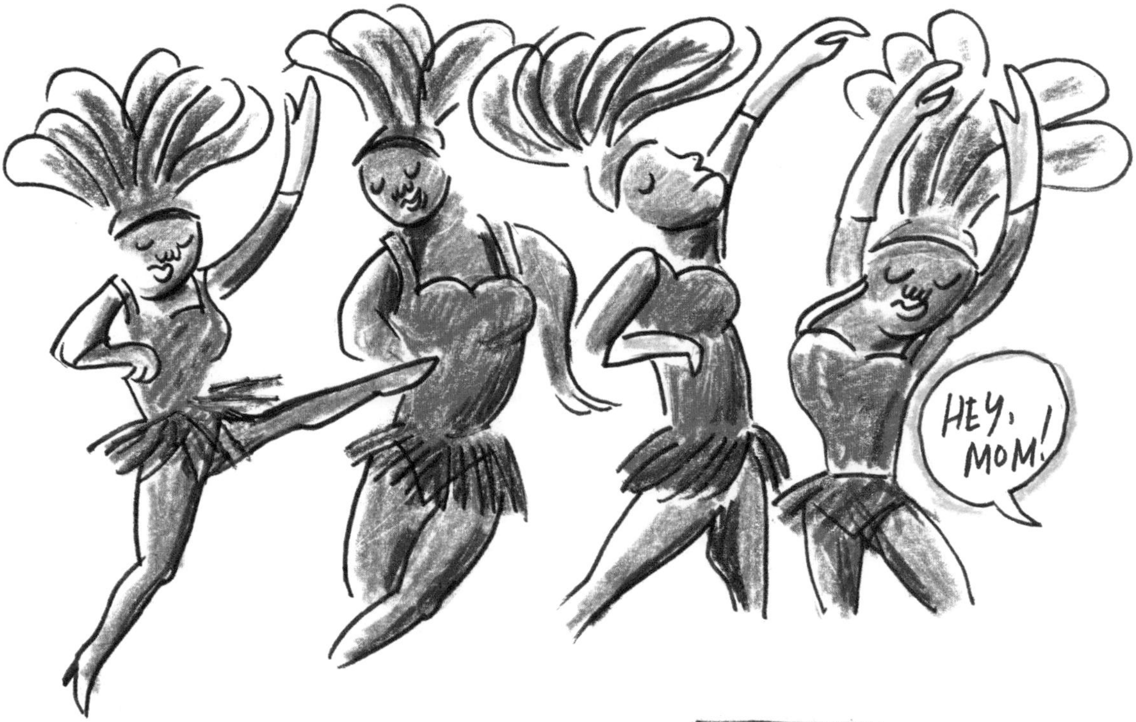
HEY, MOM!
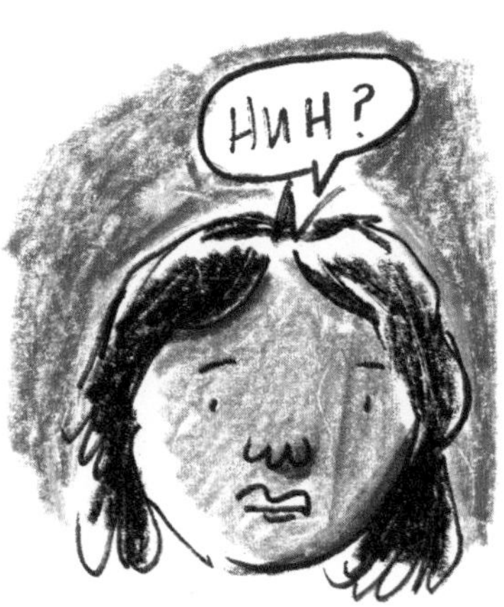
HUH?
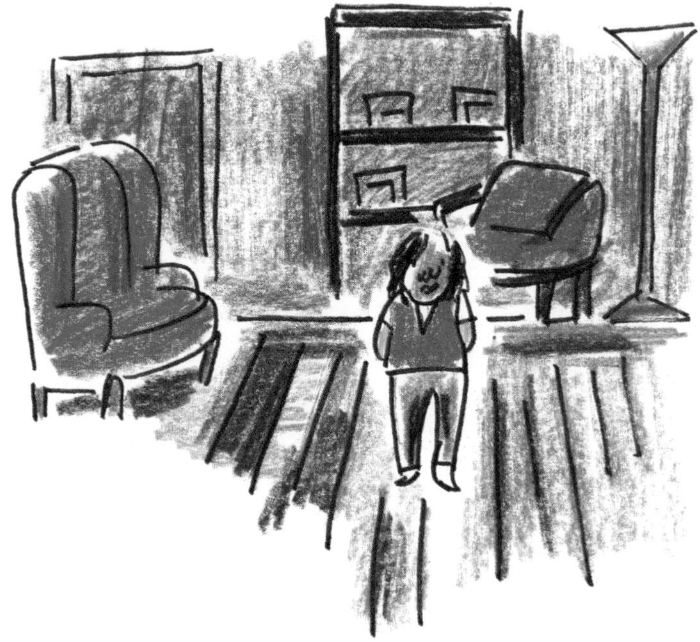

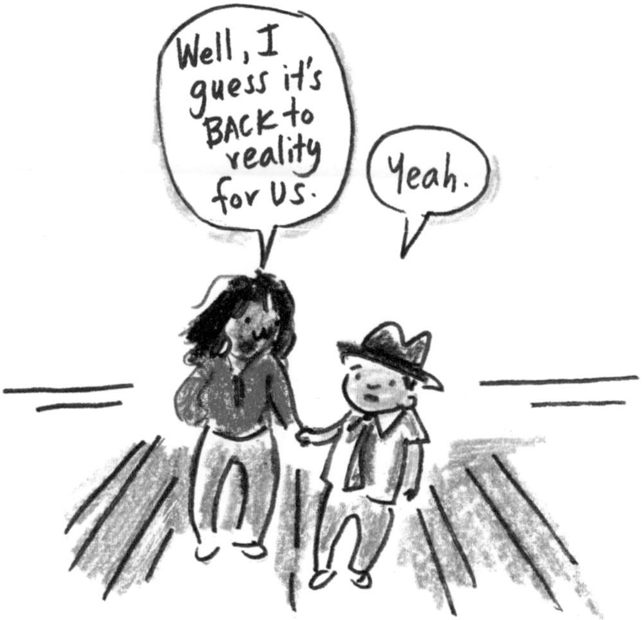
Well, I guess it's BACK to reality for US.
Yeah.

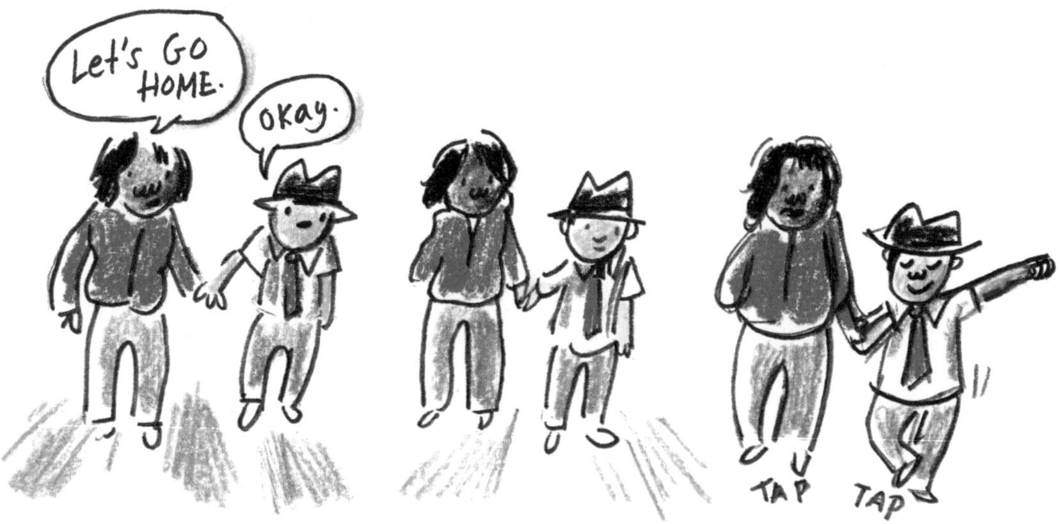
Let's GO HOME.
Okay.
TAP
TAP

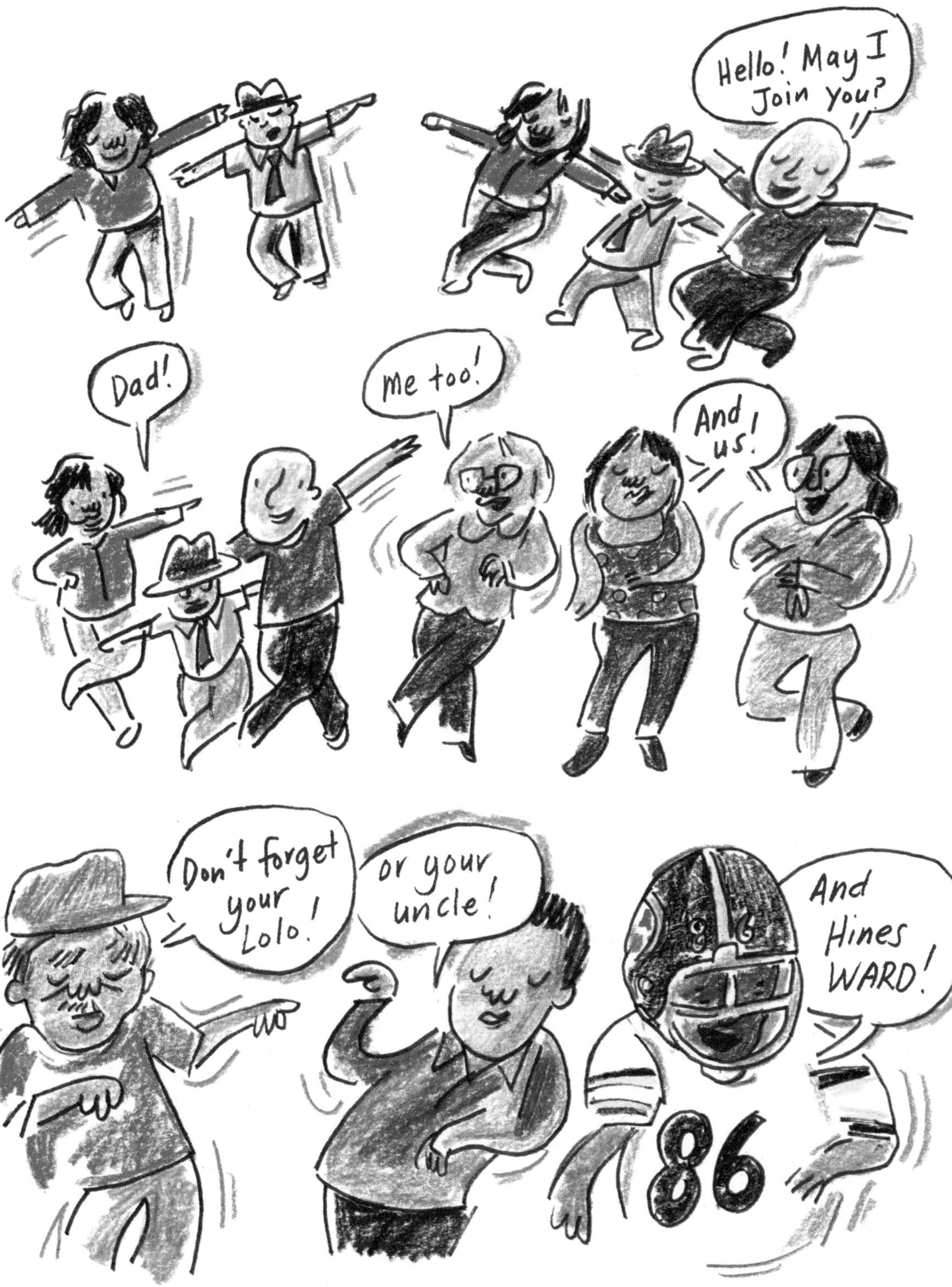
Hello! May I Join you?
Dad!
Me too!
And us!
Don't forget your Lolo!
Or your uncle!
And Hines WARD!
86

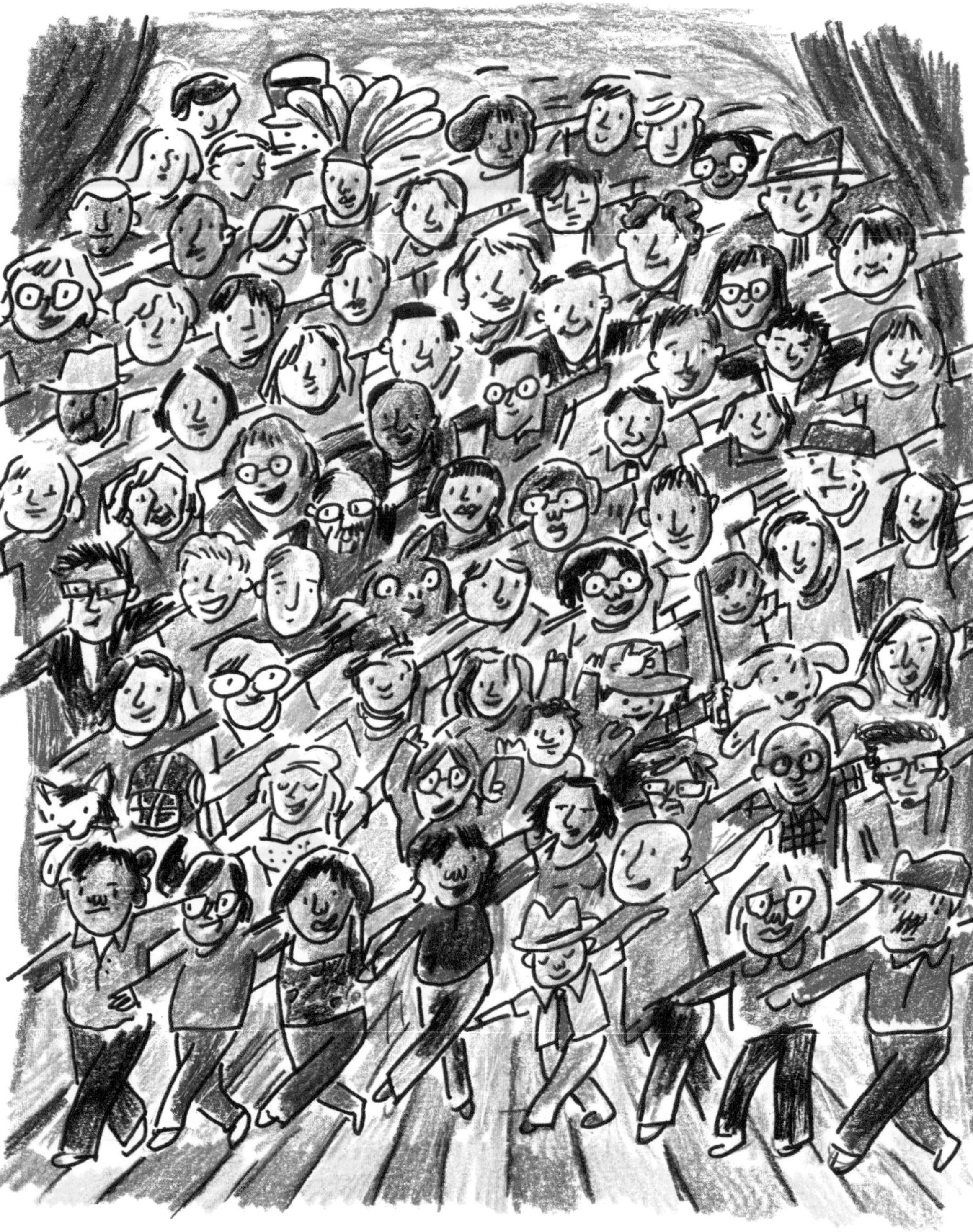

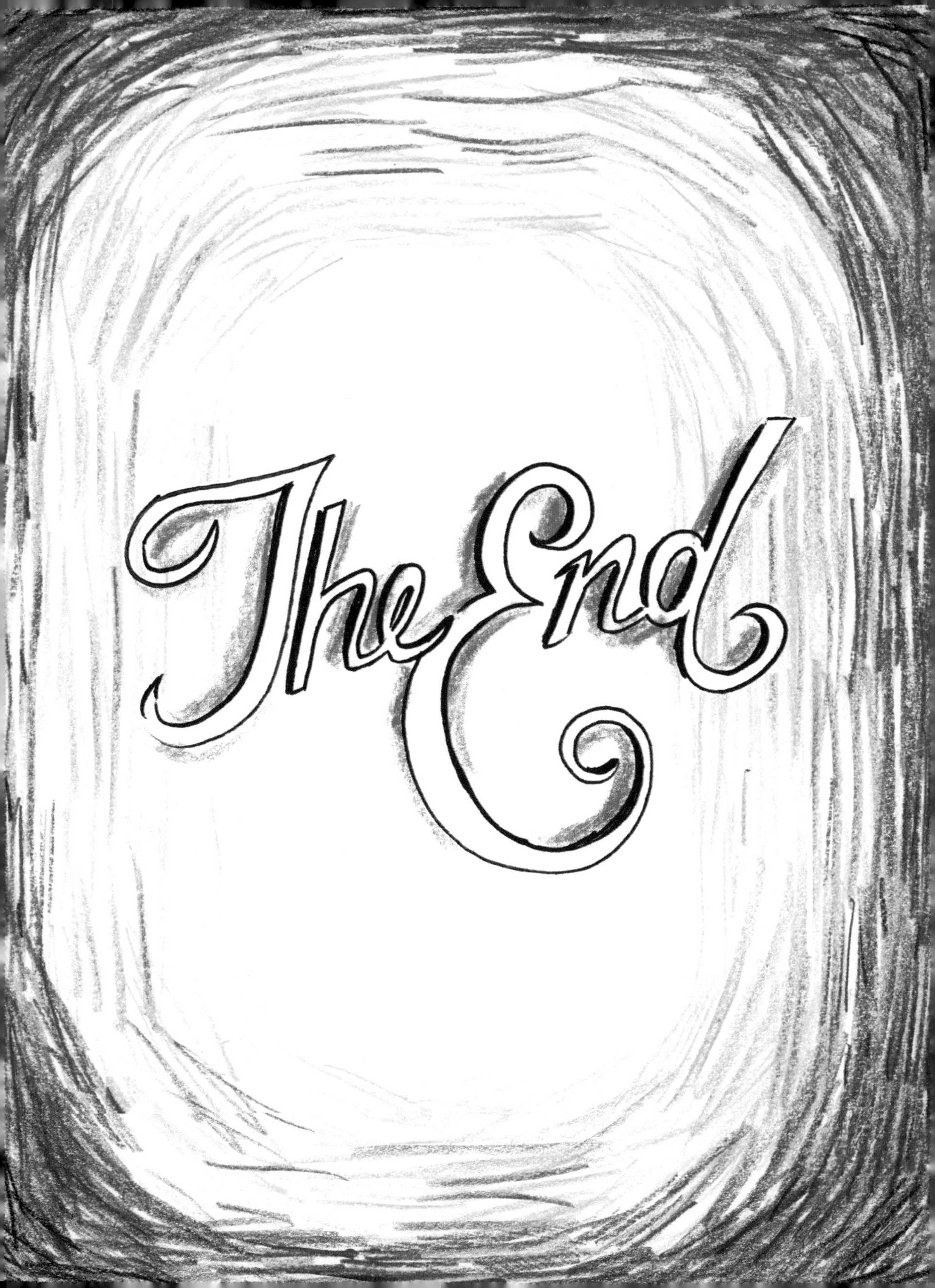
The End

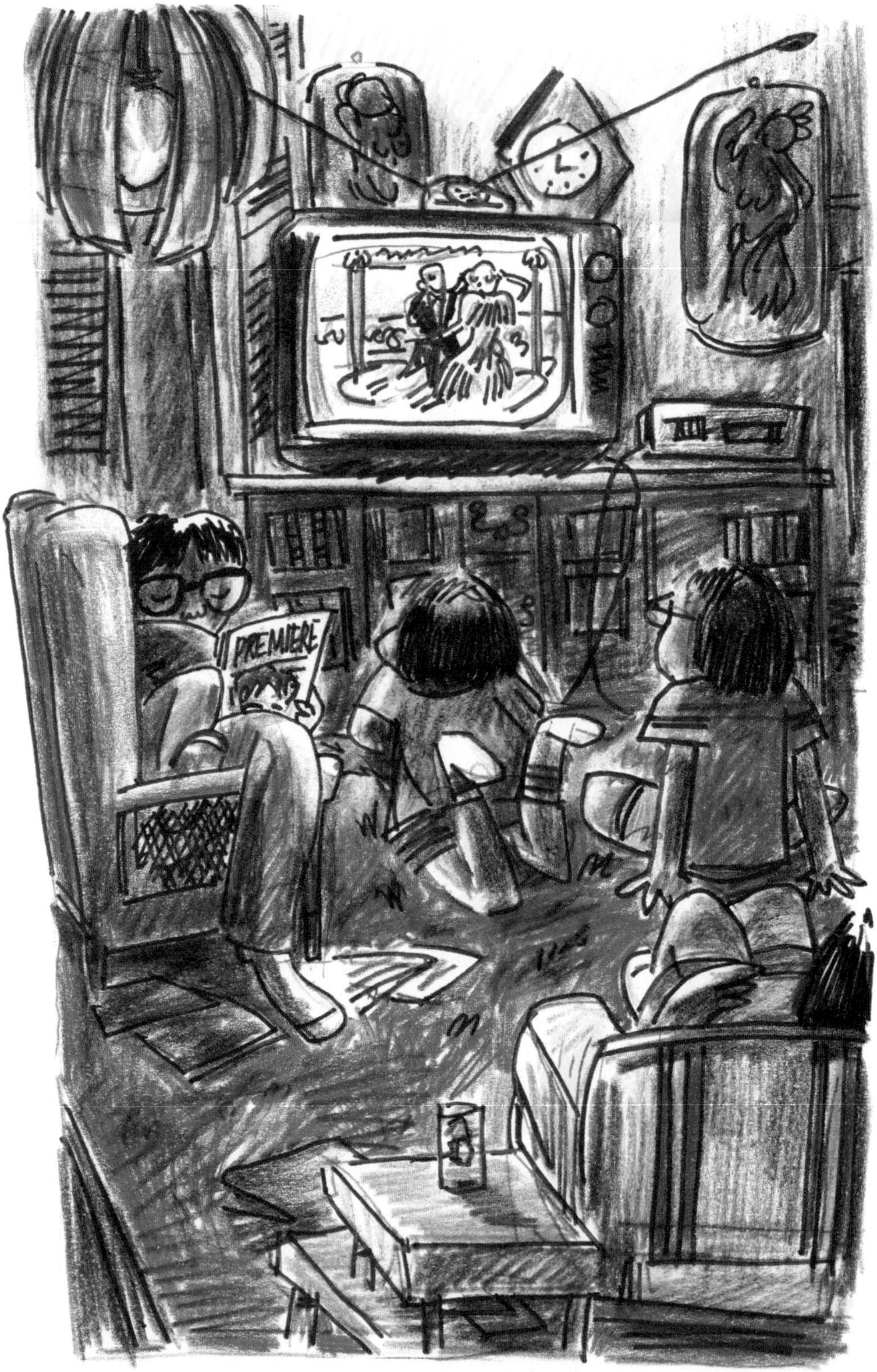
PREMIERE

THANK YOU

To Mom, Dad, Raoul, Rachelle, and Rhodora.

For all the support during the making of this book, thank you to Vanessa Davis, Josh Frankel, Renée French, Tim Hensley, Miriam Katin, Anne McGillicutty, Thien Pham, Lark Pien, Mimi Pond, Mimi Young, the amazing HMS Mirrorball, and the Piedmont Cartoonist Cabal.

Thank you to Peggy Burns, Tom Devlin, and everyone at D+Q for their guidance.

And lastly, thank you to Ken and Finn for all our wonderful craziness. ♡

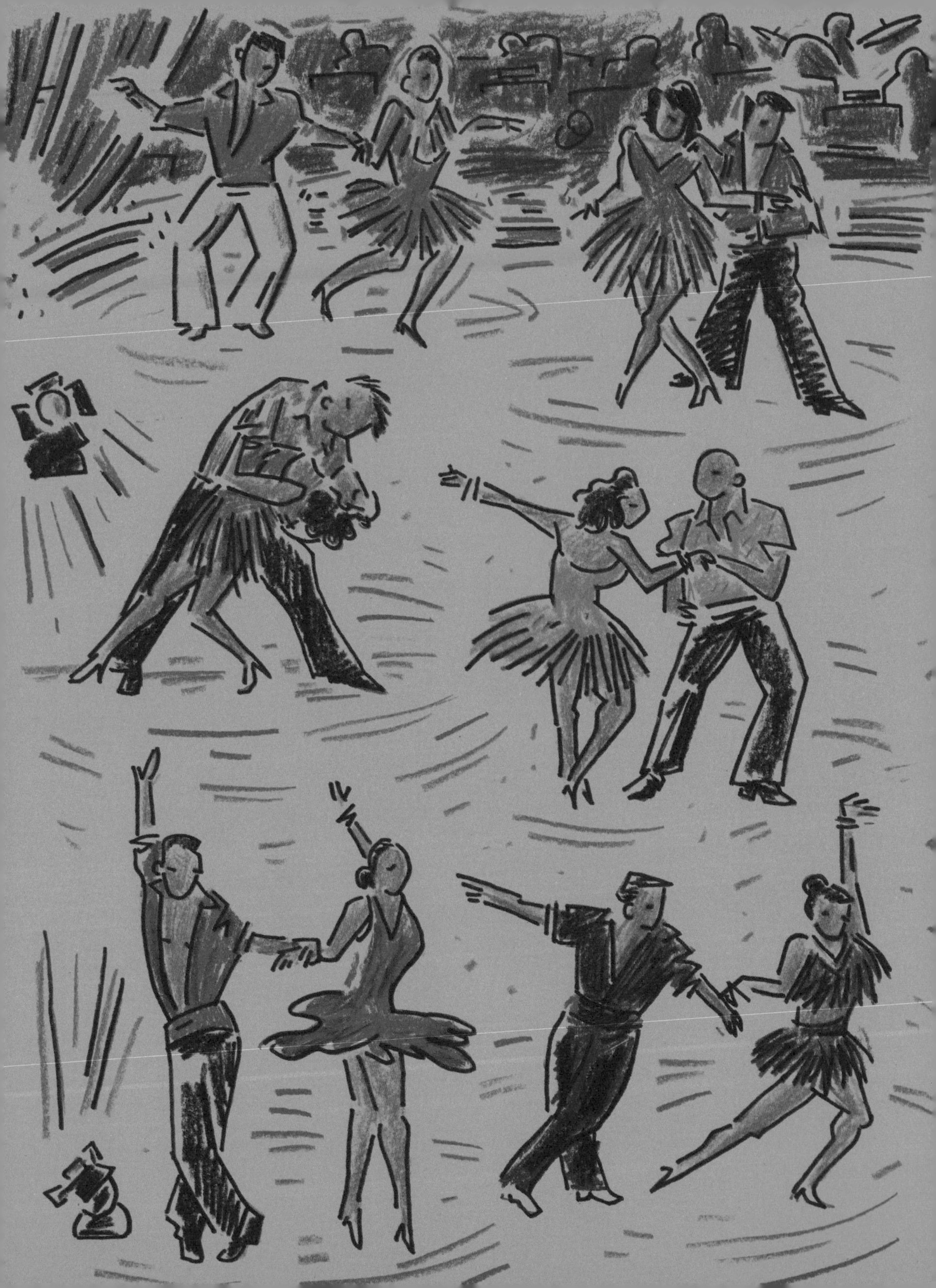